Twelve De

by Steve Wallin

With thanks to Elaine, Ian, Keith and my long-suffering wife Kate,
and special thanks for their inspiration to New Scientist and Betty.
Cover design by Keith Mellor.

Other titles by the same author:

The Disappearing Hands: An Inspector Copeland Mystery.

AN INSPECTOR CALLS.

Pleased with the way he neatly sidestepped the trail of blood, he stealthily made his way to the crouching woman near the steel door at the end of the corridor. Sensing his approach, she turned her head to stare at him. She flicked her dark hair aside, rolled her eyes and screamed, 'Hells bells, Larry! You've got the grace of a tap dancing whale!'

Looking at where her white latex-gloved finger was pointing, Larry Copeland peered behind him and saw a bloody footprint trailing him on the white tiled floor. He leaned against the wall, lifted his left shoe and examined the sole. 'Ooops, sorry,' he muttered, levering off the offending shoe. He thought any foot odour would probably go unnoticed since the whole corridor reeked like the inside of a sewer.

'Back in uniform, eh, Clare? Congratulations on making Chief, by the way,' smiled Copeland as he tottered the last few paces to join Chief Inspector Clare Harper. 'You're looking well,' he added quickly, choosing to ignore the bags under her eyes, the grey roots and, before she reminded him, that her promotion had been eight years ago.

She looked up at him dangling his shoe from a finger and shook her head. His smile faded as he became sombre and observed, 'Dead body, eh?'

She stood, rolled her eyes, pointed down and flatly said, 'No, he's just having a nap with four bullet holes in him.'

'I noticed he'd been shot,' Copeland pointed out.

'Laser sharp as ever, Larry,' groaned Clare. She lifted the blood splattered key-card hanging from the neck of the corpse and angled the photo and name towards Copeland. 'Allow me to introduce you to Dr. Jonathan Carter, biochemist and until his recent untimely demise the director at this now rather messed-up research facility, and, until probably sometime yesterday evening, in his mid thirties, six two and rather handsome before he acquired the hole in his forehead. Now, I have no idea why they've sent you here Larry, but unless you need to get your magnifying glass, pipe and deerstalker to go with that awful green raincoat and those blue latex gloves, continue to use whatever deductive skills you have left and tell me what you think happened here – preferably without contaminating the crime scene any further!'

Larry Copeland saw himself as someone who had always risen to challenges, even if those challenges had usually involved large amounts of alcohol consumption or menu items that came with a health warning. He looked down at the body propped against the frame of the slightly open door. It sat with a straight back and legs straight out, which would have been quite good posture if not for the slumped head. Copeland considered Dr. Carter's corpse. It was hard to tell if the bullet in his head or the one put into his heart had killed him. The bullets in the shoulder and the leg had not helped Carter's suit look much neater either.

First question, thought Copeland. Why is this scientist chap wearing such a sharp suit in his own lab? He thought the second question could wait. He would find out why the metal door needed a palm-print reader to open it soon enough. As he turned to investigate the scene Clare warned, 'And don't go in the work-lab, Larry. Forensics will be here soon with bio-hazard protective suits.' Good to know, thought Copeland.

Dangling his discarded shoe, Copeland retraced his route back along the bright fluorescent corridor to where the blood trail began. He stopped at an open door. The frosted glass, which had once been the upper half of the wooden door, now

3

lay shattered behind it. What remained of the door had a gold nameplate bearing the name Dr. J. Carter. The blood trail began inside the doorway with a large, oval stain on the thin blue carpet. Copeland surveyed the windowless, functional interior. Even his diminished sense of smell detected an odour of burning. In front of him was a wooden chair half-facing Carter's desk, where an unopened packet of chocolate biscuits lay next to an open laptop and, on the far side of the desk, a black swivel chair. Behind Carter's black chair, on a second desk, lay an upturned grey computer server. To Copeland's right were four comfortable blue armless chairs around a square coffee table.

Stepping over the stained carpet, Copeland went round Carter's desk and looked at the server. The back had been removed and the metal inside was still smouldering. He glanced at the open laptop on Dr. Carter's desk. The plastic keys had melted away.

Copeland closed his eyes and imagined the scene. The dead scientist chap had sat working at his desk when the killer came in. They had argued. Carter had gone to the door, thrust it wide and told his unwanted guest to leave. The killer had pulled out a gun and shot, hitting Carter in the shoulder. Carter then made a run for it to try and get to the safety of the room that needed his palm print to open it, trailing blood down the corridor. The killer was in the corridor by the time Carter had opened the door and shot again, this time hitting Carter in the leg. Carter had collapsed in the open doorway. The killer had caught up with him and finished him off. It was all obvious.

Copeland opened his eyes again. He knew that wasn't right. Something didn't fit. He looked around the office again. Besides the large amount of blood on the carpet there was something... That was it! The biscuits! Uneaten biscuits made no sense. Who works alone after hours and doesn't even eat their biscuits? Copeland knew if it had been him working late then any biscuits would not have lasted long, but then again he never worked late. Resisting the urge to do an investigative biscuit taste test, Copeland examined the empty glass panel in the open door again. A bullet was lodged in the wall behind it. He stood where Carter may have stood and worked out where the shot had come from. The killer had been an arm's reach from Carter's desk (and the biscuits). Copeland knew even he could not miss a kill shot at that sort of range. But the killer had put a bullet clean through Carter's shoulder. That was a good shot, thought Copeland – to know where to put a bullet so it went straight through Carter's shoulder. This was no amateur.

Copeland put the mystery of the biscuits in his mental pending tray along with Carter's smart suit. He left the office, peered through the long window opposite to scan the vandalised work-lab then followed the blood stained tiles down the wide corridor, passing the closed wooden door next to Carter's office and the open door with a toilet inside next to that. He imagined the shocked scientist clasping his bleeding shoulder, staggering down the same corridor to the metal door.

Without leaning over more than necessary, Copeland examined the entry wound in Carter's shoulder and the copious amount of blood around the corpse. He nodded to himself, knowing that if the first fatal shot had been to a beating heart then there would be *really* copious amounts of blood. The killer had put a shot between Carter's eyes and then one in his heart to make sure then, with Carter well and truly deceased, the killer had trashed the work lab and poured some sort of acid into the server and laptop. Copeland groaned as he stood upright.

'Well?' asked Clare, arms folded. 'Is it as obvious to you as it is to me?'

'Yes. Obviously suicide,' answered Copeland.

Clare Harper gave him a wry smile. 'Come on, Larry. The killer missed and hit Carter in the shoulder. Carter made a run for it but the killer hit him in the leg and finished him off here.'

Copeland nodded slowly as he inwardly sighed. 'So what's behind the two inch thick steel door that needs a palm print reader to open it?' he asked.

Clare held her hands out wide as she incredulously asked, 'Can't you smell?'

Copeland no longer had a great sense of smell so considered his answer carefully before responding, 'They were experimenting on shit?'

His theory was met with a sigh, a shake of the head and a rolling of the eyes. Copeland thought Clare seemed to do that a lot whenever he was with her, even back when they were young detectives working together. 'It's animals,' she informed him.

It all became clear to Copeland. 'Aha!' he exclaimed. 'The killer is an animal rights terrorist extremist chap!'

His theory was met with more eye rolling and even a palm slap to the forehead. Clare gestured for him to go through the door. Copeland looked at the gap. He looked at his stomach. Clare shook her head and gently pushed the door open further,

'Excuse me,' Copeland said as he reached his shoeless foot over the outstretched legs of the corpse. His other foot and shoe followed, as did Clare. She flicked on the light and he muttered, 'Shit...'

Pushing him further into the room, Clare nodded. 'Yes, Larry, and a lot of it. They must have got pretty scared when they realised what was going on. Their cages are full of it.'

Wide-eyed, Copeland turned to stare at her. 'Surely experimenting on chimps is illegal!'

'Well,' said Clare. 'Firstly, they're not chimpanzees, they're bonobos. They're slightly smaller. Secondly, primate experimentation is allowed for certain things, like the study of some infectious diseases, thus the bio-hazard suits, and thirdly, they've all had a bullet put into their brains.'

Copeland returned his gaze to the two rows of six cages along the far wall – one row along the concrete floor, the other on a stainless steel shelf above. Each metre cube cage was isolated from its neighbours by steel partitions and each cage contained a dead bonobo with their fur, blood and brains splattered onto the bars and the grey breezeblock wall behind them. Almost all had their limbs splayed wide and had died with a look of sheer terror on their faces. Dead humans were something Copeland was used to, but the looks on the faces of the twelve dead monkeys sent a shiver down his spine, especially the one on the top right. That one seemed to be almost smiling.

Copeland felt Clare nudge him. She flicked her head towards the corner behind Copeland's shoulder. He turned to see a high backed metal chair with leather wrist and ankle restraints. Copeland could guess what it was used for. The bonobos didn't have much of a life.

'All the mice in the room next to his office have been poisoned too,' Clare said.

'Probably not animal rights activists then,' suggested Copeland.

A deep voice droned from the doorway behind them. 'The forensics team is finally here, Chief.'

Copeland turned to see the pale face of a young man with vacant eyes staring at him, or possibly through him. Unlike Copeland and Clare, he wore a full forensic suit and was

7

replacing his white face mask as Clare nodded and said, 'Thank you Inspector Lord. We'll get out of their way. I can't stand this smell anymore anyway. Tell them to ignore the bloody footprints in the corridor – they're his.' She pointed at Copeland, who was in shock. He could not believe someone as young as this man was already an inspector.

On the way out of the building Clare pointed at the glass double door entrance, telling Copeland how four police officers with a crow bar had not been able to get them open or break the glass, which would probably need a tank shell just to crack it. Eventually she had ordered an officer to go to Dr. Carter's home in search of a spare key card. The officer had wisely told Mrs. Carter it looked like there had been a break in at the lab and, fortunately, his wife knew where her husband kept his spare key card.

By the time Clare had finished telling him this they were in the rain in the car park of the 'Science Park' with its solitary, recently blood-stained building fronted by its impregnable glass doors.

'There's one more thing, Larry,' said Clare. 'Wait there.'

Copeland waited with the forensics team hovering behind him. He watched Clare use the key-card to re-enter the building. The sliding glass doors closed behind her. The lights inside went off. Copeland waited. Clare appeared on the other side of the glass doors. She pointed to Copeland, to her own eyes, then over her shoulder down the corridor behind her and stepped back. Copeland looked. He could see hardly anything beyond the other glass door on the far side of the reception area. He put his face up against the sliding door. As his eyes got used to the gloom he could just about see as far as the entrance to Carter's office. Copeland was startled when the lights came back on again and, as soon as his eyes adjusted, he could see the whole length of the corridor to where

Carter's body was propped against the doorway of the dead bonobo room.

Clare emerged through the sliding entrance doors, handed the forensics team the key-card and asked, 'So, Larry, what do you think?'

As the forensics team went through the doors, Copeland replied, 'Hmmm... I think it's raining. Let's go to a pub.'

Copeland soon assured Clare he knew all the pubs in the area and knew one that would definitely be open as it was already after ten a.m. and, since they were both almost senior citizens, they should take one of the marked police vehicles so they could park on the double yellow lines right outside the pub to avoid excessive walking. Chief Inspector Clare Harper liked letting Larry Copeland think he had talked her into something she had been about to suggest anyway. After being in stench among dead things she wanted to leave the scene behind for a while, and she needed coffee. She also needed a toilet.

Clare waited until they had passed Tesco and were driving up the hill before she broached a sensitive subject. Without looking at Copeland, she said, 'Long time no see Larry. I'd heard you'd got fatter since your minor stroke, but you haven't. It's just a larger stomach.'

Copeland ran fingers through his silver hair and patted the protruding pod where his shirt stretched the seat belt. 'All muscle this,' he smiled.

'They said you looked ten months pregnant.' Clare said, keeping her eyes on the road and her face straight. 'But I think it looks more like you've swallowed a dinosaur egg.'

'Oh,' said Copeland as the smile melted from his face and his long-dormant conscience deep inside him said, *'Told you so, Copeland!'*

MARY WHITE.

Mary sometimes missed her old primary school friends. True, there had been times they had been cruel and taunted her. She especially did not like the way they had circled around her in the playground and sang, 'Mary, Mary, quite contrary...' until they had her in floods of tears. She always told herself they did have a nice side though, and she would always remember them every year by taking flowers to their graves.

Right now she had bigger concerns. The business of mergers, acquisitions and liquidations for a freelance operator like her was always a challenge. She never knew where the next job was coming from and for someone who had already turned thirty she really had to start considering the future. Dear husband Jeffrey seemed to know what that future held. It was simple: three children and a people carrier. Mary sometimes found herself wondering if she wanted more. 'Sometimes' was at least eight times a day and she was already considering the future when she flexed her shoulders, threw her feet off the side of the bed, clambered into her woolly onesie, slipped her phone into the pocket and sleepily staggered down into their kitchen. Hubby Jeffrey was already there. Charmingly, he had his back to her, staring out of the window, eating his Weetabix and listening to the Today programme where yet someone else was being interviewed about something apparently interminable she did not have the remotest interest in called Brexit.

'The grass needs cutting,' husband Jeffrey said. The prospect really excited Mary. It was going to be another day of fun in the White household.

Rubbing her bleary eyes she answered, 'It's the warm, wet spring. It really makes the grass grow, doesn't it, darling?'

'You're right there, honey-bunch. It's probably something to do with this global warming thing. We really do need to do something. Perhaps we should get a better mower,' he replied, still staring out of the window and watching the grass grow. 'You were late last night, darling. I went to bed once the ten o'clock news came on. Difficult meeting or a long drive back?'

Mary had not been surprised Jeffrey was already asleep when she got back at ten thirty. 'No, the meeting went mostly as expected, but making someone redundant is always a little tricky, especially when they have dependants. I had to make sure the exit package made sure all the dependents would not need anything in the future too.'

'You're so thoughtful, honey-bunch,' said Jeffrey once he had swallowed his Weetabix.

Mary grabbed a banana while she waited for the conversation to continue, but she knew Jeffrey's focus was back on the simply extraordinary length of the early spring grass. She knew he was working out when it would be best to cut it, and thinking about an appropriate time to skip the Radio 4 schedule and get the mower out. It was all fun, fun, fun in the White household. She waited. She stared. She wondered how long it could take to eat a bowl of Weetabix. 'I need to check my emails before I go to the gym, darling,' she finally said.

'I've been thinking', said Jeffrey. Mary wished he had turned round when he spoke.

'That's good, darling,' she said.

'It's our first wedding anniversary on Tuesday,' he went on and Mary felt her heart miss a beat. It missed another when he said, 'I think we should do something special to celebrate.'

'Wonderful, darling,' gasped Mary, trying to disguise her surprise. 'Perhaps a weekend away?'

'I was thinking,' Jeffrey said with an air of conviction as he stared at the garden. 'We could go for a curry. You know, to that cheap place where they let you take your own wine.'

Mary said, 'Wonderful, darling,' but wished she had not left her Berretta M9 pistol in her other house.

COPELAND AND HARPER GO TO THE PUB.

Copeland was not happy. Clare had parked in the pub car park and he had needed to walk all the way from there to the pub. She said he looked like the walk would do him good. He had been right, though, seats were easy to find in the very traditionally themed Butchered Calf public house, established 1889 and awaiting its first renovation. Besides having a very decent coffee machine, the only thing that surprised Clare was that there was no sawdust on the floor to go with the plain wooden tables and chairs. She sipped her coffee as Copeland cast aside his raincoat, gulped his pint of Minster Ale and chose brown sauce for his bacon sandwich. Clare wondered how he could eat after just leaving such a scene of mass carnage, and a human body too, but remembered if she knew one thing about Larry Copeland it was that it took a lot to take his mind off regularly filling his stomach. The only thing she could think of that had diminished his appetite was an acrimonious divorce after which he had disappeared for two years to work undercover in Northern Ireland. Clare had long since shed the guilt of introducing Larry Copeland to her friend Helen and often recalled how, when he told her they were getting married, she had rolled her eyes and tried to warn him he was not making the right choice. At least he had made the right choice today: the pub was empty. The shower had passed and the sun had broken through so they decided to sit in the quaint beer garden at the rear to enjoy the warm spring weather and have a brief moment of tranquillity gazing across the Dorset countryside.

'So,' said Clare, wincing as Copeland swigged beer to wash the sandwich down, 'you may have noticed the new science park is what one might call underdeveloped – one road in and nothing else around except a few cows in the next field. I doubt the killer even had to use a silencer.'

Chewing his sandwich, Copeland nodded, pointed to the middle of his forehead and circled his finger around. Clare assumed Copeland meant the burn marks around the bullet hole into Dr. Carter's brain showed a silencer had probably been used, at least to terminate Dr. Carter.

Clare continued, 'We do know Carter was the registered tenant of the building and it's listed as a medical research facility. We're trying to find the names and addresses of the other lab workers, but Carter's mobile phone is nowhere to be found and I suspect the computers and the server are beyond helping us either. Did you spot there was no Wi-Fi? That and the doors being virtually impregnable tell us Carter was obsessed with security, though, strangely, there's no CCTV. I suppose they thought they didn't need it with those doors. The wife has to be our number one suspect. It's usually the wife.'

Copeland considered this theory while he swallowed his sandwich. 'I thought it was usually the butler?' he ventured, got an eye roll and picked up what was left of his pint.

'Keep up, Larry. Mrs. Carter knew where the spare key-card was,' sighed Clare. 'She obviously hired someone and gave him the card key to get in once the other workers had gone home. A real amateur who hit Carter in the shoulder and leg first and was stupid enough to leave the lights on.'

Copeland wanted to go with Clare's theory. Why not? A prominent scientist with a score of awards had been killed in his own research lab by someone hired by his wife so she could get the insurance money, and just in case they were called as eyewitnesses all twelve of the bonobos had their brains blown out. Not to mention the mice which would, without doubt, have testified in court too. And after eliminating these witnesses the killer had melted the computers and smashed up the work lab because he was bored? Copeland knew Clare must have known all this and suspected the animals were killed and the lab was trashed to muddy the waters, make it look like it was more than it was and divert attention away from the wife. Copeland wasn't so sure. He took another sip of beer. He knew he was off his game. It was still his first pint. He took a long swig and felt better before saying, 'I suppose the body was spotted by the weekend cleaners?'

Clare shook her head. 'There don't seem to be any. It was spotted by a local guy. I've already threatened him with a charge of perverting the course of justice if he breathes a word to anyone. He was taking his dog for a walk along the river. As you saw for yourself, I doubt he would have been able to see Jonathan Carter's corpse from over twenty metres away if the lights hadn't been left on. Apart from the entrance doors there's not a window in the whole place.'

'Hmmm,' nodded Copeland. 'I deduce the dog walker was distracted from picking up his dog's mess when he stooped down, glanced through the glass doors and saw the body.'

Clare paused with her coffee halfway to her mouth. 'You still amaze me sometimes, Larry. How the heck did you know that?'

Copeland sipped his beer and said, 'Elementary, my dear Harper.' He thought he would not spoil the moment by admitting he had, in fact, trodden in the said mess before entering the lab. He had hoped stepping in the pool of blood in the corridor would have diluted it a little.

'You know,' said Clare rubbing her nose, 'after being in that room where all those bonobos had expelled their waste products before they were killed, I just can't get the smell out of my nostrils.'

'Me neither,' said Copeland, surreptitiously scraping the sole of his shoe on the side of the wooden bench and hastily moving on with, 'So no weekend cleaners? The killer probably didn't expect the body to be discovered until the staff came back to work on Monday.'

So, Copeland, said his cynical inner voice, *why did your so-called professional killer make the mistake of leaving the lights on? They drew the dog walker there and allowed him to see Dr. Carter's dead body, so why? Not very professional, was it?*

Copeland thought his curmudgeonly inner voice had a good point but he had a different question. He asked, 'How come you're here, though, Clare? This is Dorset. You're Devon.'

'Cross county work,' replied Clare, sipping her coffee. 'Our stations are closer so we look after the town, not that much happens here. But I could ask you the same question, Larry. Why are *you* here? I was surprised when my chief super called and said you were being sent. I heard a rumour you left the force and went to work for some secret, off-the-books security service. Is that true?'

Copeland leaned across the table and secretively whispered, 'I'm not allowed to say because no such secret organisation like The Pickfords even exists and they are definitely not in the people removal business and I don't work for them anymore either and I only did background research anyway, but I can tell you it wasn't them who killed our dead scientist because I phoned Beryl to check when I was driving here. Do you know my new car's even got a built in phone? By the way, Beryl Pickford doesn't exist either. Honest.'

'The Pickfords? Beryl? Right, I understand, I think... They don't exist...'

'Anyway,' Copeland continued, 'I work for this new Department C now, or will do from Monday morning when it's officially up and running.'

Clare's jaw had dropped again. '*You?* YOU work for MI5?'

Copeland looked across the fields and considered this. He screwed up his face and answered, 'Well, perhaps technically, but we're sort of an independent division. My job is recruiting and training undercover operatives to tackle corruption, organised crime, etcetera. Apparently, I'm some sort of alternate thinker.' He waited while Clare spluttered coffee back into her cup. Squinting, he looked at his watch and said, 'I think I'll have another pint now it's nearly eleven.' He groaned as he stood and held his back as he sauntered from the patio into the bar. Clare noticed he had avoided her question about why he was there.

He returned with another coffee for Clare, a second pint and a packet of peanuts between his teeth. He slumped back onto the wooden bench and began struggling to tear the peanuts open. Clare snatched them off him, made short work of the job and handed them back. 'So why are you here, Larry, if your job is recruitment and training? Or do they send someone from the security services every time a research facility gets broken into?'

Pouring nuts into a palm, Copeland said, 'I was supposed to be on holiday until I start the new job Monday – I'm staying at nice little hotel over in Kilmington – but the boss gave me a call and when Wendy Miller phones and says she's spoken to your Chief Super and you're expecting my involvement in this case, I don't argue. One year of working for her and my pension is...' He pointed to the sky. He watched the nuts in his hand cascade into his lap. He did not need to look to know there was some vigorous head shaking and eye rolling going on across the table. 'So, Clare, you think it's the wife hiring a hit man?' he asked as he brushed nuts off his dark blue suit and considered the wife theory as highly unlikely. The trouble was, he did not have a better one, except possibly a rival company out to steal Dr. Carter's research and make sure no research data remained by destroying the computers and splattering Carter's brain onto a metal door.

Exasperated, Copeland's inner voice huffed: *So how did this rival company's hit-man get in through those impregnable doors then, Copeland?*

JANE SADLER VISITS NANCY CARTER.

Detective Constable Jane Sadler knew exactly why she had been given this task. She knew all the other Dorset detectives had at least ten cases each and because of her particular circumstances, she had none. Even so, being sent off to the other side of Bridport on Saturday morning had not been how she had intended to spend her supposed day off. She had promised to visit her partner and the call she had made to say she had to work instead had not gone down well. Before the call was abruptly ended, Jane had been told to not bother going up that weekend at all.

She had almost reached the turnoff for Charmouth when she turned right to follow the minor road to the open gates of the large white house owned by Dr. Jonathan Carter and his wife, Nancy. Jane sat in the car for some time, staring at her hands on the steering wheel and trying to remember her bereavement training. With a sigh, she eventually got out and noticed she was being watched by someone on the far side of the garden's waist-high hedge using shears and doing a reasonable impersonation of a Mediterranean Poldark. He gave her a wave with one muscular arm. Jane raised a hand in reply, took a deep breath and rang the doorbell.

Thirty two year old Mrs. Nancy Carter opened the door, looking concerned and wearing a pink, slim-fit tracksuit. Jane thought it looked expensive, as did Nancy Carter's long light brown hair, film-star makeup and three inch heels. Jane introduced herself with her warrant card and Mrs. Carter's look of concern turned to a look of apprehension.

The Carter's lounge was large, as was the sofa where Jane sat next to Mrs. Carter to break the news there had been a tragedy at the research lab and Mrs. Carter should brace for some bad news. Even though Mrs. Nancy Carter said she knew something might be wrong after a police officer had called earlier to see if her husband had a spare key-card for the lab, she took the news of her husband's recent demise badly and spent half an hour crying inconsolably through half a box of tissues before Jane managed to tell her how her husband's body had luckily been spotted by a passing dog-walker and tactfully added the death was being treated as a murder because everything in the lab had been destroyed and Dr. Carter's brains had been blasted out of the back of his skull. Jane could not understand why Mrs. Carter began crying again. She sobbed on Jane's shoulder, repeatedly muttering, 'Murder? Why? Who?'

Holding the last tissue from the box, Nancy Carter eventually told Jane what a terrible shock it was her husband had been murdered and how she had not suspected anything was wrong when Jonathan had not returned home the previous evening because he regularly worked really late on Fridays, usually not coming home at all, but sleeping on the little cot he had in his office and sometimes even working through Saturday too. The sniffling Nancy had told Jane this as Jane sat beside her with an arm around her shoulder. Jane learned little else except Jonathan liked to keep his work and home life separate, and Nancy knew no more than the first names of the four other people who worked at the lab with him, so she really could not help Jane with their addresses. Jane wrote their first names down anyway.

Jane was not happy leaving Mrs. Carter, but she said she preferred to be on her own and her neighbour Ernie, the hedge trimming gardener, and his wife Nicola were on hand if she needed anyone, so Jane returned to her car, dutifully made notes and phoned her inspector before returning home to Weymouth. At least the inspector thanked her for her time and told her not to worry about going to interview the murder victim's co-workers as planned since Mrs. Carter had no information about them. Instead he would phone Devon Police to persuade them to have a uniform officer outside the lab to get their addresses when they arrived for work on Monday morning and she could go and interview them then.

On her way home Jane wondered how she was going to spend the rest of her weekend. She supposed she could do some more sorting and packing, but investigating a murder seemed much more enticing.

-*COPELAND AND CLARE RETURN TO THE LAB.*

Through the modern miracle of mobile phones, Copeland and Clare soon learned the computers in the completely wrecked work-lab were just as melted as the ones in Dr. Carter's office. Clare declared coffee break over with, 'No. Larry! You're not having one for the road!' so Copeland allowed her to drive him back to the scene of the crime beyond the town's fringe. By the time they were halfway there he already had a plan. He told Clare what it was. He would take his sleek new Department C issue silver BMW back to his little hotel, go for lunch at that nice bistro pub round the corner and then go back to his room for a nap. He explained how the late night he had spent drinking at the little hotel's bar with the proprietress had caught up on him. Once the friendly proprietress Nina had found out he played golf too they had spent hours exchanging golf stories until the other resident slammed her glass down and left in a huff, which was when the proprietress had invited him up to her room to see her golf trophies.

'I think she had something in her eye when she asked me to go up with her because she sort of clenched it closed and opened it again when she leaned across the bar really close to my face, but I thought looking at her trophies sounded boring so I went to bed instead,' Copeland confided as they came to a halt in the lab car park. He could not understand why Clare gave him the full eye roll and head shake before putting her head in her hands.

Once Clare had breathalysed Copeland and he was about to get into his car, the gaunt young Inspector Lord, now wearing a black, well-cut suit, approached and in an unenthusiastic slow monotone informed them, 'Still no sign of the victim's phone and the work lab has had every flask and test tube smashed, even those that were in those whirling machines that spin stuff round and round. The forensics people say it seems to be clean but I think they're wrong. There's broken glass everywhere. It's really rather untidy in there. But I did find something interesting. I used my phone to do some research. Did you know bonobos are sometimes called pygmy chimps? I'm just going to look up what pygmy means.' He wondered away, tapping on his phone.

Copeland saw a rare opportunity for some passive-aggressive revenge. He looked at Clare, shook his head and rolled his eyes.

'Don't ask,' she whispered. 'Giles is being fast-tracked with some real-world work experience until the next safe parliamentary seat comes up in a by-election.'

Copeland clasped his cheeks as he moaned, 'Which party?'

Clare leaned closer and hissed, 'His father is Baron Robert Lord of Kernow, so go figure.'

Copeland looked to the skies and did some real eye rolling. 'His father is **the** Robert Lord?' he rhetorically asked.

Copeland's plan for his Saturday afternoon did not go well.

He had left all the paperwork to Clare just as happily as he had taken the job with Department C. His previous, other 'new' job working for the ultra-secretive Pickfords doing background checks had almost driven him mad with boredom so he had accepted the Department C job, along with his salary increase and the new car too. What he had not expected when he took the job was to be told what to do by Judi Dench. Or, more accurately, by her voice. Or, even more accurately, by the voice that was meant to sound like Judi Dench's cultured smoothness. Copeland had always liked Judi Dench until she cut off his Best of Blondie, spoke to him through the car's speakers and told him he was exceeding the speed limit.

Pressing every button he could see only resulted in the car's voice volume having a louder and more irritated sounding Judi Dench. And he really did not need car-Judi to shrilly tell him the wine he had consumed with his two hour lunch had taken him over the legal limit. He tried to explain to her that it was only fifty yards back to his hotel but Judi's inbuilt breathalyser on the steering wheel would not let the car start. He luckily found some duct tape in the glove compartment and stuck it over the breathalyser, shouting, 'Let's see if a so-called intelligent personal assistant is smart enough to get that tape off, Judi!' at the speaker and drove back for his nap.

The nap was a failure. Whenever he closed his eyes the same vision haunted him. He tried to think about the lasagne he had eaten for lunch, but his 'happy thought' did not overshadow the faces of the dead bonobos. One in particular kept haunting him – the small one in the top right cage which had the different look to the others. It had the sign B11 above the cage and while the others had fear and panic written over their faces and were sprawled in misshapen positions, B11 had looked almost serene, as if it had sat and waited for the bullet in its brain. Copeland assumed the little bonobo must have been the first and had no idea the barrel of a gun could end its life. Either that or it welcomed death more than captivity and being regularly strapped to a chair. He managed to steer his thoughts back to the lasagne (with chips instead of salad) when the friendly, golf playing proprietress started banging on his door and shouted something about how he was supposed to have checked out. He thought she was not as subtle as the three previous owners who had simply emptied his room for him and left his cases in the lobby.

Spookily, the tape covering the steering wheel breathalyser had dropped off by the time he checked out of the hotel and began his drive back to his little house in Leyton. He was not on speaking terms with Judi and she seemed not to be on speaking terms with him, which suited Copeland just fine. The silent drive gave him time to think. The murder was open and shut as far as he was concerned – a hired hit man somehow gets into the research facility, kills Jonathan Carter, destroys evidence and forgets to turn the lights off. Obviously, this professional hit man had been hired by a rival company, or, as Clare thought, by Carter's wife who had given him the spare key card to get in, or it could have been one of the other workers at the lab with a grudge against Dr. Carter, or none of the above. Yes, it was an open and shut case. What bothered him more was why he had been ordered to assist the police with murder enquiries. As far as he understood, Department C was concerned with corruption, thus the 'C' in the name. He stopped for a small snack near Andover and, as he ate the best steak and chips he had ever tasted since the previous Wednesday, Copeland resolved that the first thing he would do when he got into the Department C office on Monday morning was to ask Director Wendy Miller exactly why she had wanted him to assess the crime scene.

MARY MAKES A CALL.

Mary White's phone pinged as she walked into the gym. She took it out to see a waiting WhatsApp message. Mary ignored it, deciding there was no way she was going to miss her gym session, nor the yoga class after it, nor the usual coffee she had with the gym crowd afterwards, whom she saw as reminding her what normal people were like, which was mostly mind numbingly boring.

She returned home to find Jeffrey staring out of the window looking at the grass. She surmised he had moved since she had gone to the gym because he was eating toast instead of Weetabix. He was being his usual charming self by biting into the toast and immediately taking a swig of tea. She kissed his cheek. He told her he had intended to get the mower out when it brightened up but thought it might rain again and, look, he had been proven right. Besides not really wanting to see his half chewed toast soaked in tea, Mary thought he seemed smug about predicting rain when dark clouds were billowing and he had probably heard the radio weather forecast three or four times, so she left him to his contemplations and toast mastication while she went upstairs to make a WhatsApp call. End to end encryption and convenience all in one thought Mary as the call was answered and she heard silence.

'Your message said to call you. What's wrong?' she asked.

She paused and listened while the voice on the other end of her call spoke.

'That's impossible,' Mary said, dubiously.

Another pause while the voice spoke.

Shaking her head, Mary said, 'But no one goes anywhere near the place. It's the other side of the railway tracks from civilisation.'

A longer pause followed before Mary sighed and groaned, 'A dog walker? Just bad luck then, is it? Perhaps I should visit him to find out for sure? I'd like to ask him how he could even see down that corridor.'

Quite a long pause.

'Right then! I won't go to see him then, not if your bosses want me to speed things up and ruin my timetable. I had got other things planned, you know. I already wasted a whole evening killing those bonobos.'

Pause.

'What do you mean, what bonobos? The bonobos that were in the extra room built at the back. There were twelve of them. You said to get rid of all the... Are you crying, Atticus?'

Long pause.

'Finally! Yes, I suppose it is sad, but please don't blow your nose down the phone like that, Atticus.'

Pause.

'Yes, I do realise it's not your real name, Atticus. You're using one of those voice distorters anyway.'

(Sigh.) 'Yes, you are, Atticus. And saying honest isn't going to convince me you're not either.'

Longer pause.

'Yes, Atticus, I did know a fake name is also called a nom de plume.'

A silent pause was followed by a longer pause as she listened to Atticus.

'I'm sorry, Atticus, I have no idea why a different name translates literally as *name of feather* either...'

Pause.

'Very well, Atticus, I'll try to find out for you. It's not like I have anything better to do is it?' Mary said sarcastically. 'Now, you are transferring the next part of my payment aren't you?'

Pause.

(Annoyed) 'That's not what we agreed, Atticus! You said once Carter...'

Pause.

'Oh, just following orders are you? Very well, then, if that's the way it is. I'll speed things up, but the whole lot had better be in my account as soon as the job is complete, Atticus.'

Only half content with his reply and not liking her employer withholding her money, even if his bosses did say so, Mary ended the call. She looked at her phone and shook her head. What was the rush? Mary thought. They all lived so close. Wasn't that why she had persuaded Jeffrey to move near the Dorset coast? Mary was sure she had covered every angle, and with all the computers now destroyed there was no way to find the addresses of the other workers. The kindly Dr. Carter had confirmed as much when she had shot him in the leg so he'd have a nice sit down while she poked her Beretta's smoking hot silencer into the hole in his shoulder, just after he had so thoughtfully opened that big metal door for her.

She huffed and tapped her phone to find the locations of the trackers she had put on the other lab workers' cars, knowing she would have to abandon her plan to go shoe shopping and go to work again instead.

2. Sunday, March 17th.

COPELAND.

Free of Judi at the golf club Sunday carvery lunch, it was constant pings from his phone that now annoyed Copeland. Clare kept sending him updates about the cold-blooded murder of a man and twelve helpless primates, not to mention a few dozen even more helpless white mice. Although he hated cruelty to defenceless animals, the young lamb carvery lunch was excellent so he resented being disturbed, especially since the continuous texts from Clare told him nothing except they had nothing: the acid used to melt the computers and server was probably untraceable, there was no trace of any chemicals or biological agents at all in the trashed lab, the shots fired from the Beretta M9 pistol did not match anything on record and the dead animals had been carted off to Exeter for tests. All they did have was that Dr. Jonathan Carter had been killed by a bullet to the brain fired at close range (he could have told them that) and Carter's office had so many fingerprints, fibres, hairs and such stuff the forensics people did not know where to start. At least that told Copeland something: Dr. Carter's office was not cleaned very well.

Another message from Clare told him they had finally persuaded Dorset Police to send officers to interview the other lab workers to take their statements and their fingerprints. This annoyed him most: a dead body shouldn't have to wait for cross-county wrangling, he thought, then decided it probably could, especially since the message went on to say that because the labs computers were destroyed, there seemed to be no way to find out who the other lab workers were, but an officer would be outside the lab waiting for them when they arrived for work Monday morning.

It didn't help when his phone pinged again while he ate his cheesecake. If she dared interrupt the cheeseboard too he would denounce Clare as Emily's godmother! The golf club captain, no less, had a quiet word in his ear about mobile phones and clubhouse protocols. Resignedly, Copeland went outside to phone Clare from underneath his umbrella, determined to tell her to stop texting him, when his phone pinged yet again. He was about to say a very naughty word when he saw there was finally something to act on. Some sad Dorset detective without a life had done some internet digging and she had discovered who actually financed the lab. Even better, the head office of the lab's owners, Uroboros Rejuvenation Limited, was near Slough, only ten miles from the temporary offices of the new Department C.

His inner voice sarcastically said, *If it's that close, I wonder which idiot they'll send there Copeland?*

MARY WHITE.

Inside Mary White's larger than average handbag was a photograph. She took it out and looked at it. No doubt someone had printed it off, intending to frame it and hang it on the wall – perhaps even Dr. Jonathan Carter himself, though Mary doubted it. There he stood at the centre of attention, smiling and holding the small plate in both hands. His subordinate co-workers flanked him. To his immediate left and right stood Reema Sharma and Alison Taylor, holding high a hastily scrawled banner with the word EUREKA felt tipped across it, while the fourth of the quartet, Wang Linpeng grinned broadly in his white coat with a thumb up.

Three down, one to go, thought Mary as she studied the face of the quartet's remaining survivor before slipping the photograph back into the side of her handbag. She noticed the third silencer lying in the bottom of the bag. It was the only one she had left. Silencers did not last long and she had buried the two that were recently ruined by overheating in the back garden of her other house already, but one should be enough for now. She could always get replacements.

Tucked into an inside pocket of the handbag was the crumpled tissue that interested her more. She took it out and unfurled it, holding its contents in the palm of her hand. They looked like ordinary plain aspirin tablets, but she knew they must be something far more if Carter and his team had placed them on a small plate and given them pride of place in their group photo. She was not sure what to do with them now. Her instructions had been to remove all the evidence, so she had removed the little white tablets, wrapped them in the tissue and put them in her bag just before she had trashed the lab.

As she stared at the tablets she reflected on how hard it had been to shoot the bonobos. After she had shot the first one the others had started jumping and twirling frantically around inside their cages. They had been quite difficult targets. Killing them had taken longer than she had anticipated and she blamed the dead bonobos for disrupting her evening so much she had not eaten until much later than was really healthy, and now this dog walker spotting Carter's body had disrupted her weekend schedule even more thanks to Atticus and his bosses' unnecessary panic. A dog walker? The chances of anyone like this dog walker going near the lab was remote, and how did he even see the body when it was lying at the end of that dark corridor? She had left it there because she knew it was practically invisible. Even if the sun shone outside there was no way someone could have seen it once she had turned the lights off. She wished she had dragged it into the room with the dead bonobos, at least then she would have finished the job on her own schedule and not have missed her Sunday morning yoga, but the police finding the body had clearly spooked her paymasters and provoked them to get Atticus to hurry her along. Bloody Atticus with his ridiculous nom de plume! Mary stopped herself. Atticus' employers were rich enough to pay her more than she had ever dreamed of when she became self-employed so if Atticus wanted a nom de plume then Atticus could damn well have one – as long as she was paid in full, of course, with some extra for the annoying animals. If not she would inscribe the name Atticus on a new tombstone.

Mary folded the little white tablets back inside the tissue and slipped it back into the inside pocket of her handbag. She took her Beretta out, checked the magazine, checked the spare magazine and double-checked the silencer fitted. She took out the photo again, looked at it, and once more set off to silence the elusive fourth photogenic scientist.

DETECTIVE JANE SADLER GETS A CALL.

The expectation was that the colleagues of Jonathan Carter would arrive for work as normal on Monday morning and be met by a uniformed officer in the car park. He would take their names and addresses and send them home to await the arrival of a CID officer who would interview them. They would leave for home and wonder what was going on until Detective Jane Sadler arrived.

Waiting by her phone, Detective Sadler researched Jonathan Carter and Uroboros Rejuvenation Limited, just as she had done throughout Sunday once she had discovered they owned the research lab where Dr. Carter (Ph.D.) was murdered. She did not care today was supposed to be her day off in lieu for working both Saturday and Sunday – any chance of visiting her partner had passed now normal people's work weeks had begun. By nine fifteen she was looking at her watch and wondering what to do with the rest of her day. She presumed the constable waiting outside the research lab had found the co-workers all lived in Devon so had passed the addresses on to the Devon and Cornwall CID rather to her at Dorset Police. She knew the alternative was unsavoury. Twenty minutes later she was just about to ask her overworked sergeant if there was anything she could help him with when the phone on her desk rang.

She answered it and said, 'Hello, Detective Jane Sadler, Dorset CID.'

There was silence. Jane thought it was another one of those computer generated calls and a voice would soon come on telling her all about the government scheme to replace the gas boiler which she did not have. She was about to hang up when a voice said, 'Hello.'

'Detective Sadler,' Jane repeated.

'How can I help you?' asked the voice so slowly Jane thought whoever this was she would recommend him to the insomnia society.

'Er, you phoned me,' said Jane.

'Ah, yes,' droned the voice, now with a hint of sentience. 'It's something to do with the workers at a research lab. I wrote it on a post-it somewhere... Did you know pygmy means small?'

'Actually, I did,' replied Jane. 'Who is this?'

The voice on the other end seemed to think about this for a few seconds before saying, 'Inspector Giles Lord, Devon and Cornwall Police.'

Jane sat up straight as she said, 'Sorry, Sir.'

'Apology accepted, Detective. What are you apologising for?'

Two whole sentences from the voice on the phone almost sent Jane comatose so she was not expecting a follow up question.

Giles asked, 'Now Chief Harper has been promoted to Super, do you think they'll let me have her old desk? I could put it by the window.'

Jane responded to the query with, 'Are you phoning me to tell me none of Dr. Carter's fellow researchers turned up for work, Sir?'

'Er, let me check this post-it note... Well, I say! How did you know that?' asked Giles.

'Female intuition, Sir,' said Jane, resorting to what she was often accused of using whenever she stated the bleeding obvious.

'Well, you're right, Detective. The receptionist lady did not show up either. We reckon they probably live in Dorset so it's over to you. I have to go now. I'm supposed to be meeting someone.'

By the time Giles had finished saying this Jane had looked at her watch twice and already logged on to the Uroboros Rejuvenation Limited web site to get their number. 'Very good, Sir,' said Jane and put the receiver down.

Within ten minutes, Jane had phoned Uroboros Rejuvenation Ltd. and got them to phone back with the addresses of all employees at the research lab. At first, they had denied knowing anything about any facility near Axminster but Jane had been quite persuasive and, in a friendly, informative way, she had explained how many years the sentence was for conspiracy to withhold evidence. Ten minutes after that, Jane had already informed her sergeant she was off to see the co-workers of the murder victim and was on the road to Bridport in an unmarked vehicle.

COPELAND GOES TO THE OFFICE.

Copeland arrived at the temporary, cold, damp offices of Department C a little later than first thing on Monday morning. Some might have said it was a little later than second thing. He could have blamed his lateness on lots of things, such as not getting up very early, but the Department C Director, Wendy Miller, told him she understood how difficult it was getting from the other side of London and that was exactly the reason they were putting him up in a local hotel during the week. Copeland remembered she had indeed told him that. He was glad he had absent-mindedly left his case with all his holiday stuff in the car boot and only taken his toiletries bag out, along with the only bottle of wine that remained. Perhaps something inside him, some inner voice, had reminded him he was staying at a hotel and he had left his case there on purpose: it definitely wasn't just because he hadn't bothered taking it out. Honest. He was glad he always packed too much and most of the clothes were clean anyway. Somewhere in his case he even had a spare dark blue suit, just like the one he was wearing and the other ones in his wardrobe.

At Director Wendy Miller's suggestion, and because it had not occurred to him to do so, it was decided Copeland would not phone ahead to warn Uroboros Rejuvenation Ltd. they were about to get an official visit. His face had probably not hidden his look of despair when Director Miller went on to tell him he would be met there by someone from Devon and Cornwall Police, who were, for some reason, insisting on having an officer present since it was their murder enquiry. He expected the eye-rolling, head shaking Clare to be tapping her foot impatiently by the time he got there. He had his chance to ask why Department C was even getting involved in a murder enquiry at all but decided to avoid rocking any boats. Rocking boats had often ended up with him being the only one getting wet and, besides, a visit would get him out of arranging new furniture in an office that had not seen heating for five years. It would also get him away from the other recruits he had met on his 'Orientation Day'. They all seemed to have the gregariousness of a dead slug. None of them even drank at lunchtime. At least Wendy Miller seemed an OK boss. Although she was even taller and greyer than Copeland and looked like she bench pressed Olympic weightlifters before breakfast, she seemed to laugh readily, especially when Copeland was around.

Copeland left the cold, damp offices near the M4 junction roundabout and drove through Windsor, then, with his back to the London smog, on towards the address he had put into his satnav. Car-voice-Judi was very helpful with directions and he found himself on the outskirts of Bricknall in front of a four story white building with mirrored glass windows. It looked more like a state of the art hospital than an office block. 'Aha!' thought Copeland. 'It's *that* Uroboros Rejuvenation Limited.'

His inner voice came back with, *IS there another one? And I told you to Google it first, but you had to have just one more pint and then a brandy at the golf club last night, didn't you Copeland?*

Copeland thought his recently reawakened conscience was being a bit harsh. He had intended to Google the company that morning, but his new healthy breakfast regime was more time consuming than his old one. The previous system had allowed him time to wash and shave while the bacon and eggs fried gently before he slapped them into four rounds of bread, dowsed them in brown sauce and consumed them with a mug of sweet tea. The new healthy regime consisted of going continental, so now he had to put the packet of croissants into the microwave, watch them go round, slice them down the middle to put the butter and jam on and afterwards spend time with a dustpan and brush getting all those flaky bits off his kitchen floor. What was worse, he felt hungry within an hour, rather than the two hours the old regime had engendered, so he'd been relieved to find that nice little cafe near the office where he could pick up bacon and fried egg sandwiches on the way to work. Besides, now he had realised Uroboros Rejuvenation Ltd. was the same as U.R. Ltd he knew so well he did not need to Google it. He knew more about U.R. Ltd than Google ever would and for a moment he suspected that was why Wendy Miller had given him the case, until it occurred to him she had sent him to Carter's research lab before anyone even knew U.R. Ltd. owned it – before that sad Dorset detective had spent her Sunday finding out.

Copeland got out of the car and had a quick look around. There was no sign of Clare so he got back in and waited for the 'Devon and Cornwall liaison officer' to arrive. He watched the drizzle fall and watched droplets of water trickle down his windscreen. It was soothing. He closed his eyelids. He awoke to the sound of tapping on his car window. He wound the window down while he rubbed his eyes and braced himself for some Clare eye rolling.

'I suppose old people need to take a nap quite often,' said the deep monotone male voice.

Copeland prised his eyelids open to see the thin deadpan face of young Inspector Giles Lord smiling at him. 'Oh, God!' muttered Copeland, looking at the man whose skin appeared to have not seen sunlight since birth and who might possibly have no reflection in a mirror either. Copeland would soon learn it was likely his parents had locked him in an attic through shame, sent him to boarding school as soon as he learned to speak, paid extra for them to keep him there over Christmas and only kept him around in case one of his siblings needed an organ transplant. Copeland sympathised with Giles' father for doing what he had done, but only very briefly.

'Nice seats in these new BMWs, aren't they Inspector?' Giles said, almost enthusiastically.

Copeland opened the car door. Unfortunately, Giles was nimble enough to step back quickly. 'The roads were awful. Sorry it took me almost until lunchtime to get here, Larry,' apologised Giles as he trotted behind the striding Copeland towards the rotating door of Uroboros Rejuvenation. Above the door was the all-gold company logo – the letters UR inside the ancient uroboros symbol of the snake eating its own tail. Copeland had not needed to be reminded either by Giles or the snake that it was almost lunchtime.

THE DARK MAN.

The man in the dark raincoat and black fedora hat stood opposite Copeland's small semi-detached house in Leyton wondering what to do. He had arrived too late and had seen Copeland drive away in his shiny new BMW. He had considered his options. He knew he was getting wet but Copeland was his first priority. He was determined justice would be served, even if it meant pointing a gun at Copeland's head.

COPELAND.

Once Inspector Giles had gone round the revolving door twice he flashed his police identity warrant card with the flourish of a stage magician before the Uroboros Rejuvenation Ltd. receptionist could open her mouth, and when he told her they were there to see whoever was in charge the receptionist beckoned an elderly man wearing a 'Volunteer Helper' badge over and told him to take them to Dr. Lynn's office. Copeland was glad they used the lift up to the fourth floor, not for his own sake, of course, but for the sake of the elderly guide.

When the guide deposited them at the entrance to what was clearly a medical waiting room, Copeland put his hand firmly on Inspector Giles' shoulder, stopped him in his tracks and whispered, 'Let my experience handle this, my young protégé!'

Giles shrugged and hung back while Copeland approached the outside curve of the chest-high reception desk. The middle aged woman with short dark raised her thin, spectacled face as he approached. She stood, looked him up and down and said, 'Sorry, Sir, liposuction is on the third floor.'

Copeland felt inside his jacket pocket for his ID as he said, 'We're here to see Dr. Lynn.'

'Ah,' said the receptionist. 'Consultation before having the actual liposuction, is it, Sir? It doesn't hurt much at all, honest, and they'll have you in trousers two waist sizes smaller in no time. If you and your young boyfriend would like to take a seat, I'll check what time you're booked in George.'

Now searching his side pockets, Copeland distractedly said, 'I'm Larry, not George.'

'Of course you are,' whispered the receptionist, 'I know how you famous people like to go incognito. It's amazing how they can make you look slimmer and even handsome on screen these days, isn't it, er, **Larry**?' She laughed behind her hand.

Copeland finally produced his credit card size ID from his breast pocket and handed it over to her. She took it. She brought it closer to her spectacles. She squinted. She lifted her spectacles up, held it very close and squinted harder.

Copeland had vaguely glanced at the ID card when Director Miller had given it him. He had been more interested in the BMW key she had given him at the same time. He recalled the ID had a holographic picture of a crown in the top left corner with the words HM Government across the top. Underneath that it said Department C, with his name on the next line and his official number under that, then a space where he was supposed to have signed it and two lines at the bottom saying how the identification had been issued according to Home Office regulations and all necessary guidelines. Given that everything beneath the holographic crown and HM Government banner headline was alongside a driving licence size photo of his face, Copeland had not bothered to try to read much of it. He remembered he had intended to get a magnifying glass especially for the job, so was not surprised the receptionist was having trouble.

'MI5?' she asked, still squinting.

'Where does it say that?' asked Copeland, trying to lean over the reception desk.

'Under your photo,' replied the receptionist.

'I thought it just said Department C,' countered Copeland, aware that Giles was next to him and stroking the top of the reception desk with the palm of his hand.

The receptionist had the card almost to her nose and said, 'No, it says Section C and... Hang on... Do you know your number?' She looked up at him as she let her glasses fall back onto her nose.

Copeland stroked his chin and tried to sound confident. 'Er... Yes, er, well, has it got a seven in it? Perhaps a zero as well?'

With wide eyes, the receptionist leaned towards him over the desk, handed him the card back, winked and touched the side of her nose. She whispered, 'Lots of zeros, then a gap, and then two more zeros followed by a seven. Please wait a moment while I let Dr. Lynn know you're here, double o seven.'

'Er, OK,' said Copeland.

The receptionist turned, took two steps, banged three times on the door behind her, opened it as little as possible and went inside. Copeland looked down at Giles' fingers stroking the front of the reception desk. 'This is solid wood,' Giles informed him. 'Beautiful finish. Not like the cheap stuff in that lab.' Copeland nodded to show he understood as his inner voice shouted, *Who is this idiot? Even I want to go to the pub!*

The receptionist reappeared, took Copeland's ID back from his hand and re-disappeared through the door behind her. With feeling, Giles said, 'With workmanship like this, I think it must be Swedish.' Copeland did not know much about furniture, but he also thought the reception desk was probably from IKEA.

Thankfully, Dr. Lynn had good eyesight because the receptionist soon returned, handed Copeland's card back and haughtily said, 'Doctor Lynn says it should say Officer and not Inspector in front of your name even if you are a new section of MI5.'

'We are allowed to keep our old titles if we want,' Copeland said, hoping that was true but believing it was probably a printing error.

The receptionist pointed at the desk-stroking Giles and asked, 'Does **he** have a card?'

Copeland gave Giles a nudge. After looking surprised, Giles eventually worked out Copeland's gesticulating eyebrows meant he should hand over his warrant card. The receptionist looked at it in its wallet size leather case with the crown prominent on the inside cover and went back through the door again. She was back before Giles had stroked the top of the desk more than twice. 'Alright,' she said with her nose in the air. 'Phones off. That's the rule. Take a seat and Dr. Lynn will see you next.'

From the seating area behind him, Copeland heard a woman's voice loudly proclaim, 'Bloody Hell! More waiting?'

Turning to view the waiting area as he took out his phone and flicked it to airplane mode, Copeland saw two rows of six black, airport-style, plastic seats; the sort without legs, held aloft by stanchions and a metal bar underneath. They faced each other at right angles to the reception desk. Most of the seats were occupied. To his left were four men in their early twenties at most and, judging by the pronounced muscles of the arms emerging from their matching black polo shirts, they were not averse to keeping fit. The thought of exercise made Copeland feel a little queasy and he decided he would take a seat on the row to his right where the protesting woman sat. She was no older than the men opposite her and sat with her arms folded and a scowl on her face, which Copeland thought was a shame since she seemed such a nice young modern lady holding her bag and black leather jacket in front of her low-cut sleeveless white top and short, lopped-off denims, though he thought the circular steel earrings dangling in front of her chestnut brown plaits looked somewhat on the large side. Three of the four men opposite her were staring open mouthed at her. The fourth, who had rather unfortunate acne, was staring at Copeland until Copeland met his gaze and the man mouthed the words 'fascist copper' at him, accompanied with a sincerely meant V-sign.

Copeland returned his gaze to the woman, who blew a chewing gum bubble in his direction until it popped. She seems nice, Copeland thought before his attention was suddenly fully absorbed by the book reading man sitting on the far seat, an empty seat beyond the gum chewing girl slash woman. Copeland felt the cop equivalent of his Spiderman Sense start tingling as soon as he saw the book held in front of the obscured face. It was called 'Why Aliens Built Atlantis'. The fact that the man was wearing a pink check surgical gown and his short, skinny bare legs dangled above the floor further aroused Copeland's suspicions. When the book was briefly lowered and Copeland saw the collar length peroxide blond hair and immense green rimmed glasses, Copeland knew his worse suspicions were confirmed. The man saw him looking and immediately raised the book high and turned to hide his face completely behind it.

The receptionist nudged his shoulder. 'Just go and sit next to Elton John,' she said with a laugh. Without turning Copeland nodded and mumbled, 'Sit next to Mini-me Elton John? Yes. Great.'

Copeland plucked up the courage and walked slowly over to sit in the seat between Miss Big Steel Earrings and 'Sir Elton John'. Miss Earrings scowled at him and shuffled away in her seat. Mini Elton was so thin he did not need to shuffle an inch.

Copeland turned to his left to face Miss Earrings, holding his hand out and saying, 'Hi, I'm Larry.' He thought using the word 'hi' was very modern of him and was impressed. He was even more impressed by the way Miss Earrings resolutely held his gaze with her big brown eyes, blew another chewing gum bubble, let it burst, sucked it through her full red lips and said, 'Piss off.'

He smiled a tight, toothless smile at her and dropped his hand into his lap. He sighed as he realised Giles was still at the desk, trying to get round to the receptionist's side as he stroked his hand around the corner. Copeland found it hard to believe Giles was the son of the notorious Robert Lord. 'Inspector Lord! Giles!' snapped Copeland. 'Come and sit down!'

Miss Earrings took in the situation instantly. She put her bag and jacket on the other seat next to her but Giles sat on the end one anyway, leaving a spare seat empty. Copeland watched as Giles stared into space before he bit the bullet and started to turn to the mini Elton man on his right. In mid-turn he stopped and looked at the four Miss Earrings-staring men opposite. Besides noticing the one on the end with the nose ring was actively drooling, Copeland also noticed a white logo on their black polo shirts. It said English S.S. He looked at his shoes, thought they needed a good clean and pondered... A series of bizarre coincidences had led him here. He had for some unknown reason been recruited to this new Department (slash 'Section') C, had gone on holiday a few miles from a town where a scientist's murder had taken place (not to mention the dead mice and the pygmy chimpanzees), had not been able to see the owner of Uroboros Rejuvenation, Dr. Lynn, straight away, and had, by the dice roll of Lady Luck, sat opposite four members of an ultra right neo-Nazi terrorist group. He wished he had his gun, but remembered they had not given him one since he'd left the last two on the train. Fortunately, they had never given him any bullets.

For goodness sake, Copeland! his inner voice shouted. *How can they be neo-Nazis when one called you a fascist? The S.S. must stand for something else!*

'Excuse me, gentlemen,' said Copeland.

The shorter one at the far end turned to him and said, 'We get this all the time. It's about the S.S. on our polo tops isn't it? We're the English synchronised swimming team. Don't ask. It will be an Olympic sport for men too soon. We're here for a medical. They're going to sponsor us.'

'And pay us to be blood donors, Mike,' enthusiastically added the spotty one who had given Copeland the V-sign.

Copeland nodded, smiled and let them go back to drooling at Miss Big-Earrings. He was not convinced, but ultra right extremists were not his problem. Not anymore. And certainly not so close to lunch time. He would send a message to his old Chief at S.O.15 and leave it at that. In the meantime he turned his back on everyone to offer his hand to the book reading mini Elton John. 'Hello, Elton,' he whispered.

The book was not lowered as a voice hissed, 'I'm John Elton! I had to change my identity after the last time!'

Copeland twisted back to face forwards again, but leaned to one side, towards mini Elton. He whispered, 'This leaning sideways is killing my back, but I have to say the wig and glasses really suit you.' He paused to bite his lip when a snigger came out. 'So, how're you doing, Tom Benson?'

'Pretend you don't know me!' the voice behind the book hissed. 'My life has been Hell since I got involved with you and that poison gas thing.' He held the book in one hand while he raised the index finger of the other to go into quotation mode as he whispered, 'Hell is other people!' The finger went down. 'You're one of the other people, Larry. I wish I'd never helped you! Have a mint.'

Copeland looked down. A packet of extra strong mints was in front of him. He took one. The packet was withdrawn. Copeland wondered why his mint-offering erstwhile friend was quoting Sartre and where someone wearing only a pink and white check surgical gown could possibly keep a packet of extra strong mints. Logic told him there weren't that many places. Before logic got to storage places where logic should not go he bit into the mint and swallowed it as quickly as he could.

'But...' began Copeland, pausing to cough, clasp his overheated throat and squeeze his burning nose then having his next words cut short by the receptionist calling his name.

Shaking his silver-haired head, he turned away from mini-Elton and saw the back of a man in a motorised wheelchair leaving the waiting area. The receptionist beckoned Copeland towards her. He stood, hesitated, chose to leave the book reading incognito mini-Elton in peace, rounded the feet of Miss Earrings, gave Giles a slap on the shoulder, flicked his head for Giles to follow and went past the reception desk into the open door beyond.

JANE SADLER.

Jane decided to start her interviews of the colleagues of the deceased Dr. Carter with the only other male on the team, Wang Linpeng since she had to pass near his home in Bridport on the way to the other addresses. She rung the bell and rapped the door of the smart detached house but no one answered. She looked through the front window and saw toys scattered on the floor but no one home.

She paced the path up the front garden a few times, went into the road and looked up and down, went back and tried the locked garage door, shouted in case someone was in the garden. She concluded the children were at school, Mr. Linpeng's partner was probably at work and Mr. Linpeng himself was probably in a GP surgery waiting for a cancellation. What other reason could there be for him not to go into work except illness?

She waited for him to return and googled him while she waited. Mr. Linpeng was not Mr. Linpeng. He was Dr. Linpeng and almost as notable a biochemist as Dr. Carter. While waiting she looked up her next appointment. Would it be Ms. Alison Taylor or the child prodigy genius, Dr. Reema

Sharma? Not the receptionist, Erica Young. She lived furthest away in Axminster itself. Alison Taylor was chosen for the next visit. Jane would come back later to interview Dr. Linpeng.

As soon as Jane approached Alison Taylor's door she knew something was wrong. The old terraced house in Charmouth had letters and pizza flyers sticking from the letterbox. Jane went up to the door anyway. Jane knocked anyway. She looked through the window anyway. She waited for ten minutes anyway. She began to suspect.

A cold shiver ran up Jane's spine as she sat in her car. She slapped her thigh, closed her eyes and clenched her fists. They might both be sick on the same day, she told herself, but something inside her said that was nonsense. Their boss was murdered, scores of animals killed, the work-lab trashed and they both just happened to be off sick the next working day? She shivered again, went back to Alison Taylor's door and banged ferociously, hoping she was just taking a bath and would answer, looking surprised and wondering what the fuss was about. Jane banged again. No one came. A lump began to grow in her throat.

She moved on to Lyme Regis to visit the home of the brilliant, multi-doctorate Reema Sharma. She drove the grey Ford slowly, not really wanting to get there. She stopped outside the gateless drive of the house almost opposite the entrance to the golf club. She pulled slowly onto the gravel and parked alongside the four white Land Rovers parked there. She was reluctant to get out of the car but knew it was her duty. She clenched her fists, got out, closed the door quietly and crunched over the gravel towards the house. There were four cars on the drive... Someone had to be home, didn't they? A shiver ran down Jane's spine.

Jane got to the solid oak door. She did not ring the bell. She did not knock on the door. She leaned against it. She had meant to knock but she had looked down. She had seen her feet were standing on a doorstep. It had once been grey stone. Now it was stained red. She thought about the toys she had seen through the window earlier. A tear filled Jane's eye. Her ears buzzed. The tear fell.

COPELAND.

Copeland was not sure what to expect anymore. When he had first arrived outside the clinic, and just before he had nodded off in his new silver BMW, he had expected to be meeting someone in a plush fourth floor office looking towards the London skyline. Once he had arrived at the waiting room his expectations had changed and he had assumed he would be walking into a consultation room much like his own GP's. The room he entered was neither and both. The half which he and Giles walked into was the plush office with deep burgundy carpet and a large, ornate wooden desk with the mandatory closed lap top on top and the mandatory book shelves and framed diplomas behind. To his right there was the expected large window. It looked out towards three large blocks of decrepit flats. The other half of the room to his left was purely medical, with cream tiled flooring, an examination bed, heart monitor, ultra sound machine and something with a chin rest that looked straight from his optician's. The room was not as he had expected.

AND you expected Dr. Lynn to be a man, didn't you, Copeland?

Copeland resented his curmudgeonly conscience virtually accusing him of being misogynistic. He believed in equality. Hadn't he accepted it was the twenty first century and women were now allowed to join his golf club? He had to agree though, Dr. Lynn did appear to be a woman and, even if a slightly smaller, slighter version than the average, looked quite professional – in her late forties with straight, bob-cut, mid-blonde hair falling around her serious, round face to touch the collar of her retro white coat. He thought there was a vague resemblance to his ex-wife. He put that down to her steely grey eyes already judging him.

But it was true. He had expected Dr. Lynn to be male. One of his last tasks while working for the secretive Pickfords was to do boring, painstaking background research into UR Ltd but he had not come across a single photograph of its owner, Dr. E. Lynn. He knew exactly what they did and where their other two lucrative 'face and body enhancement' clinics were in west London, and even that the company was squeaky clean down to the last penny of their taxes, but Dr. E. Lynn himself, or herself as it turned out, had been elusively imageless.

Copeland advanced across the plush carpet towards the large oblong desk, from behind which Dr. Lynn was reaching forward with a proffered handshake. He leaned across the wide desk with some difficulty and took her hand as he introduced himself. 'Inspector Copeland,' he said. Her steel-blue eyes narrowed as if she was trying to see into his soul. 'And this,' continued Copeland as she finally released his hand, 'is Inspector Lord.' Giles shook her hand but looked down as he did so, as if trying to avoid her gaze.

Dr. Lynn looked at Copeland. 'He's very young for an inspector, isn't he?'

'That's what I thought,' replied Copeland. Dr. Lynn smiled at him as she sat back on her black chair.

'Please, take a seat, inspectors,' said Dr. Lynn, sweeping her arm wide to indicate the two leather upholstered chairs facing her desk. 'Now, to what do I owe this pleasure?'

Copeland locked his fingers together in front of his light blue shirt, dark blue jacket and expansive stomach. 'I understand you do plastic surgery and stuff like that, Doctor, but I also understand you own a small research facility near Axminster. Is that correct?'

Doctor Lynn laughed. 'It hardly warrants the police and a new department of MI5 to investigate it!'

There was something Copeland did not entirely trust about her. It might have been the dyed blonde hair. It might have been the similarity to his ex, Helen. He decided to tread carefully and judge her reactions. Even though her clinic owned the ransacked laboratory, perhaps this Jonathan Carter was about to sell some shocking new discovery to a rival and Dr. Lynn had paid someone to remove Carter from the equation? He shuffled in his chair. 'I'm afraid the research lab was vandalised on Friday evening,' Copeland told her.

'And...' began Giles. Copeland elbowed him, not wanting Giles to show their hand too early.

'Oh, dear,' said the doctor, putting her hand to her mouth with shock. 'Do you think it may have been terrorists looking for something they could use as some sort of bio-weapon?'

Copeland said, 'Pardon? You have your hand in front of your mouth.'

Dr. Lynn moved her hand down. She clasped her hands together with her elbows on the green leather top of her really expensive looking desk and said, 'It was purely medical research there with nothing posing a security risk... Wait a moment...' He steel eyes narrowed again as she bit her broad bottom lip. 'Dr. Jonathan Carter runs that lab. Why are you here and not talking to Jonathan?'

In line with his softly, softly, one step at a time approach, Copeland tried to think of a reason.

'He was shot in the head,' said Giles.

Great! So much for your oblique approach, Copeland. Mind you, it probably wasn't going to get us anywhere, was it?

Copeland ignored his inner voice and held his hands wide. Giles beat him to the next word with, 'Well, to be accurate, Dr. Carter was shot in the head and the shoulder and the leg and the heart.'

Dr. Lynn clasped her face. She bowed her head and put her hands in front of her eyes. Copeland stared at Giles. *Elbow him again, Copeland! Really hard this time.*

As he turned back to the apparently shocked Dr. Lynn, Copeland briefly worried about whether his inner voice, which he believed those of a more religious inclination might call a conscience, was getting more aggressive of late and possibly going a little senile. Copeland clutched his thighs as he turned back to Dr. Lynn to apologise. 'I'm so sorry for my associate's bluntness, Doctor,' he said softly. 'He's a new inspector who's being fast tracked so he can become an MP. Apparently, his father is a lord.' He hoped that explained everything adequately.

A short silence followed. A longer one followed it. Dr. Lynn regained her composure and looked up at Copeland. 'So Jonathan was murdered and the lab was vandalised? What about the other staff?'

'They're fine. They'd already gone home,' Copeland said reassuringly, feeling relieved Giles had gone back into his default silent mode, staring at the desk. 'Of course, a specialised team was sent round to break the news to Dr.

Carter's wife, but she was only able to provide us with the first names of her late husband's colleagues so we had someone at the lab waiting for them when they turned up for work this morning.' A pale looking Dr. Lynn nodded. 'But... and this may come as a shock Doctor,' continued Copeland, 'I'm afraid the animals were killed as well.'

Dr. Lynn was not shocked, but she was surprised. Her brow furrowed. 'They killed the mice?' she asked incredulously.

'And the bonobos,' said Giles.

'Bonobos?' repeated Dr. Lynn. 'Bonobos?'

Giles was keen to explain, 'They're sometimes called pygmy chimps. Pygmy means...'

'Right, Giles!' snapped Copeland, glaring hard at Giles. 'Not another word from you!' He turned back to see the Doctor had risen from her desk and was pacing back and forth in front of the shelves of medical books and the framed diplomas. He gave her a moment. She shook her shiny mid-blonde hair and leaned on the back of her high leather chair and said, 'I didn't know they had primates. He said he knew someone who could get him some but I told him the mice were enough and I refused to support his application for a licence. The fool! I warned him animal rights activists could be violent if he used primates... Hang on! They would just have set them free, wouldn't they? Primates! Damn! The mice should have been enough until the human trials...'

'Trials of what, Doctor?' asked Copeland.

Copeland stole a glance at Giles: he was staring at the desk.

'So, Inspector,' Dr. Lynn said, taking a deep breath, easing round her chair and sitting again. 'Have you heard of Viagra? Of course you have. Everyone was bombarded with emails and adverts in the not too distant past, weren't they? But do you know how much it's worth? No? Sales were two billion dollars in its first year and have been about one point five billion a year since. What if someone made the next generation Viagra?'

Giles stirred. 'I've heard of Viagra,' he said, almost excitedly. 'It's a big waterfall in America. People go there for their honeymoon.' His head sagged into hibernation mode again.

Dr. Lynn looked at him and raised her eyebrows. She closed her open mouth and turned back to Copeland. 'That's what Dr. Carter and his colleagues were trying to make in that lab, Inspector. Viagra two point zero.'

Copeland looked thoughtful, stroked his chin, thought he needed to get a better razor and said, 'So all this is about pills that let men get...' He stopped. There were just some things he would rather not think about. He felt his cheeks flush.

Dr. Lynn grinned.

Copeland found himself smiling back.

Dr. Lynn grew more sombre. 'That cheered me up,' she said, 'but let's remember a brilliant scientist and his unfortunate test subjects have been killed.'

Very seriously, Copeland said: 'Are you suggesting the drug company that makes Viagra may have had your lead researcher killed and destroyed all the evidence of his work, Doctor?' asked Copeland. 'The killer seems to have poured acid into the computers too. Their insides are melted.'

If Copeland had not spent years interrogating suspects he may not have noticed Dr. Lynn virtually fall off her chair at the news the lab's computers had been destroyed. He pretended not to notice.

Giles pointed at Dr. Lynn as he said, 'That upset her.'

Copeland decided the best strategy was to pretend Giles was not with him and asked, 'So who do you think might have killed Jonathan Carter, Dr. Lynn? Another drug company who had found out their product would become obsolete?'

Dr. Lynn held her hands up in defeat. She sighed. 'No, not Pfizer. That's absurd. If they knew about it they would have made a financial offer, not resorted to violence. In fact, that's what my investors and I were hoping for. A bid of a few hundred million would have made us happy. But the work wasn't finished. We planned to leak the news as soon as it was, then wait for the highest bidder.'

'Hmm. You're being very honest, Doctor,' said Copeland, suspecting she was not.

'And why shouldn't I be honest? It's all gone now. Jonathan was one of those scientists who would not share partial results. Not even with me, supposedly his employer. He was paranoid about secrecy. That's why he wanted to move from Cambridge to a lab built so far off the beaten track. In fact, I was the only one who knew it was there. He made me swear to not tell anyone else – not even the other investors.' She huffed. 'You know, Jonathan was so obsessed with secrecy I sometimes doubt he even let his team have access to all the data!'

Copeland thought that fitted in with the bonobos behind the metal door which required Carter's handprint to open it and the computers' server being in Carters office. If Dr. Lynn was right, then all the information from each computer in the work lab would have gone to that single server in Carter's office, to be accessed by Carter alone. 'So,' mused Copeland, 'if only Carter had access to the research data for your new Viagra two point zero, he had you over a barrel, didn't he?'

Dr. Lynn's steely eyes bore into him again. 'So you think **I** might have had him killed? That may be a good theory if he **had** actually got something and told me about it. Two years of work and all he's told us investors for eighteen months is that he was getting close and would soon have something ready for human trials. At times I've suspected he may have been more interested in keeping his huge salary going than getting his bonus for finishing the work. Jonathan has worked for me before, Inspector. That's what he did for over a year then – he strung it out. Look, I honestly can't say I liked him much. He liked himself well enough though. Bit of a ladies' man from what I've heard, though of course **I've** never had any direct experience of him turning on the charm and, well, you know, getting personal. Honest. I'm a married woman. But he was damn good at his job and if it wasn't for the dead animals and wrecked computers then the others... the others...' She trailed off, head sagging and lost in her thoughts.

Copeland waited. He leaned forward. 'The other members of the team may have finished your new Viagra?'

Dr. Lynn looked up and clasped her hands together. 'The last time Jonathan worked for me he produced revolutionary appetite suppressants,' she replied, evasively. 'Would you like a free sample, Inspector?'

He could see her eyes on his open jacket as she started opening a desk drawer. He shook his head as he patted his robust stomach, heard it rumble a complaint that lunch should have been delivered by now, and said, 'All muscle, this.' Dr. Lynn opened her mouth to speak. Lost for words, she closed it again. 'So,' Copeland continued, 'if not a rival drug company, then who do you think might have wanted Dr. Carter dead, along with the monkeys, mice and computers, of course?'

The doctor looked at the top of her desk. Copeland hoped she wasn't going into a Giles-like desk staring trance as well, but she looked up at him, fixed him with her steel-blue eyes and said, 'I really have no idea.' This would have satisfied most people, but Copeland noticed a barely perceptible tension in her shoulders before she answered. He also noticed she had noticed he had noticed. She held her hands wide, shrugged her shoulders and asked, 'Have you spoken to

Jonathan's wife? He once told me she had threatened to kill him if she ever found out he was being unfaithful, and she has a temper so may be vindictive enough to want to destroy all his work too.' Copeland nodded. He stood up. He wished he did not utter a groan every time he did that these days. 'Thank you Doctor,' he said, his hand stretching across the table.

She took it, held it and said, 'You're right. The rest of the team could finish our new Viagra. Reema Sharma is beyond brilliant, so it's possible. But I suppose I should phone the other investors and let them know what's happened. Good luck finding the culprit, Inspector Copeland.'

Copeland looked at his hand in hers, smiled and said, 'I'll leave my card with your receptionist in case you think of anything.' His inner voice said, *You don't have a card, Copeland!*

Giles had not stood. He raised his head to say, 'I have a question, Doctor Lynn.' They waited. Giles put his hand on the desk. They waited while he stroked it. Copeland was glad only one full minute had passed before Giles asked, 'Is this desk early nineteenth century French?'

JANE AT THE HOME OF THE SHARMAS.

By the time her first tear fell from her cheek and splashed on the blood-stained concrete step Jane had pulled herself together. She whirled, ran to her car and thrust open the boot. She grabbed her stab vest, threw it on over her black jacket and zipped it up over her white blouse. As she ran back to the door she patted her sides to make sure her baton and tazer were in place. She stopped, breathless, full of adrenaline, staring at the door. She clicked her radio on, held it to her mouth and as calmly as she could, said, 'Detective Jane Harper at the address of Reema Sharma. Threat to life suspected. I'm going in.'

'Wait for back-up!' shouted a voice on the other end of the radio.

Jane switched the radio off and clipped it back onto her stab-vest. She kicked the door. It shook. She kicked again. It burst open and swung in. She whipped her baton free and extended it. She was about to shout out when she saw she did not need to. The body of a middle-aged man lay on his back in the hallway. His blood had run along the wooden floor and under the door from the hole in his chest, where it had congealed to dark red on his white shirt. Jane guessed this was once Reema's father. She took a deep breath and sidled stealthily through the doorway, her baton at the ready. Moving along the side of the hallway, she glanced down at the body as she passed it. A shot to the forehead and another to the chest had ended Mr. Sharma's life with a look of surprise still on his face. Jane knew he had opened the door to the unexpected caller, saw the gun and stepped back. The bullet penetrating his skull had knocked him back further.

Jane had already seen the second body at the end of the hall. The dead woman, possibly in her mid-twenties, was on her side. Her fluffy white sweater and jeans were as blood soaked as her long black hair. Jane paused at the doorway where the body of Reema Sharma lay. She glanced quickly into the kitchen beyond before kneeling in Reema's dried blood to feel her pulse, knowing it was pointless. The wrist was cold. Reema had a bullet hole in the side of her skull and two more in her ribs. Jane guessed Reema must have heard her father fall in the hall and come to the kitchen door to see if he was alright. Seeing her father was far from alright and seeing a gun pointed at her she had turned to run, only to receive a bullet in the side of her head before she had taken her first step.

Jane stood and surveyed the kitchen. Chopped onions, herbs and a half chopped carrot lay on the large, free-standing oval work-surface between Jane and the double cooker beyond. Jane stepped carefully around Reema's body and edged slowly around the island work-surface. Mrs. Sharma had met the same fate as her husband and daughter. Her head was wedged against the base of the cooker with her neck at an impossible angle. The chopping knife lay in her blood beside her. Jane checked her pulse and remained behind the work-surface to unclip her radio and whisper, 'Multiple homicides at the scene. Get that back-up here fast!'

She waited for the stunned voice at the other end of the radio to say, 'On its way, Jane,' before she switched the radio off. She knew there was a fourth member of the family and hoped Reema's eighteen year old brother was still alive. She hoped he was out, but the four cars in the drive told her it was a forlorn hope. She went from the kitchen through the door near the cookers and found herself in a spacious but empty dining room. She moved through it and checked the lounge before leaving by the far door and finding herself standing over Mr. Sharma again. She leaned over his body and pushed open the door opposite. The small toilet under the stairs was empty.

Placing her feet sideways on each step, Jane went step by step up the stairs, listening for the slightest sound of movement. She heard her heart thumping in her ears. She paused halfway up, gripped her baton and put her hand on top of her tazer to reassure herself it was still there. At the top of the stairs, the bathroom door was open and she could see nothing unusual inside. The door next to it required the doorknob to be turned to open it. The doorknob squeaked.

Jane clenched her teeth and, crouching low, pushed the door open. It appeared to be the master bedroom, but then she looked harder and saw framed posters of Einstein, Hawking, Franklin and, with pride of place above the bed, Dorothy Hodgkin. Jane realised it was Reema's room and her heroes, just like her, had fought against the odds to succeed. They were odds which Reema would fight no more. Jane knew she should have been upset, or at least angry or afraid, but a strange calmness had overtaken her. She moved carefully along the upstairs corridor.

The next room along could not have been more different. Clothes were scattered on the floor and the singers in the posters had far less clothes than the scientists in Reema's room. Jane was about to move on to the other bedrooms when she noticed the headphone wire from the sound system was plugged in and hanging down the far side of the bed. A police siren grew closer as Jane looked over the bed. Reema's brother had probably been totally unaware what was happening as he sat cross legged on his bed and the killer entered from behind. His brain would have exploded inside his skull before he had even realised he had been shot. He had ended up face down on the floor beside the bed with his legs still half crossed and his headphones still on his ears. The killer had put two more bullets in him just to make sure.

Jane slumped onto the end of the dead teenager's bed just as she heard a man shout, 'Police! We're coming in!' followed by a second voice shouting, 'Bloody hell!' Jane thought his description was appropriate. It was indeed a hell of blood. With moist eyes she almost laughed as she stood and shouted for them to stop outside until forensics swept the house.

Jane put her baton away, closed her eyes, rubbed her forehead and went down to join the two uniformed officers outside the house. She contacted her inspector to get him to send officers to the homes of the other colleagues of the deceased Dr. Jonathan Carter and Dr. Reema Sharma. He already had.

'Good work, Jane,' he said.

'Thank you, Sir,' replied Jane, thinking it was far too late for praise now considering the last two years. She turned off the radio and threw it in the open car boot. She took her stab vest off. She walked to the side of her car. She leaned against the passenger door. She bent over. She vomited until yellow bile dripped from her lips. She heard one of the uniformed officers exclaim, 'She's totally nuts! The shooter might have still been in there!'

She heard the other calmly reply, 'I think she knew that.'

TOM BENSON.

On the way out of her office-come-surgery-come-consultation room door, Copeland crossed paths with John Elton in his peroxide wig, immense green-rimmed spectacles and pink and white check surgical gown. 'Nice to have met you, Inspector,' said John Elton, aka Tom Benson, as he shook Copeland's hand.

As Benson approached Dr. Lynn's door, Copeland clasped the paper smuggled into his palm during their handshake and turned to look at skinny little Tom Benson. He thought someone should have told Benson his gown was not tied properly at the back and he really should have kept his underwear on. He thought perhaps that was why the receptionist was following Benson's exposed posterior to Dr.

Lynn's door, but she stayed at the threshold only to inform her boss the English synchronised swimming team were waiting.

Copeland waited until he was outside the waiting area and was waiting for the arrival of the long-awaited lift before he opened his palm to see what Benson had smuggled into it as they shook hands. It was a piece of toilet tissue. Fortunately, it was unused. On it was an address, the time 7 p.m. and, in capital letters, the words IMPORTANT INFORMATION!

Copeland wrapped his hand around the message again as Giles, standing beside him said, 'I was sure it was an early nineteenth and not late eighteenth century. I suppose you know my degree was in furniture history, Larry.'

Copeland forced a smile in Giles' direction. 'I guessed it was your only interest, Giles.'

Giles looked hurt. 'Not at all!' he protested. 'I have an interest in upholstery too!'

Inspector Giles Lord sulked until he and Copeland were inside the lift when he turned to Copeland and monotonely said, 'So no one knew the lab was there except Dr. Lynn – apart from the people who worked at the lab, probably their families and friends, the people who did the lab workers contracts and those who do the payroll, the people who deliver things there like the mail and bonobos, the people who built the extension to house the bonobos and any passing dog walkers.' Copeland was impressed Giles had grasped all this and thought Giles might not be as dim as he appeared until Giles added, 'So it must have been Dr. Carter's wife who killed him.'

MARY.

Still troubled by how a passing dog walker had seen Dr. Carter's body where she had left it at the end of the long, dark corridor, Mary was trying to put it behind her and focus on another exceedingly boring day. Just like the day before, the day was being spent wandering the streets of Charmouth so she could repeatedly walk along the road where the three bedroom terraced house belonging to molecular biologist Alison Taylor stood. Each time she passed the house, Mary glanced sideways to see the new police notice still on the door. She had seen them kick the door open and go inside with tazers at the ready and had seen them wait for the locksmith to turn up to fit a new lock. She had watched and waited while they put the laminated sign on the door, telling Alison Taylor where to phone to get her new key, watched them leave and then waited for Alison Taylor to return. But just like the day before and the day before that there had been no sign of Alison Taylor. Mary could not understand why Alison's red Audi A3 cabriolet was parked outside Alison's house. The tracker Mary had put on it had told Mary that Alison had returned home in it after leaving the lab on Friday afternoon, just like she had done every Friday afternoon for the last four weeks. The car had not moved since and Mary was fuming. Where the hell was Alison Taylor? Why was she not at home? Where had she been since Friday evening? Why couldn't she just play the game and come home and be killed so Mary could finally get her money? Mary decided Alison would die much more slowly for wasting most of her Saturday evening and the last two days.

Mary knew Alison had not planned to go away. Wang Linpeng had told her so and she was sure Wang had told her the truth. According to Wang the rest of the research team would still be going to work as normal. Mary had got on well with Wang. He had been one of the more interesting members of the gym's coffee drinking group because, unlike the others, he did not talk about how wonderful his children were – at least not all the time. Mary also knew that Alison was always in on Saturday evenings and rarely went out on Sundays unless it was to complain to the Waitrose driver who delivered her groceries like clockwork on Sunday afternoons. Straight after the Sunday Waitrose delivery would have been when Mary would have met Alison for the first, and last, time. Mary's plan had been simple: wait for the delivery van to depart, knock on Alison's door, enthuse with her about the quality of Waitrose food for a few minutes and shoot her in the head. But because the police had found Jonathan Carter's body Atticus wanted the timetable moved up, and Alison was proving to be really most annoying by not following either the old timetable or the new one by being somewhere other than home.

Pretending to be an old university friend name Bella, Mary phoned Alison's parents and asked if she was visiting them because she was supposed to have been meeting her for drinks on Saturday evening but had not turned up. 'Bella' told Alison's parents how she had tried to call Alison several times but all she got was a message saying the number was unavailable. (Mary did not tell Alison's parents she had got Alison's number by cloning Wang Linpeng's phone while they drank coffee together at the gym.)

Alison's parents were very helpful. They were keen to tell 'Bella' the police had also phoned and asked if Alison was there with them, and had later called back to assure the worried parents they had checked with local hospitals and the missing Alison was not in any of them. Alison's parents could only tell 'Bella' the same as they had told the police: they had not heard from her, which, they went on to say, was not unusual. They were quite surprised Alison still had a friend from university because she certainly didn't have any others and asked 'Bella' to try to have a word with Alison about her personal hygiene when she saw her. Alison's mother went on to helpfully tell 'Bella' that Alison was not visiting the only remaining aunt who still spoke to her either. They had phoned and checked after the police had rung. 'Bella' assured Alison's mother she was sure Alison was safe and well, which was true and would remain so, at least until 'Bella' and her Beretta M9 found her.

Mary was tempted to go to the lab to see if Alison was there but she knew that would be risky. Even though the uniformed officer was no longer standing outside it was still an active crime scene and investigators or forensics might arrive there at any time. She could not afford to be seen, not when she was so close to getting the rest of her money.

Alison Taylor would turn up sooner or later, Mary told herself, but she still felt at a loose end. She knew she always felt better if she did something creative and decided to start planning a special first wedding anniversary event for husband Jeffrey.

COPELAND HAS A VISITOR.

Within moments of walking back into the drab offices near the M4 exit, Copeland realised Wendy Miller was not in her usual jovial mood. The clue was in the way she bawled at him with her forefinger pointing nearer and nearer his eyeball until he was pinned against her filing cabinet. He gathered the gist of what she was saying: he gathered she wanted to know where he had been for so long. He thought that was what she was asking, but it was not that easy to follow due to the frequent expletives used.

'At the clinic,' was his reply as he sank further down the front of the filing cabinet. 'I had to wait for Inspector Lord to arrive.' He thought it prudent to leave out the two hours having a quiet, late pub lunch in Eton on the way back, though he was tempted to inform her how generous they had been with the smoked salmon.

Then there was some screaming in his general direction about him having his phone off. At least, by this stage, she was storming around her office and had removed the finger from his face. He explained it was because of the no-phone rules in the clinic. Prudence again called for him to be tactful and not mention the pub did not have any such rules.

With his tail between his legs he followed Director Miller's instructions to leave her office and switch his (expletive) phone on. He scrolled through the list of messages left by her and cried, 'Oh, what? I don't believe it! Damn! It looks like Tesco sandwiches for dinner...' before he rushed out of the office.

With Tesco Express out of everything except a totally unacceptable 'healthy choice', mayonnaise free, tuna and cucumber, Copeland returned to his hotel room to grab some clothes. By the time he had opened his door and remembered his case was still in the boot of his car he thought, since he was the wrong side of sixty, he would just use the bathroom before he drove back down to Dorset to help solve, as ordered, the homicides of Reema Sharma, her family and, by the time he got there, probably the rest of Dr. Carter's missing research team as well.

Although it was a hotel chain, he quite liked the hotel room with its firm double bed and wall mounted widescreen. He was not sure what the desk could be used for but he liked the toilet seat. It moulded itself well when he sat on it. But the bathroom's motion sensor light was annoying. He did not like making it stay on by having to occasionally wiggle something about while he sat on the toilet.

When he emerged from the bathroom and into the short corridor that led from the main door past the recently used ensuite, the built-in wardrobe and on into the main bedroom, Copeland realised something was wrong. It may have been he was sure he had switched the corridor light on and now it was off, or it may have been the click that sounded just like a pistol hammer being cocked, or it may have been the voice behind him saying, 'Privet, Tovarishch Copeland. Do not turn round. I have a gun pointed at your head.'

Without Copeland wiggling something appropriate, the bathroom light timer expired. Everything was plunged into the dim glow of the street lamps two floors below. Copeland put his hands above his head and thanked the gods he had just used the comfy toilet seat. He swallowed hard and said, 'Vasily?'

'How are you, Larry?' enquired the voice in the gloom behind him.

'Not so good as five minutes ago,' replied Copeland. 'Five minutes ago I was having a really good...'

'I do not have much time old friend,' said the cultured voice of Colonel Vasily Goraya, former KGB, currently Russian SVR, Order of Lenin, Order of the Red Star, also known as the Killer of Kamchatka, etc.

'Just shoot and get it over with,' said Copeland. His inner voice shouted, *Don't encourage him, Copeland!*

'What?' asked Vasily. 'Oh, this gun? Just a precaution in case you shot me on sight after the last time.'

'I thought you were dead, Vasily,' said Copeland, feeling his arms start to ache and hoping Vasily would let him put them down soon before he was begging to be shot instead.

'You thought me dead?' said Vasily, surprised. 'Oh, yes, that food poisoning outbreak at the embassy. They could not track the source down, but you and I know better, don't we Larry? I was on a diet and not eating anything sweet at the time. Shame about young Nikolay, though. Still, that is all water under the ducks back as you English say.'

Copeland had not heard much of this. Most of his mind was preoccupied with having a gun pointed at him and the purely coincidental need to use the really comfy toilet seat again. The rest of his mind was focused on trying to keep his arms above his head.

'Now,' ordered Vasily. 'Very slowly, put your firearm on the floor.'

Just take it out, whirl round and put a bullet between his eyes, Copeland, suggested the ever-reliable inner voice. Copeland would have done as his better self suggested except a) he could no longer hit a barn door at ten paces and b) he did not have a gun (two left on the train, remember?). These reasons made it difficult to comply with either Vasily or his inner voice so he asked, 'What do you want, Vasily?'

'Your gun please, Larry,' repeated Vasily.

'They don't let me have one anymore,' said Copeland. 'You know, Vasily, you should not say please. It makes you sound imploring. You should use thank you. It implies expectation of compliance. I did a course.'

Hey! I'm not totally senile! Shut up, Copeland! He has a gun pointed at you!

'Hmm,' hummed Vasily. 'That is good advice. Thank you put down your gun. Hmmm, that does not sound right.'

'I don't have a gun,' Copeland told him. 'They stopped me having one after I left mine on a train seat for the second time. I blame these new waist holsters. The gun sticks into my stomach when I sit down.'

'Hmmmmm, with a stomach like yours that does sound about right, Larry,' Vasily said after a few moments.

Are you going to take that insult, Copeland? Shoot him!

'I don't have a gun,' Copeland reminded everyone present.

'I said I believe you, old friend,' said Vasily. 'You may put your arms down and turn round.'

'Ooooh,' said Copeland as he lowered his arms and rubbed what was left of his aching biceps. He turned round and looked at the short, stocky man who had been trained to snap necks like twigs. 'What's that in your hand, Vasily?' Copeland asked, peering in the gloom.

'The light switch for your desk lamp,' said Vasily, clicking the switch a few times. 'I took the plug out. I don't have a gun either. I thought I would click it. It sounded quite realistic, did it not? Just like a pistol being cocked. I need your help, Larry. We birds in the weather must stick together, eh?'

Besides the cramp in his biceps, Copeland was more or less thinking clearly. He guessed it was after six. He was supposed to get to Dorset and help sort out the Sharma homicides mess there, and he had the nagging feeling there was somewhere he was supposed to be at seven besides the hotel bar. Copeland looked at the dim figure in the raincoat and fedora hat sitting on the chair at his desk.

Why is he wearing a raincoat and a hat in a hotel room? asked the inner voice.

'Thank you sit down,' said Vasily, taking Copeland's don't use "please" advice a tad too far. Copeland looked around the little corridor for a place to sit down. There was always the possibility of opening the built in wardrobe door and sitting in there.

'The floor will do,' said Vasily, pointing the light switch at him menacingly.

The floor! Is he kidding?

Copeland decided his inner voice was not as senile as he thought. The floor was a long way down. He said, 'I'm okay standing, thanks.'

'Very well,' shrugged Vasily. 'I am out of favour, my old comrade in arms, and so I turn to the man I can trust. I need to kill two birds with one brick, as you English say. I need to make peace with you and find my niece.'

'Your niece?'

'Yes, nice girl. Very English in many ways. She likes tea and has no moral qualms regarding foreigners. Born to my sister when she worked at the embassy as a translator. Dominika was schooled here under a false name until she was ten, then she went back to the Motherland to be educated properly. She was an excellent student. Very talented. She carried out many missions. She was sent back here. She had learned to wear two bonnets but got some bees in her hat about something and went off the grid, as our American friends say.'

What the hell is he talking about, Copeland? You need to be somewhere that I can't remember at seven and be back in Dorset for the crack of dawn at nine. When are we going to eat?

'I see a great deal of concern in your eyes, Larry,' Vasily said. Copeland knew he was lying. It was Vasily's default position. It was too dark to see anyone's eyes. Vasily put down the threat of the clicking light switch and leaned forward onto his knees. 'Please help me find her, Comrade. For old time's sake. And for twenty thousand pounds.'

Copeland became a little more interested. 'You found me, Vasily. Why can't you find her?'

'You were easy to find, Comrade. I broke into your home, logged into your computer and read your emails. By the way, you need better passwords than Larry1 and Larry2. There was an email from your new boss, Wendy Miller, whom I have crossed knives with before. It told me you were booked into this hotel near the temporary offices until your new ones are completed in The Onion.' Vasily paused. 'Why are your offices going to be in something they are calling an onion? Are they smelly?'

'It's near The Gherkin and the building is shaped like an onion,' Copeland explained, hoping Vasily would get to the point soon so he could get to his appointment at seven, which he knew he could just about make if he remembered where it was and who it was with.

'This new Onion of yours must be costing a fortune, Comrade Larry. A tsar's ransom, as you English say. And you British are brick broke, are you not? But to get back to my niece. She is hard to find because she is an expert at disguise and was provided with many false identities. Do you know how easy it is to hack into your birth, marriages and deaths and get national insurance numbers? Dominika is one of... er, many agents we have here who are slumber agents.'

'Sleeper agents,' Copeland corrected.

'No, slumber,' Vasily reiterated, shaking his head and frowning. 'They are easily woken up. If they were sleeping then when we woke them they would be all, you know, bleary eyed and needing the toilet. Dominika was the best of our best slumber agents. She was not only deadly, but able to use her skills to get us any secret. Unfortunately, I fear I may not have been able to discover all the false identities she has available and now I will soon be cast out like a piranha.'

'Like a little fish with lots of teeth?' asked Copeland, scratching his silver-haired head. *He means pariah, Copeland!*

Vasily was laughing. 'I have no teeth. My new orders arrive soon, Comrade Larry. I am expecting to be sent to Siberia. It has taken them three years to do the paperwork, but it must be soon. The new ambassador has told me it is all happening for me any week now. I need to find my niece before that or my sister will make my life worse than the deepest salt mine.'

Copeland thought he would probably not enjoy an evening with Vasily's sister. 'Ok, Vasily,' he said. 'Even though we've had our ups and downs... *(When were the ups, Copeland?)* If you give me what you have, I promise to help. I know how important family can be. I haven't seen my daughter Emily since...'

'I am not interested in your daughter, Larry. Why would a colonel in the SVR be interested in a tall, skinny, dark haired artist?'

'She's an artist?' asked Copeland.

'Post graduate now,' Vasily said. 'Does sculptures. Good at hockey. Attractive, but some eczema on the side of her neck.'

Just like on the bottom of your foot, Copeland! Nice to know she inherited something from you, eh?

'Yes, Comrade,' continued Vasily. 'They once wanted to use her against you after that thing at the port, but I said no, Comrade Larry. I said the noble Russian SVR do not threaten children! We only kill everyone else! Of course, she is older now...'

Copeland found himself leaning against the wall with his heart and mind racing. This was about family. There was nothing more important than family. And despite everything he and Vasily had gone through... Damn it! This was about family! His inner voice went on red alert. It shouted, *It's about family, alright, Copeland! Yours!* And Copeland said, 'OK, Vasily. I'll find your niece for you.'

JANE.

A twelve hour, full-on day without a break for more than a bottle of water was not unusual for Jane, but one where she had seen a multiple homicide, crept round a corpse filled house fearing for her life, then rushing to the other homes of Dr. Carter's team to meet uniformed officers who had broken front doors down was not her average day. At least there had been no more dead bodies like the Sharmas, which the forensics team estimated had been dead since possibly early Saturday evening, and they had got one solid clue – a clear footprint in the Sharmas' kitchen, no less, and forensics was already certain it did not belong to any of the victims. But that was all.

As for the other lab workers' homes, the news was mixed. Alison Taylor's car was outside her little semi and her home had no signs of a struggle or, thankfully, any signs of blood. The same lack of anything was found at the receptionist's small flat near the centre of Axminster, with its very nice outside balcony overlooking the Co-op car park. But, just like Ms. Alison Taylor, Miss Erica Young was not at home. Jane had thought both homes strange in different ways. Alison Taylor's had lots of photographs on walls, on mantelpieces, shelves and even in the bathroom. They were all selfies of the same person: Alison Taylor. If her photographic vanity was not a big enough clue, Jane had gathered a lot from what Alison had posted about herself on LinkedIn, especially that

Alison was the best thing since sliced bread and would have been a top model or film star if she was not such a brilliant molecular biologist, at least according to Alison herself.

The other flat, rented by the non-driving receptionist Erica Young, did not have a single photograph of anything. It was more like a holiday home and if it had not been for the burned baked beans saucepan on the cooker and the half eaten pizza on the plate beside the sink, Jane might have thought the flat unoccupied. The young P.C. who had broken the door down had quickly looked for a dead Erica Young and had made a discovery. Before Jane arrived, he had looked through the contents of the wardrobe and the chest of drawers and subsequently shown Jane some of the clothes he had found. At first Jane thought Erica Young must have two jobs. Not only was she a receptionist at Uroboros Rejuvenation Limited's research lab, but the clothes suggested she must also be working at night in a less than respectable profession. Then Jane remembered this was Axminster and unless the locals had all been drugged to leave their TVs, Miss Erica Young would not have made much money. Jane thought that thought was unfair. She knew at least one person in Axminster who had the internet. At least he did have before Jane had arrested him for shoplifting in Bridport. It had been one of her most exciting days.

Those two abodes had brought no further evidence and the hard pressed Dorset constabulary did not have the manpower to keep a constable outside each door until Ms. Taylor or Miss Young might or might not return. The police budget could only just about afford to pay a locksmith to put new locks on the doors the officers had forced open, and civilian staff were needed to make phone calls to determine the missing workers were neither with relatives nor admitted into any hospital.

Unlike the untouched homes of Miss Taylor and Miss Young, the third home was disconcerting. The lovely house of Wang Linpeng had been completely ransacked. Clothes were strewn across bedrooms, toys were scattered everywhere, curling tongues were plugged in and still singeing the carpet, half eaten sandwiches were left on plates. The kitchen was reminiscent of the infamous Marie Celeste. Most worrying was both Mr. and Mrs. Linpeng's cars were in the garage. Jane had checked the garden to see if dead bodies were behind bushes, but found nothing except a little swing and a miniature trampoline.

Jane believed everything pointed to the Linpengs being abducted and that, clearly, the killer had been ransacking the house in search of something when the Linpengs returned home and they had walked in on him. The whole family had seen his face. The killer had put a gun to one of the children's heads and made Wang or his wife drive them all to some secluded spot. There the grizzly deed was done. There was where their bodies now lay...

Jane woke up with a stiff neck. The sofa she had fallen asleep on had high arms and her neck was not happy. She could smell blood. She tensed. She realised it was on her clothes from when she had knelt in Reema Sharma's blood. So young, so gifted, so beautiful, thought Jane, holding back the tears as she sat up, rubbing the back of her neck. She laughed a sad, hollow laugh, recalling the curt text message she had received offering her counselling. She knew the waiting list even for her rural constabulary would be so long she may as well not bother.

Still rubbing her neck, Jane recalled her inspector telling her no senior officer was being assigned because a new division of MI5, called Department C, had already taken over the case and one of their operatives, designated double o seven, would be arriving in the morning. Jane wondered two things – why had a division of MI5 taken over the case, and whether the new double o seven would finally be a woman? More likely it was another Daniel Craig, Pierce Brosnan or Sean Connery. She hoped it was not another Roger Moore. He was her favourite and she worried how she would react if someone who looked like Roger arrived in the morning. Jane need not have worried. Copeland was on his way.

COPELAND VISITS BENSON.

Copeland drove towards Bricknall with the piece of toilet paper from his jacket pocket on the passenger seat. The pocket was now occupied by a flash drive with everything Vasily knew about his niece, Dominika. When he put the flash drive in his pocket Copeland had been surprised to find a piece of toilet tissue there, but once he had looked at it he remembered who had given it to him and where he was supposed to be at seven. Copeland was nearly on time. It was only half past, and stopping off to see Tom Benson was more or less on his way back down to Dorset, and if Benson had some important information it was best to check it out, especially now it was a multiple homicide. Copeland was sure Benson must have learned something on the dark web from his fellow conspiracy theory obsessed nutcases.

The address written on the sheet of toilet tissue took Copeland to a warren of terrace houses on the less than affluent southern fringe of Bricknall. Copeland was happy it would mean a short drive to the M3 and on to his hotel with the friendly, golf playing proprietress and it was only when he found somewhere to park his shiny new, broodingly silent car that he wondered exactly why he was so happy. It did not take long for him to work out what it was. He had heard news about his estranged daughter Emily and she was doing a postgraduate course, no less. He felt proud she was excelling, even if it was in art.

He was not pleased with the voice inside him which kept saying, *Vasily telling you he knew all about Emily was a badly disguised threat so you would help him find his niece, Copeland!*

Copeland refused to listen. Vasily was capable of many things, but killing a child was not one of them. His inner voice reminded him Emily was now twenty three, or possibly twenty four. Copeland stopped worrying when he arrived at the address Tom Benson had scrawled on the toilet tissue.

The plain, paint peeled wooden front door of the address Tom Benson had given Copeland was half open. The sounds from inside were ominous.

Copeland! The killer has got to Benson first!

Instinctively, Copeland's hand went inside his jacket before he remembered he did not have a gun anymore, but he was pleasantly surprised to find that really nice pen he thought he had lost was in his inside pocket all along. He pushed the front door back with an extended arm, sheltering to the side as he did so. He listened for anything suspicious.

Suspicious? Really? Listen, Copeland!

He heard what sounded like someone trashing a room, with things smashing against the walls, though it was trying to be disguised by loud rap music. Treading lightly for someone of his height and waist size, Copeland slowly ventured onto the threadbare carpet of the hallway. A hooded youth came stomping along the hallway towards him. Copeland froze. He braced himself. He remembered all those martial arts sessions. He wished he had sometimes gone to them.

The hoody barged past, muttering, 'First on the right upstairs if you're Mom's next client.' Copeland thought the upstairs of a terraced house was a strange place to situate a chiropodist. What else could it be? His chiropodist had always referred to him as a good client whenever she had given him that cream for his rash, smiled and took his payment in cash. But an odour stirred by the youth's wake triggered Copeland's one remaining olfactory nerve and it struck him that the youth's mom was probably something far more exotic, such as an aromatherapist. Further speculation was halted by the continuing sound of things being thrown against a wall in the front room on his right and the blasting music from the room further down the hallway from which the hooded teenager had just emerged. Copeland realised the noises were not connected and this was a two up, two down, with each door having a different letter. Since the two rooms on the ground floor were marked 'A' and 'B', Copeland used some clever deductive reasoning and worked out Benson's flat 'D' was most likely upstairs, along with the aromatherapist lady. Copeland sniffed to see if he could detect any pleasing aromas, then remembered his olfactory nerves were pretty much permanently out to lunch since his (minor) stroke and gave up. To be fair, no one else would have smelled anything through the sickly reek of cannabis left behind by the hooded youth either.

At the top of the stairs Copeland regained his breath and saw he was half right. Room D was indeed there, at the front of the house along the landing, but the nearer room C was clearly not being used by an aromatherapist, but a masseuse. The lady's name and price list was written on a sheet of paper pinned to the door. As he passed toward Benson's apartment D, Copeland briefly scanned the price list. He felt as if the world had passed him by with all these new-fangled, new-age ideas with their healing crystals and bottles of diluted water and consequently he had no idea what some of the types of massage on the price list might entail, but he could see Mistress Sadie seemed to offer a wide array of services. He recalled Clare had once told him she had once gone for a massage that had really hurt and how her shoulder had been stiff for days afterwards. The heartfelt cries coming from behind Door C confirmed to Copeland that massages sounded like a painful way to get rid of stress.

He knocked on Door D. He waited. He knocked on door D again. Door E opened. Copeland realised the box room was also in use. A bearded, long-haired head peered round the door and, in a haze of smoke, said, 'If you're after the little bald guy, he's in the shower.' Door E closed again. Copeland heard a guitar being softly strummed until something else smashed against the wall downstairs, a cry of pain came from Room C and the next rap song blared.

As the smoke from Room E billowed around him, for some reason Copeland suddenly felt quite happy and in need of crisps. Smiling, he retraced his steps along the landing to the closed door facing the top of the stairs. He was about to knock on the door when it opened and Benson appeared in a cloud of steam and a white towelling bathrobe.

'Inspector Copeland! Larry!' cried Benson once he had raised his steamed-up glasses. 'You came! Thank goodness!' He raised an index finger and solemnly quoted, 'I can no other answer make but thanks, and thanks!'

'And oft good turns are shuffled off with such uncurrent pay,' grinned Copeland, staring at his own inexplicably raised index finger. 'Now, can we leave Shakespeare quotes out of this?' he said and, for reasons unknown, began to giggle.

'Come in, Inspector,' said Tom Benson frowning, sniffing the cannabis in the air and negotiating his small frame between Copeland's chuckling girth and the banister. He took a key from his bathrobe pocket and unlocked Door D.

Tom's room was exactly as Copeland had suspected, no more than a bedroom rented out as 'a compact luxury apartment with shared bathroom and kitchen facilities'. It seemed functional enough with its four metre square magnolia walls, a wardrobe standing on the laminate floor opposite the door, a single bed with a Star Wars poster above it, a bedside table beside it and, along the wall behind the door, a tall white bookshelf alongside a work desk with an old kitchen chair tucked under it. The central showpiece of the room was a large pink rug.

Thinking the rug was really cool, Copeland stepped further into the room and asked 'So, Tom, what's so important you had to smuggle me a message on a piece of toilet paper?'

Benson closed the door. Benson put a finger to his lips. Benson locked the door. Benson slid the top bolt across. Benson slid the bottom bolt across. Benson shushed Copeland with, 'I don't want Jesus to hear.'

Copeland thought Jesus was probably not listening and certainly unlikely to hear anything with screaming swear words coming from the room below, a thumping bass coming up the stairs and cries of anguish from the man getting his massage. 'It's what I call, him,' explained Benson, throwing his towel onto his bed. 'The bearded guy who never leaves Room E. We followers of the truth, who **you** people call conspiracy nuts, think he's hiding out in there. He doesn't know the Romans have gone. Do you mind averting your eyes, Inspector, while I dress?'

As Tom started rummaging in his wardrobe, Copeland nodded slowly. The thought of Tom removing his bathrobe quite abruptly cleared his mind. After a quick right turn he sauntered past the desk, where a sleeping laptop sat beneath an obscure space film poster featuring a woman who looked like she would be very cold wearing that costume in space. He stopped and studied Benson's bookshelf. Copeland was not surprised it was mostly full of books with conspiracy theories, but he was surprised how many different secret societies and extra terrestrials seemed to be responsible for really running the world and the assassination of JFK. He browsed the titles on the shelf labelled by a taped scrap of paper as "Rulers of the World". All the usual suspects were there – the Freemasons, the Family, the Illuminati, the Yale Bonesmen, Voldemort's Death Eaters, the Davos Group, and, with 'UNTRUE' labels stuck on their spines, Facebook and Google. Copeland took one off the shelf and flicked through it as if he could see perfectly well without his glasses on and thought he would keep the conversation conversational with, 'I thought you were... in a relationship with Beth, Tom?'

There was a pause. 'She got a plum job up north,' sighed Tom with a cracking voice. He coughed. 'But let us not burden our remembrances with a heaviness that's gone.'

Without turning to look, Copeland knew Tom had his index finger raised again. 'We said no more Shakespeare!' laughed Copeland. 'One more Shakespeare quote and I'll sit on you. And that's a fate worse than death.'

Tom laughed a mirthless laugh. 'To quote Tom Baker then – quite often a fate worse than death is life.'

Definitely time to change the subject before he tops himself, Copeland!

'You like magic, then, Tom?' asked Copeland, changing the subject.

'Level twelve wizard with a really mean fireball spell,' enthused Tom. 'Oh! You mean the books? I thought you meant my character in Runeworld Revisited Yet Again Six. I have to log on at nine or my fellow adventurers might be eaten by a dragon... Er... Yes, the books... Written by people who do all those sorts of things on TV shows where they appear to read minds and hypnotise people and stuff. Do you know I've learned to tell when someone is not telling the truth by reading their micro body language?'

A plastic beaker was thrust in front of Copeland. It contained something red. Copeland lost his interest in the books. He tossed the one in his hands onto Tom's desk, took the beaker and smiled at Tom, now dressed in a plain grey sweatshirt and jeans. Smiling back up at Copeland, Tom said, 'I got a bottle of red in case you came. I hope it's a good one. It cost me nearly five pounds. Don't worry about the white stuff in the bottom. It's just the glass I use to rinse my mouth when I clean my teeth.' He touched his plastic glass against Copeland's. Copeland smiled and swigged. 'How is it?' asked Tom.

'Great,' said Copeland, grimacing as if he had swallowed vinegar.

'Aha! Your micro body language gave you away! You don't like it!' Tom moved to take the plastic cup back.

'No, it's great. Honest!' said Copeland, guarding it like a vulnerable baby.

'Aha!' said Tom Benson. 'Saying **honest** is always a sure sign of lying!'

Copeland swigged the toothpaste flavour wine and said, 'I'll get used to it. Hon... Er, right. Now, Tom, tell me why I'm here. What's this important information you need to tell me?'

Tom looked over his shoulder. He looked over his other shoulder. He leaned towards Copeland. He whispered, 'It's a jar,' and nodded his balding head wisely.

Copeland looked down at Benson's large, smiling teeth. He looked at his shiny cranium. He looked at the wall over his bed with the picture of Yoda. Copeland could understand why Benson liked Yoda – Yoda was one of the few people Tom was taller than – but he could not understand the cryptic message about a jar. After seriously considering the white wardrobe, Copeland said, 'A jar?'

'Yes!' exclaimed Tom, downing his wine with gusto. 'Pandora opened a jar, not a box. It's a common misunderstanding. I heard it on the radio. I think it was something with Melvyn Bragg. I thought it was important you knew after that last case we worked on all revolved around something that came from Pandora's Box.'

Copeland bit his lip and squeezed his nose before he said, 'Er, well, not really. It was made by people.'

There was a pause. 'Oh,' said Tom, clearly deflated.

'I'll be going then before my car tells me I've had too much drink to drive again,' said Copeland, putting the half-full beaker down next to the discarded book on the desk. 'Glad to see you're well.'

Copeland! How can you say that? screamed his inner voice. *He was at the clinic. He might not be well. He may be terminal! You owe him!*

'You are well, aren't you, Tom?' asked Copeland as his hand subconsciously reached back towards the half tumbler of cheap wine. It subconsciously picked it up and subconsciously raised it to his mouth. His mouth subconsciously opened and, wanting to be one of the team, his throat subconsciously swallowed.

Tom was looking at his feet, which were ensconced in furry white slippers. They had a rabbit face on them. 'What? Am I well? Yes. Fine. Oh, the clinic? Just a full medical before I start my new job.' He perked up. 'I was head-hunted for a PR company! Oh, yes! There is something else. Why were you and that Inspector Lord there, seeing Dr. Lynn?'

Copeland considered the confidentiality aspects of an ongoing murder enquiry and, alternatively, how long it would take to play twenty questions with Tom. 'Why?' he asked before making a choice.

'Well,' said Tom with his squinty eyes as big as they could go, 'she was on the phone when I went in...'

'She had to phone some of her investors, Tom. One of her top scientists was murdered at a lab in Dorset.'

So much for confidentiality, Copeland!

Tom's eyebrows raised. 'Murder, eh? Well, Larry, she was telling someone not to worry because you'd swallowed the Viagra story hook, line and sinker.'

'Really?' said Copeland with eyebrows raised. 'Hmmm... Tell me, Tom, do you have more wine and perhaps some sticky tape?'

After Benson had told Copeland about Dr.Lynn's Viagra story being some sort of ruse, Copeland made Benson repeat the story twice from the beginning while he finished the bottle of 'Ripe and Rich' red wine (from an undetermined country), took Benson's only roll of tape and left. Benson had really wanted to ask him how he had got a BMW with the enhanced intelligent personal assistant but Copeland had insisted he needed to get to Dorset for an early start investigating the very hush-hush murder of Dr. Carter, Dr. Reema Sharma, her family, twelve bonobos and lots of mice in a secret lab, so Benson had helped him down the stairs and waved goodbye. Benson instantly knew he should have mentioned how Dr. Lynn's micro body language had further revealed itself. He knew he should have told Copeland how the Doctor's secretary had come into the consultation room to tell Dr. Lynn she had forgotten to mention someone name Erica Young was also there to see her. Benson had noticed the subtle body language changes that told him the good Doctor Lynn was not pleased. She had sworn vehemently at her secretary for not telling her this Erica was there. Then she had clenched her fist, waved it about and sternly ordered Benson to go and wait outside again, all of which Benson thought a little inconvenient since she had just started examining his prostate.

Benson found himself regretting his omission and standing in the doorway looking out into the street long after Copeland's rear lights had disappeared. When he shut the door the house was strangely quiet. He knew that meant the couple in Room A had run out of mugs to throw, the guy in Room B had gone out to sell what little cannabis he had not smoked himself, the massage parlour was between customers and Jesus was keeping himself to himself, possibly in case there were any Romans around.

It was not until Benson sat down in front of his laptop and logged on to save his fellow on-line gaming avatar adventurers from the dragon that he realised he had omitted something far more important than Dr. Lynn's anger about someone name Erica. He stared at the packet of extra strong mints lying beside his laptop, and said, 'Oh! Dear me! And I forgot to warn him about that Alison Taylor and why we all need mints...'

DOCTOR LYNN HAS A HOME VISIT.

With her arms folded, the circular steel earrings swung as she looked from Dr. Lynn to her husband Jeremy Lynn and back again. 'You wanted me to come to your house late so **he** could be here. You want me to sign another twenty page legal contract, right?' earring girl asked before resuming her gum chewing.

'Not at all, Erica,' smiled Dr. Lynn across her ten seat dining table. 'We wanted somewhere private and for our housekeeper Finch to have retired to his room before you came.' She nudged husband Jeremy sitting next to her.

'What?' said Jeremy. 'Finch? Yes! Brilliant chap! Super chef! Found my jacket for me again earlier! What? Er, yes, quite... I'm just here to see fair play, you know. That's what we lawyers do. We just make sure everything is fair.'

Erica tutted and shook her head. The earrings waved about in sympathetic motion with her her brown pigtails. 'Fair?' she said, arms folded. 'Fair? You said I was going to be a receptionist. You didn't say anything about being a cleaner, tea-maid, errand girl, and zookeeper.'

'I've told you already, Erica, we didn't know they had bonobos,' Dr. Lynn soothed with her hands clasped together like a sincere preacher or snake-oil salesman.

'The monkeys are why I came to see you earlier...'

Jeremy interjected with, 'Your contract clearly states you would never contact Doctor Lynn personally or ever visit the clinic, Miss Young.'

Erica scowled at him for a few moments. Still looking at him, she asked, 'So, Doc, was he stupid and looked like a balding grey haired skeleton with a beak for a nose when you married him?'

Doc Lynn waved a finger at the young woman across the table, as a mother would to a naughty toddler, saying, 'Just because my husband is old, thin, unattractive and had a head trauma so knows nothing about anything except contract law there's no need to get personal, Erica.'

'Then tell your old pervert husband to look at my face when he's talking to me,' snorted Erica.

Every time Erica spoke Dr. Lynn half expected her to spit on the floor afterwards, but at the moment she needed her so she turned to look at husband Jeremy. His eyes went up to Erica's face without a word needing to be said.

'Good,' said Erica, for once sounding like her words were not going to be followed by an unsavoury globule of projectile phlegm. 'I want more money. Sneaking into that creep Carter's office every few weeks to download his files is one thing, but cleaning out monkey shit is another.'

Jeremy began, 'You were right, Evie! She doesn't know about...' before Dr. Lynn kicked him under the table, smiled and calmly said, 'I take it you have not been back to the lab since Friday, Erica.'

Erica chewed her gum, shook her earrings and said, 'Not going back again either without a pay rise. I want either half as much again or an extra fifty percent.'

'That's the same thing,' Jeremy observed.

A chewing gum bubble exploded in Jeremy's direction. Erica's red lipstick lips sucked the gum in. 'I know that, granddad, but I wasn't sure you did,' she said as she chewed open mouthed.

'A pay rise might be in order, Erica,' agreed Evie Lynn. 'But do you have another flash drive for us? It's been a few weeks since you sent the last one, and you said another was ready.'

Erica sat chewing, looking as defiant as a fifteen year old and gazing up at the ceiling.

Jeremy tried to be helpful. 'You know, dear girl, the flash drive? Sometimes called a USB stick for some unknown reason. It's that little plastic thing you stick in the side of the computer every few weeks, click on the little icon with the file picture, click on copy to external drive, take it out, put in a padded envelope and post it special delivery to me at my solicitor's office? I now it's all very technical for a young lady without any qualifications whatsoever like you, but just try to focus and think if you did it recently. By "did it" I mean download the data onto the flash drive. Not the other did...'

Erica fixed him with her round brown eyes, chewing menacingly in his direction. Jeremy shuffled in his seat. Dr. Evie Lynn said nothing. She liked the way Erica could make the so-called stronger sex shrivel. Along with her high IQ scores and being penniless, her looks were the main reason Dr. Lynn had selected her: she expected Erica's looks to be more than enough to have the well-known philanderer Jonathan Carter eating out of her hand. But even though Carter's head did not seem to have been turned (before he received a hole in it), things had still worked out and after a couple of months Carter had trusted his new receptionist enough to sometimes leave his laptop on when he left his office and Erica had proven to be opportunistic enough to download all his files every few weeks. Dr. Lynn had decided it was the only way she could be sure the obsessively secretive Carter and his team were not taking the clinic's money – her money – and doing next to nothing to earn it. The infrequent postal deliveries of flash drives sent by Erica had convinced Evie Lynn her money was most certainly not being wasted. Now, through that tubby Department C man and that idiot inspector, she had discovered Jonathan Carter and his team were using primates as test subjects and the data Erica had been sending had all begun to make sense. Dr. Lynn had always wondered why some of the mice had been given different, colour coded designations with the letter B in front of them. Now she knew the B really stood for bonobo. While she looked at Erica and tried to stop herself from laughing at Jeremy's squirming discomfort, Dr. Evie Lynn suddenly understood the significance of subjects B9 and B10, and that new understanding thrilled her. Carter's team had been close... Before she had realised it, Dr. Lynn had slapped her hand on the table, shown Erica what a real glare looked like and snapped, 'Erica! Do you have the latest flash drive?'

For a moment Erica lost the rhythm of her gum chewing, but soon regained it to say, 'Chill out, Doc. But now you've mentioned it, that's my other new demand. I'm not going back to the lab to work as your spy unless you give me expenses for buying and posting those flash drives.'

Jeremy was indignant and retorted, 'We already pay you enough! And Carter was paying... Er, I mean **is** paying you as his receptionist because he's very much still alive and well and...'

Dr. Lynn put a hand on his arm. She squeezed tight. Jeremy got the message. Dr. Lynn could not believe Jeremy could not see it was all irrelevant. Carter was dead, the mice were dead, the bonobos were dead, and worst of all the computers were dead. If Erica had one more flash drive then all of Carter's team's research so far would be in her hands. They just might have finished, but if not Evie Lynn was confident the rest of the team could finish the work without Dr. Carter. She was sure Alison, Wang and especially Reema could complete the work. Why couldn't they? She flicked back her straight blonde hair, smiled at Erica and asked, 'Do you think two hundred pounds cash would cover your costs so far, Erica?'

'That'll do,' said Erica, standing up.

'Do you wear that dress for work, Erica? It's rather short and, well, quite tight,' commented Dr. Lynn holding her hand out for the flash drive to be placed into it, noticing Jeremy was trying to look anywhere except at Erica's dress.

'It's my favourite black dress. I'm going clubbing,' said Erica, now chewing while standing. 'And no, I don't wear this for work. I did at first, but that snotty Alison woman said it put Jonathan off his work and she made me wear boring jeans and blouses. But that reminds me of another thing.' She folded her arms again. 'I want to see that modelling contract you promised me with that friend of yours. I'm not going back to my old job and, you know like, stuff. Our contract is up next month and I'm not working for that slime-ball Jonathan and stuck-up Alison one day longer than I need to, like. I've done my year as we agreed, and that's despite the bloody monkey shit!'

'You'll have your modelling contract and I told you I didn't know about...'

'And they'd better pay me for all that stuff I bought too like or I'm charging you for that as well, Doc Lynn!'

Doc Lynn further extended her hand for the all-important flash drive. Smiling as sweetly as she could, Doc Lynn said, 'May I have the latest flash drive please, Erica?'

'Over a hundred pounds they owe me! My credit card's maxed-out!' Erica huffed. She used her finger to pry stuck chewing gum from a tooth. She leaned forward onto the table. 'Do you know, Doc, last Wednesday they sent me to get cakes and champagne like and when I came back with Tesco's own brand! Well! The looks I got! I thought we were one happy family – I even clean their toilet for Christ's sake – and then they don't even invite me to their little champagne and cakes party. Come and take a photo, Erica, they say – not even a please! – and then it's just like that'll do and now go back to your reception desk Erica. At least Reema brought me a cake afterwards. She's OK, she is. Wang's a laugh sometimes too. He invited me round to his house and let me play with his little kids one Sunday. I think it was so I could meet his wife so she could see I wasn't some sort of threat to their marriage. I was wearing this same dress so I'm not sure that worked out so well... But Wang is devoted to her and his kids, you know?

He doesn't strip me with his eyes like Jonathan does every day and like your husband is now. But that stuck-up aren't-I-lovely Alison and Jonathan are like clean the bonobos out Erica or like shave the mice Erica or like carry in the new delivery and like put it in the fridge Erica. I'm not working a day after the end of April with those two shits so get me that modelling contract by the end of the month or I'll find my own lawyer and sue. I've got grounds.'

Jeremy was dumbfounded. 'You actually read your contract?' he asked. 'In our standard font size six?'

Dr. Lynn had only one thing on her mind. She stood and thrust a palm towards Erica. 'The flash drive, please!' she insisted.

Erica changed stance. She put her hands on her hips. Jeremy groaned. She took her chewing gum out and, perhaps just in case she visited the Lynn's home again, stuck it to the side of the dining table. 'All this fuss for Viagra mark two?' she scoffed. 'There's nothing wrong with Viagra mark one. I can tell you that. Works on everyone as far as I can tell. And it's definitely not like your husband needs it like. Look at how he's looking at me. Totally ga-ga. I know where his brain is right now. I told you. I'm fed up paying for the postage.' She held her hand out to mirror Dr. Lynn. 'Give me my money and I'll post it. I transferred the files while they were having their little party in the work-lab.'

Dr. Lynn's mind whirred at top speed. She replayed the last few minutes. She dropped her outstretched hand, controlled her breathing while she counted to ten (very quickly) and said, 'That's so sad, Erica. You fetched all the things for their party and you only got invited in to take a photo. I think that's so sad. Honest.'

'I know!' Erica agreed with an eye roll. 'You know, I thought it was a surprise party for me when I saw the banner.

It was my twenty first birthday. I just thought they had spelled my name with a k by mistake. Then I realised it didn't say Erica. It said... you erika.'

'You erika? Eureka?' said Dr. Lynn, eyebrows raised.

'That's it!' said Erica. 'They had a little plate and some of their new Viagra tablets on it. Smarmy Jonathan held it, they all grinned and I took a photo on Alison's phone.'

Dr. Lynn swallowed hard. 'And you were left out of the party and went and downloaded all their latest research while they were enjoying the champagne you'd bought,' sympathised Dr. Lynn, quite convincingly.

'Yeah,' said Erica. She stared at Jeremy, who was intently staring back. She stuck her tongue out at him. 'You know, I used the little plastic thing you stick into the side of the computer and download the files onto.' She turned back to Dr. Lynn. 'It's still in the grotty Axminster flat I pay you rent for. Now you've agreed my pay rise, I'll go back tomorrow and post it before I go into work and suffer that insufferable Jonathan ogling at me until Alison comes along and then he's all like Oh, Hi Alison, you look so good today and stuff. I mean she's okay, like, two eyes a mouth and a nose, like, but a bit on the large side like and not like model material like me, you know? Reema calls her Miss Piggy!'

'Yes, quite,' said Evie Lynn, thinking Erica had better post the flash drive before she got into work and found out Jonathan would never ogle at her again, not unless the police had left him lying in the lab with his eyes still open, when some ogling may have still been a possibility given Erica's figure. Dr. Lynn thought she had better make sure. 'Our contract is at least one data download each month, Erica, so if you don't post it **before** you go into work then there will be no modelling contract and definitely no pay rise. And text

Jeremy the tracking number like usual. We'll give you an extra hundred.'

Erica shrugged. 'Fine, Doc. An extra hundred will do,' she said as Jeremy, horror-struck, looked in his empty wallet.

Evie Lynn sent Jeremy upstairs to fetch the three hundred pounds. He used his initiative, borrowed it from their servant Finch and returned to grudgingly place it in Erica's hand. Dr. Lynn pretended to graciously usher Erica out and returned to her dining room. Jeremy was drinking a very large Scotch. He looked very flushed as he said, 'She has no idea Carter and all the lab animals are dead.'

'I gathered that,' said Evie Lynn. 'But you know what this means, Jeremy?'

'I do, Evie. It's terrible. We have to pay her an extra fifty percent,' said Jeremy. 'Plus postage for the flash drives. How are we going to explain that on my tax return?'

Not for the first time that evening, Dr. Evie Lynn really wanted the contact details for a contract killer, but, deciding to let husband Jeremy live for a little longer, she resorted to the method that had worked ever since they had married and said, 'Shut up, Jeremy.' She despaired how, once upon a time, someone could get a law degree from Oxford as long as they had the right connections. They had even invented the 'Lower 3rd class' category just for Jeremy. At least Jeremy had stuck to his oath and never admitted which college had accepted the large 'annual donation'.

Jeremy said, 'Hey, Evie, I meant to mention it, but did you know Baliol College is getting a new library?'

Dr. Lynn gritted her teeth, tried to remember what Jeremy used to be like before he had suffered the head trauma which had apparently damaged one of his two brain cells, and said, 'You must realise Carter and his team finally did it! That flash drive in Erica's so-called bijou modern apartment overlooking the Co-op car park has the answer to untold wealth.'

'I thought you said it was something that would make people not worry anymore,' Jeremy reminded Evie Lynn, wiping the sweat from his brow and pouring a second calming single malt.

Dr. Lynn pulled the front of her hair and screamed, 'Yes Jeremy! But they still have to pay for it!'

Jeremy looked like he was thinking hard. He went to fetch ice. Evie Lynn heard him in the kitchen hacking it out of the ice-tray. She paced along the side of the dining table while she waited. Jeremy returned to the dining room, sat with his large Scotch, looked meaningfully at his wife and said, 'I understand now, Evie. Men do worry about that sort of thing, don't they?' Evie Lynn sighed and waited. Jeremy said, 'You know I don't usually drink so I may be getting a little confused here compared to my usual razor sharp self, but isn't Erica right and the current Viagra does what is says on the tin? Does it come in a tin?'

Resignedly, Evie Lynn sat. She put her head in her hands. As calmly as she could she said, 'How many times do I have to tell you, Jeremy. It is not – I repeat – NOT Viagra! And they made it. They had tablets! They tested it on bonobos. They probably even took it themselves. They celebrated their success. It works!'

Jeremy thought about this. He scratched his thinning grey hair and said, 'You know I don't quite understand all this sciency stuff anymore, Evie, but I get it. It's not Viagra. What you're saying is Carter and his lot have made a really good **new** sort of Viagra.'

The side of Dr. Lynn's fists banged the table as she shouted, 'I've told you a hundred times, Jeremy! It **never** had anything to do with Viagra!'

ERICA YOUNG.

While Dr. Lynn tried to explain everything again to Jeremy, Erica enjoyed her evening clubbing. She had not bothered to check into a hotel. She knew it was cheaper to use a local leisure centre, go for a swim, then shower and change there. She had left the rest of her things in the car she had managed to buy with a thirty percent interest loan. Jeremy Lynn had told her having a car was necessary when she had been interviewed for her job as receptionist and spy. She liked the car. It was an automatic, which was lucky really because Erica had never driven a car before so she had soon got the hang of it. The man in the back street garage who took her deposit had not asked her if she could drive so Erica had not bothered to mention it either and it had not worried her since. Neither was she worried about where she was going to sleep. Whenever she went out clubbing she always got plenty of invites back to people's homes.

What she had not told Doc Lynn (besides the minor thing about the driving) was that she had meant to bring the latest flash drive with her but had, like, left it on that little table with the empty blue plant pot on it right by the door. She had put it there, by the front door like, so she did not forget it when she left the house to drive up to confront Doc Lynn about her pay rise, but had then remembered to phone in sick like and she had walked right past it while she was unsuccessfully trying to leave a voice mail message on lecherous Dr. Carter's phone like.

Besides the driving thing and Jonathan Carter's phone being out of order, what she had not told Doc Lynn either was that she quite liked the bonobos, and she got overtime pay for staying behind after Reema and Wang had gone home. That was when Jonathan or Alison would open the metal door for her to feed and clean out the bonobos. Erica was especially fond of the two old ones called B11 and B12, which she had named Betty and Barry. It had been so cute, the way Betty had leaned against the side of her cage and pushed her arm through the bars so her hand could reach over the stainless steel shelf for Barry to reach up and hold it. She hated Jonathan Carter even more because he had got rid of both Betty and Barry last week and replaced them with two young bonobos, just like he had B9 and B10 a few weeks before. Erica thought the new B11 and B12 bonobos were not nearly as nice as Betty and Barry. The new ones just sat there looking depressed, even when she hosed out their cages.

4. Tuesday, March 19th.

COPELAND GOES TO THE SHARMAS'.

When he woke up in the room he had reoccupied at the little Lyme Bay View Hotel in Kilmington, Larry Copeland was faced with a dilemma. By the time he had driven down to the hotel, stopping off for toiletries, a chicken sandwich and a couple of bottles of now empty red, he had not quite got round to looking at the contents of the flash drive Vasily had given him. And Boss Wendy Miller had arranged for him to meet the officer investigating the murder of the Sharma family at the crime scene at nine. Copeland lay in bed with a lot on his mind. He had difficult decisions to make. He carefully weighed up his priorities. He stared at the bedroom ceiling and calculated all possible alternatives. He came to a conclusion. He needed to get up if he wanted breakfast before the kitchen closed.

In some ways he wished he had not bothered and stuck to plan A and gone back to sleep. Nina, the usually affable golf playing proprietress, was still quite terse with him and seemed to be paying him little attention compared to the only other guest in the small dining area opposite the equally small bar. He did not even get his usual second pot of tea, let alone his usual extra toast. He recognised the other guest, whom proprietress Nina called Mrs. Smith, as the woman who had slammed her glass down on the bar and stormed off on Friday night when he and proprietress Nina were talking golf. Copeland remembered he had commented Mrs. Smith was clearly not a golf fan and Nina had pulled a face and told him Mrs. Smith was a regular at the hotel. Thcn Nina had apparently got something in her eye again because she kept squeezing it closed and opening it again as she told Copeland (whom Nina had decided to call 'Big Larry' for some reason) that Mrs. Smith was a Friday night regular, always came by taxi and usually had the same room – the upstairs one furthest from the stairs – where she waited for (more one-eye closing and opening) Mr. Smith.

Well! This is outrageous, Copeland! There's no Mr. Smith here now, is there? So why is she getting a second pot of tea and we're not?

Jane's watch had been scrutinised several times as she paced the gravel drive in front of the Sharma house. Finally she went inside to rehearse what she was going to tell the undoubtedly sophisticated M.I.5 Department C genius they were sending to solve the case. She walked herself through her rehearsed description of the crime scene, which now seemed comparatively sanitised after forensics had finished and the bodies had been removed. She stopped in the kitchen, ignored the blood stained slate tiles near the door and those near the cooker, and stood near the door leading to the conservatory. She knew this was their big break. The killer had seemingly left not a shred of evidence except for this. He had got careless and stepped in Mrs. Sharma's blood, leaving this one clear footprint near the conservatory door. Jane rehearsed what she was going to tell the dashing Department C officer. She had learned the preliminary forensic findings off by heart but, just to be sure, she cleared her throat and said it out loud: 'Male size eleven trainer footprint, Sir. The forensics people say it was worn by someone weighing no more than eleven stone, Sir. So we're probably looking for a tall thin man, Sir. He must have taken the shoe off straight away because it's the only footprint, Sir,' Jane nodded contentedly and looked at her watch again, wondering where this hotshot Department C person had got to.

Her phone rang. She took it from her jacket pocket, fully expecting it to be the expected James Bond clone from MI5. It wasn't. It was her sergeant. At least it was some good news at last. A neighbour of the Linpengs had seen the police notice left on the Linpengs' door telling them to contact the police for a new key for the replaced lock if they returned. The neighbour had reported they had gone on holiday. He knew this because he had given them a lift to Bristol airport on Friday evening to catch their flight to Malaga and it seemed they were all well except for Dr. Linpeng having his usual pre-flight upset stomach. Jane's inspector had confirmed with the airline and the Linpengs were definitely on the flight. Jane had not slept well thinking about the fate of Wang Linpeng, his wife and especially his children and as she put her phone back in her pocket a wave of relief swept over her. She almost laughed. She knew what a state she left her apartment in when she packed to go on holiday. The Linpengs, it seemed, were even worse.

While Jane was inside the Sharmas' house rehearsing for the arrival of the MI5 Department C young hotshot special agent whom she had already decided would definitely look like Roger Moore, Copeland arrived. He parked across the drive, got out and introduced himself by handing his card to the uniformed officer standing behind the yellow tape. Copeland felt pleased with himself. He may well have forgotten to transfer his ID to a different dark blue suit if he had not cleverly put on the same dark blue suit he had worn the day before. The officer squinted at his ID and went to fetch someone he called 'Detective Sadler' from inside the house.

Copeland sat back on the bonnet of his BMW. Detective Jane Sadler came out of the house in her black trouser suit and white blouse and crunched across the gravel with his ID card in her hand and the uniform officer at her side. As he watched her approach, Copeland's first thought was how warm the car bonnet was keeping his backside. His next thought was that she was too innocent to have ever seen a corpse in her life. (Jane Sadler, not his car.) Her jaunty step, rosy cheeks, gleaming, straight smile and most of all the pony-tailed (and undoubtedly dyed) daffodil-blonde hair cried 'millennial snowflake!' As she strode closer in her black trouser suit, Copeland realised she was as tall as he was. Then he realised he was leaning back on the bonnet and she was probably closer to average height.

She's a lot slimmer than you are though, Copeland! the inner voice pointed out.

She was already holding out her hand to shake his and introduced herself with, 'Detective Jane Sadler, Sir. It's a real pleasure to meet you, Inspector Copeland.'

'Where's the S.I.O?' asked Copeland, arms folded.

Still holding out a hand and looking confused, Jane said, 'Er... That's you, Sir. I've been told you are the senior investigating officer.'

Copeland raised an eyebrow and took out his phone. There was a text message from Director Miller. It had been sent at seven a.m. He vaguely remembered hearing his phone ping before going back to sleep. It seemed he was indeed the S.I.O. It did not surprise him. Why should it? Nothing else about why he and Department C were even involved in this case surprised him any longer either. He was past caring. It got him out of the cold damp office, out of the London smog, back to clean air, and to where his favourite pubs were. He put his phone away and refolded his arms.

Jane said, 'It's fairly standard practice for the security services to be involved when there is a break-in at a scientific research facility which might possibly be producing potential biological agents that could be used by terrorists, isn't it, Sir?'

'It is?' said Copeland.

Jane took this as a statement rather than a question and, still with her her hand held out, she smiled and said, 'I thought as much. I'm assigned to assist you, Sir. '

Oh, great! Here we go again, Copeland!

For once, Copeland had to agree with his despairing inner, better, but possibly increasingly senile self. The six mile drive from Kilmington had taken almost an hour. Most of it had been spent opposite the farm shop waiting to pull out to turn right on the A35, but sitting watching an endless stream of vehicles had given him a chance to reflect on his feelings. He had found them mixed. He might have just about coped working with Clare again, despite her eye rolling, but he would not miss working with Giles Lord. He was certain about one thing, though. He did not really want to work with anyone at all – it cramped his laser-like investigative style and usually restricted how many meals he could get in during the day. Another Inspector Giles was not what he needed, yet here was another young detective foisted on him against his wishes and he fully expected her to be as intellectually sharp as dreary Inspector Giles Lord. He reminded himself the last thing he wanted right now was someone looking over his shoulder and getting under his feet at the same time. He had his own priorities: he had to find Vasily's niece Dominika before Vasily's veiled threats against his daughter became unveiled threats. And it had been too long since breakfast.

Detective Jane Sadler held her handshake hand higher. She looked down to see if he was responding. Copeland hit on a foolproof plan to get rid of his new chaperone. He kept his arms folded above his generous stomach, looked as contemptuous as he could and said, 'So which charity shop did you get your black suit from, Blondie?'

Copeland! Seriously? That's your plan? To insult her?

The uniformed officer coughed and discretely retreated. Jane's smile dropped as did her hand when Copeland ignored it as he groaned, rose from the car bonnet, turned his back on her and went round the car to get into the driver seat. Detective Jane Sadler was already in the passenger seat with her seatbelt on by the time Copeland had got his legs under the steering wheel.

'Driver, your door is still open,' said the pretend Judi Dench voice.

He slammed his door closed and looked across at his new chaperone. She sat stony faced, staring unblinkingly at him with her big blue eyes.

Good God, Copeland! What's she doing? Nobody salutes anymore, do they? Certainly not to you!

'My apologies, Sir,' Jane said with her hand sideways on her forehead. 'A handshake is not an appropriate way to greet a senior officer. Please forgive me, Sir.'

Copeland bit his lip to stop his jaw from dropping, but could not think of a plan B to make her storm off out of the car and request another assignment. He reasoned Theresa May had never had a plan B for Brexit so why did he need one? Safe and secure, just like dear Theresa, he stuck with the same plan. He sternly said, 'Don't think I'm going to hold your hand, Detective. I'm not impressed by young high fliers who think they know it all. What are you? Twenty four, twenty five? Thinking you will rise up the ranks to Chief Constable by the time you're forty, I suppose? It'll take more than a pretty face. I've never believed any woman should ever make senior rank. They should be at home raising children and cooking and cleaning and...' He ran out of anything else. 'Ah, yes!' he said, still trying to sound convincing, 'Yes! Cooking and having babies, and not going around to murder scenes and seeing things that makes a young slip of a girl like you all teary and needing to...' He searched for the right word. What was it? '... Er, yes, all teary and needing to swoon! Yes, swoon! I don't need a pretty young sidekick chick who swoons at the sight of blood!' He was quite pleased with the phrase sidekick chick – that should do it!

But Jane Sadler had not lowered her salute. 'Permission to speak, Sir?' she asked. Copeland had run out of put-downs so he nodded, thoroughly dismayed the inspired 'sidekick chick' comment had not been enough to get a slap or an official complaint, or at the very least an empty car. He felt too deflated by his failure to get rid of her to even listen. His mind panicked and turned to more important things like elevenses. His eyes glazed as she said, 'I'm forty two, Sir. People say I just have one of those young complexions. I have no plans to rise in the ranks, Sir. I recently handed in my resignation. I'm going back to being a teacher, which I was for a few years after my first stint in the force. I thought the attitudes of the force towards lesbians would have moved on and been better by now, but I was wrong. As you must know, my last evaluation said I was often too matter of fact and overenthusiastic and how I didn't grasp questions and got answers. I thought it was a bit contradictory. The sight of blood does not bother me, Sir.'

Copeland thought she had probably finished whatever it was she was saying so turned away from her, put the BMW in gcar and pressed the accelerator. Nothing happened.

The silky, suspiciously similar to Judi Dench voice said, 'Not wearing a seatbelt is against the law.' He ignored the smooth voice until it added, 'Sir.'

The car said, 'Driver seatbelt required,' in its suspiciously similar to Judi Dench voice.

Copeland stared at the speaker on the dashboard. He stared at Detective Sadler, who shrugged and said, 'Some people think I sometimes sound a little like an actor called Judi Dench, Sir, but usually at twice her speed.'

Copeland knew when he was outnumbered. He put his seatbelt on and growled, 'Stop saluting and put your bloody hand down, Detective.'

'Very good, Sir! May I ask where we are going, Sir?'

Copeland sighed, 'I've been driving for an hour, Detective. I need coffee. And maybe a cake. I thought Lyme...'

'I thought you'd want to see the evidence first, Sir?' said Jane with her hands in her jacket pockets. 'The footprint, Sir?'

Red alert Copeland! She said footprint not footprints! And when I say red alert, I mean RED alert!

Copeland was annoyed. He had heard just fine. He almost wished he had read the reports now, but he had always found that coloured his thinking. He always liked to approach all evidence with a fresh mind so he could draw his own conclusions. To see things fresh, not have things tainted by...

Be honest, Copeland! It's because you would rather be in a pub than reading reports!

Jane said, 'Size eleven but with not much pressure so we're looking for a tall thin man. Here's a photo on my phone, Sir.'

So much for not being influenced by evidence, Copeland... but look...

Copeland was looking. How could he not look? Detective Sadler had thrust her phone in front of his face. He could also see something that confirmed his suspicions.

'Strange, though, Sir,' commented Jane, contemplatively. 'There's only this one, single footprint after he had got Mrs. Sharma's blood on his trainer's sole, but it points towards where her body was, not away from it. Why would the killer step into the blood and walk directly backwards? Why is it a good three paces from her body, even for someone as tall as you, Sir? Surely there would have been one more footprint even if he did step back?'

Copeland stared at the phone picture and said nothing. He was waiting for his inner voice to tell him this detective was not cut from the same cloth as Giles Lord.

'Can I put my phone down now, Sir? My arm is starting to ache leaning across like this.'

Copeland slowly nodded.

Slipping her phone into her jacket Jane said, 'I think it's a ruse, Sir. A footprint intentionally planted. I don't think it's a tall thin man at all.'

Copeland thought, *Don't you dare say it!* to his inner voice. His inner voice knew when to be silent. Either that or it was having a nap. Putting his hands on the wheel and staring out of the car windscreen Copeland quietly said, 'I've seen this before. It's an old KGB trick. It usually throws the local police off the trail when they've assassinated someone. The KGB, not the local police.'

Jane's eyes widened. 'Ah, it's Russian SVR. That's what they're called now. Most people think they're called the FSB because of films, but the SVR are their external secret service. Aha! That's why MI5 is involved!' exclaimed Jane. 'Oh! I mean, involved, **Sir**!'

Copeland considered this. Firstly, Department C was definitely not what he would consider 'traditional' MI5. It had no security mandate, as far as he knew, but was set up to tackle corruption in the form of organised crime – drugs, people trafficking, gun running, etc. One of the few things he already knew was that the team he was meant to recruit would first be dealing with illegal animal smuggling and his opposite number, Natalie, would be leading a team infiltrating gun runners in Bristol. He reflected on this. That was actually two things he already knew. Yet, still, why had Wendy Miller got him involved with tracking down a Russian SVR operative murdering people? Surely that was the proper MI5's job?

Unless it's a trained Russian agent who has gone freelance, Copeland, said his more thoughtful self, giving him a clue. *Perhaps one who has gone off the grid, as our American friends say. Someone whose uncle Vasily...*

Yes! I got it, thought Copeland.

'Are you alright, Sir?' asked Jane. You seem to have gone into some sort of trance. But forgive me for saying so, Sir, but why would the Russians want to kill the Sharma family? They owned restaurants and Reema – poor, young Reema...' Jane sighed, '...Reema was working on a new sort of Viagra from what Inspector Lord's report said. And killing her brother was just vindictive.'

Copeland stared out of the windscreen. *Everything is connected to everything else, Copeland, just like da Vinci said and...*

Copeland snapped, 'Shut up! I'm thinking!'

Jane swallowed hard. 'Sorry, Sir,' she said.

'What? Not you detective,' Copeland said turning to look at her. 'Sometimes I sort of have internal discussions with myself.'

Jane beamed. 'I do that too, Sir! Sort of throwing the pros and cons across the net of logic!'

Copeland had never thought of it like that. Then again, logic had little to do with his inner voice and he really did not want to be committed to a psychiatric ward so he smiled and nodded.

'I thought it was just me,' enthused Jane. 'Like a split personality or something!'

Copeland nodded in a more fatherly way. 'No, it's quite normal, Detective. Why are you gripping my wrist?'

Jane gripped harder and said, 'I've heard of you, Sir.'

HA! That's a first! scoffed his more logical inner voice.

Copeland was not stupid. He had to admit Detective Jane Sadler was not either. It was blatantly obvious to Copeland that she had read his case files when she knew he was coming to solve the case. But he knew he had to be careful. He had, after all, signed the Official Secrets Act, so said, 'I suppose you know about my involvement in Ireland then. My undercover work with those Loyalist extremists is classified, and my part in securing the Good Friday Agreement is exaggerated, you know.'

Jane's big blue eyes widened and stared at him. A voice said, *She has no idea what you're talking about, Copeland.*

Copeland said, 'Or that thing with the Russians taking over London docks..? Er, not that either? Perhaps the shoot-out in the warehouse? There were only five of them and back-up came within the hour, so that was not such a big deal... Er, no..? Possibly the thing at Harrods then? I know my plan saved maybe hundreds of lives, but you definitely should forget you ever heard of that or my last employers, who don't exist and who call themselves The Pickfords because they are in the removal business – removing people, not furniture – will take a dim view and... Not that either? Ok, well, I didn't do any of those things, or all the other things, and the Pickfords definitely do not exist or have secret offices above a bank in Kensington and it's all classified anyway so forget I said anything.'

Jane smiled. 'I really have read everything about you, Sir. I first came across you when I was in uniformed copper on my first stint. I found out everything I could. There was so much redacted they must have used ten black marker pens. You really are one of my heroes. Well, sort of. I was expecting Roger Moore...' (Who? Copeland thought) 'But what you've said about Russians, organised crime and loyalist extremists aside, the bravest thing you ever did was standing shoulder to shoulder with that young detective back in the mid-eighties when she made sexual harassment claims against a senior officer. If not for you she would have left the force and would never have become a superintendant. And she was just the first. I knew that stuff you said when we met was just to get my back up and get rid of me. Why would someone like you want some raw detective like me cramping your laser-like investigative style?'

Copeland was more than a little surprised. 'Clare's become a superintendant?' he asked.

'As of yesterday morning, I hear,' Jane assured him. 'She's Superintendant Harper now, and just before a chief super retires, so who knows? I just know she would have left the force if you hadn't stuck your neck out and backed her, Sir. Although, from what I hear she's a bit unorthodox and cuts corners.'

I wonder where she learned that from, eh, Copeland?

'And there are rumours she gets confessions by, you know, er, applying pressure...'

OK, I can't blame you for that, Copeland.

'Sorry, Sir. Not my place to say, is it? I just wish you'd been there for me too, Sir... Can we go to the lab, Sir? Parking is a nightmare down in Lyme anyway so we could get coffee in Axminster. I know a pub that does great coffee. I'd like to see the scene of the murder of Dr. Carter and those poor animals. Devon Police have given me his key card to get in already. I went down to Honiton to fetch it early this morning. That Inspector Giles Lord is a bit strange isn't he, Sir? Oh, darn! That's in no way a criticism of a senior officer, Sir!'

At least Giles talked less, Copeland.

Copeland sighed. He said, 'Giles Lord is the son of Robert Lord.'

Jane's enthusiasm was curtailed. Her face fell. Sombrely, she said, 'The one who got away with all the insurance swindles? Er, allegedly...'

COLONEL VASILY GORAYA.

The large, ornate desk which the Russian ambassador was propped against would have kept Inspector Giles fascinated for a whole week but Colonel Vasily Goraya was not interested in the desk. He was not interested in the ambassador either. All he was interested in was the piece of paper the ambassador held in his hands. As soon as he had seen it the hairs on the back of his neck had stood up. He knew that flimsy piece of paper in the ambassador's hand had his future written on it. Why else would he be summoned into the ambassador's presence wearing full dress uniform and all his very heavy medals? Why else had the ambassador stared at the sheet of paper and kept him standing there at attention?

'Let us speak in English, Colonel,' suggested Ambassador Yashin. 'I need to use it more and, as you told me these English say, I need to do more than dip my toe in the bath.'

'Absolutely, Mr. Ambassador, Sir,' Vasily said as formally as he could as he stared at the paper. Vasily respected this new ambassador, Yuri Yashin. Ambassador Yashin was not one of the usual corrupt oligarchs who had risen to power on the back of bribes. Ambassador Yashin was a bona fide self-made businessman who had negotiated many successful deals in his time and made his fortune legitimately, trading in natural products grown on his own farms near Omsk. But besides his heroin business, Yuri Yashin had built solid commercial connections throughout the gambling and prostitution industries too and was generally regarded as someone who could negotiate to bring rival groups together to reach mutually beneficial goals – such as dividing a city up with strict territorial boundaries and the fewest possible fatalities. Ambassador Yashin was generally regarded as a liberal.

'Tell me, Colonel,' said Ambassador Yashin, flourishing the sheet of paper. 'How is your task going? Have you found all of our sleeper agents yet?'

Vasily hesitated. He thought it best not to correct the ambassador and tell him they were slumber agents, not sleeper agents, because if they had been asleep then... 'There is one still remaining, Mr. Ambassador.'

Yuri Yashin held the fate-bearing sheet of paper to one side as he rubbed his chin with his free hand. 'Tell me, Comrade, as one patriot to another, is it true all these red sparrows call you Uncle Vasily?'

Not correcting the slumber agent mistake was one thing but Vasily could not let that go. 'If I may, Sir, but they are not red sparrows. That was just in the book and...'

'And the film,' the ambassador interrupted. 'Jennifer Lawrence should have been nominated for an Oscar for that!'

'I agree, Sir,' said Vasily, having no idea there had been a film or who Jennifer Lawrence was, 'but I was going to point out they are not called red sparrows, Sir, but red cuckoos.

They were put in the English nest like a cuckoo lays eggs in other birds' nests.'

Ambassador Yashin hummed and nodded. He said, 'Thank you, Colonel. I sit corrected.'

'As for your question, Sir, the answer is yes. They all called me Uncle Vasily. It was a term of endearment and respect, you might say. I spent some time tutoring the red cuckoo recruits. Nothing major, just getting them to resist torture if they got caught. You know, a few weeks of water-boarding, electric shocks, submerging in ice-water – just the everyday sorts of things. They had the option to quit at any time. All they had to do was say "Please stop Uncle Vasily". They knew if they said that they would be out of the red cuckoo programme and be set free. Quite a lot chose to quit the programme.'

Ambassador Yashin was curious. 'And were they set free?' he asked.

Vasily thought about this. He answered, 'Yes, Sir, they were. At least their spirits were set free. Those that passed made their first kill by eliminating their friends who had failed.'

When Yuri Yashin had stopped laughing he said, 'So there is one left?' He grew very serious. 'Please do not tell me it is the one called Dominika?'

'I'm afraid it is, Sir. When I contacted them the rest came to the rendezvous points and they are back in the Motherland, but Dominika did not show up. She has been freelancing for some time and seems to have decided to cut her ties with the glorious Motherland for the decadent West. She was always one of the smarter ones. But now I have duped a top British agent to track her down for me.'

Ambassador Yashin frowned. 'Do not upset the British, Colonel. This is a delicate time. You know as well as I do that the President sees Britain as being our best ally soon. This EU thing has stolen our Baltic states, Poland, Romania... The United Kingdom will be the first to take their place, not counting Chechnya, and parts of Ukraine and Georgia of course. They will soon do this Brexit and turn their backs on the rest of Europe. They will need new partners, new car manufacturers... We will soon have Lada and Gaz factories in every city!'

'I understand, Sir. This is why we are terminating all the red cuckoos as a sign of good faith in our new friendship to sell them our gas and oil.' Vasily shuffled uneasily. 'But may I ask..? Are those my new orders, Sir? On that paper in your hand?'

Ambassador Yashin glanced at the paper. He shivered. He said, 'This paper says you have a new assignment, Colonel Goraya.' Vasily heard his heartbeat fill the silent void. Vasily began to sweat, thinking about the harsh winters of Siberia. Ambassador Yashin flourished the sheet of paper. 'I was going to tell you, but it can wait, Colonel. I have spoken to the President. I'm sure he has bigger fish to fly, as the English say – flying fish? – but he agrees with me and you should finish here first. It is important you find Dominika and eliminate her for her treachery. You are to remain in England until you have found the last of these red cuckoo sleeper agents. After you have found the traitorous Dominika then you will, er... get your new assignment in mother Russia. I hope you have a very warm coat, Colonel.'

Vasily saluted, wanting to tell Ambassador Yashin they were *bloody slumber agents!* and feeling very differently motivated about finding Dominika.

COPELAND AND JANE.

Despite protests from his stomach, Copeland relented to Jane's requests and reconnoitred the house that had once been the home of the Sharmas. He saw the suspicious size eleven footprint for himself and Jane enthusiastically told him what she thought had happened there – father opens door, steps back, gets shot in head, he falls back, killer puts another two in his chest, Reema comes to the kitchen door and... Copeland angrily snapped, 'I've got it Detective Sadler! Thanks!' and stormed out of the house. The uniformed officer took him to one side just before he got in the car. Copeland gestured for Jane to get into the car before he joined her. Jane sat in the car and waited. She saw the uniformed officer point to the car and saw Copeland look towards her with his eyebrows raised.

They drove in silence towards Axminster. Partly because of what the uniformed officer had told him about Jane entering the house unarmed and partly for losing his temper with her, Copeland felt so guilty he was actually giving up his elevenses.

The Judi Dench-like car voice soon announced, 'ATTENTION DRIVER. YOU ARE EXCEEDING THE PERMITTED SPEED LIMIT.'

Copeland looked at the speedometer. Two miles an hour faster than the speed limit was hardly a crime. *Actually, Copeland, it is.* Exasperated by the inability to escape the car's voice, his inner voice or the (not as young as she appeared) detective, Copeland thought he would use one of them against another. 'Your first order, Detective, is to change the damn voice of this car and limit it to telling me things I don't already know.'

'Really, Sir? asked Jane, surprised. 'I saw your ID card, Sir. Judi Dench is James Bond's boss and you are the new double o seven, Sir.'

Copeland was quite pleased. He had actually heard of James Bond. He looked at Jane. Was she smirking? He could guess who had programmed the voice. It had to be his real boss, didn't it? He imagined her smirking too. 'Change the voice, please,' said Copeland as he secretly thanked Wendy Miller for knowing him well enough to have put some duct tape in the car too.

Jane opened the glove compartment in front of her passenger seat and took out an instruction manual.

Did you know that was in there, Copeland? I didn't!

Less than two miles later, Jane pressed a few buttons on the control of what Copeland had assumed was a part of the radio and said, 'Annoyingly the instructions manual tells you at the end everything can be done by just speaking to the advanced personal assistant, Sir, but I've limited the car's voice to level red instructions only, Sir. They can't be turned off. Now, which simulated voice would you like? They have lots of actors, and of course I include female ones in that gender neutral category.'

'Make the car a male's voice,' he said.

'Very well, Sir,' agreed Jane, pressing buttons and, by the time they reached the remote car park of the isolated Uroboros Rejuvenation research lab, the car had a new, louder voice.

'Behold the Gates of Mordor! Parking brake on, young Master Frodo!' boomed the Sir Ian McKellen-car when Copeland pulled up outside the lab.

Copeland looked at Jane. She shrugged and said, 'You said you wanted a male voice, Sir. Gandalf is a male. Consider it a gift in return for your sidekick chick comment.'

Copeland folded his arms and glared at her. A smile broke onto his face. 'You can call me Larry, Jane,' he said.

Jane shook her pony tail. 'That would not be appropriate, Sir,' she said, frowning.

'Very well, Detective Constable Sadler,' Copeland groaned. 'But I suppose I should bring you up to speed. I don't think they were really making some sort of new Viagra here at all.'

P.C. REDMAN.

After twenty lengths of the garden, P.C. Redman ducked under the yellow tape across the deceased Sharmas' drive and stood next to the road to watch vehicles going to and from Lyme Regis. P.C. Redman liked Lyme. Shops there sold really good fudge. Taking some home always made him the best dad ever, at least for ten minutes or so. He looked at his watch to see there were two more hours until he was relieved of the boredom. He watched some very nice cars pull into the golf club entrance a stone's throw away from where he stood. He was just turning to go back under the tape and do laps around the drive when a car pulled up a few yards away. A man holding a little notebook got out. A white van pulled up behind it. A man and a woman got out. The man put a large camera onto his shoulder. The woman was holding a microphone. P.C. Redman quickly ducked back under the tape before the reporters assailed him.

He was trying to get his radio working when a microphone was thrust over the top of the tape and into his face. A whole series of questions bombarded P.C. Redman's ears before he had chance to speak. When he did he said, 'No comment.'

He felt the camera zoom in on him as the reporter said, 'So you're not denying there were four people killed here. We have a neighbour who's told us...'

'No comment,' commented P.C. Redman, feeling like a rabbit with headlights coming at him, and they were the headlights of a twenty tonner.

'And can you confirm, Constable, the victims were of Asian descent?'

'No comment.'

'Was this an attack by far right extremists?'

'No comment.'

'So you refuse to deny the police believe this was a racially motivated attack, then?'

'Er, no comment?'

JANE AND COPELAND VISIT THE LAB.

'There's not a single window in this place,' Jane observed when they were inside the isolated research facility. 'Except for the glass double doors into the foyer and the glass door from the foyer into the corridor, there's not a single window. You were right, Sir. It was really dark before we put the lights on. It was so dark without them that dog walker would never have spotted Jonathan Carter's body.'

Copeland hoped he had not misjudged Detective Jane Sadler. A five year old could have told him there were no windows and how it was really dark until they flicked the light on in the reception area and it lit up, along with the fifteen metre corridor leading to the metal, bonobo room door. Copeland sauntered apathetically behind Jane as she examined Jonathan Carter's blood stained office carpet, where she hummed ponderingly and muttered, 'Interesting. Nancy Carter told me her husband sometimes slept overnight on a cot in his office, but there isn't one. So why would she tell me that?'

Copeland shrugged, more interested in the empty desk now being devoid of chocolate biscuits.

Jane followed the trail of dried blood up the white fluorescent corridor to the thick metal door where Jonathan Carter had met his own grim reaper. After a pause to examine the palm print reader she went through the doorway to look inside the now empty bonobo cages and scrutinise the bad imitation of a Jackson Pollock smeared on the grey wall behind them. Copeland went over to the high-backed metal restraint chair near the corner and noticed a previously unnoticed hose pipe and electric cattle prod in the corner. He thought he might have the answer to why bonobo B11 had died smiling – a life being squashed in a cage, electro-prodded into a restraint chair and injected with who knows what was enough for it to have welcomed a bullet. He shook his head and turned to see Jane approach the nearest cage and hold her forefinger and thumb like a gun pointed towards the bars. 'Difficult shot without hitting any of the bars,' she commented before dropping her hand. 'Especially when all the bonobos were young, healthy adults like it said in the autopsy report.'

'Autopsy report?' muttered Copeland, realising Jane was already past him and through the doorway. He followed her back down the corridor, where she pushed the little toilet door open and peered inside, then did the same with the door to where the mice had been kept. She put the light on and went in. It was bigger than Copeland had realised. On the long, six metre wall to the right were about sixty empty cages, and facing them along the opposite wall were open storage cupboards where animal food was being kept, but the wall carried on around the end of the toilet next door to where there was a metre square maze sitting on a surface with more cupboards with mouse food beneath. Jane saw him looking and explained, 'The maze is to test the mice to see how fast they learn or how well they remember. Er, sorry, Sir. You knew that, didn't you? For a moment I forgot what your degree was in. But it's one more thing to indicate they were not making Viagra mark two.'

'Unless,' ventured Copeland with a grin, 'they were seeing how fast the male mice could catch the females.'

Jane stared and nodded solemnly as she passed him to leave the mice room, go further down the corridor and through the door into the main lab. He followed her inside, realising he had not given it more than a cursory glance on his previous visit after Clare Harper had said something about bio-hazard suits. But even after forensics had done their work it was as if a tornado had swept through, as if someone had vented torrents of rage at every test tube and flask, leaving them all smashed across the work benches and floor. The lab bore little resemblance to Copeland's school chemistry lab with its high wooden benches, Bunsen burners and fume cupboard. This one had a glass topped central work area with similar work surfaces on top of similar white cupboards down each side. His old school lab had not had the high-tech microscopes and the centrifuge either, nor did it have what looked like a stainless steel magician's disappearing person box fitted flush with the worktops near the padlocked fire escape on the far wall. Noticing something else he did not recognise, Copeland switched it on. The base vibrated up and down. Copeland thought it would have made an excellent cocktail mixer if it was not so loud. Shaken, not stirred, he mused to himself in Sean Connery's voice. He switched the jolting machine off and turned, intending to ask Jane if she liked cocktails but catching himself when he saw Jane holding a large piece from a smashed glass flask and staring at it. She was about to stroke the forefinger of her other hand over what would have once been the flask's inside.

'Detective! No!' Copeland shouted. 'Not without protective gloves... OK. Too late. Remember I told you they were experimenting on primates and it might not be Viagra mark two. It might really be something like a contagious disease... Don't smell it! Aren't you listening? And... No! Don't lick your finger! OK, you've licked it...'

Jane tossed the remnants of the broken flask aside. It smashed on the floor and joined the other myriad shards of glass. 'Just like the forensics report said. Every piece of glass they examined had no trace of anything, not even water.'

'The initial forensics report said that?' muttered Copeland.

'You're right to correct me, Sir. I should have said the **initial** forensics report. It said it was as if no experiments had ever happened here. Maybe it's like you told me and Dr. Lynn was right to be suspicious about the team here just taking her money and doing no research.'

'Or they were very good at cleaning up after themselves,' joked Copeland.

Jane's eyes momentarily widened before she pointed to the head-high silver door of the steel cabinet sitting halfway down the side the work area facing the door. 'Now, what's in there?' she rhetorically asked, crunching over the broken glass as she walked around the central work bench and tugged at the door's lever handle. It did not move. 'Still not unlocked,' she said, turning to face Copeland.

'That's a shame,' said Copeland.

Jane whirled to face the door again as she said, 'You're right, Sir. It is. They were supposed to bring an oxyacetylene torch to cut this lock out, but it's just a simple number combination lock so...'

She punched four numbers in. She tried the handle. It did not move.

'Not Mrs. Carter's birthday,' she said.

She pressed another number combination. 'Hmmm,' she said when the handle did not move again.

Copeland! She's bloody well memorised all their birthdays!

Another four numbers were entered. The door lever moved and she pulled the door open, saying, 'Alison Taylor's birthday. That's interesting.'

'Why?' asked Copeland, looking over her shoulder to see what was behind the door.

Jane looked carefully inside the white wall interior of the empty metal cabinet. She tapped the walls. She pulled on the white rails that ran the metre length to the back of the cabinet. 'Oh, yes, sorry Sir.... Despite what she says about herself on LinkedIn and Facebook, she was hardly going to set the world alight was she? She didn't even finish her Ph.D. and apart from making that perfume no one buys despite all the ads, she's got no real track record for anything. Compared to the others she really shouldn't have been here, so why is it her birthday for the code?'

'Maybe she was the one who had to get things out of there,' Copeland suggested.

Looking sceptical, Jane pulled her head out. Her little blonde pony-tail whirled as she looked left and right. She went to the side of the metal box, kicked some glass away, got on her knees and reached between the cabinet and the work-top. The metal box hummed. A light inside flickered on. A cold blast of air hit Copeland still standing in front of the open door.

'It's a fridge,' he said.

Jane laughed as she stood and brushed her palms on her thighs. 'I got that one. Very droll, Sir. You already knew that when you saw the temperature dials above the door.'

Copeland looked above the door. Oh, yeah! Temperature dials!

Talking to herself, Jane asked, 'Why was it unplugged?'

'It's empty,' Copeland observed.

Jane looked at him. She clasped her hands to her rosy cheeks, exclaiming, 'This is why you're a genius, Sir!'

It is? thought Copeland.

Ha, ha, ha! said an inner voice.

Jane's hands were clenched and shaking with enthusiasm by her sides. 'Sir! Don't pretend! You say things to provoke people to hit on the answers – answers you already know. Yes! You were right, Sir, they've cleaned up. Yes! You're definitely a genius, Sir!'

She's winding you up, Copeland, suggested the inner voice as Copeland watched Jane sniff around the lab. She turned her face to him as she sniffed a worktop. 'Lemon furniture polish,' she informed him.

Copeland sniffed and got nothing.

Pacing, bending, sniffing, Jane said, 'You said "she" when you referred to the killer earlier, Sir. Does that mean you agree with Inspector Lord's handover report? It says the best theory is the wife is the murderer.'

Copeland saw a big flaw in that theory – its author. Copeland was amazed that Giles had the skills to think and type at the same time. 'Inspector Giles Lord did a report and said he thought it was Mrs. Carter who had Dr. Carter killed?'

Jane wrung her hands together nervously, stared at him and said, 'I know. I read it too, Sir. What did you think? You know how Inspector Lord's report says how it was an amateur such as his wife who tried to kill poor Dr. Carter in his office, missed and hit him in the shoulder, then had to chase him down the corridor, firing and missing again when she hit him in the leg, and how it was only when Carter was immobile on the floor that the shooter could get close and put one right between his eyes. I've seen the initial post mortem report and photos. It really was right between the eyes.' She stopped wringing her hands and took a notepad from her inside pocket. She flicked a few pages. She read, 'I measured it on the photos and worked out the shot was exactly thirty seven point three five millimetres from the centre of each eye.'

Copeland said, 'O kaaay... well measured, Jane.'

'Thank you, Sir. I like numbers,' she said, putting the notepad away. 'I think Inspector Lord's jealous wife theory is wrong and your ex Russian SVR assassin theory is right Sir...' She stepped forward and grabbed Copeland's shoulders. 'This is so exciting! It was a real professional – an ex-Russian assassin! And a *she* ex-Russian assassin! Each shot had a meaning. It provoked Dr. Carter to do something... Well, not so much the one in his heart to make sure he was dead, but the first three did – one in the shoulder to show she meant business, then one in the leg after he had used his handprint to open the door, then she propped him up like a doorstop and put one in his head, killed the bonobos and put a shot in Carter's heart to make sure. Once Inspector Lord's report eventually finished describing Dr. Carter's desk, it said the bonobos were shot at close range through the bars and how anyone could do that, but they were all hit with a single shot in the head, and that's not easy when they must have been jumping about in their cages. Why was it so important to get into that room and kill the young bonobos? And whatever was in that sugar that poisoned the mice must have been undetectable by them and if it was something common then the forensics people would have found it in them by now, wouldn't they?'

Copeland's was happy to agree with Jane and nod, hoping that would be enough to stop her gripping his shoulders. He thought she seemed pretty strong.

'Except...' Jane continued, 'I was the one who told Nancy Carter about her husband's death and she told me he slept here on a cot in his office. There is no cot there. So why did she lie? And why would she want the Sharmas dead? Ah! I see! Only Reema was meant to be killed! She was having an affair with Dr. Carter... Her family were innocent bystanders! She had to get rid of the witnesses. Nancy Carter **is** the ex Russian assassin! Yes, that's it!'

Copeland had been thinking while his shoulders were having the life squeezed out of them. He saw Jane's eyes moving left then right. To some she might have seemed half demented. But Copeland could see she was in her pros and cons mode, but with everything she was thinking verbally spilling out with overwhelming enthusiasm.

Copeland opened his mouth to speak but Jane gripped harder. Her eyes were wide as she said, 'But why would she do that? Lie to me about her husband having a cot here? If she's the killer, or hired the killer, then why would Nancy Carter risk a lie about something so obvious? We need to see her!' She finally stopped and took a breath. Her hands suddenly dropped despondently to her sides. 'I don't think it's the wife, Sir. I was the one who told her about her dead husband and she would have to be a pretty good actress to react like that if she was behind it.'

Resisting the urge to rub his shoulders, Copeland looked towards the entrance, nodded sagely, and asked, 'How did we get in, Detective?'

Jane thought Copeland was having a senior moment and answered, 'Er, through the door with Dr. Carter's spare key card, Sir. I told you I picked it up...'

'And the fire escape is padlocked and has not been forced. Clare told me those glass entrance doors were almost impregnable without a key card,' mused Copeland still staring at the two sets of glass doors.

'Except for Alison Taylor's we have them all now, Sir. The other cards were all in the homes of the other employees. It's all in the...'

'So,' said Copeland, finally turning to face Jane standing beside him, 'nearly all the cards are accounted for now, but where were they on Friday evening?'

Jane twiddled with an ear-lobe as she said, 'I see... Any one of them could have given the killer their card, including Nancy Carter who could have given the killer her husband's spare. Though poor Reema Sharma seems an unlikely suspect to have hired the killer given the circumstances... Unless she was reneging on the payment...'

'Yes, it could have been any of them, Detective Sadler,' agreed Copeland. 'But one thing has bothered me from the start. Why was Jonathan Carter wearing a top-notch suit in his own lab on Friday evening?'

Jane stared at the unbreakable doors beyond the reception area. He let her think until she eventually said, 'The killer may not have needed a key card, Sir. Not if Dr. Carter let him, I mean her, in.'

He let her think some more. She said, 'Dr. Carter was in his Sunday best for a meeting, Sir. Whatever they were making, he was selling out to a rival drug company but the killer was a Trojan Horse.'

Copeland was impressed. Especially so since his new, current theory was that Dr. Carter was smartly dressed because he was meeting someone he did not want his wife to know about when the hired killer, Dominika, had arrived with his spare key card, given to her by jealous wife Nancy who had discovered his illicit intentions.

So you were agreeing with Inspector Giles were you, Copeland? Idiot! What about the melted computers, dead animals and trashed lab? The lab which, by the way, was spotlessly clean and has no sign of anything being made there at all, let alone new Viagra!

Jane groaned, 'You must think me doubly stupid, Sir. My Trojan Horse theory is rubbish. A rival company would have stolen the research from the computers, not just destroyed them. Of course you know the tech people say they managed to determine the computers had not been turned on for days.'

'They can do that?' said Copeland.

'Oh, you knew that, Sir. How clever,' said Jane, oblivious to the question and Copeland's look of surprise. She sighed and said, 'We need a break, Sir. It may not be my place to say this but we deserve a pie and a pint, Sir.'

This was music to Copeland's ears. Copeland thought he might just be falling in love. His inner voice spoiled the euphoric moment with, *And if our hired ex-Russian hit-man, or, more likely, hit-woman, was so smart, why did he, or she, not discounting a cross-gender possibility, allow some passing dog-walker to see Carter's dead body by leaving the lights on?*

MARY.

After loitering in Charmouth for two days, enough was enough for Mary. She knew Alison Taylor would surface sooner or later and, needing to release some energy, she went to her gym in Bridport. The two classes on Tuesday morning were her favourites, next to the Saturday ones, the Monday evening ones and the one on Friday which she had annoyingly missed last time because she was otherwise engaged in a certain isolated laboratory killing things. In truth, Mary was quite upset. She knew this would be the last chance she had to attend any of her usual classes, which was why she had ignored the new message on her phone from the man who called himself Atticus. It told her to call him urgently (again), but she really did not want either to be late for her last keep fit classes or to be harangued about why Alison Taylor was still breathing. Calling Atticus could wait until after her classes, after her shower and after enjoying lunch with her exercise class friends, who were as mundane as ever and seemed to be only able to talk about how a family had been gunned down in their own home a mere ten miles away, and wasn't it just *so* terrible and would anyone like another cappuccino?

Mary only had one cappuccino. She returned to her car to phone Atticus. What Atticus said through the voice distorter surprised her.

'What? Someone else?' said an astonished Mary into her phone.

Pause.

'That's what I thought you said.'

Pause.

'No, it won't be a problem, Atticus. I'm very thorough. I can locate her whereabouts in no time.'

Pause.

'Today? How much? I have plans with my husband this evening. It's our first wedding anniversary.'

Pause.

'Thank you for your congratulations.'

Pause.

'No, I'll keep my address private, if you don't mind, so you needn't send a card. Now, how much are you offering for killing this extra one?'

Pause.

'No chance! If it's so urgent I want double that. And especially if you want it messy again like the others. And I want it in my account **before** I do the job after the way you screwed me with the last payment.'

(Long pause for apologetic explanation.)

'Listen, Atticus! I don't care if it was your bosses who decided that. Read my lips. I don't care!'

(Sigh.) 'It's just a figure of speech. I know you can't actually see my lips, Atticus. Just tell your bosses in this family business of yours I want the money up front this time.

'I know, Atticus. You've told me that, but Alison Taylor **will** be taken care of and you **will** transfer the rest of my money for the extras for the first job once she's terminated. It's all in hand.

'Good. Talk to your bosses then, Atticus. By the way about the nom de plume... Tut! He's gone.'

'Right,' Mary said to herself as she swiped and tapped her phone. 'Let's see where that other tracking device says you are, Erica Young.'

COPELAND AND JANE.

The euphoria Copeland had felt at the imminent prospect of finally having a light snack in the form of pie, chips and peas was short lived. Once back in his shiny new car in the lab's car park Jane had insisted on visiting the abode of Erica Young again. He would have pulled rank and insisted they go to the pub, but she had imploringly gripped his forearm as she pleaded more fervently and even Copeland's stomach had agreed he should avoid having his arm broken before he ate, reasoning he would need intact bones to use a fork.

At least the journey was short and a mere minor diversion on the way to The Butchered Calf. They parked the BMW Gandalf-car in the service road and Jane produced the door key for Miss Young's replaced lock from her pocket. Copeland thought they may have needed something called a search warrant this time since there was no suspicion that Erica Young was inside and possibly coming to harm, but Jane was already up the flight of metal steps and through the door bearing the prominent, laminated police notice telling Miss Young the number to phone to get her new key. With his stomach protesting about being ignored and his legs protesting about having to climb steps up to the apartment, Copeland went further into a dark mood when Jane showed him round the one bedroom of the apartment and the open plan kitchen-diner-sitting room and said, 'See? There's nothing to see. Not even a photo.'

On the way out Copeland did see something. It was near the front door, lying on a low little table next to a plant pot. He picked it up and put it in his pocket.

'Sir! You can't do that!' Jane indignantly exclaimed.

'It might be interesting,' shrugged Copeland.

Jane was not swayed. 'It may well be, Sir, but we don't even have a search warrant and there are specific guidelines regarding private possessions which were put in regulation number...'

Copeland held up a hand to stop her, took the pilfered flash drive from his pocket and replaced it next to the empty blue plant pot.

Jane's phone pinged. 'Oh, well,' Jane sighed, reading the message and putting the phone back in her pocket. 'I suppose the news of the Sharmas had to leak sometime. Poor P.C. Redman has got himself on local TV. They want us to stay well away before they have to explain why double o seven is involved, Sir. Is it nearly time for lunch?'

ERICA.

Soon after Larry Copeland and Jane Sadler had departed, Erica Young arrived home at her one bedroom apartment overlooking the Co-op car park, climbed the metal steps and tried to push her key into the lock. She had to ram it in. It did not turn. She forced it. It began to bend. 'Bastards!' she swore, tugging the key free. 'Bloody Doc Lynn and her weirdo husband have changed their minds and double crossed me! The tight buggers have decided not to give me the pay rise I asked for after all! They've had the lock changed and locked me out of the flat expecting me to grovel and call them. Bastard landlords! I bet they waited until they thought I'd posted the flash drive on the way to work and then sent someone round to change the locks! Bastard Lynns!' She kicked the door, hurt her toe and wished she had got there earlier, but the house she had ended up sleeping in the night before had a very appreciative middle-age widower she felt sorry for. She twiddled the emerald ring on her finger. It reminded her how appreciative he had been for her sympathy. 'Right!' she said as she pulled down the sides of her black leather jacket.

She went back down the metal steps and passed the two young teenage boys who often seemed to linger there after school, sitting on the concrete at the bottom of the steel steps. Ignoring them, she went to her car and got the handle of the carjack from the boot. Going back up the steps, she stopped two steps up, turned to the two teenagers, brandished the jack in their direction and said, 'Not a word, right?' They nodded as they stared up at her. She continued up the steps and casually smashed the glass from one of the four small windows in the top part of the door. She was damn certain she was going to get her clothes before she found a lawyer to sue the crap out of sodding Doctor and Jeremy Lynn for breach of contract unless she got that modelling job they had promised. She carefully reached through the little broken pane, turned the latch and opened the door.

Still seething, she strode in, immediately grabbed the flash drive from the little low table beside the empty blue plant pot and thrust it into her wrist bag, which she thought matched her black leather jacket, which she thought went well with the three inch black stilettos and the little black cocktail dress she was still wearing because she had not had chance to change it since she had left that nice, generous man's house after he had appreciatively made pancakes for brunch before she left.

While considering how much she would charge deceitful Dr. Lynn for the lab's data on the flash drive she stuffed her clothes into two Tesco bags. They were small and did not take up much space. (The clothes, not the Tesco bags. Though, if you scrunched them, the Tesco bags did not take up much space either.) Her shoes filled another three bags. She had to make three trips down to her car, passing the boys sitting at the bottom of the steps each time and wondering why one of them was holding his laminated homework sheet so close to his chest.

Erica threw the bags into her car boot and texted Jeremy Lynn. Her text said, 'If you want it then I want five thousand pounds and my modelling job.' She thought that should be sufficient to make them to pay up for the stupid flash drive and show she wasn't going to just roll over. She checked she still had the cash Jeremy and Lynn had given her. It was still there under the mat in front of the passenger seat. It was off-season and she knew she could probably find a little hotel away from the coast where the money might pay for two or three nights stay. She could always sell her new ring to raise more cash if the Lynns had not relented and paid up by then.

As she pulled away she briefly glanced up at the door to her flat, discounting the idea of staying there any longer. The Lynns owned the flat and she did not want to let them get the upper hand by getting herself arrested for breaking and entering and squatting.

To remind them to stay quiet she waved a fist at the two boys, who were now sitting on the bottom metal step. They waited until she had gone round the corner of the access road before one of them showed the other what he was holding to his chest. 'Cool, eh?' he said. 'I'm going to put it on my bedroom door. See? It says to phone the police for a key if you want to get in. It'll keep my mum out!'

'Forget that,' said his friend. 'Did you see how short that dress was again?'

COPELAND AND JANE VISIT NANCY CARTER.

Copeland's neck strained as he turned his head to see The Butchered Calf whizz by. 'Er..?' he said.

'Beautiful to drive, isn't it, Sir? Thanks for letting me. That was the pub I was thinking of going to for lunch later. It's called The Butchered Calf.'

'Later..?' groaned Copeland.

'After we've visited Nancy Carter, like we agreed Sir.'

'We agreed..?'

'I'm glad you remember, Sir. There's still the question about why she told me her husband had a bed in his office when he didn't and we don't have an alibi for her yet and there's no time like the present is there?'

Unless it's lunchtime, thought Copeland.

Nancy Carter was not alone when they arrived. The Poldark lookalike gardener-neighbour and his wife were there. The neighbour-wife did not look like anyone in particular except a young and possibly more attractive Angelina Jolie wearing a black cashmere sweater. Copeland took an instant dislike to her because as soon as they entered Nancy's conservatory come dining room Mrs. Neighbour told him and Jane they should have arrived twenty minutes earlier when they could have enjoyed their "***wonderful*** buffet lunch" with them but now, as they could see, it was "sadly too late" and they had just cleared the table and were about to start an exciting game of Scrabble.

Nancy Carter smiled her white-teeth toothpaste advert smile, swept a hand in the direction of her neighbours and said, 'Allow me to introduce my dear neighbours, Nicola and Ernest Rebus. They have been my saviours in this difficult time. (Little sniff.) I don't know what I'd have done without them. (Little sob.) They even came with me to identify Jonathan's body.' (White-teeth smile.)

Copeland caught Jane's glance in his direction. He knew she was thinking the same as he was – the recently widowed Nancy Carter did not seem like a typical grieving wife. Besides her breezy introduction, her flowery dress did not exactly convey a sense of mourning and she had not taken much time off from doing her make-up and hair either. She saw the look on their faces. 'Look,' she said, pulling back chairs at the dining table so they could sit next to her neighbours and opposite each other across the scrabble board, 'it's no good crying over spilled milk is it?' Copeland and Jane slowly sat. Copeland uncertainly shook his head in response to Nancy's question. Jane glanced about to see where the milk had been spilled.

'Shame though,' said Ernie Rebus, scratching his neck.

'Humph!' said Nicola Rebus, glowering across the table at her husband and folding her arms across her top-of-the-range sweater. 'You're just annoyed because you've lost your Saturday night drinking partner. No more pretending to do a barbecue while you two get as drunk as lords together.'

'Ahem,' Copeland coughed as politely as he could. 'We're here to ask you, Mrs. Carter... Where's she gone?'

'Just here, in the kitchen getting you two public servants a nice cool glass of lemonade,' called Nancy cheerily from somewhere in the adjoining kitchen.

Ernie Rebus leaned across the varnished table and confidentially told Copeland, 'It's very good lemonade. The cloudy sort. We brought it round. It's an old family recipe.' He gave a thumbs up and leaned back as Nancy reappeared with two tall glasses brimming with cloudy lemonade and ice cubes. She placed them in front of Copeland and Jane and sat herself at the head of the table.

'We're sorry to have to call on you,' began Jane, 'especially in your time of, er, grief, Mrs. Carter, but when I came on Saturday to give you the news about your husband being shot several times you mentioned he often stayed at the lab on Friday evenings.'

'Yes,' nodded Nancy, adding, 'Damn it! I've got all vowels here! Yes. He had a little cot bed there so he could work late and crash out in the early morning. As I said, he sometimes stayed there all Saturday too.'

'Humph,' interrupted Nicola Rebus. 'But he always got back in time to get legless with Ernie every Saturday evening, didn't he, no matter how exhausted he was?'

Ernie frowned at her. 'Give it a rest, Niks. The poor chap has been shuffled off the mortal coil and all that.'

'Er, yes, right,' Jane said trying to regain her line of thought. 'Well, the thing is, Mrs. Carter, it seems there was no bed in your husband's office at the lab, so why did you tell...'

'Ex husband,' corrected Nancy curtly, showing how much she felt the full depth of her recent loss. She shrugged. 'It's what he told me. But it wouldn't have been the first lie out of his mouth.'

Nicola Rebus reached across Copeland and placed her hand onto Nancy Carter's. 'You should tell them, Nancy. Otherwise they might think you had something to do with his murder.'

Nancy Carter looked at Nicola Rebus. She turned her head left and looked at Jane. She turned it right and looked at Copeland. She turned it left and looked at Ernie Rebus. Ernie nodded his agreement. Nancy Carter sighed. She looked back at Jane. 'I was going to divorce him,' she admitted. 'I was waiting until he finished whatever it was he was making. He'd told me he was getting a huge bonus when they'd finished making whatever this new miracle drug was – way much more than he got for that appetite suppressant even. Once he had got his payout I was going to take the conceited turd to the cleaners.'

'But when I told you, you seemed so upset!' protested Jane.

Nancy gave another shrug. 'I was a bit miffed about losing half of his bonus. Besides, I thought it was appropriate. You seemed nice and I didn't want you to think I was heartless. I thought I'd let you have some job satisfaction succeeding to console me. I've done a bit of acting in my time and know how to turn on the tears when I want to. I just think about the tortoise I had when I was a kid.' Tears filled her eyes. 'He got eaten by a fox.' Tears rolled down her cheeks. She smiled and said, 'And after divorcing him I intended to go back to civilization and do toothpaste adverts again.'

Selling toothpaste clearly needs a wide repertoire, eh, Copeland?

Ernie Rebus laughed. 'I'm probably more upset than Nancy is. I've lost my drinking partner,' he grinned, prompting Nicola Rebus to fold her arms tighter, scowl at him and say, 'At least we won't have to carry him to bed after his interminable boasting. He really couldn't hold his drink. Now, are we going to play scrabble or not. I've got some really good tiles here. Do you two want to play too?'

'What? No, thanks,' smiled Copeland, enjoying his lemonade more than he had expected considering he had been expecting to be drinking a more beer-like liquid called beer by now. He finished the lemonade and stood. 'We'll leave you to it,' he said, but noticed Jane staring at him, wide eyed, and giving him 'go on, go on' sideways nods of the head. 'Oh, yes,' said Copeland, placing his empty glass down and feeling like a real detective by throwing in the all important question just when the suspect least expected it and would be totally thrown off guard. 'Where were you on Friday evening during the time of your husband's murder, Mrs. Carter?'

'With us next door,' replied Niks Rebus.

'Oh,' said Copeland.

'Friday evening is always a games evening with Nancy, Inspector,' added Ernie. 'Monopoly, wasn't it, Nancy?'

'And you cheated!' laughed Nancy, wagging a finger at Ernie. He laughed. She stood and leaned on the table, pretending to scowl at Ernie. 'And I shall get my revenge before you bugger off back home, Mr. E. Rebus!' They all laughed; Jane and Copeland joining in half-heartedly to be polite.

Jane was still smiling until Nancy Carter closed her front door, then she slammed the car door and growled, 'I hate rich, beautiful people! They can be so heartless! Playing Scrabble days after her husband's murder? What's that about?'

Copeland nodded understandingly and said, 'You're in the driver's side again, Detective Sadler.'

Jane slapped both hands on the steering wheel and gave Copeland a hard stare. She growled, 'After meeting those people I need a stiff drink and I'm going to go very fast to that pub to get one. Any objections, Inspector Copeland?'

Copeland shook his head. He never objected to going to a pub.

Copeland almost fell in love with Detective Jane Sadler when she offered to pay for his pie and pint at The Butchered Calf and was head over heels when she rooted in her jacket pocket and found a fifty pence piece for the pool table after she had come back from washing her hands. They threw their jackets over the backs of two chairs and set the balls up. He had expected the first game to last until the pies came. It didn't. Jane potted the black down the length of the table before Copeland had potted three balls.

Getting his phone out of his trouser pocket he said, 'I'm just a little rusty.' He took out the twenty pound note he kept tucked in the little slit pocket of the phone case, next to the slit where he kept his credit card and, more importantly, his Tesco points card. (Copeland always made a point of carrying cash in case he forgot his pin number.)

'So,' said Jane after Copeland had returned from the bar with a second pint for each of them and a few fifty pence pieces for the pool table, and after she had put two red balls down from her break.

Copeland waited until she was just making her second shot before he said, 'So, what, Jane?' His question had the desired effect. The cue ball missed the easy red into the side pocket and hurtled down the table. He smiled. The ball passed between two of his yellow balls, rebounded off the cush and hit the red on the way back. As the red fell into a hole, Jane explained how having the white ball end up where it did made her next three shots easier. Copeland was glad they were not playing for money.

While Jane removed all the reds from the table, she talked Copeland through her theories. A red went down as she said, 'Theory one. The killer had to have a key card to get in so must have been hired by one of the remaining members of Dr. Carter's team – Alison Taylor or Wang Linpeng – to kill him and the others and destroy all evidence of their work so he or she could sell the research to another company. My money's on Wang. Alison Taylor is in a shallow grave somewhere.' She missed potting the black. 'Or, two, Mrs. Carter hired the killer to kill her husband because she thought he was having an affair and the trashing of the lab and killing the animals is a red herring. Great shot, Sir! And being the jealous sort, Nancy Carter also paid the killer to get rid of her husband's lover, Reema Sharma, despite what she says about divorcing him after he's got his bonus. Super shot, Sir! Or, theory three, Dr. Lynn sent someone posing as a buyer for the new wonder drug. That would explain why Dr. Carter was wearing his nice suit, Sir. She already has the formula for whatever wonder drug they had worked on and killed off Jonathan Carter to prevent him from giving the formula to another company, not to mention not having to pay him his bonus. Wow, Sir! You're cleaning up! That fits in with them finishing there and the lab being cleaned and the computers not being switched on for days. The killer then made sure no one else except Dr. Lynn got the research by killing Reema Sharma – she was brilliant and might know too much.'

Copeland listened to Jane and thought it was all too easy. All his yellow balls had been left suspiciously close to pockets each time Jane had potted one of her reds.

'If you go for that one first, Sir, it will leave you a good angle to pot the other one and end up in a great position for the black,' Jane suggested and confirmed his suspicions. He didn't really care that she was letting him win. He believed in the old saying: it's not the taking part, but the winning that counts.

As the black ball finally dropped into a pocket and Copeland celebrated like a Wimbledon champion, Jane collected their pies, chips and peas from the bar and set them down beside their empty pint glasses and cutlery on the table near the pool table. Happily watching steam rise from his pie, Copeland said, 'Or option four, Carter and Sharma were killed because... er... I've got nothing. Fancy another pint?'

'No more beer for me,' Jane replied. Copeland's heart almost broke. 'I'll have wine with my food, thanks.'

Copeland's heart soared. 'Make it a sauvignon if they have it.' It fell again. She liked white? Copeland had never seen the point of white wine. It may as well have been water.

It did not take long to get served since they were the only people eating lunch at 4 p.m. and the barmaid told him she would be in the back and 'to ring the little bell on the counter if he or his pretty young granddaughter wanted anything else.'

Jane had tucked a serviette into the neck of her white blouse and was liberally sprinkling salt onto her chips when he said, 'We have an elephant in the room, Jane.'

Jane looked over her shoulder as he sat down. 'There's only us,' she said. 'Oh! That's a saying isn't it?' She laughed nervously. She leaned forward and stage-whispered across the table, 'You should know, but I don't believe in drinking on duty. I'm only drinking because I've decided this is now my afternoon off. I wouldn't want you to think I'm one of those people who would break the rules. But you carry on, Larry. I'm not judging.' Copeland took her at her word and swigged his beer. He thought she did have a point though, and decided he would move on to wine next as well. He had noticed a nice Rioja behind the bar. He thought it would go well with the apple crumble. He thought most wines went well with apple crumble and Rioja went well with any food so it was a perfect match. What could be better than apples and grape juice? He resolutely still believed the secret to a long and happy life was consuming lots of fruit, as long as it was fermented or in a dessert.

'So, about this elephant... Besides the snazzy suit there was a packet of strangely untouched biscuits...Pass the salt, please,' he said as thick gravy oozed from his pie. 'Hey! You called me Larry a minute ago.'

'I'm not on duty, am I, Larry?' she smiled and emptied her large glass of Sauvignon.

By the time they had finished the pies, desserts and two more glasses of wine, Copeland and Jane had found besides Jonathan Carter being murdered in his best suit and inexplicably leaving uneaten biscuits, there was more than one elephant in the room. The room was, in fact, getting quite crowded. It had not been made any better by the arrival of some building site workers and a steady influx of locals. Copeland was back to beer and Jane had moved on to fruit cider and when the noise got too much and they moved into the beer garden where all four of the wooden picnic-style tables were unoccupied in the chilly twilight. It took Copeland a little while to judge how far down the wooden bench was before he sat and he thought it was time to be sensible and stop drinking beer. After his current pint it would be strictly wine.

Unflattering as it was to someone who thought she should be a super model, film star, or TV presenter, another elephant in the room was Alison Taylor. If she wasn't already dead, where was she? Reema Sharma was dead, Wang Linpeng was holidaying in Spain, but Alison Taylor was still missing. Unlike the brilliant Reema, Ms. Taylor was more of a plodder and it was unlikely she would contribute anything vital to the research. Jane's background checking had revealed Ms. Taylor had only worked on one noteworthy project before, and that was making a new perfume for L'Argent, the French owned cosmetics company.

The next elephant was why only them? There were five dead bodies, twelve dead monkeys, lots of dead mice and a trashed lab which had been in pristine condition until the killer had trashed it, yet the whole case had seemingly fallen into the laps of just two people. Jane and Copeland soon concluded it was because of Wendy Miller. Despite the new Department C still recruiting and not even having desks yet,

Director Miller had for some reason used her influence to take over the case and the under-resourced local police had been more than happy to hand it over to a section of MI5. This conclusion did not help explain exactly **why** Wendy Miller had taken over the case and thrust it onto Copeland. In contrast, Jane knew exactly why she was there – she had been virtually twiddling her thumbs before she left the force for a second time, so she was the obvious person to dump the role of police liaison officer on.

The biggest elephant was the lights being on. If this was a professional killer who could put a bullet in exactly in the right places to go clean through Dr. Carter's shoulder and in the back of his knee so he collapsed into an opening doorway like a doorstop, then why were the lights left on? If not for the lights being on, the dog-walker would not have approached the building and the body of Dr. Carter would have lain undiscovered until his wife began worrying and phoned the police, who would probably have told her to phone again if he had not come home by Sunday lunchtime.

'OK,' said Copeland, starting to feel peckish again. 'If we are assuming this was a hired professional, probably ex-Russian SVR trained killer called Dominika, then why did she leave the lights on? Ah, yes, about Dominika...' Copeland trusted Jane. It was either that or the influence of the amount of alcohol he had consumed, but he decided to confide in her about Vasily's niece, the missing rogue slumber agent, Dominika, and about the flash drive Vasily had given him to help find her.

'You think it might be her?' Jane asked, excitedly.

Swaying a little, Copeland said, 'Well, none of this is subtle is it? Dead bodies shot everywhere. I suppose she doesn't need to be subtle if she can just move on to another new identity. And it was professional and then there's the footprint she left, the old KGB trick she would have learned in her SVR training. Take another shoe, put your foot in it and press. Throws the local police off and acts as a warning to us.'

'A warning, Larry?'

'To counter intelligence services. It sort of means this is nothing to do with you or national security so back off or else. Nothing important really.'

Jane looked up at a tree branch swaying in the strengthening breeze and swallowed hard. 'Back off or else..? So this is why you took over the case, because of this Dominika's involvement..?'

Copeland screwed his face. It made his nose feel funny. 'Naa,' he said, scratching his nose. A shirt button pooped off. He ignored it. 'Wendy Miller knows nothing about Dominika. I really don't know why I'm here investigating dead scientists. My first case was supposed to be tracking down a ring of illegal animal smugglers, so why I got sent to the lab I've no idea, but I like it here and the beer's good so I'm not complaining. Er, why have you got your head in your hands, Jane? Oh, yeah... animal smugglers... dead bonobos...'

Jane lifted her head and nodded as she groaned and again said, 'You're a genius, Sir.'

TOM BENSON.

Without much to do before starting his new job at the PR and management company, Tom Benson was trying to keep himself busy. Keeping busy mainly consisted of being in the communal kitchen and acting as marriage guidance counsellor to the couple in room A; explaining how to maximise profit margins to the cannabis entrepreneur in room B; acting as surrogate father to the teenage son of the masseuse in room C (by giving him meaningful talks about who really killed JFK, why aliens built the pyramids *and* Atlantis, the secret organisations running the world and how Elvis was really working in a chip shop in Cardiff). He also gave the teenager a sleeping bag so he could sleep in the kitchen. Tom always cooked twice as much as he needed and took some to the reclusive Jesus in Room E. Tom had soon learned young Jesus was not just afraid of Romans but afraid of everyone and he vaguely remembered a time when he was somewhere else and they had called him Brian, but they had shuffled him through the door with a bag of tablets and without a watch to tell him when to take them.

Such experiences made Tom want to leave the real world behind, but Tom's prowess on-line as a level twelve wizard with a mean fireball spell was unused because Loreni the Elf had not shown up with her mystical bow for days so there had been no adventuring for Tom and his little group of fantasy game adventurers. He longed for the old days of working with Copeland and being shot at.

Bored, Tom half-heartedly logged into the Dark Web chat room frequented by the other members of his TIC group, but most of his fellow members of the conspiracy cover-up revealing 'Truth Investigation Council' seemed to be busy with actual, real work and the dark web forum site was barely ticking along with even the most common conspiracy theories for the TICs to get their mandibles into. Tom was still miffed the 'TICs' had never accepted his suggestion to rename themselves as the Anti-Conspiracy Executive so they could call themselves the ACEs. His most recent suggestion to rebrand the group as the Federated Union of Conspiracy Killers had not gone down well either.

The conspiracy forum was so quiet even the oldest chestnut was barely getting a comment. The Masons, the Illuminati, The Order of the White Lotus... The names for the secret organisation which really ruled the world went on and on, and had done for hundreds of years. The latest contender was 'The Family'. Tom had been bothered enough to find out this so-called 'Family' were nothing to do with The Fellowship or the Mafia and had even paid good money for a book about them, but had given up such pointless research because he was already convinced the world was run by aliens from Alpha Centauri.

Tom sighed, moved the book Copeland had tossed on his desk to one side, and waited for another visitor to the conspiracy forum. He thought he would while away time by researching the young, vacant looking detective inspector who had accompanied Copeland to Uroboros HQ. It did not take long for Tom to find he was the first and only son of Robert Lord, Baron of Kernow. Tom knew all about **him**. Who didn't? Robert Lord's insurance company had gone bust some years before, just when it was being taken to court for selling insurance policies that did not seem to insure against anything. Tom had personal knowledge of falling foul to the small print of a Lord's Insurance policy when the front of his car had hit a tree one icy morning. His claim had been refused because he had fitted a generic headlamp and not one made by VW so Lord Insurance had said this constituted a modification he had not informed them about which breached the contract. Tom had got zero money to fix the car despite paying ten years of premiums. Home insurance, life insurance and every other sort of insurance from pets to boats all seemed to have clauses somewhere which meant no payments were ever made, except the payments to Robert Lord's massive salary and his astronomical annual bonuses. When the company suddenly went bust there were rumours about a vast fortune going into an account in the Cayman Islands.

Tom stared up vacantly at the poster above his desk. It was his prize possession: an actual cinema poster for his favourite ever space film, 'Invaders from Esbos'. The poster was a collectors' item, especially as the film was generally considered so bad it had never been released in cinemas. He asked himself what the film's star, Rachel Duvall, would do. She had defeated those purple aliens by doing the right thing and, after the big fight in space, had won the peace by appealing to their better nature. Tom decided he would do the same. He would track down this son of Robert Lord and persuade him to convince his father to pay up, at least to the widows and widowers who had relied on the life insurance to pay their mortgages. Back on the TICs Dark Web chat room he typed, 'Anyone know where I can find Detective Giles Lord?'

The laptop said nothing. He waited. He was just considering getting the DVD of the 'Invaders from Esbos' from under his bed when a message came up on his screen.

Dear John Elton,
He's in Honiton investigating a shoplifting epidemic in the local area: Remember to guard yourself against the diabolical machinations of the most evil woman in the universe, Alison Taylor!
Hope you are well. ☺

Ignoring the capital letter after the colon, Tom considered his response. He typed, 'Thanks. OK.'

A response immediately appeared:

Alison Taylor was the brains behind Midnight Intoxication!!! Don't go anywhere near her without your mints to protect you!!!

Tom scratched what little hair was left above his ears. He adjusted his NHS plastic spectacles and read the message again. He leaned closer to the screen and read the name of the sender. He shook his head. The message was from 'Mint-Saviour' again. Tom sighed. Mint-Saviour had provoked a lot of forum discussion among the TICs on the Dark Web. Whoever Mint-Saviour was, he or she had been the first person to share a new conspiracy: a new conspiracy which most of the other conspiracy theorists had completely rejected, and that took some doing. Tom had gone along with it for a while, but had finally come round to the majority opinion that Mint-Saviour was some sort of obsessive nut, and, therefore, obviously quite unlike the rest of the TICs. Mint-Saviour had tried to convince everyone that the new perfume, invented by Alison Taylor and sold by L'Argent, called Midnight Intoxication (currently only available in the UK) had some sort of added ingredient and that the perfume actually did what the adverts said it did and it really could 'Bring out the Beast in YOUR Man'. This claim was what had turned most of the conspiracy theorists against Mint-Saviour's conspiracy theory: every conspiracy theorist knew that anything in an advert was a lie, so if Mint-Saviour was saying the adverts were true then, ergo, Mint-Saviour must be wrong. Benson had been one of the last true believers and had religiously kept his extra strong mints handy in case he caught a whiff of Midnight Intoxication and possibly turned into a werewolf – though to be fair to the adverts, the beasts that men were turning into looked more like six foot two models who wore dinner jackets, which Tom would have not minded turning into, but failing that the werewolf thing might have been OK too if it meant he grew hair on top of his head again.

But before making up his mind, and because he had a lot of spare time, Tom Benson had conscientiously studied the Midnight Intoxication adverts on YouTube. He may have been the first person ever to watch a whole advert and not bother with what came after it. His research had nothing to do with the supermodel known simply by the name Colfetti being in them. Honest. It had nothing to do with, for some reason known only to advertising men, her needing to use the perfume wearing only a bikini. Honest it didn't. Yet despite the magnetism of the advertisement campaign, a few hours earlier Tom had finally decided to join the opinion of the majority, leave Mint-Saviour in a minority of one, and had put his extra strong mints in his desk drawer.

Tom considered his response to Mint-Saviour and typed, 'Thanks for the advice. I agree, Mint Saviour, Alison Taylor is a threat to civilization and something must be done to stop her. I'll keep my mints handy and watch out for her. Honest,' and signed out of the chat room. *Phew,* Tom thought. *Is that guy paranoid or what? Worrying about perfume when there are aliens living among us? Phew!* But at least he had somewhere to start in his quest to right the wrongs of insurance fraud. Mint-Saviour had given him a starting point. He would go to this place called Honiton, wherever it was, and confront Giles Lord about his father's misdemeanours. He knew he needed something to stay focused on to give him some pointless purpose before the dark thoughts came back again, enticing him to do something rash now the love of his life had chosen her career before him. Tom stopped the dark thoughts before they took over again. He looked up at his favourite poster and reminded himself Rachel Duvall was the real love of his life – Rachel had kicked that purple alien's ass and saved the galaxy! Tom pulled himself together. He quit the Dark Web conspiracy chat room. He thought he needed cheering up with some fiction instead. He logged on to the BBC news, taking full advantage of his intention to eventually get a TV licence and feeling determined to get his money's worth in the meantime.

The news showed a helicopter hovering over a rather nice house. Tom was not terribly interested until the words 'multiple murders' and 'neo-Nazis' were mentioned. He watched and listened. People who worked at restaurants were interviewed, all saying how lovely the late middle-age Mr. and Mrs. Sharma were, and the son's headteacher said what a model student he was, but none of the dead daughter's co-workers could be found to be interviewed. Tom's ears pricked-up when the reporter gripped his microphone, stared intently at the camera and said, 'So where are Wang Linpeng, Jonathan Carter and Alison Taylor?'

MARY AND JEFFREY WHITE.

'This is a lovely idea of yours, Mary,' said Jeffrey, 'to walk along the beach and see the sunset. Shame it's pouring down with rain. At least we've got our waterproofs and a nice flask of hot tea.'

'You bring out the best in me, darling,' said Mary looking out to the grey sea. 'We always liked coming to Portland and strolling in this cove. It's always so quiet here, especially when the weather is inclement. This wind is so fresh, isn't it darling? Have some more tea, dearest.'

'Don't mind if I do,' said Jeffrey, pouring more into the flask's plastic cup and offering it to Mary.

Mary smiled and raised a hand, 'Not for me thanks, my love. I had a large mug before we left the house.'

Jeffrey swigged the tea and swayed a little as the wind tried to push him into the sea. 'I remember,' he said, 'when I had that idea about you opening a shop here.'

'The sea shells shop,' smiled Mary as she inwardly groaned.

'Yes! That's right. I wanted to call it *She Sells Sea Shells by the Sea Shore*. I thought it was a catchy shop name.'

'But your bank wouldn't give us a loan would they, Jeffrey?'

'I know. I was amazed when they said they couldn't see how the shop could ever make money selling sea shells next to a beach where people could pick them up for free. I tried to explain to them the other woman who did it must have succeeded.'

'Yes you did Jeffrey,' sighed Mary, hoping the tea took effect soon. 'But the saying is based on the song about Mary Anning, and she sold fossils really, didn't she?'

'I feel a bit sleepy,' yawned Jeremy. 'I've had a hard day behind the counter in the bank again. It's a fascinating job, though. You never know what's going to happen. It was exciting today. Someone came in with a bag of change.'

'Wow! That **is** exciting,' said Mary. She noticed Jeffrey drop the vacuum flask. 'And you must be tired after doing that quiz on Radio 4 before we left the house.'

Swaying, Jeffrey sleepily said, 'It was the repeat of Brain of Britain. I always get more answers right when it's the repeat. I think I'll just have a sit down.'

Feeling her creative impulses were finally being met, Mary let go of Jeffrey's arm and watched his legs wobble as he tried to sit down on the wet sand. She waited for him to topple onto his side before she pulled the front of her waterproof's hood forward, turned and strode off towards their car, less than two hundred metres away.

She opened the boot and took out the flimsy orange inflatable dingy she had put there earlier, along with the electric pump to inflate it. With the pump attached and the dinghy inflating she knew this was where a little luck would help.

'Hey, love!' shouted a man from the shelter of his front doorway. 'You're not going out in that in this weather are you? You know the tide is strong here and with the wind blowing, well...'

Mary smiled, thanked luck, but only half turned to face the man, pulling her hood as far over the side of her face as she could. 'Don't worry,' she shouted back. 'My husband and I are only going knee deep for a charity bet.'

'Even so, best someone stays in the water and hangs on to it,' shouted the man.

'Good advice. Thanks,' called Mary, putting her gloved thumb up. She risked a glance and saw him shake his head at her madness before he returned into the warmth of his house. Satisfied the dinghy was sufficiently inflated she hung on to its rope as she returned the pump to the boot and locked the car. She knew the next part would be the hardest. She would have to carry and drag the dingy along the roadway, under the old castle's archway and down the concrete steps to the cove, and all with the wind trying to rip it away from her.

The first part was easier than she had expected, but the last forty metres, between the beach huts and across the beach itself was harder and she had to grip the rope on the front of the dinghy before it flew off into the sea. Eventually, the dinghy was at the side of the slumbering Jeffrey, who looked so peaceful on his side, snoring in the torrential rain and howling wind. Mary jumped into the dinghy to keep it on the ground, leaned over its side and slowly hauled Jeffrey on board. He was heavier than she had anticipated and once his sleeping body was in she needed to sit on the side of the dinghy for a few moments to catch her breath before she grasped the rope and swivelled the dinghy round to point towards the sea. The piles of pebbles were just where she had left them that afternoon and she took a few handfuls and dropped them into Jeffrey's pockets. Just to be on the safe side, she added a few handfuls more.

The sea was cold, but not as cold as the ice-water Uncle Vasily used to submerge her in when she was training, and she wasn't tied to a chair like she was then either. By the time the sea was up to her knees the wind had already swivelled the dinghy, with Jeffrey in it, over the waves and was trying to take it out to sea. By the time the water was up to her thighs she could feel the current pushing against the backs of her legs. She leaned back and pulled on the rope to stop the dinghy heading for France. There was one final thing to do. While hanging grimly on to the dinghy's rope with one hand she took the safety pin she had fixed to her waterproof trouser pocket and opened it. She grimaced as she pulled the dinghy closer and stabbed the pin's point into it. Then she let the safety pin and the dinghy go.

She waved as the slowly deflating dinghy picked up speed and bravely made its way out into the dark, rolling sea. 'Bye, bye, Jeffrey,' she said quietly. 'Happy anniversary.'

After pouring the drugged tea into the sea, filling the flask with water and hurling it into the waves Mary left the cove by the other route through the woodland and the ruins of the old church. It was only an eight mile walk to the bus stop in Weymouth where she could catch the bus to her 'other' house and dry clothes. While she walked she wondered how long it would be before the man who had warned her from his doorway would see her car still there and report how the 'crazy woman' had probably got herself swept out to sea with her 'daft husband' and drowned.

Her reasoning for the evening's creative enterprise was simple. The man who called himself Atticus only knew her as 'Mary White' and after delaying the agreed payment she no longer entirely trusted him with the knowledge of that identity. She was glad she had given him the account number of one of her other 'Mary' aliases. Mary Black would become richer by a large six figure number once the elusive Alison Taylor was disposed of. It had occurred to Mary that Atticus might welsh on the deal and hire a different killer, but since her aliases made up over half of the contract killers on the Dark Web she knew she had a better than fifty fifty chance. She supposed she had another reason for the deflating dinghy excursion. Jeffrey was boring.

ALISON TAYLOR.

Alison Taylor had been worried. Now she was in a state of blind panic. Jonathan had often told her Nancy Carter got jealous easily. Alison recalled how he described how Nancy had gone ballistic when he told her he had done some work with an old acquaintance named Beth Spencer, and even though Jonathan had only briefly met with Beth twice it was enough for Nancy to threaten to kill her if she ever contacted Jonathan again.

With an ear on the TV twenty four hour news channel, Alison peered from behind the bedroom curtain to see everything was still quiet in the road below. The news was not being much help with only sporadic reporting on the murder of Reema Sharma and her family. Most of the news seemed to be interviews with politicians about things called 'hard Brexit' and an 'extension'. Alison did not pay much attention to such transitory matters. She had more important, long term things to think about such as the millions she was about to lose now everything had gone pear-shaped at the worst possible time.

The bed sagged deep as she sat on it and ran her fingers back through her strawberry blonde hair. She knew very well what was going on. At first she had thought Jonathan had stood her up and was not meeting her for their usual Friday night tryst. She had given him plenty of time before she had snapped, squirted on more perfume and got a taxi. It had dropped her off around the side of the lab in case Nancy Carter had shown up to check up on Jonathan. Alison had known that even though the main lights were off in the lab, Jonathan and Nancy might be in Jonathan's office, probably screaming at each other, so Alison had crept around the side of the building to peer through the entrance doors. There was not the slightest hint of light but she knew Jonathan had not gone home. His car was still in the otherwise empty car park where he always left it on Friday evenings. She knew Jonathan always got a taxi to meet with her for their rendezvous at the secret location, just like she always got a taxi there from her little house in Charmouth. They had decided long ago that it was best no one would spot their cars and guess they were together.

Alison had stood outside the dark entrance to the lab, hesitating, until she had finally snapped for a second time that Friday evening and used her key-card to go inside. As soon as she had switched the lights on and saw Jonathan's body at the end of the corridor she just knew Nancy had found out about them. The next thing she'd done was run.

In some ways Alison was not sure if she had made the right decision to drop her phone from the bridge into the river when she was walking back, but something had warned her that phones could be tracked and she needed to play it safe: Nancy was capable of anything. This was clear when Alison's worst fears were borne-out and the news reported Reema's death. At first, Alison was relieved. She had mentally clapped her hands with joy. Hooray! Nancy had killed Reema, thinking it was Reema who Jonathan was cheating with! Excellent! Then it occurred to Alison that Jonathan was cheating on Nancy with Reema **as well**! How could he be so unfaithful to her? She was **so** upset! But... maybe Nancy had found out about both of them? Alison felt herself shaking again. She poured another full glass of vodka and drank it in one, slammed the empty glass down and paced the room. Alison had not known Jonathan was having an affair with Reema as well as her but, obviously, Nancy knew. Alison could think of no other reason why Reema would be killed. And in a fit of blind rage Nancy had killed Reema's whole family too!

Of course Alison had considered contacting the police, but she had no proof Nancy was responsible and the police would question Nancy then let her go and then Nancy would kill her, just like she had Jonathan and Reema. On the whole, Alison thought it safer to lay low and wait for the news to tell her Nancy had been arrested. Until then Alison was going nowhere. She was certainly not going home.

DR. LYNN AND JEREMY.

'That was delicious, as usual Finch,' Dr. Evie Lynn complimented. 'Once you've tidied the kitchen and brought us coffee you may retire. I won't be requiring your services any further this evening. Remember to change the beds tomorrow.'

'Yes, Ma'am,' Finch replied with a little bow.

Across the dining table from Dr. Lynn, Jeremy's beady eyes watched the servant disappear into the kitchen before he whispered, 'I had a text from Erica.' He fumbled in his pockets, left the table and came back with his suit jacket and his phone in his hand. He pushed it across the table to his wife. 'My PIN is still my birthday,' he reminded her.

Dr. Lynn glanced through the archway into the kitchen, smelt coffee and heard their dessert dishes being scraped. She tapped the PIN in and read the text. Jeremy leaned his bony face forward and said, 'It's a bit bold of her isn't it? To ask me for five thousand pounds for it?'

Dr. Lynn looked across at Jeremy and put her finger to her lips as the clangs in the kitchen ceased. Finch appeared with two black espressos, placed them next to his employers and said, 'I'll be going to my room then Ma'am, Sir. See you both in the morning.'

'You will indeed, dear boy,' said Jeremy, smiling up at him. 'I have an early meeting with people from the Ministry of Defence about some big new cleaning contract I've somehow managed to land. It's a bit hush-hush. Nuclear subs and whatnot. They're coming here so the press don't get wind of anything.'

Finch nodded to Jeremy. Dr. Lynn waved him away.

They sat in silence until they heard silence. Dr. Lynn was first to speak. 'We need to be careful. Finch has been with us for years but we've talked about not letting him hear more than he should. Now, as far as Erica is concerned, just agree. I don't know why you haven't already. Text her now and tell her you'll give her the five thousand.'

Jeremy looked confused. 'But we're married,' he said. 'That's why I showed you her text. I'd never, you know, do that.'

'Jeremy..? Do what..? Oh! You thought...' began Evie Lynn. She sighed. 'The *it* she's referring to in her text is the flash drive, Jeremy. She'd want far more from someone like you if the **it** was what you thought she meant.'

'Oh, the flash drive!' Jeremy said. 'Hold on a mo old thing... What do you mean she'd want more than five..?'

'Just pay her the five thousand, Jeremy,' Dr. Lynn told him. 'Erica must have found out her boss was murdered at the lab. Damn it! I told her to post it before she went into work! She must know the research data is worth a lot more now that Carter is dead... Or she may know nothing and is just getting greedy. But just pay her.'

Jeremy huffed. 'Five thousand? For a flash drive? You're not serious, Evie! Do you think my law firm has that sort of money lying about in petty cash?'

'Yes,' replied Evie Lynn. 'Put it down as expenses or something.'

'Expenses? That would be a very nice client lunch. The auditors would soon spot it. The other partners would play merry hell.'

'Forget it then,' said Dr. Lynn. Jeremy breathed a sigh of relief until she added, 'Pay her from your personal account.'

Jeremy considered for a moment. 'No,' he said, folding his arms angrily. 'We've paid her enough. She can go to hell and starve for double crossing us. You already have nearly a dozen flash drives from her with information and data and stuff about what Carter and his scientist geeks were doing in that lab – which you own, incidentally! I say! All this excitement! I feel quite flushed!'

Evie Lynn thought seeing his gaunt, grey skin going red was not a pleasant sight after eating Eton Mess for dessert. 'Listen, Jeremy,' she said, 'tempt not the hatred of my spirit, for I am sick when I look on thee.'

'That's very poetic,' Jeremy observed, fanning his bony face with both hands.

'It's sodding Shakespeare, Jeremy! Now, if you've finished your little tantrum... Pay her the damn money!' She added a glare for good measure.

Jeremy swallowed hard. 'How come you can't pay her, Evie? You've got millions.'

Dr. Lynn had hoped she could leave the dining table without counting to ten for once. She had needed to count to twenty before she managed to say, 'You may recall how we have discussed this on several occasions Jeremy. There should be no financial links between Erica Young and myself. We don't want anything traced back to me, do we?'

'Like what?' asked Jeremy.

'Like the fact I was paying her to spy on my own research lab, Jeremy.'

'Ah, yes. I remember. The lab where they're trying to make that new sort of Viagra!'

Dr. Lynn held her head in her hands. 'Jeremy, you stupid... It is bloody well not... Oh, forget it. All you need to remember is that Jonathan Carter and his team may well have cracked it and their final formula is probably on that flash drive and it could be worth... Well ! Who knows how much! So just transfer the money to her account and tell her as soon as we get that flash drive the modelling contract is all ready for her signature.'

'Is it?' asked Jeremy.

'Now she wants five thousand? Of course not!' screamed Dr. Lynn.

ERICA.

After waiting all day, the text agreeing to the five thousand pounds for the flash drive had taken too long to come through as far as Erica was concerned and it added to her distrust of the Lynns, so in case they decided to descend on Axminster with a team of lawyers, Erica had decided to be discrete and had travelled a whole twelve miles down the A35 to Honiton. Erica liked Honiton. The shopping there was good. There were lots of shops without security cameras.

She found a budget hotel on the edge of the town. The hotel was near an Aldi so she decided to stack-up on food and chewing gum for the evening. She always wondered why shops everywhere kept chewing gum so near the tills and made it so much easier to steal. As she slipped some into the pocket of her black leather jacket she stopped. She asked herself why she was stealing gum again. Her usual answer was that she quite liked gum, but on this occasion the question was more esoteric and one level of answer was because she had a zero bank balance, drove a shitty old car that she was paying extortionate loan interest on, had a maxed-out credit card and apparently no longer had a job. She put the chewing gum back on the rack, partly because she had a new desire to better herself and partly because the woman on the checkout was staring at her and shaking her head.

While she sat in her budget hotel room eating her Aldi egg sandwiches and drinking tap water, Erica read the magazine she had surreptitiously slipped inside her jacket. She flicked through it, looking at the models in the adverts. She stopped turning the pages when she came to the one advertising 'Midnight Intoxication' with the perfect Italian model known only as Colfetti surrounded by four soave men in dinner jackets. She stared for a few moments then threw the magazine across the room. The Lynns had changed the lock on her flat's door, hadn't they? They had taken half the day and most of the evening and still had not responded to her text asking for the five thousand, hadn't they? The message was clear. She sat at the dressing table and looked at herself. She pushed her nose to the left and wished the end did not have that little droop. No matter what others said, she knew she was just not perfect enough to ever be a model. She knew the Lynn's were never really going to get her a modelling contract, even if their mysterious friend who owned an agency even existed.

As she brushed her teeth before bed her phone pinged. It was a message from Jeremy Lynn, finally agreeing to pay her the five thousand and give her the modelling contract.

Erica knew this game. She had played it too many times. She had made her best money making promises she never kept. She found an appropriate emoji to text back to Jeremy Lynn. She hoped he was young enough to know what 'the finger' was. She followed it up by texting, 'You took too long. I want the five thousand in my account before I post you anything!'

5. Wednesday, March 20th.

The morning after their late night at the pub, Copeland woke up on his back with Jane lying next to him. He watched his little hotel room slowly get lighter as the sun began to rise outside. He felt Jane move and saw her arms emerge from under the duvet, stretch out in front of her and fall back down. He had to admit his recollection of the previous evening was more than a little hazy; more like snapshots rather than a stream of continuous memory. Their talk in the beer garden had ended when the torrential rain started and they had rushed back inside. He had sat at the bar with a bottle of red and Jane had played pool and flirted with the men from the building site, except when she was downing tequila shots and flirting with the men from the building site. She seemed unaffected by how much she'd drunk but Copeland knew he had drunk too much when he paid for Jane's burger as well as his own. He vaguely remembered someone saying something about no taxis at that time of night and someone else offering to give them a lift back to the Lyme Bay View Hotel. After that he remembered hardly anything. He yawned.

'Are you awake, Larry?' whispered Jane, knowing he was.

Copeland grunted.

Jane nudged him and said, 'You were brilliant last night, Larry. So thoughtful...'

Copeland grunted again before he asked, 'Can I ask a personal question now that we've slept together, Detective?'

Jane giggled. 'Of course, Larry. Now that we've slept together we should have no secrets.' She giggled again.

Looking at the ceiling Copeland said, 'Since my mini-stroke my sense of smell has not been what it was. So my personal question is... Do my feet smell?'

Jane turned her head to one side. She sniffed and replied, 'Not as far as I can tell, but you did put two pairs of socks on after you said I could go under the duvet and you'd sleep on top. It was very gallant of you. I was surprised you had two extra sweaters and two jogging bottoms to put on top of your suit though.'

'British weather,' moaned Copeland, glad he had found out why he could hardly move. 'Always pack enough is my motto.'

'Quite right, Sir,' agreed Jane looking at her watch. 'I need to get up and use the bathroom now. I only have my bra and pants on, so do you mind not looking?'

'Of course,' said Copeland, having no intention of looking at Jane now he knew she was only wearing underwear. He closed his eyes really tight.

Hey, Copeland! You know there's something really wrong with you, don't you?

Jane got up. Copeland heard her stop, level with the bottom of the bed where his head was. He turned his head and squinted to see what was wrong. He quickly turned his head back and squeezed his eyes tight again. When he heard Jane start sobbing he raised himself onto an elbow to see Jane staring at herself in the wardrobe mirror, but looking down. Copeland remembered a course where he had been told to not think of anything yellow and he had instantly thought of a banana. He could not help himself. He raised himself higher and looked down at Jane's lower legs.

Copeland? Really? an exasperated inner voice sighed. *She's in her underwear and you're looking at her knees?*

Jane must have sensed him looking. She whirled, pointed at him and screamed, 'You promised you wouldn't look!' She put her face in her hands, turned and sat on the end of the bed with her back to Copeland. Head sagging, she muttered, 'I have lymphedema. It's type two. It's also called Meige disease. It's a hereditary thing to do with my lymph nodes. My legs swell up because of lymph collecting in my subcutaneous tissue. It's awful. It started just after I left the comp I was at and went to the sixth form at the grammar school. We had to wear dresses. Preg-legs was my nickname. I hated it. That's why I did a biology degree – the seventeen year old me naively thought one day I would find a cure.'

Copeland thought she needed cheering up so said, 'The rest of you is very nice, though.'

'I need to massage my calves,' announced Jane determinedly as she stood up and bent over to start massaging. Copeland remained silent as Jane bent and massaged. Suddenly feeling quite warm, he took one of his two pullovers off. He lay flat and examined the ceiling again. It had an interesting little crack in it. 'I can't do this,' said Jane, still trying. 'Usually my partner does it.' She stood and turned to look at Copeland. 'Sir, would you mind doing it for me? Massage and exercise are the only things that can keep it in check and I haven't had the chance to go for a run for days.'

'Er, Ok,' said Copeland, feeling it only common courtesy to look at her while they spoke. 'I'll certainly give it a try.'

She looked at him. Her eyes narrowed. She put her hands on her bare hips. She tilted her head. She folded her arms under her half-cup bra. She said, 'This is not a sexual thing, Sir, so please don't think I'm leading you on here. Remember I told you I was lesbian?'

'You did?' said Copeland, astonished.

'I'm glad you remember, Sir,' said Jane, again not picking up on his intonation. 'I'll grab a shower and then you can do my calves for me. My partner usually raises each leg one at a time to massage while I lie on my back. But don't worry, Sir, since it's you, I'll slip back into my underwear after I shower.'

'OK,' gulped Copeland as Jane went into the ensuite. When his pulse slowed a little he called, 'But if you're a... Er... you know... why were you flirting with those men from the construction site – all that pool and tequila shots? They were like bees around honey!'

Jane put her head round the open door. 'That was work, Sir. Eight months ago some of those same workers did modifications on the research lab for what we now know was the bonobo room. They told me that had just finished when a truck came and they were paid cash to clear off quick. One of them remembered the name on the side of the truck. I think you have a lead on your animal smugglers, Sir.'

By the time he had finished the professionally bonding experience of massaging Jane's calves Copeland needed a shower. He let the water run as cold as he could take it. When he came out wearing a fresh dark blue suit identical to the one he had slept in Jane had his second cup of tea waiting. She was still wearing the light blue shirt he had given her when she came out of the shower, but had now tucked it into her trousers, explaining she could not wear her white blouse for a second day running and how she needed to go home to get fresh clothes. Hesitantly, she handed Copeland his tea. As he took it she leaned forward and planted a small kiss on his cheek. 'That's for being so thoughtful,' Jane said. 'Putting my heel on top of your stomach while you massaged my calves was pure genius, Sir.'

'This partner of yours is a lucky man,' Copeland said, embarrassed by the kiss. Jane looked at him, smiled and shook her head. 'Oh! Right,' said Copeland. 'I mean lucky woman.'

'I'm moving in with her,' Jane said. 'That's why I got the job back in Bricknall.' She looked thoughtful, found something amusing and laughed. 'Trouble is she currently shares the flat with this other crazy girl. She's an art student. First year. We call her Bee. She looks a bit like a young Britney Spears!'

Copeland smiled benignly. He had no idea who this Britney thingy was. He said, 'Vasily told me that my daughter, Emily, is art student. Postgraduate. I'm not sure where though.'

Jane put her hand on Copeland's shoulder. She knew why Copeland had got so drunk the previous night. She had heard about Vasily's threats towards his daughter Emily. She had also heard a lot about his marriage break up, the court's restraining order because he 'associated with violent criminals' and his estranged daughter while she was trying to get his two pullovers on over his suit after she had helped him up to the hotel room. The pullovers had been easier to put on than the jogging bottoms but he had insisted he needed two pairs because he seemed to feel the cold more these days. In the cold light of day, she'd thought it best to let him think he had still been capable of dressing himself for bed and, recalling his tales of his divorce woes, Jane thought it best he had something to cling on to so said, 'Maybe your daughter is at Bricknall art college, Sir. I'll ask my partner and Bee if they know anyone name Emily Copeland.'

'She kept her mother's name,' Copeland told her. 'She's Emily Richardson.'

Jane nodded and quickly turned away before Copeland noticed her turn pale. She could feel his eyes on the back of her neck. She felt her heart start pounding in case he guessed.

'You know this partner of yours?' Copeland said. Jane felt her heart start to race. She hoped he was not going to ask what her name was. Copeland said, 'I'm sure she'll like it like that.'

'What?' asked Jane, confused, as she pretended to tidy the used tea bags and empty sugar sachets.

'Your hair,' said Copeland. 'You said it's naturally blonde and goes curlier like that if you don't use hair straighteners after you've washed it. I think it looks good. It's all I looked at while I was massaging your calves. Honest.'

'Thank you, Sir. Perhaps I will keep it curly,' said Jane, relieved. 'I'll just wash my hands again and we'll go and get some breakfast.'

MARY.

Mary White was now Mary Black. She liked to keep the name Mary. It was the one she had grown up with before being taken to Russia. Over half of her twenty fake identities had 'Mary' as her first name. None of them had 'Dominika'. Dominika was not a name she responded to: it rekindled nightmare memories of her training with Uncle Vasily.

While she waited for Atticus to agree to her terms to pay, Mary took the time to completely change her appearance and become Jennifer Green. With a long platinum wig, blue contact lenses, a larger nose and a little beauty spot on her cheek, she briefly visited her shop in Lyme. It sold sea shells. It also sold fossils. When Mary had opened it under the name of 'Jennifer Green', Mary had not known selling fossils could be so lucrative. It was also home to her charity, dedicated to preserving the fossil coastline of West Dorset, mainly so her shop could get most of the best fossils. Mary Black, in her persona of Jennifer Green, was very grateful to Jeffrey and Mary White for recently rewriting their wills and leaving all their worldly possessions to the charity once they were eventually declared legally dead. Both Mary Black and Jennifer Green were patient sorts of people who knew how to wait.

But Mary's visit to her Jennifer Green shop was a fleeting one. Atticus texted to offer a ludicrous amount of money for what he called "strictly payment by results" and Mary rushed home to change before going to significantly change the life of Erica Young.

COPELAND AND JANE HAVE BREAKFAST.

Nina the hotel proprietress was more than happy to serve an extra breakfast for an extra cost. She leaned on their table and said, 'You should have told me you were in a relationship, Larry. When I invited you up to my room the other night I thought you were being racist – me being Puerto Rican and all.'

Copeland had had no idea Nina was Puerto Rican. He thought she was from Torquay. He looked at Jane and saw her eyebrows were raised.

Nina had not finished. She smiled at Jane 'And you are such a young pretty one too. Larry must have depths I have not seen. Good for you, Big Larry.'

There was a brief moment when Jane wondered why Nina called Copeland 'big' Larry, but Nina's friendly pat on Copeland's robust stomach answered her curiosity.

'No Mrs. Smith this morning, then, Nina?' asked Copeland.

Nina shook her head. 'She's still here. She's paying me extra to do room service. She's shut herself up in there. I think she's upset her Mr. Smith did not show up. Shame. The poor woman was very upset yesterday evening. She had just been telling me how she could have been a film star or a top model when the news came on. At one point she almost burst out crying. Still, that was upsetting, wasn't it? A whole family murdered in their own home just a few miles down the road. I think they were restaurant owners. Who would want to kill a family like that? The news said it might have been a far right group who attacked them just because their name was Sharma. They go on about Muslim extremists, but these neo-Nazis, eh? I think I'll keep my last name to myself. So, it's full English twice with extra toast. Double bacon and three eggs as usual for you is it, Big Larry?'

Several cups of tea later, they got a taxi to The Butchered Calf, got in Copeland's car, stuck tape over the inbuilt breathalyser to avoid it telling Copeland how much he'd drunk the previous evening and drove to the Sharmas' house to try to retrieve Jane's car. It was hopeless. The media circus was there in full swing. A helicopter circled overhead. Three bemused uniformed officers were keeping the news crews at bay while a fourth more senior officer was trying to answer rapid fire press questions. 'Hell's bells!' groaned Copeland as he navigated through the cars and TV vans. He went a little further down the road and turned round in the entrance to a caravan park.

The Gandalf-car said, 'Fool of a Took! This is not a hobbit walking party. Make your mind up next time, Driver!'

Copeland was impressed the car quoted the book rather than the film Gandalf. He was getting quite fond of it now he had realised the acronym for intelligent personal assistant was IPA. Decent beer, IPA, he thought as he drove Jane to her flat in Weymouth and waited outside while she did a quick change and threw some things into a holdall. They had been summoned to the Department C office for a meeting with Director Wendy Miller.

ERICA.

After a late hotel breakfast of stale croissants and suspiciously smelling milk, Erica checked her bank account had five thousand pounds more than it did the day before and went to a post office to buy a jiffy bag and post the flash drive special delivery to Jeremy Lynn at his solicitors office, just as she had done for many months. Like many 'modern' post offices, this one was at the back of a shop which sold everything from frozen food to alcohol. It also sold newspapers. On her way out she noticed the headline of the Devon Gazette. The headline 'Four Killed in Lyme Terror Attack' annoyed her. She knew Lyme was in Dorset, not Devon, so felt the Devon Gazette was out of its area and stealing stories that should belong to the Dorset Herald. She bent over to look at the newspaper photograph of the smart detached house taken above the heads of three police officers and the strip of yellow tape across the drive. She started to read on.

'Ahem! Excuse me, Miss,' said a voice behind her.

Erica looked over her shoulder. According to the sticker on his shirt, this was 'Bob' and he was 'Shop Manajor'. Erica stared at the label. She thought the word 'manager' was spelt differently, but she wasn't certain. She had not paid much attention to English lessons even before she had left school at fourteen when she ran away from home and her step-father. Of more interest to her were the three more than middle-aged women standing behind the 'Manajor'. They stared at her. They had their noses in the air. They had their arms folded. They looked cross.

'It's my little black dress, isn't it?' innocently asked Erica. 'Has one of their husbands had a heart attack when I bent down? It happens all the time. I suppose you want me to zip my jacket up too?'

The 'Manajor', straining to keep his eyes on her face, said, 'They are not with their husbands, er, fortunately. But my wife sent me over to ask if you're going to buy that news... Please don't look at me like that, Miss.' He swallowed hard. His legs wobbled. He stammered, 'J-j-just t-take the n-newspaper and go. No charge!'

Erica took a copy of the paper and stood. To thank him, she gave him a kiss on his cheek. As she left the shop he was having his shins kicked by the woman from behind the counter so Erica took the opportunity to grab a chocolate bar on the way out.

With the newspaper in her hand, Erica found a coffee shop. It was crowded. The over fifties were there in force. She waited for an interminable age while the woman in front of her decided if she wanted chocolate sprinkles on her cappuccino. Erica finally got her large straight black. She had always liked a large straight black. Sometimes she liked two. As she held it between her hands she looked for a seat. There seemed to be only one available, right by the window. An elderly frail woman resembling Miss Marple in an old mustard cardigan was slowly heading towards it. With the newspaper under her arm, Erica beat the little old woman to the seat and sat opposite a young man in a black suit. She thought he looked like an extra from a Dracula movie. One of those who had already had his blood drained. She sat and placed her coffee down. The man did not look up. He seemed to be more interested in the table.

'Mind if I sit here?' asked Erica. Since she had already put the coffee down and sat, she really did not know why she was asking.

The pale man shook his head without looking up. He very slowly said, 'Fascinating table this. It seems to have a heart shape actually in the wood grain itself.'

While he had been speaking Erica had had time to take her phone out, send a text message to Jeremy Lynn to tell him the package had been posted and put her phone back into her jacket pocket. She leaned forward to look at the alleged strange heart shape ingrained in the table. She saw young vampire victim man was correct. The table did indeed have something resembling a heart shape on the surface. Erica said, 'The heart seems to have the words Harry and Megan above and below it too.'

Vampire victim man leaned closer to the table. 'I say! You're right! This is amazing. This composite MDF table seems to have somehow strangely brought this forth. It's just like the Turin shroud.'

Erica stuck a finger in her ear and waggled it about. She looked around. She wiped her nose on her wrist (the one without her wrist bag) and said, 'Maybe someone carved it there.'

His pale face looked up at her. He got excited. She could tell by the way he spoke at almost normal speed. 'My God! You may be right! That would mean **they** were actually here!'

'OK... Right... I'm going to read my newspaper now,' said Erica.

She managed to read enough to know Reema Sharma and her family were killed by right wing neo-Nazi extremists, that the paper had tried to find her co-workers but Alison Taylor was apparently in hiding from the press and a Mr. Wang Linpeng was, according to a neighbour, holidaying with his family somewhere in Spain. (*So much for it supposedly being a secret lab*, thought Erica.) She read on and learned a lot about the Sharmas' house, their restaurant business and where they had bought their cars. Much, much further down the piece, the newspaper told how Nancy Carter, the wife of Reema Sharma's boss, would say nothing except her husband had recently been murdered too. Erica raised a recently plucked eyebrow. She did not know much about journalism but suspected this was not the most experienced journalist or the best newspaper editor.

'I'm Giles,' said vampire victim number one on the other side of the inscribed table.

Erica was trying to absorb the significance of two people she worked with being murdered and wished she had stolen more gum so she could blow a bubble at vampire victim and tell him where to go, just like she had done to the tubby old police dude who had tried to shake her hand when she was waiting to see Dr. Lynn. Recalling that reminded her she had seen Giles before. He was the same guy who had been with that tubby police dude at Lynn's clinic. Currently lacking gum, Erica had to resort to the V sign.

'Aha!' said Giles. 'I admire Winston Churchill too. I'm going to be a politician like he was. I'm just a police inspector at the moment so we can say I've had real world experience. I've interned at the Ministry of Health too. My father is Lord Kernow and he has a bit of influence so the next safe seat is mine. He expects Maidstone will be available soon, you know, when *she* resigns.'

Erica became somewhat more interested. 'Your father... This Lord Kernow...'

'Kernow is just an old name for Cornwall,' said Giles. 'He owns a few hundred square miles of it around our stately home.'

Erica became even more interested in the thin pale man across the table. She thought he was starting to look quite handsome.

'It's all just worthless moorland really,' said Giles.

Erica started to lose interest.

'If his insurance business hadn't made quadzillions I'd just be the heir to lots of wet bogs,' said Giles, doing something which might have equated to a laugh if he was a bullfrog.

A little more interested again, Erica asked, 'Insurance business? What's your father's name..? Er, Giles, is it?'

Giles thought for a moment before he said, 'Oh, yes! It's Robert.'

'Robert what?' asked Erica.

'Robert Lord,' said Giles. 'You know, Lord Insurance.'

Erica thought, **_Holy shit!_** and, with a big smile, said, 'You're right. This table is amazing. I love tables. Men who like tables are so interesting. '

'I really like desks,' said Giles.

'Wow! You do? They're my total favourite. Honest,' enthused Erica. 'I love classical...' She thought quickly. What had she never been able to afford? 'Italian,' she said.

Giles stared at her, open mouthed. She gave him her best look. He stared. He swallowed. His eyes watered. His throat made a noise resembling a dying geriatric tortoise. He said, 'Er, Miss, my father says the Home Secretary job is in the bag, but I need a wife to become Prime Minister, just like Donald has his Ivanka. But for some reason which alludes one, I don't seem have much success with totties from the weaker sex. Are you married, er... do you have a name?'

'Erica,' said Erica, quickly deciding to strike while the iron was hot and adding, 'All I've ever wanted is a family, so, yes, I am available to marry you, er, Giles, is it?'

Grinning, Giles clapped his hands together. 'I must take you to meet dear Pa-pa!'

Erica winced. 'If I'm visiting a lord I might need a new wardrobe.'

Giles waved a finger from side to side to allay her concern as he said, 'Don't worry. I know an excellent carpenter.'

Erica closed her eyelids momentarily before she rolled her eyes behind them. She thought Giles had all the attributes to be Prime Minister. She opened her eyes, tilted her head to one side and gave Giles her better than best smouldering look, 'I might need new clothes as well,' she said.

'Of course,' said Giles earnestly. 'We'll go to my apartment in Kensington tomorrow and shop in Knightsbridge.' He leaned forward to whisper, 'I just have a case here to finish off today. I'm on the trail of a shoplifter. The new Superintendent sent me here. She said it had to be me who got sent a long way away from her office because it was a case of the utmost importance. Don't worry. I'll catch her soon. The shoplifter, not the Superintendent. I've got a full description now.' He got a notepad from the inside pocket of his black Savile Row suit, flicked a few pages and said, 'She's about five feet eight tall, brown hair, centre parted with pigtails, wears large circular steel earrings, rather attractive and something about her brown eyes being smouldering according to the male witnesses.' He put his notebook away and returned his attention to Erica. 'Weren't you wearing earrings a moment ago?' he asked.

Erica chose distraction tactics. 'We should seal our engagement with a really big diamond ring and possibly a small kiss,' she said, leaning forward and offering her cheek. She was surprised Giles knew what to do, but he thrust his head across the table and kissed it. The coffee shop window shattered as brains splattered onto Erica's favourite little black dress.

MARY.

Mary did not know why Erica Young needed to die. She did not really care. She was mildly curious to know why Miss Young had not been one of her original targets and why she was now. After all, Miss Young was only a lowly receptionist in the corrupt capitalist system which Mary enjoyed so much. Mary wondered where else she could make so much money doing what she had been trained to do. Certainly not with the Russian SVR which expected her to live in southern England on the same money as the average worker in Minsk. That money hardly covered her gym membership.

Having discarded Jennifer Green and her flowery dress in favour of a black padded jacket when Atticus had offered an outrageous amount when the job was done, Mary sped to Honiton and parked in a shoppers' car park off the high street to keep her car some distance from where she would kill Erica Young and briskly walked the kilometre to where her phone was telling her the tracker on Erica Young's car was. She soon found it parked diagonally across two parking bays outside a budget hotel. Mary went into the lobby, hoping to ask which room her dearest friend Erica was in. There was no one there. Mary shook her head and put her steel attaché case down. All this on-line booking annoyed her. It seemed gone were the days someone could simply turn up at a hotel and expect someone there at reception unless you had told them what time you were arriving. Mary quickly swivelled to turn her back on the young woman in the short black dress and black leather jacket who came from the self-serve breakfast area towards her. Even if Mary had not recognised the face the telltale brown plaits and immense circular steel earrings would have told her this was Erica Young.

Picking up her attaché case, Mary followed Erica's three inch stilettos out of the hotel and along the road to the high street. Mary wondered how anyone could walk so fast in such shoes but kept up with her target until she went into a shop which doubled as a post office. Mary waited outside, knowing post offices often had a hidden CCTV. Target Erica was some time in the shop. Mary was running out of things to pretend to look at in the shop window by the time Erica Young came out eating a chocolate bar and with a newspaper under her arm. Mary followed again, hoping her target would go down a secluded alley somewhere. Mary patted the base of her spine to check her hunting knife was ready to be drawn from its sheath fixed to her belt under her jacket. Her employers wanted it messy to make a statement, they said, and what was messier than a slit throat? Unfortunately – or fortunately if you were Erica – Erica Young did not go down a secluded alley but into a coffee shop a few doors from the post office.

Mary pretended to be reading the price list next to the door while she watched her target wait for her coffee then barge past a little old lady with a grey hair bun and sit in a window seat. Mary smiled and looked across the road. The flat above the stationers shop opposite was ideal. It still had sash windows.

It took moments for Mary to go down the side road, go down the alleyway, pick the shop's back door lock and silently carry her case up the back stairs. She readied her hunting knife but the flat above the stationers was empty. She found the best window for a good view of Miss Young, who was being so accommodating by taking the window seat. Mary opened her case. She glanced across the street to see the target reading her newspaper. Mary took the components of her sniper rifle from the case and screwed them together, not needing to look what she was doing but watching to make sure the target stayed where she was. Mary loaded a single bullet, opened the window, rested the end of the barrel on the window ledge, nestled the stock into her shoulder and put her eye to the telescopic sight. Mary felt somehow cheated. The side of Miss Young's head was such an easy target at this range, especially now she was making it easier by leaning forward, as if offering her head as a target.

Mary took a breath. She held it. She began to squeeze the trigger. Her phone whistled. She squeezed the trigger. The shot hurtled across the street, smashing though the coffee shop window. She looked through the telescopic lens and saw Miss Young was no longer sitting where she had been.

By the time people in the shop started screaming, Mary had already closed the window. By the time the coffee drinkers were hiding under tables the rifle had been dismantled and put back in its case. By the time wailing people starting to pour into the street Mary was out of the back of the shop and casually going back into the high street, checking her phone.

The message that had disturbed her concentration for a split second was from Atticus, who else? It said, 'Termination contract on Erica Young cancelled: effective immediately.' Mary was staring at the screen and thinking it was a bit late to tell her that now when she collided into a little bald idiot who wasn't looking where he was going.

JANE AND COPELAND MEET WITH WENDY MILLER.

Copeland and Jane had a very informative meeting with Wendy Miller. They returned to the new, replacement car in silence and drove to the hotel near the Department C office without a word. The replacement car said nothing either, perhaps because it detected the tension or because it was a ten year old Fiat 500. Once Copeland had tried yet again to see if the driver seat could go back any further so the steering wheel did not press into his stomach, they sat staring through the windscreen at the murky vacancy of the hotel's underground car park.

Jane finally broke the silence. 'So Wang Linpeng is dead. He was probably dying before he got on that plane to Spain. The hospital ran tests for two days before he died! What sort of poison can be that undetectable?'

'One developed by the old KGB probably,' Copeland said wearily.

Another car pulled into the car park. They watched the elderly owner get out, take a large case from his boot and catch the lift to the hotel lobby.

'So now we know you were initially sent to the lab because of the bonobos, Sir,' remarked Jane.

Copeland managed a hollow laugh. 'Apparently, but I don't remember phoning the Liverpool police early this morning to get them to raid that haulage firm's premises though, Detective. You wouldn't happen to know anything about that, would you?'

'You were a long time reading that newspaper on the toilet this morning, Sir.'

'I was having a shave as well.'

'For an hour, Sir?'

'And I had a shower.'

Jane glanced at him. Her eyes went down. 'I can see why a shower might take a long time, Sir.'

'All muscle this,' Copeland said, patting his stomach, 'and if you're inferring it takes me a long time to shower because I have a lot of stomach to wash...'

'I thought you should take the credit for the arrests of the animal smugglers, Sir. As I said, I've already handed in my resignation.'

'You have?' said Copeland. He tried to recall what Jane had told him the first time they met, when he wasn't really listening. He remembered. The memory shocked him. He said, 'You're forty two?'

'Please don't rub it in, Sir,' said Jane.

Copeland sighed. 'It's good to know I wasn't supposed to be working the case on my own though. All ten of the team would be helping if Natalie hadn't got that tip off about gun runners and they all had to go to Bristol. But that still leaves just the two of us trying to solve a multiple homicide. If only Clare hadn't got that promotion.'

'Hmmm...Quite,' mused Jane. 'If Chief Inspector Harper's promotion had not gone through surprisingly earlier than expected then the Devon and Cornwall Police may well have carried on with the case, but once she gets sent to Plymouth it miraculously gets handed over to my lot and... Well, they must have been overjoyed when the Home Office called them and they were asked to hand it over to Department C.'

'I know what you're inferring, Jane,' said Copeland, still staring out of the windscreen.

Jane stared at the side of his face. 'Oh, come on, Sir! Director Miller gets me to sign that combined official secrets act and non-disclosure agreement, shows me a file about me with details even I'd forgotten... For Pete's sake – second place in the sixth form fifty metres breaststroke!'

'Third,' said Copeland. 'The winner was wrongly disqualified.'

'Let's not get into that again, Sir. But you know my point. Clare Harper's promotion was fast-tracked as soon as I found out Uroboros owned the Axminster lab. I know there are cutbacks everywhere, Sir, but did you already know your Department C was mostly financed by private companies like Uroboros? Dr. Lynn obviously used her influence and got Wendy Miller to get Clare Harper promoted to make sure you investigated her own lab in case something was found they didn't want found!'

'Director Miller pointed out Uroboros and the other sponsorship companies are all vetted meticulously,' pointed out Copeland.

Meticulously, Copeland? You were the one who vetted Uroboros and Dr. Lynn when you worked for the Pickfords, and you didn't even know Dr. Lynn was a woman!

Copeland cleared his throat. 'And, like Director Miller said, the money the companies like Uroboros gave to set up Department C are only loans only until we're self-sustaining from the seizure of assets of the criminals we bring to book.'

Jane tutted. 'So now you're defending this private finance initiative of law enforcement? Is it because they're paying for your new offices at The Onion or is it because you get massive bonuses based on the assets you seize?'

'That has nothing to do with it,' said Copeland.

Really? I think the bonuses are a good idea, Copeland, commented his inner voice.

'And,' Jane huffed indignantly, 'Now we've been ordered to tread carefully. I don't suppose one of Department C's sponsors being Uroboros Rejuvenation Limited has anything to do with that either, does it? Damn it! They're our main suspect!'

'They are?' said Copeland.

'I'm glad you agree, Sir,' said Jane. 'Now we know Wang Linpeng has been killed as well then the jealous wife hypothesis is completely out of the window. That leaves us with the killer being hired because of whatever they were doing in that lab. So it must have been someone who knew what they were doing. So besides the two remaining people who worked there – Alison Taylor and Erica Young, whom I suspect must both be in hiding after last night's news about the Sharmas, that's if they are actually still alive – the only person who even knew where it was *and* what they were doing was Dr. Lynn, and she owns Uroboros Rejuvenation. She has to be the prime suspect. She's certainly rich enough to hire a killer.' She paused to reach between the seats and retrieve the manila folders Wendy Miller had given them. She flicked rapidly through and said, 'Erica Young certainly couldn't afford to hire a killer... Here's her bank statements. It looks like she's clever enough not to tell anyone she was being paid twice for the same job but still doesn't have two farthings to rub together on that wage.' She flicked more sheets over. 'Here's Alison Taylor's. She was doing OK. Let's see... She got a big payment from L'Argent Cosmetics nearly three years ago but it looks like she used most of it towards the deposit for a house at about the same time Jonathan Carter must have hired her to work at the Axminster lab a few months later, though I still can't believe she got the job. Let's look at the wife. OK. She probably could afford it. She keeps a lot in her account – just under six figures. But there are no big payments out to hire a hit-man, or a hit-woman. So we're left with mega-rich Dr. Lynn, aren't we? The woman we think already lied to you about what her team were actually making at that lab. Remember the lab was in pristine condition? I think they cleaned everything because they had already made whatever it was they were making and Dr. Lynn wanted them silenced so she could be sure to have a monopoly on it. It's option three, Sir. Dr. Lynn has to be our chief suspect.'

Copeland thought there was something strange about Jane. It would have taken him an age to look through sheets of bank accounts and grasp their significance like she had, even with his spectacles on, but she had seemingly absorbed the meaning of the numbers by some sort of brain osmosis. He looked at his watch and sighed deeply. 'Time we went to see Dr. Lynn,' he said.

Jane was amazed. 'Really? Sir! We haven't had lunch yet and I'm starving!'

TOM BENSON.

Armed with his old car insurance policy inside his waterproof poncho, Tom Benson walked from the railway station down Honiton High Street to the police station. By the time he got there he was feeling quite determined to right the wrongs and confront Inspector Giles Lord about the misdeeds of his father. He banged on the counter and demanded to see Inspector Lord, quoting Russell Crowe in Gladiator with, 'I shall have my vengeance in this world or the next!' He was told Inspector Lord was out for coffee and he should come back in a few hours time.

Aimlessly strolling back along the High Street, Tom rehearsed his speech ready for his eventual confrontation with Inspector Lord when he would demand justice for the misdeeds of his fraudulent father and his rip-off insurance company. Tom's aimless strolling stopped when all hell broke loose. He looked diagonally across the road and quickly ascertained some young hooligan had thrown a stone at a coffee shop window, shattered it and caused mass panic inside. The patrons were swarming out onto the pavement.

Curious, Tom walked slowly along his side of the road to see what was happening. The next thing he knew he was on his backside on the pavement. He looked up at the person who had barged into him.

'Sorry,' said the woman about his age dressed in the padded black jacket and black trousers. She put her attaché case down and held a hand out to him. He took it and she helped him up. He did not expect to be pulled so quickly and found himself standing far too close to her.

Tom Benson did not notice her swept back, short, thick, auburn hair, her high cheek bones, her full lips, or that she was his height and almost as thin. He did not notice she was still holding his hand. He did not hear the sirens in the distance. All he knew was one thing. He whispered, 'You have the most beautiful green eyes.'

Looking slightly puzzled, she stared back into Tom's eyes and, with a husky voice sounding as if she had a slightly sore throat, she said: 'You are so very cute...'

This should have come as a shock to Tom. It was the biggest compliment he had ever received since his mother had called him 'gnome face' and his father had called him 'friar tuck'. But it did not come as a shock because he did not care about anything except her eyes. The sirens got closer. He shuffled his feet and asked, 'Would you like to go for coffee?'

COPELAND AND JANE VISIT UROBOROS REJUVENATION.

There was disappointing news from the woman behind the main reception desk in the lobby of Uroboros Rejuvenation Limited. After first trying to direct Copeland to the waist reduction department the receptionist told them Dr. Lynn was not there. The receptionist explained the good doctor usually worked weekends but gave herself Wednesdays off instead. Copeland told the receptionist not to worry because they had her home address, then he looked at Jane, smiled, raised his eyebrows and nodded encouragingly. She rolled her eyes and said, 'Yes, Sir, **I** do have her home address.'

See that, Copeland? I wondered how long it would take before the eye rolling started!

Jane nudged Copeland. He saw she was reading the board on the wall behind the reception desk. The location of all the departments was there. He had heard of some of them, or could guess what they were, such as liposuction, laser hair removal, forehead lifts, Botox, but had no idea what things like brachioplasty, botulinum toxin, plasma therapy, flap or vaginoplasty meant. Curious, he turned to Jane and asked, 'What does flap mean?'

'Moving tissue with the blood supply intact, but I was looking at the arrow to the restaurant, Sir. I have a high metabolic rate and need food, Sir.'

Copeland did not argue and a few minutes later they were duly being turned away from the restaurant. 'What?' asked Copeland, innocently looking at Jane. 'All I did was ask how much things were. There were no prices on the menu.'

'I think if you have to ask then you probably can't afford to eat in there, Sir. I saw quite a few celebrities. Let's just go to the self-service down the other end like the waiter in the bow tie suggested.'

The bustling, staff filled self-service was just within their price range and had a choice of salad, salad or salad. Jane chose a walnut and avocado. Copeland chose three 'healthy-life' desserts. At least the tea was more their cup of tea and they made sure they grabbed a good handful of sugar sachets before they sat down on plastic chairs at a Formica table. They ate sombrely, becoming increasingly depressed with each mouthful until they both pushed half eaten remnants away, looked at each other and stood.

By the time Copeland had almost reached the revolving exit door Jane had disappeared. He retraced his steps and saw her curly blonde hair down the end of a side corridor. He approached from behind and tapped her on the shoulder. She turned with her finger on her lips and whispered, 'We may have some extremists to arrest, Sir. There are four young men wearing English S.S. polo shirts in there, Sir. I saw them go in and followed. They're sitting at the far end, beyond all the other young people.'

Jane frowned sceptically when he told her they were the English synchronised swimming team. He pointed to a sign on the wall. 'Look,' he whispered, pointing. 'They told me they would be paid to be blood donors if they passed their medicals.'

Jane looked where his finger was pointing and saw this was indeed the waiting area for blood donors. She also saw there were a lot of them, perhaps over twenty counting the black shirted members of the S.S. and, just like the S.S., they all looked in their prime. A passing nurse was leaving the waiting room, her eyes fixed on the screen of a computer tablet as she passed Copeland and Jane. Jane put a hand on her forearm and gave her a smile when she looked up. Copeland realised he had failed to notice how innocent Jane could look with her curly daffodil-yellow hair haloing her round, rosy cheeked face as she smiled at the nurse and looked at her with her big, child-like blue eyes. Butter wouldn't melt in her mouth, thought Copeland. No, not innocent, thought Copeland, it's more like naive. No, more than naive... more like... ***Bloody hell, Copeland! She's making herself look as vulnerable as a*** *puppy so she can plug information out of this nurse!* Oh, I see, thought Copeland.

'You seem to have a lot of young blood donors, nurse,' smiled Jane, still with a hand on the nurse's forearm.

The nurse looked at Jane. She smiled. She looked at Copeland. She nodded. 'Only the best,' she said. 'I see you've brought your old dad with you to show him the quality of the young, fit stock we harvest the blood from. So don't worry, your dad will be getting blood from the very best.'

Vampires! thought Copeland, I wonder if Tom Benson knows about...

The nurse laughed and placed a hand on Jane's shoulder. 'Listen to me!' she chuckled. 'I make it sound like vampires don't I! But I'm sure you've read the pamphlet so you know there's nothing, you know, like, spooky about it.'

'Pamphlet?' enquired Jane.

'From reception,' said the nurse, concerned. 'Don't tell me they forgot to give you one when they knew you were here about the plasma therapy? Typical! Now, if you don't mind...'

Jane gave the nurse's forearm a final squeeze, widened her smile and said, 'Thank you for your help, nurse,' and they watched the nurse continue down the corridor.

Jane looked at Copeland. She wasn't looking quite so innocent, naive or vulnerable any longer and her wide blue eyes had narrowed. 'We need to get a pamphlet,' she said and was off.

The woman at the reception desk had been replaced by a man who happily handed over a pamphlet to Jane and another to 'her dad who looked like he needed it sooner rather than later' and with a pamphlet each they sat in the old two door Fiat 500 and read.

As soon as he had put his spectacles on, Copeland instantly baulked. 'Ten thousand pounds!'

Jane was equally stunned. 'And that's every month if you want it to keep working, Sir. Oh, hang on... It says that includes overnight stay in a top hotel with dinner if you're flying in for the treatment and if not you can get the tenth treatment free.'

'It's a bargain then!' huffed Copeland. 'If I'm reading this right, Jane, they take blood from these young healthy people, extract the plasma from it and inject it into old people?'

'Old, rich people,' Jane said, still reading. 'It says here that people feel twenty years younger and tests have shown the heart and other organs work better too. What's this asterisk mean? Aha! The small print at the bottom says these effects have been found in tests on mice.'

Copeland took off his glasses and held them closer to the small print. 'It also says the blood plasma injections may cause nausea and vomiting for up to a few days. This sounds great! Ten thousand quid to get injected with someone else's blood plasma and then you throw up for days! I don't even like needles!' He replaced his glasses into his top pocket and looked at Jane. 'You're not listening, are you, Detective?'

'Pardon? Oh, yes, needles... Tests on mice, Sir!'

Copeland hoped Jane would expand on that a little.

She looked at him. Her curly blonde head began nodding. 'The lab, Sir... The mice... What if they were trying to get around the injections..? Sir! We need to go and see Dr. Lynn!'

Copeland thought he would have a go at being enthusiastic as well. He raised two fists to shoulder height, groaned, and monosyllabically said, 'Damn it, Detective Sadler, you're darn right! Let's go!'

'Er, OK, Sir. Right. Yes. OK. But before we go to Dr. Lynn's house shall we get some proper food?'

ERICA.

Sharp pains from her left shoulder and arm felt somehow distant to Erica as she lay on her side with Giles Lord on top of her. As Giles' kiss almost reached her cheek sheer revulsion had kicked in and she had baulked back, but his slavering lips had followed her. Then the coffee shop's window had sprayed at her and his head had crashed into hers and knocked her sideways. The journey to the floor had seemed to last an age. Memories of her happy childhood had faded into the slow death of her mother, the abuse by a step father who had told her it was 'all natural and girls used to get married at twelve', to the guilt, to being in trouble at school, to being told she was attention seeking when she confided in a teacher, to running away just after her fourteenth birthday and living on the London streets.

She lay on the coffee shop floor with something warm and sticky stinging her eyes, making her wince. Her head hurt on both sides, from where the head of Giles had crashed into her and from where the other side had banged onto the floor with his full, dead weight on top of her. In a daze, Erica told herself she was a survivor. She had survived the London streets, she had survived the one and only night she had stayed in a hostel when all her belongings had been stolen, she had survived living on charity outside the supermarket, never knowing if hunger or cold would take her first and wishing whichever one it was it would come soon. But that was then, and right now she lay on the floor desperately wanting to live. She knew from the screaming all around her that something sudden and terrible had happened, just like the night when she and a friend had injected that cheap heroin and she had been the only one to survive. She managed a smile. Maybe she would go to hospital again, just like when they found her beside her dead friend. That was the first time her body had been clean in two years and, when she left the safety of the hospital in clean second hand clothes, it was the first time she had got a job.

Erica could hear a siren. At first it was a long way away. Then, suddenly, it was closer. Was she in an ambulance? The siren faded into a grey mist. She woke again to see a light being shone into her eyes as someone said, 'She's not in there. Definitely concussion – could be a haemorrhage. Forget the wounds, get her down for a brain scan.'

Erica saw fluorescent lights flashing above her head. Was she on a trolley? The bright lights reminded her of her first job, working in a so-called 'Gentleman's Club' and earning moderately good money for a few years but paying most of it in rent to her employer. A machine whirred around her head as she tried to recall Jeremy Lynn coming into the club, telling her he did not want a lap-dance or any of the 'extras', but wanted someone willing to use their charms to steal information from a scientist. She remembered how she thought it sounded like a good deal, and how she'd be doing more or less the same as she did at the club but with a steady income.

As she was wheeled away from the brain scanner she felt herself rising, either to her judgement day or in a lift. Erica laughed and cried simultaneously as she remembered eating dinner with Jeremy and Dr. Lynn while their handsome young manservant waited on them and Dr. Lynn explained what she would have to do and she had shrugged and signed the contract Jeremy presented to her. She wondered if she would have signed the contract if she had known then that her signature would result in her head being scanned after someone had just tried to kill her. Her eyes shot open. Yes! Tried to kill **her**! Dr. Carter was dead, Reema and her family were dead, snotty-cow Miss Piggy Alison was missing, the man opposite her in the coffee shop was shot dead... But he shouldn't have been should he? Erica was not too concussed to realise it should have been her.

COPELAND AND JANE HAVE A VISITOR.

After chicken and bacon rolls eaten in the car, Jane checked into the hotel near the M4 junction and got a room on the same floor as Copeland. They had both decided a quick shower and change of clothes was in order before they visited the home of Dr. Lynn to confront her about what the research lab was really doing.

Copeland was just about to get in the shower when there was a knock on his door. Curious and with a towel around his waist he went to answer it. It was Detective Jane Harper, spruced and ready in a new black trouser suit and white blouse. In the scheme of things, Copeland didn't think he had spent all that long sitting on the comfy toilet seat. He did not like the disdainful look Jane was giving him for not being ready, or the way she was staring unbelievingly at his stomach protruding over the top of the towel. He backed quickly away and sidled back into the bathroom, quite glad he had used the fresh air spray. Beyond the rapidly closed bathroom door he heard Jane shout, 'I'll just wait then, shall I Sir?'

He was as quick as he could be and did not even bother rubbing his 'Silver Glory' colouring into his hair or put the moisturiser on the eczema rash on the bottom of his foot, but he had not expected Jane to be so speedy and had anticipated getting dressed in his bedroom. Holding a towel around his waist he stepped out of the bathroom. He stepped back again.

That draught was cold, Copeland! She's left the bloody door open! Bravely ignoring the draught from the hotel corridor, Copeland padded out of the bathroom, turned left and shut the door. He heard a click behind him. 'Hands up, Comrade Larry,' said an all too familiar voice.

'I'd rather not, Vasily,' said Copeland. 'I've only got this towel and I definitely don't have a gun. Just a second. You don't either. You're just clicking my light switch again aren't you?' Clutching the towel, Copeland turned round. He said, 'Nope. You really do have a gun this time.' He put his hands up.

'Comrade,' said Vasily after a moment, 'if you do not pick that towel up again then I really will shoot you.' Copeland grinned sheepishly and picked the towel up. He walked slowly down the short hallway past the bathroom towards the bedroom and to Vasily sitting on the armchair in the corner, with the reading lamp on the table beside him still very clearly plugged in. Jane was kneeling on the floor at the foot of the bed, with her hands up, a few feet away from Vasily and the barrel of his pistol.

Vasily pointed the pistol at Copeland then pointed it at the floor. Copeland got the message. He knelt by the side of the bed. He glanced at Jane. She was staring wide eyed at Vasily. *Perhaps she's wondering why he's still wearing that raincoat and a hat...* suggested the inner voice.

Vasily exhaled slowly. 'Comrade Larry, I must throw caution to the breeze, as you English say, and ask if you have found my little niece Dominika yet?'

'Well...' said Copeland.

Vasily's eyes narrowed, 'Perhaps I should visit your daughter, Comrade Larry. Yes?'

'We know where she is,' Jane quickly said. 'She's living in the Lyme Bay area and we have people checking CCTV footage against the photos of her on the flash drive you gave Inspector Copeland.'

Clever girl, thought Copeland. That should buy us a few days.

'Hmm,' said Vasily, pointing the gun at Jane. 'And where is my flash drive with the information about her now?'

Copeland answered, 'It's in my jacket pocket, Vasily.'

Vasily's arm straightened and the gun pointed closer to Jane's head. 'Do not play games, old friend, or I will blow your pretty blonde friend's curly head off. I have already checked your suit. It is not there.'

'It's in his other suit,' said Jane quickly. Seemingly untroubled by the pistol nozzle an arm's length from her forehead, she turned to Copeland. 'Remember, Sir? You put a fresh suit on this morning. You left the other suit with the flash drive in it at the other hotel.'

Clever girl, thought Copeland. She has the flash drive up her sleeve, that's why her hands are straight up like that, in case it falls out.

Waving the gun slowly up and down Vasily said, 'I fear, Comrade, that I have sent you on a wild duck chase. I came here to get the flash drive back, hoping you had not looked at it yet. I no longer want my dear niece to be found. But it seems you already almost have. So now I will have to kill you both. Sorry. Oh, yes, I mean thank you.'

Damn! He'll never believe us now if we tell him we haven't even looked at his flash drive yet! We're in trouble, Copeland!

Copeland glanced at Jane. She mouthed the word 'sorry.' He did eyebrow gestures to get her to get the flash drive from her sleeve. She mouthed the word 'what?'

Er, Copeland... It really IS still in that other suit...

Copeland looked back at Vasily's gun. He thought quickly. He was double o seven, wasn't he? He could get out of tight spots like this.

That's it Copeland! Do what James Bond would do!

Copeland said, 'Please don't shoot us, Vasily.'

'Why not?' asked Vasily.

Copeland! Goldfinger! Or maybe it was Thunderball! Who cares? The laser was going to split James Bond in half!

Copland said, 'Er, well if you shoot us, Vasily, then... Well, it might hurt... And we would just get replaced by other agents, like double o eight.'

Blimey, Copeland, you cut that close!

Vasily thought about this. 'Then I'll kill them also.'

Damn! Did Goldfinger think of that?

Jane sighed. 'Mr. Vasily, Sir, can you shoot me first please. My arms are killing me.' Vasily smiled, nodded, tilted his head, closed an eye and looked along the top of the barrel. He started to squeeze the trigger. 'But,' said Jane, 'maybe we can help each other? Perhaps we could make sure all the information about your niece Dominika gets accidentally lost? We can negotiate a fair price for our services. You may not get a better offer from our replacements and, sooner or later, someone will locate your niece before you can kill them. So what's it going to be? It's either my deal or no deal.'

Vasily's eyes narrowed as he stared at Jane. He sat back in the chair. The pistol's barrel sagged. He said, 'Very well. I will not look a gift horse in the teeth. Shall we say five thousand pounds?'

Copeland! Haggle! He offered you twenty thousand to help him last time! Copeland was too scared to tell his erstwhile conscience the minor current difference was that

Vasily had an actual, real gun this time. 'OK,' said Copeland. 'I'm in for five thousand.'

'Sir! I was going to haggle!' protested the kneeling Jane a few feet away.

Vasily looked at them both. He looked at them both again. He laughed. It was the laugh of someone enjoying the misfortune of others. He said, 'In return for a mere five thousand pounds you will lose the flash drive and make sure anyone looking for her on the CCTV footage stops looking. I do not ever want Dominika found. The day she is found will be the day your daughter dies, Larry, and it will be your fault she will be kicking up the... those little yellow flowers... kicking up the daffodils!'

Copeland tried doing the eye-narrowing thing too as he said, 'Forgive me for bringing it up, Vasily, but I thought it was your mission in life to find this niece of yours, for your sister.'

Vasily laughed his hollow laugh again. 'Ha! I have no sister! It **was** my mission to find Dominika, but I have learned that once that mission is over then I am reassigned.'

'Ah! To the salt mines of Siberia,' said Copeland.

'Exactly, my towel wearing kneeling comrade friend. By the way, you need to do something about that stomach, Larry. It looks like you have swallowed a giant egg. Has no-one told you this?'

'I've sort of heard it,' sighed Copeland. 'So, let me get this straight, Vasily, you wanted me to find Dominika so you might get back in the Kremlin's good books but now you find out your transfer to Siberia is on hold until you finish finding all your red cuckoo slumber agents?'

'Yes, Comrade... Dominika is the last. She was the best. The bee's ankles. But wait! How did you know they were called our red cuckoos? Do you have a spy inside the SVR? Perhaps in the Kremlin itself, eh?'

Copeland felt his heart pounding behind his man-boobs. He gripped the towel around his waist tighter. He grimaced as he said, 'The truth is, Comrade, I don't actually know which. I just know it's someone really, really high up in the Kremlin. Damn! Now I've already told you too much by letting that information slip as well, Comrade.'

'Hmm... Very well,' said Vasily. 'I will give you the benefit of the snout... So, we have a deal, yes? I give you forty eight hours to return the information about Dominika and make sure she is forgotten. Now I will go for vodka in the hotel bar. Just one for the street. I will give them your room number, Larry.'

Vasily stood. He walked around the kneeling Copeland. He paused. He said, 'One last thing, Comrade Larry.' He pushed the barrel of the gun against the back of Copeland's head. He said, 'HANDS UP!'

'Oh my God!' screamed Jane.

Vasily left, laughing heartily.

TOM AND MARY.

The phrase, 'It was nice bumping into you,' kept popping into Tom Benson's head. Was that the best he could come up with when he had just met the most beautiful woman in the world? The fact that any woman who actually spoke to Tom instantly fell into the category of the most beautiful woman in the world did not occur to him. When the beautiful mystery woman looked into his eyes he was sure she was going to agree to go for coffee, but all she said was she was in a bit of a hurry and, stunned, he picked up her case and handed it back to her before watching her walk hastily away without turning back. With a heavy sigh, Tom plodded off in the other direction, deciding it was time to see if Inspector Lord was back in the police station yet, even though his heart was not really committed to the endeavour anymore now that the aforesaid heart had been stolen by the previously mentioned most beautiful woman in the world. As he plodded and sighed melancholically towards the police station two police cars and several running officers passed him in the opposite direction. Tom briefly thought the Honiton police certainly seemed to take vandalism extremely seriously and were reacting very speedily to catch whoever had thrown that stone through that coffee shop window, but his thoughts soon returned to the face of the new love of his life.

After waiting for nearly two hours on a hard plastic seat in the deserted police station and amusing himself by staring into space, Tom gave up his attempt to confront the young Inspector Lord about his Lordship father's financial treachery, decided he was in danger of missing his train home and trudged off back through the town to the train station. He only just made it in time to catch the train, having been forced to take a detour around the High Street because of the yellow police tape and flashing blue lights. Tom nodded his balding head righteously and suspected Honiton must be one of the quietest towns in the country if the whole police force was swooping down to catch one young hooligan.

Long before Tom Benson had boarded his train, Mary was home in her 'other' home and placing the silver case with the sniper rifle back into the false wall and closing the wooden panel. Two questions were on her mind as she had driven back. One was why the termination of Erica Young had been so suddenly cancelled and, since she had killed young Erica anyway, would she get paid? The other question was who was that charming little man? Every time she thought about his ridiculous 'Nice to have bumped into you' comment she smiled. By the time she had parked outside her house her smile had turned into a sporadic giggle and she had begun wishing she had thrown caution to the wind and agreed to go for coffee with him. Before she turned off the engine she had scolded herself for giggling and having such thoughts and had reminded herself there was no room for humour or personal feelings in her line of work.

Mary soon changed into a flowery dress and went down into Lyme to call in at her 'She Sells Sea Shells' shop. It cheered her up. Her shop manager had just paid two hundred pounds to a tourist for half of a fossilised ichthyosaur head. Mary knew it would sell for at least twenty times that amount. Her satisfaction lasted until she got home and sat with a glass of Chablis watching the early evening news. It told her there had been a shooting in Honiton. She sort of knew that already. There was one dead and several others injured by flying glass. She sort of knew that too. Mary was disappointed the TV did not name the deceased as Erica Young but supposed they would have to inform her family first. She was also surprised when the face of the suspected murderer appeared on the screen. It was a photo taken on someone's phone and the blurry image had clearly been enlarged. Mary leaned forward and squinted at the fuzzy image on the screen. She flopped back into her chair and shouted, 'Damn!' as she flung her wine glass across the room.

The toaster in the communal kitchen never ceased to amaze Tom. Every time he used it he had to clear out the burnt bits of Rizla cigarette paper and swore he would have a strong word with all those responsible for using the toaster to light their joints. As usual, they had turned the toaster dial up as well, and, as usual, Tom's evening meal was baked beans on burnt toast shared with Jesus. As he sat alone at his desk eating, he was telling himself burnt toast did not taste that bad and convincing himself someone in the house probably had a TV licence so it was perfectly legal to log on to the late evening BBC news. All chewing ceased as the news led with a shooting in a coffee shop in Honiton and Tom, aghast, realised there was no stone throwing vandal as he had thought after all! Agog, he watched as the TV screen scenes switched from the scores of police and forensics teams in the High Street and went back to the presenter in the studio, who sternly advised viewers of a sensitive disposition not to watch for the next two minutes. Tom regarded himself as having a semi-sensitive disposition so shut one eye. With the other eye he saw a short montage of mobile phone videos showing the scenes of chaos inside the coffee shop and the ensuing pandemonium in the street outside. The BBC, in its wisdom, was not showing any clips with the merest hint of blood, or the glass-lacerated bystanders or, for that matter, someone's brains splattered across a coffee shop floor. Tom opened his closed eye and started chewing again as the presenter reappeared and told his audience a suspect was already being sought. Tom said, 'Good!' and forked beans into his mouth. The presenter explained the suspect was known to have made enquiries about the whereabouts of the shot victim earlier in the day and several phones had captured the image of the perpetrator in the background, lurking directly across the road from the coffee shop, with some eyewitness claiming to have seen him holding a silver attaché case which police believed contained the sniper rifle. Tom swallowed and said, 'Good!'

'So,' said the news presenter with extra gravitas, 'if you know this callous, cold blooded murderer do not approach him but immediately call the police on the hotline number shown below.'

Tom got a pencil and paper from the desk drawer, ready to jot down the number. He stopped chewing and stared at the face on the screen. Baked beans trickled down his chin. A knock came at his door. 'It's me,' called a voice, and, to clarify, the voice from the other side added, 'It's Jesus.'

Tom's eyes stayed fixed on his laptop screen. 'Er, I'm eating. What can I do for you?'

The hushed voice of Jesus from the other side sounded as if it was coming through the keyhole as it asked, 'Do you know there's a photo of you on the BBC news?'

COPELAND AND JANE VISIT
JEREMY AND DR. LYNN.

Arriving at the Lynn's mock Elizabethan house at the end of the cul-de-sac in the affluent east of Bricknall, Copeland and Jane looked at each other. They raised their eyebrows. 'Nice,' said Copeland.

'I'm surprised it's not bigger, Sir,' commented Jane. 'At least a mansion. Dr. Lynn must be worth a fortune.'

'Hmm,' said Copeland. 'Are you sure you're up for this, Jane? You spent some time throwing up in my hotel toilet after Vasily had held that gun to your head.'

'Fine, Sir,' said Jane, forcing a smile. 'It was the most traumatic experience of my life. The gun, I mean, not seeing you naked when you let go of the towel. Honest.'

'Don't worry, I knew that,' said Copeland with his hand hesitantly hovering above Jane's shoulder. He gave it the lightest tap. 'Listen, Jane, we'll just go back to Dorset tomorrow and get the flash-drive Vasily gave us and just give it back to him.'

'Don't worry, Sir, I won't tell anyone you let it slip about the mole we have in the Kremlin,' Jane said reassuringly as she moved Copeland's hovering hand back onto the steering wheel.

'The mole?' asked Copeland. 'Oh, the double agent! Aha! There isn't one! The name red cuckoos just popped into my head. You know, red sparrow, red cuckoo.' Copeland laughed. 'The Russian FSB will waste months trying to find a double agent now.'

Jane chuckled. 'Let's go and see Dr. Lynn before we miss dinner and supper too, Sir.'

The door was answered by a tall, thin man with sharp features beneath his thinning grey hair. He looked at Jane. He looked at Copeland. He shut the door. They knocked again. He opened it again. He wagged a finger in their faces as he haughtily said, 'I've told you people before! I'm not interested in your magazine and if there are only one hundred and forty four thousand people in heaven then I'm not interested in living somewhere the size of Bolton! Have you been to Bolton? Jesus H. Christ! Er, no offence.'

Jane produced her warrant card and, after some rummaging, Copeland produced his plastic driving licence and said, 'I wondered which suit I'd left that in.'

Jeremy Lynn changed demeanour. 'Aha! Copeland!' he exclaimed. 'Heard all about you from the wife, dear boy. She described you to a tee, you poor old chap. Do come in.' He turned to Jane. 'And we have a very nice antique bureau in the study you might like to examine later, young Inspector Lord. Come in.'

'Detective Sadler,' said Jane as Jeremy Lynn disappeared down the short hallway, in which Jane and Copeland waited and shuffled their feet for a few moments before Jeremy reappeared and cheerily said, 'Finch is getting us coffee and biscuits or, if we're lucky, a few muffins. Come into the sitting room.' He was gone again, but this time they followed him through the door on the left and into the lounge.

Jane and Copeland sat on a pink sofa facing the stone fireplace and Jeremy sat on a sky-blue one at right angles to them. Both sofas clashed equally well with the lime green carpet and beige walls.

'Er, is Dr. Lynn here?' Copeland asked Jeremy Lynn from the far end of the sofa.

Jeremy's brow furrowed. 'It's Wednesday,' he said.

Copeland felt Jane's eyes glance at him. They waited. 'And is Wednesday significant in some way, Mr. Lynn?' asked Jane.

Jeremy nodded meaningfully. 'She spends it in her new lab in the basement,' he said.

Jane asked, 'New lab, Sir?'

'Please try to keep up, young lady. I'll repeat myself, shall I?' He spoke more slowly to Jane. 'In the new lab in the basement. Not here. Over in her place where she has her office. Where all those people who fly into Heathrow go to get their faces tucked and buttocks lifted. To be honest I don't know why they spend all their money trying to look good. I mean, what's the point? I don't bother and look at me. I'm over fifty, you know.'

Copeland and Jane glanced at each other. Copeland smiled benignly at Jeremy and said, 'The clinic told us she had already left for home, Mr. Lynn.'

Blimey, Copeland! That's a first. You being tactful and not mentioning she had not been there all day.

Jeremy looked at Copeland as if he was stupid. 'She likes to get the bus,' he told Copeland as if the news usually appeared on the front of the Daily Mail.

'The bus, Sir?' asked Jane.

'Big red thing with seats inside. Yes, the bus, young lady. Please listen more carefully. She says it helps her think,' Jeremy said. 'You know, think about the trousers.'

'Trousers?' asked Jane.

'Do I have to repeat everything? Yes! Trousers!' snapped Jeremy, leaning forward and gesturing a bony index finger as if giving a lecture. 'I don't understand all this science stuff. I'm just a named partner. What do solicitors know about science, eh? Nothing after an aeroplane has hit them on the head, that's what. But I do know she has a lab where they look at jeans inside cages. And they have jeans for gnomes too. Don't ask me why they cut them up.'

Copeland rubbed his forehead. 'We're here about the...'

'No! Not just gnomes! Genie gnomes!' exclaimed Jeremy as if a mist had been lifted from his eyes. 'Magic genies inside little prison cages. They have them down in that lab. They slice them up.'

Tom Benson would love this guy, Copeland...

'Ahem,' said Jane. 'Excuse me, Mr. Lynn. But do you mean Dr. Lynn has a lab in the basement which is looking at genes inside cells and is splicing genomes?'

Jeremy Lynn's raised finger went left. It went right. He said, 'Possibly. Now you mention it, Inspector Lord. That indeed may well be what Lynn has tried to explain to me a few times. Oh, here's the coffee. And one of Finch's special home-made muffins each, I see! Well done young Finch!'

In open neck white shirt, black trousers and very shiny shoes, Finch had entered and stood with a tray of two espressos in one hand and a tray of small plates with blueberry muffins on in the other. Copeland had not heard much since the muffins entered the room and hovered near his end of the pink sofa. Neither did he hear the slim, dark haired, very clean shaven man called Finch say, 'Dr. Lynn has just returned, Sir. I believe she has just popped up to her bedroom to freshen up before joining you. And you left your phone in the kitchen again, Sir.'

'Excellent, Finch, my good man,' said Jeremy. 'Listen, old chap, let's just give everyone a plate and a muffin and our guests their coffee shall we?'

Finch did as ordered and Copeland learned what hell was like. He watched Jeremy bite into his muffin. In one hand Copeland held a saucer with an espresso and in the other a small plate with a blueberry muffin. Hell was not having a third hand to enjoy either. He glanced at Jane. He could tell she was at least in purgatory too as she looked around to work out where she could put the cup or plate.

Barefoot Dr. Lynn entered wearing a blue blouse and some jeans with a 'j'. She did not speak. She simply flicked aside her hair as she nodded to Copeland, looked to the heavens and walked between the sofas. She fetched a small table and placed it in front of Copeland and Jane, gave them a smile, and sat herself next to her husband, tucking one leg under her and holding the shin. 'I had an investors meeting,' she said with another flick of her hair.

Copeland put his coffee on the little table. He nodded his thanks to Dr. Lynn, smiled and lifted the muffin. A third of it disappeared without further ado. He decided all his work into researching Uroboros Rejuvenation Ltd. was spot on and the table-providing Dr. Lynn was indeed a saint. The blueberry muffin was just right and, better still, there were more than enough blueberries to exceed his 'five-a-day' fruit.

While Dr. Lynn smiled enigmatically and Jane waited for Copeland to swallow, Jeremy said, 'Inspector Copeland and Inspector Lord are here about the magic genies in your lab, Evie.'

Copeland said nothing. He had just taken another bite of the muffin.

Evie Lynn sighed and smiled weakly at Jane and Copeland. 'An aeroplane hit him on the head,' she said.

'He told us that!' said Jane, wide eyed. 'But how did he survive?'

Dr. Lynn held up her hand. 'It was a model plane, but it still did some damage.'

'Who to, Evie?' asked Jeremy Lynn.

Jane nodded her understanding and put her muffin down. She sipped her espresso and waited for Copeland to take the lead. When he took another mouthful of his muffin she gave up and asked, 'We know it wasn't a new Viagra, so what were Carter and his team **really** making in that lab, Dr. Lynn?'

Lyn's smile faded. She said, 'You wouldn't understand even if I told you, Detective Sadler.'

'Try me,' said Jane. 'It wouldn't be something to do with blood plasma, would it, Doctor?'

'I understand,' replied Dr. Lynn, shuffling, 'that as well as Jonathan Carter, Wang Linpeng is now also dead, along with Reema Sharma and her family, and Alison Taylor is still nowhere to be found. As I told you in my office, Inspector Copeland, no one except myself and Carter's team knew what they were doing and also knew where the lab was, so the question you should be asking is who found out and hired a professional killer to execute my team?'

'Axminster,' said Jeremy.

'What?' said a startled Dr. Lynn, turning to her husband.

'The lab was in Axminster,' Jeremy said as if he was telling his staring wife something she did not already know. Jeremy touched a finger to the side of his nose. 'Axminster was always the postmark on the jaffa bags Erica Young sent the flash drives in.'

'Jiffy bags,' mumbled Copeland, putting a hand to his mouth to excuse himself for speaking with a full mouth. He swallowed. 'I think you mean jiffy bags, Mr. Lynn,' Copeland said, putting the remainder of the muffin between his lips and picking up the plate with Jane's muffin on.

Jeremy bowed his head to Copeland. 'I stand corrected. Thank you, old chap.'

Dr. Lynn's forehead was resting in the palm of her hand. She shook her head and looked at Jane. 'I'll explain about Erica in a moment,' she groaned. 'But I suppose the location of the secret lab was not as secret as I thought.'

'And,' Jane pointed out, glancing at her muffin going into Copeland's mouth, 'we don't know if Carter's team or members of their families told anyone, and the criminals who delivered the bonobos knew, and the workers who did the alterations for the bonobos knew...'

Jeremy laughed loudly. He wagged a finger up and down. 'Jonathan Carter knew,' he said, ending with the finger pointing at Jane.

Evie Lynn shook her head again. 'We know that, Jeremy,' she sighed.

Jeremy laughed again. 'Boring bugger, he was. Remember he came here once, Evie? All your new Viagra team did. For dinner. I think it was lamb or beef or – No! It was a whole salmon. Two glasses of wine and he was boring me with how brilliant he was – at everything – and how he made those appetite suppressant pills. Carter, not the salmon. Yes! It was salmon!'

Dr. Lynn clenched her teeth, sunk her head and clutched at her scalp. After a deep breath she turned to Finch, who seemed to be dumb struck watching how fast Copeland could consume a second muffin, and ordered, 'Finch, get me a notepad and pen.'

Dr. Lynn smiled an embarrassed smile at Jane. Jeremy looked vacantly around, rubbing his hands together like a schoolboy who had just got the right answer to one plus one. Jane stared sceptically back at Evie Lynn. Copeland sat with cheeks puffed out like a hungry hamster. Finch returned with a notepad and pen and handed them to Dr. Lynn with a little bow and a 'Ma'am.' Dr. Lynn scribbled furiously. Finch disappeared and reappeared with a plate of two more muffins. He held them in front of Copeland. Copeland stared at one. He stared at the other. Jeremy leaned forward and inappropriately patted Jane's knee as he asked, 'Would you like to see the antique bureau now, Inspector Lord?'

Jane looked at him. Copeland had a little choking fit. Finch slapped his back. Copeland winced and gave Finch a thumbs-up. Evie Lynn tore off the sheet from the notepad and handed it to Jane. Jane glanced at it. Her jaw dropped. She held it out for Copeland to read. He said, 'I can't read that without my glasses,' and went back to studying which of the two new muffins to have. He chose another blueberry, saving the chocolate one as afters – but staring at it to make sure it did not go anywhere and ignoring what Dr. Lynn was saying to Jane until she said, 'So,' as if in conclusion and raising her eyebrows as Copeland lifted the chocolate muffin from the plate, 'you have everything you need to check it out, Officers. You'll see everyone's doing it these days. Now, if you don't mind, I need an early night. Finch, take this notepad and pen and see our guests out.'

The street lights went laboriously past as Jane clasped the paper Dr. Lynn had given them between her hands and her stomach. Copeland had glanced at the sheet of paper Dr. Lynn had scrawled on. He was in a good mood. The chocolate muffin had been excellent. Finch was Copeland's new best friend. 'Brilliant muffins. Good cook, that Finch bloke,' Copeland said to underline his new friendship and whistled along with Mozart's Eine kleine Nachtmusik.

Having resisted the head shaking, eye rolling and heavy sighing for far too long, Jane did all three at once as she held up the paper Dr. Lynn had given them and tried to read it again as the street lamps went by. She wanted to get back to the hotel and read it properly and was annoyed Copeland was choosing this time, of all times, to stick to the speed limit. She gave up trying to read what Dr. Lynn had written and, through gritted teeth, asked, 'I'm not sure if you were listening, Sir, but do you believe what Dr. Lynn said?'

Pausing his whistling, Copeland looked across at Jane with a deep frown. 'Are you nuts, Detective? Of course I don't believe her. She's just made the word up! What the hell is senolytics? See? I heard just fine. I'm always completely focused! Did I just go through that light on red? Never mind. No harm done. Pinocchio would have been proud of the lies Dr. Lynn just told us. Senolytics? It's as big a porky-pie as the one she told me about a new sort of Viagra. You may have thought I wasn't listening and distracted by the muffins, but it was just my pretence so she let her guard down.'

'So what do you think about Dr. Lynn having to send Erica Young to the lab to spy for her, Sir?'

'Did she tell us that? Ah, whatever,' said Copeland as they finally arrived back in the underground car park of their Slough hotel. 'It can all wait until later, Jane. It's time we had something decent to eat.'

MARY BLACK.

Methodically cleaning her guns and counting her ammunition had calmed Mary down. She had done it so many times it was now a type of meditation, where her mind could switch off entirely and float into serenity. It was the calm, emotionless state her years of conditioning in the Moscow training academy had trained her for. She swept up the remnants of her hurled wine glass and smiled to herself. The shards of broken glass reminded her of her last training mission. She had been tasked with the elimination of a nasty Colombian drug dealer who was trying to take over the heroin trade of a good patriotic Russian drug dealer. The Colombian's tight security had prevented her smuggling any sort of weapon into the Los Angeles hotel where she was spending an intimate week with him, so she had improvised with a champagne glass and left him and his two bodyguards with their jugulars pumping blood over the previously very nice carpet. After that, all she had to do to be fully accepted as a Red Cuckoo was to kill the friend she had spent the last four years training with. Mary had found killing her fried Katarina a difficult thing to do. Katarina was almost as good as she was and had almost got the better of her. It had taken a double-ricochet shot to hit dear Katarina in the back of her head. Happy days, thought Mary as she emptied the broken glass from the dust pan into her waste bin.

With a new glass filled, Mary put the twenty four hour news on her TV. The face of the little balding man with the cheap plastic spectacles was there and the TV informed her he had been identified as Thomas Benson. Police were ruling out terrorism and working on the theory the murderer had a personal grudge against the unnamed, murdered police officer, though police were refusing to confirm this was the same Thomas Benson who had been previously linked to the murders of two Russian gangsters. Mary laughed as she thought it was highly unlikely that someone who ended up on their backside after the slightest collision in the street could be some sort of assassin, then she realised what she had just heard. Murdered police officer? Really? Mary felt annoyance growing inside her. She took a deep breath. When she had been hired by Atticus to kill Erica Young there had been no mention that Miss Young was an undercover police officer! And why did the police think this little Thomas Benson had a personal grudge against Erica Young? Mary turned her attention back to the TV. It was now reporting that a paramedic had said the shot must have killed the police officer instantly and he would not have felt a thing. Mary sat bolt upright. He? He! The dead police officer was a he? Mary shrugged and relaxed back into the chair. This time she resisted throwing her full wine glass across the room. Since the contract on Erica Young had been cancelled it made little difference whether she was alive or dead. Whoever she had killed was irrelevant. But what was still relevant, just as much as it had been when she had seen the face of Thomas Benson on the news earlier, was that Thomas Benson had seen her face when she had hauled him up from the pavement. He had seen her silver attaché case too. He was a liability. Mary did not like liabilities. Liabilities were best if they were removed. But in this case there was a problem. Mary quite liked

Thomas Benson. She had decided he was cute. That made things awkward. She had a rule about killing people she liked. She always tried to make their death a painless one.

COPELAND AND DETECTIVE JANE SADLER.

Copeland loved it when a plan came together. And over dinner at the hotel, he had come up with a foolproof plan. One part of the plan involved Jane being in her hotel room, busily working on his laptop, checking the information on the web sites Dr. Lynn had scribbled down on the piece of paper she had handed to them. Copeland fulfilled his part of his plan by sitting at the hotel bar and playing it safe by ordering a second bottle of the ever-reliable Cabernet Sauvignon. It was not as if he was not mentally active. His mind buzzed with mathematical exactness as he gave a rating of seven point four to the chips he had eaten with his steak.

He spotted Jane entering the far end of the bar, looking her usual effervescent self. Copeland reluctantly asked for a second wine glass which was placed on the bar next to him just as Jane leaped onto the bar stool and flipped open the laptop. She put her hand over the glass as Copeland went to pour. She shook her curly blonde hair and said, 'No wine for me.' Copeland inwardly smiled, then frowned as she added, 'I'll have a double brandy... No, make it a treble! It's all bloody well true, Sir!'

Copeland stared at her. He turned, emptied his wine glass and stared at her again. 'Listen, Detective Sadler, we went through this in the car on the way back. It's all nonsense. If this was true I'd know about it. Hell! **Everyone** would know about it.'

Since they were virtually the only two people in the bar, the barman had already placed a large brandy in front of Jane before she screwed her face at Copeland and with some sarcasm said, 'Of course, Sir. Just like **everyone** knows eating lots of fruit and vegetables, limiting red meat, getting exercise, avoiding alcohol and not smoking is good for them too.'

Copeland reflected on his steak and chips, his second bottle of red, needing a rest on the way from the car park and the cigar he had just treated himself to on the patio. He filled his wine glass. 'What's your point, Jane?'

'People have to *want* to know things before they know them, even when it's staring them in the face... Sir.'

Copeland noticed she was looking at his stomach, which was doing its usual superb impression of a basketball. He shrugged. He shook his head. He rolled his eyes. To add emphasis, he tutted. 'The internet can say anything,' he pointed out resignedly.

'Look,' Jane encouraged, clicking and pointing at the laptop screen. 'It used to be resveratrol developed by Sirtris Pharmaceuticals, but one of the big boys bought them and killed them off in 2013...'

'Aha! More murders, eh?' grinned Copeland sarcastically as he peered at the screen. 'Hmm... It says red grapes are a good source of natural resveratrol. Excellent!' He took large swig of his Cabernet.

Jane sighed and downed her brandy. She had suspected it was going to be a hard sell and knew the brandy would help, at least marginally. 'Now it's mostly all about senolytics – drugs that get rid of senescent cells.'

'I see. Senescent cells, eh?' repeated Copeland, staring at the screen. 'What does senescent mean?'

'Old! Like senile!' Jane snapped. 'Bodies get rid of them naturally until they can't anymore. Senotherapy is the new Holy Grail, Sir! It keeps bodies younger for longer. All those old age aches and pains, even heart disease, arthritis... You name it! All that stuff you get when you're over sixty – no offence, Sir – it can all be held off for another twenty years. How much will that save the NHS, Sir, if people don't need treatment for another twenty years? How much will American insurance companies save?'

Copeland scanned down the screen. 'It says that's just in mice, Detective Sadler. It's about as real as waving a magic wand. It's just quackery.'

Jane replaced the screen with another. 'What about this then, Sir? It's called mTOR. The R stands for rapamycin, a drug originally developed as an immunosuppressant for transplant patients.'

Copeland read a little until he said, 'That one worked on worms. Brilliant!'

'And this U.S. company,' Jane pointed at a new screen, 'are marketing something in a couple of months time using an mTOR inhibitor and it doesn't have to go through trials because the US Food and Drug Administration already regards the ingredients as safe. And this company in Florida, Ponce De Leon Health, is about to start selling one called Rejuvant.'

Increasingly apathetic, Copeland read. His brow furrowed. 'It's being sold as a health supplement? Oh, it works for worms **and** mice. Brilliant!' He stopped reading, suddenly stunned. He blurted, 'How effing much? Just for one packet?'

Laughing, Jane showed him another screen. 'Another idea dates back to 2005 with Thomas Rando at Stanford University. Stanford and Harvard have been successful with GDF11 studies.'

Just don't ask, Copeland, said the trusty inner voice, which, like Copeland himself, was losing the will to live. They took more notice when Jane enthusiastically said, 'A 2017 trial with a company called Ambrosia in Washington DC was charging people eight thousand dollars – just to take part in the trial!'

'Eight thousand? Okay...' groaned Copeland, 'What's GDF11?'

Jane's eyes lit up. 'Growth differentiation factor eleven,' she replied. 'It's found in young blood, or, more accurately, in the blood plasma of younger people. Younger people like the English synchronised swimming team, Sir!' She pumped a fist in the air.

Copeland stared at her before pouring the last of the bottle into his glass, swallowing it, wiping his lips and muttering, 'There's a lot of money in this staying young lark, isn't there Jane?'

'Not sure it helps us find out who hired a contract killer though, Sir.'

'No, it doesn't, Detective. And, the question is, if all these companies are starting to make these rejuvenation pills, why bother hiring a contract killer to bump off Jonathan Carter and his team?'

6. Thursday, March 21st.

COPELAND AND JANE.

A seed of despondency grew in Detective Jane Sadler as she tossed and turned restlessly until dawn. She got up and scoured through the suspects' manila folders Wendy Miller had given them. She hoped to find something but found only hopelessness. At breakfast, she looked over Copeland's shoulder at the subtitled TV news. It showed clips of the murder of a police officer the day before in Honiton and Jane's dark mood submerged into full blown depression. She read the subtitles on the silent TV and learned how the 'young and brilliant' Detective Inspector Lord had been callously shot by someone named Thomas Benson. *Him again*, thought Jane, recognising the culprit's face as one that had appeared on wanted posters just after she rejoined the force. Jane tried to start a conversation by asking who would want to kill Giles Lord but Copeland raised an eyebrow and ended the conversation by replying, 'Who wouldn't?'

By the time Copeland finished helping himself to the self-serve breakfast, Jane had seen the news clips re-run three times and had sunk into the depths of despair. Her mood of desolation continued to worsen and worsen and by the time Copeland started the car she felt a little bit on the glum side. She did not speak until they were over halfway back to Kilmington to retrieve the flash drive to give back to Colonel Vasily Goraya before he became less friendly and shot Jane, Copeland or Copeland's daughter Emily, or possibly all three.

Copeland had been quiet for different reasons. First he had woken up halfway through the night and stared at the inside of his eyelids trying to get a thought floating on one side of his brain to connect with a thought on the other. He knew he had heard someone say something which fitted with something someone else had said, and once he joined the mental dots the whole case would become as clear as a mountain day with some early morning mist, but he could not get the two nebulous memories to combine before he drifted back to sleep. He got up still trying to put the memories together and his sense of unease was only soothed by the comfy toilet seat. His contemplative quietness soon returned when he went down to breakfast and was confronted by the variety of things the buffet breakfast offered his plate. He was particularly enjoying the fried black pudding when Jane poked his shoulder and pointed to the TV screen behind him. At first he was tempted to tut and shake his head at the sad loss of Giles Lord, then he was tempted to burst into laughter when Tom Benson was named as a stone cold killer (again), but when he noticed a small, slight figure with a grey hair-bun shuffling out of the coffee shop at the edge of the screen (and his inner voice shouted, ***Bloody hell, Copeland!***) Copeland went quiet for a whole new reason. He stayed that way for some time before he went back to his room to get the car key, submerged his face in a sink of cold water and told himself such things were not his concern anymore.

Watching the turn off for Yeovil go by, Jane stared out of the passenger window as she groaned, 'We're not getting anywhere are we, Sir?'

'We've just passed the sign for Yeovil,' Copeland pointed out. Failing to get a much needed laugh he added, 'Dear God!'

'All we know,' Jane said seriously, 'is Carter and the team at the lab were probably working on making some sort of senolytic longevity pill. But it's just like other labs are doing around the world, so why were they targeted?'

Copeland rammed the little Fiat into second gear to get up a gentle hill and said, 'Maybe, they really had cracked this immortality pill lark.'

Again, he waited for a laugh but only got, 'Really, Sir! How many times? Modern senolytic research is no longer about living longer, it's about keeping people healthier before they die. Senolytic remedies help people get rid of old, zombie cells that pump out inflammatory proteins so they can be replaced by new ones. And before you ask, it's nothing to do with zombies, they just call them that. Besides, I read a book. It's amortality, not immortality. People could still be killed.'

Copeland shrugged as much as he could while wedged behind a steering wheel of what he regarded as a Noddy car with a roof. 'You say tom-ayto, I say tom-arto,' he said with a smile.

'I never say tom-ayto,' huffed Jane. 'And what have tomatoes got to do with it? We still have no idea who hired this Dominika hit-woman to kill everyone. We don't even know whether Doctor Carter let her in or if she'd got a key card. What do you think, Sir? I know that's all you've been thinking about since we left Slough.'

Shaking his head, Copeland said, 'I've actually been thinking about whether I agree with these buffet-style breakfasts at these modern hotels. On the one hand you can eat as much as you like but on the other hand they're far too American, aren't they?'

Jane finally laughed. 'I don't usually understand jokes but that's a good one, Sir! As if you'd be thinking about food at a time like this! I know you've really been thinking about who hired this Dominika. The thing is, even if others knew the lab was there, getting in was impossible without a key card and the secrecy regarding what they were actually doing at the lab was pretty tight. The other investors knew they were working on a new drug, but didn't know where the lab was. So, besides Dr. Lynn, only the people who worked at the lab knew both where it was and what they were trying to make. Even her husband thought it was Viagra. She stressed all that yesterday evening.'

'Really?' asked Copeland. 'When?'

'When she was writing down the web sites we should look at to show us senolytics was really a thing – while that Finch fellow was offering you another muffin.'

'Ah, yes. Home-made, you know, from a family recipe. He told me so. Perfection on a plate... I was a bit distracted for just a moment when he was offering me another blueberry one or a chocolate one. I couldn't decide.'

Jane grinned. 'Is that why you had both in the end, Sir?'

Copeland waited for his inner voice to say something sarcastic. It didn't, but he was sure he could hear it chortling. He decided to say something meaningful. He was tempted to suggest they stopped for lunch. It really was nearly lunch time – mainly because he had got up late and spent two hours eating the buffet breakfast while he decided if he liked it or not. Avoiding mentioning food, Copeland hummed thoughtfully. What did he think about who had hired Dominika? He nodded sagely. 'Yes, Detective Sadler, you're right. Whoever hired the killer had to be someone who knew the lab was there and what they were making in it, but also someone who knew they had actually finished. I don't think it's Dr. Lynn who hired our friendly neighbourhood ex-SVR assassin. I don't think she knew about the bonobos and she was shocked to the core when she found out the computers and the data had been destroyed. Then she comes clean about what they were trying to make in the lab. I don't think she knows they had actually finished making their new drug and she had a lot to lose if they didn't finish it... Er, unless she knew they had finished because Erica Young had sent her all the data she needed and she'd decided not to pay them their huge bonuses. Her husband Jeremy doesn't know the difference between a gene and a genie so I think we can rule him out... Unless he's not as stupid as he seems. Nancy Carter was waiting for her husband to get his big bonus before she divorced him, so she had no real motive, and she was quite convincing when she said she had no idea what they were doing in the lab... Unless she's a good actress, which she is... Erica Young was working for Lynn but has no science background so if she went to another company they wouldn't take a receptionist seriously... Unless she'd copied the data onto another flash drive to show them. Which is possible... That leaves Alison Taylor. She couldn't afford to hire an assassin but another company would believe her and maybe hire an assassin to get rid of the opposition... But not before they had tested the drug themselves. Hmmm... I've got it! Let's find Dominika and ask her to tell us who hired her... Jane? You look like you've seen a ghost.'

'Money,' said Jane. 'You're still a genius, Sir. All the motives come back to money. It's all about how much someone could make from this drug or by selling out to a rival. I couldn't sleep last night, Sir.'

'And..?' Copeland said, swiping his thick silver hair back and feeling Jane had somehow just given him a third corner to his unmatched thoughts puzzle. *Oh, come on, Copeland! She's right. It HAS to be about money, what else?* sighed the inner voice. Copeland turned to see Jane furiously tapping and swiping her phone.

'I couldn't sleep, Sir. I looked at all those financial statements again, Sir. Hang on. Yes, it's an insurance company that... Golly gosh! It specialises in life insurance.

This ad says it gives treble for accidental death and... ten times for deaths resulting from a crime.'

Copeland laughed. 'I'll take out a policy before Vasily visits us again then! Oh! You're telling me...'

'I'm just looking at the cost and benefits payable on my phone. She was paying in... let's see. Monthly contribution... Payout.... Times ten. My God, Sir! She's in line to get over ten million!'

Copeland sighed. 'Nancy Carter is a suspect again isn't she?' he groaned.

Jane stared through the windscreen. 'It's like that film with Tom Cruise. You kill lots of people to distract from the fact that only one of them is really the target.'

MARY.

In keeping with her policy of (relatively) painless deaths for people she liked, Mary had rummaged through the big wooden box in the cellar of her 'other' house and found the ideal thing to help Tom Benson move on to the next life, if he happened to believe in one. It was a small canister, no bigger than a bottle of Pepsi. (Other brands are available.) The nerve gas inside it (the canister, not the Pepsi) would render Tom Benson immobile and, after some very interesting hallucinations where his deepest, darkest, most terrifying fears would manifest themselves, he would pass peacefully away. Providing his fear did not cause his heart to explode first of course. Underneath the canister, Mary found a syringe with a liquid version of the gas and momentarily wished she had put that in Wang Linpeng's water bottle at the gym instead of the slow acting, untraceable poison that had left him in agony for days, but then again she had only *quite* liked Wang so maybe the excruciating poison was about right. She recalled that day two months ago when she had bought Wang a coffee after their four stage aerobics class, and he had never bought her one back so, yes, the days of agonizing pain before death was about right to even things out. Tom Benson had not done anything as bad as not get her a coffee when it was his turn like Wang, but he had seen her face after she had just shot some PC Plod when she had tried to kill Erica Young. Something milder for cutie Tom was required.

Mary doubted the police would find Tom Benson as quickly as she had done. It had taken even her until just after dawn. His driving licence, national security information, bank details and his TV licence all said he lived just south of Lincoln, where until recently he'd cohabited with someone name Elizabeth Spencer. The police would be searching for him there, but Mary's advanced hacking algorithms had thrown up an anomaly. A Mr. Thomas Benson had recently had a medical examination at the private Uroboros clinic according to their files, and even though the consent forms seemed to have been signed by someone name John Elton, Mary had crossed referenced the signatures with those of Thomas Benson and confirmed it was undoubtedly the handwriting of the same person.

Arriving at the house where John Elton (Tom Benson) rented a room, Mary got out of her car, pulled the black hood of her black hoody over her wavy auburn hair, slid her hands into her black satin gloves, tucked her favourite Beretta into the back of the belt of her black jeans, pulled the bottom of the hoody over it and picked up the canister of poison gas and plastic tube. Approaching the house, she wondered why the front door was already open. She wondered why a teenage boy was curled up in a sleeping bag in the hall, she wondered why he was surrounded by broken crockery, and she would have wondered why there was a vague smell of cannabis, but there was nothing vague about it. She did not wonder about the price list pinned to the door of 'Apartment C' because she knew how much a good massage cost these days. She found the door marked D, unwound the plastic tubing from around her shoulder, fixed one end to the gas canister and slowly pushed the other end under the door. She stopped when she heard a sound coming from inside. It was a voice. It was chanting, 'Owoom, owoom, owoom...' or something like that. Mary was a little impressed that Tom Benson got up so early to try to meditate and felt glad she had chosen the paralysing, fear inducing nerve gas so that, before he floated off in clouds of mystic lotus blossom to Nirvana, Tom Benson would have the experience of something unique. And what could be a better unique experience than having your immobilised body surrounded by imaginary cobras or vicious rats or being trapped in a confined space under freezing cold water? Mary swallowed hard and remembered being in a box and submerged was her own worst fear, not Tom Benson's. Tom Benson had never been subjected to the training of a Red Cuckoo meted out by 'Uncle' Vasily, so his imagination could never envisage what being doubled up in a box and simultaneously freezing and drowning felt like. No, Tom would just have to put up with the cobras, giant spiders or whatever dark demons emerged from the Pandora's Jar of his mind.

Mary edged the tube further under the door. She made sure the other end was secure on the nozzle of the gas canister and pushed the little red lever across. She heard a faint hissing sound. She waited. The hissing stopped. She pushed the red lever back and pulled the plastic tube back from under the door. She sat on the floor and waited in the silence.

Downstairs, something smashed against a wall. Voices were screaming rather unpleasant words. Children cried. Rap music began to blare. A half dressed male emerged from Room C. Mary watched him from the shadow of her hood. He looked at her sitting on the floor and tried to put his red gown and powdered wig on straight before he rushed down the stairs. Mary put an ear to the door of room D. She waited. She heard a thump. She sighed. She hoped cute little Tom Benson had enjoyed his last moments with the snakes, or spiders of whatever. Satisfied, Mary nodded, crossed herself just in case Tom Benson had been of that bent, stretched her arms, flexed her shoulders, did her early morning facial exercise, ran her fingers through her thick auburn hair and stood, glad it was nearly time to go home and sleep.

ERICA ESCAPES AND LIES LOW.

It had been easy for Erica to slip out of the hospital unnoticed. Despite still feeling semi-concussed, she had intended to keep herself awake all night and leave when the opportunity arose. The night staff had made staying awake less problematic than Erica had anticipated by making sure neither Erica nor anyone else got any sleep by shouting such niceties as, 'Is there a spare bedpan down your end?' and using said bedpan and other metallic percussion objects to create an ongoing cacophony throughout the night. When dawn came and the thoughtful staff crashed the medicine trolley into every available bed-frame along the ward Erica saw her chance and was dressed and gone in minutes. She'd seen no reason to stay. They had cleaned and stitched the wound at the base of her neck from the shard of glass and had dug out all the glass from the wound in her shoulder and Erica was not stupid.

No, Erica was not stupid. She did not know it because no one had ever told her, but she was very far from stupid. Once her mind had begun to clear after her concussion it did not take her long to figure out what was going on. Her fellow workers at the lab were being killed, one by one. Slimy Jonathan Carter was dead, thoughtful Reema was dead, and Miss Piggy Alison Taylor was nowhere to be found. True, Wang Linpeng was supposedly holidaying in Spain and probably not yet dead, unless he had been poisoned before he left, but it didn't take a genius to work out that if future-husband Giles Lord had not leaned forward to kiss her cheek at that exact moment, it would have been her brains and not his that would have ended up splattering her favourite little black dress. She tried not to think about that since she'd had to put the same dress back on to slip out of the hospital and, besides, she had managed to scrape most of the grey gunge off her black faux-leather jacket and zip it up.

It was not far to the cheap hotel and, finding her car just where she had left it, Erica took the car key from her wrist bag and was about to press the unlock button to get the rest of the cash from under the passenger mat when she caught herself mid-action. She put the keys back in her wrist bag and took out her mobile phone instead. (She was glad she had brought her larger size wrist bag.) She lay on her back, extended her arm and took photos of the underside of her car. She moved to each side of the car and to the rear and did the same. She brushed the car-park grit from her bare legs and examined the photographs. She was relieved to not see any photos revealing an explosive device but spotted something she thought should probably not be there. She went to the back of the car to where she occasionally put fuel in and felt underneath the wheel arch. The magnetic device was not hard to pry loose. She knew exactly what it was: a former male 'acquaintance' she had once known in her professional capacity had found one attached to his car when his wife, curious about his frequent cash withdrawals, had hired a private investigator to find out if he was seeing someone else. The device Erica held in her hand was a tracker. She dropped it on the floor and kicked it across the car park. If she needed any more proof that she and the others from the lab were being hunted down, that was it. She briefly considered trying to get a warning message to Wang in Spain but realised she was out in the open and the killer knew where her car was... Which also meant the killer might be in her hotel room waiting for her. Fetching her belongings was out of the question. She was in the driving seat and gone within ten seconds.

As she accelerated out of the car park, Erica considered going to the police, but knew the media were already all over the story of the dead and missing lab workers and the last thing she wanted was to advertise her whereabouts to someone who was trying to kill her. Her first priority was to get as far away as possible from the tracker she had just ripped off her car. Leaving Honiton behind, Erica went on autopilot and soon found herself heading back towards her old flat in Axminster. It was only when she got nearer that it occurred to her that going back to her old flat was not the best idea ever if someone was trying to kill her. She pulled off the road into a farm shop to rest and work out what her options were. She parked in the shade of a tree, well away from the shop and the other vehicles, reclined the driver seat as far as it would go and settled back to regain some much needed sleep.

JANE MEETS MRS. SMITH.

While Copeland trudged up to his Kilmington hotel room to fetch the all important Dominika flash drive to give back to Vasily, Jane passed the note left by Nina saying she had gone to play golf and went into the little three-stool bar where she knew a jug of water would be waiting to quench her thirst. One of the bar stools was already occupied by a woman. She was wearing a red dress made for someone two sizes smaller. Jane presumed this was the woman Copeland and Nina had referred to as Mrs. Smith, a reasonable presumption since there were no other residents currently at the hotel. Not wishing to judge too harshly, the most flattering description of Mrs. Smith that first sprung into Jane's mind was 'heavy set', but she moderated it to 'robust'. Then Jane thought Mrs. Smith reminded her of someone and the temptation to call the lady with the make-up layer and unwashed, dark-rooted strawberry blonde hair 'Miss Piggy' popped into her mind.

Sitting with an empty stool between them, Jane tried not to judge as she pulled back the sleeve of her black jacket, glanced at her watch, glanced sideways at the half empty bottle of Jack Daniels sitting in front of Miss Piggy – Damn! Mrs Smith – and glanced at the half empty half pint glass in Mrs. Smith's hand. It was not half empty for long. This did not seem to be a problem for Mrs. Smith. By the time Jane had got a glass and reached for the water jug Mrs. Smith's glass was half full again. Then it was empty again. Mrs. Smith turned her piggy eyes and looked along the bar at Jane, who was frozen in the act of picking up the water jug. In a harsh nasal voice, Mrs. Smith snarled, 'What are you looking at, Curly?' Jane smiled back. Mrs. Smith consumed the current half tumbler of Jack Daniels. She leaned across the empty stool and put a hand on Jane's shoulder. 'He's dead, you know,' said Mrs. Smith moving her mouth, which was strange because most of the words came down her nose. 'The love of my life is dead. I know what you're thinking. You're thinking I shouldn't worry – that a woman with my looks and figure will soon find another man.'

Jane wasn't thinking that at all. She was thinking something else. She looked down around her feet and said, 'Have you seen a cat? It smells like one has pissed somewhere in here?'

Leaning further across, Mrs. Smith looked down as well. Jane had to push back against the chubby hand pushing against her shoulder. Mrs. Smith's head was almost on Jane's lapel. Jane sniffed. She realised there was no cat. The smell was coming from Mrs. Smith. She tried to heave Mrs. Smith back towards her own stool. With a final shove Mrs. Smith was upright again, where she was able to pour more whiskey into her glass and say, 'Have a drink, Curly,' and pour the whiskey into Jane's water glass before Jane could stop her.

'I'm sorry to hear about your bereavement, Mrs. Smith,' consoled Jane.

Mrs. Smith guffawed and spat Jack Daniels across the bar. 'Mrs. Smith! Baaa!' she spluttered. She fixed Jane with her piggy eyes, pointed at her and offered some advice. 'You could do with losing a few pounds, young lady.' She winked. Jane felt her fist clench. Mrs. Smith looked over the vacant bar stool. 'Especially off those hips,' she added helpfully. Jane had two fists ready and hoped Copeland would reappear soon and rescue her. 'I know what you need, Curly,' nodded Mrs. Smith. She leaned over to get something from the pink handbag propped against the far side of her stool. She disappeared over the side of the stool with her chubby bare legs slowly rising to the horizontal. Jane grabbed her arm and tugged her back upright. 'There!' announced Mrs Smith, placing a small glass bottle on the bar. The bottle was the size and shape of a perfume bottle, which was appropriate because it was a perfume bottle. It had the words 'Midnight Intoxication' on the label. Mrs Smith pointed to the bottle and nodded. She took a time out and gulped more Jack Daniels. She tried to remember where she was. She looked surprised when she saw Jane. 'Ah, yes! You just try some of that if you want to get your man,' advised Mrs. Smith.

Jane thought quickly. Did she really want to get into a conversation about sexual orientation with a drunk, obnoxious, plump, smelly woman? (She had decided the time for nice adjectives was long gone.) Jane bit her lip. She picked up the perfume and sprayed some on the back of her hand. The cat was back and its bladder had been well and truly emptied. Jane held her hand at arm's length before her eyes started watering. She guessed why sales of Midnight Intoxication had not done as well as expected.

Mrs. Smith boasted, 'You know, Curly Top, I'm not just gorgeous enough to be a top model or a film star, I'm also a total genius. I invented that.'

Jane stared at her. Jane's hand flopped onto the bar. Jane's jaw dropped. Jane picked up the tumbler of whiskey and emptied it. Jane stared at Mrs. Smith. 'Alison Taylor?' she stammered.

'Aha! And I'm famous!' shouted Mrs. Smith happily.

'You, er, don't look like you do in your photos, Miss Taylor,' Jane said uncertainly. 'You look, er, less muscular in your photos and your face is... Oh, my gosh! Crikey!'

Alison Taylor glared at her. 'It's Ms. Taylor to you, child,' she said. 'And let me give you some more advice. Try Photoshop, dear. It will take those pounds off your hips without any need to diet. You could add some cheekbones too. And more up top would help.' She turned away, stuck her nose in the air, filled and emptied her glass again. She swayed and toppled from her stool like a felled tree.

MARY AND THE OCCUPANT OF ROOM E.

Mary wondered if she had done the right thing. Was gassing someone who could identify you as a murderer the right thing to do? Now Tom Benson was dead she regretted what she had just done. Gassing him like that was so wrong. She wished she could turn the clock back and undo the last half hour. She wished she had made Benson's death look more like an accident, or possibly suicide, but it was too late now and heart failure or undetermined causes would just have to do. She shrugged and was about to leave when she had an idea. She was about to turn the door handle when the hairs on the back of her neck stood on end. The feeling she'd had that she was being watched was confirmed when she turned and saw an eyeball staring at her through the slightly open door of room E. She was about to snatch her Beretta from the back of her belt when the door of room E was pulled open wide and the grinning occupant cried, 'Wow! It IS you! How did you find...'

Before Tom Benson had finished his sentence, Mary's hand was on his chest forcing him back and she was in room E with the door closed behind her. She hoped the senior police officer coming up the stairs had not seen her face under her black hood. She dropped the canister and tubing and with a hand behind her back on the handle of her Beretta, she closed her eyes and focused her highly trained hearing to detect if the policeman was coming to room E. The highly trained hearing heard, 'You're early today, Chief Superintendant. The usual number four massage, is it?' followed by the slamming of a door. Mary opened her eyes. Tom Benson was grinning an arm's length away. Mary knew he was an arm's length away because she still had her palm pressed against his bony chest. Hadn't she just killed this balding, shiny domed witness? Hadn't she just heard his body crumple to the floor? She had a few questions she needed answering. She started with, 'What the hell are you wearing?'

Tom somehow managed to answer without the need to stop grinning. 'My pyjamas,' he grinned.

Mary was conflicted. Part of her knew she should pull her pistol out, screw the silencer on the end, let Tom Benson shake with fear for a few moments, and put a bullet between his eyes. Another part of her was thinking how cute the gap between his two front teeth was. Lowering her palm from his chest, she chose a middle ground and said, 'You wear pink pyjamas? Are you..?'

'Yes I am!' answered Tom. 'I'm reclaiming the colour for men, just like it used to be in Victorian times. Pyjamas are just the start.' Tom's finger went up. 'The past is just prologue!'

Mary's brow furrowed. 'That's a quote, isn't it? From a play called The Tempest written by Vasilii Shakespeareski from Leningrad?'

'Er, almost right,' said Tom, lowering his raised quote-finger slowly.

Mary was aware they were standing in a room just wide enough to stand in. The rest of the room was occupied by a single mattress on the floor. It had a thin green sleeping bag heaped on it. 'This is your room?' she asked, looking around at the bare mouldy walls and the bare floor boards.

'Depends what you mean by your,' Tom said, wincing. He brightened up. 'But you're here! I've been thinking about you since we met – by the way it wasn't me who shot that police officer in the coffee shop. But you know that! And now you've found me you can tell the police it wasn't me because you saw me and I didn't have a gun or anything! Is that why you've found me, so you can be my alibi?'

Mary looked intently into his eyes and slowly said, 'I'm here for something else.' She let go of the handle of her Beretta in the back of her belt while she took hold of Tom's shoulders and turned him sideways. Pushing down on his shoulders, she forced him onto the mattress on the floor.

'Wow!' said Tom, sitting cross-legged on the mattress and looking up at Mary. 'Even that really good dream I had about you last night wasn't this good! We went for coffee first.'

Mary's hand went behind her back. It pulled the Beretta from her belt. Tom looked from the gun to Mary's face. He winked. Mary took the silencer from her pocket and began screwing it on the barrel. 'Erm,' said Tom, 'I don't mind the gun and stuff if it's your thing – I love the black spy outfit by the way – but shouldn't I at least know your name?'

Mary thought about this. She supposed he had the right to know the name of the person who was about to put a bullet in his brain. 'I am Dominika. I am an assassin. I was trained since I was ten by the Russian SVR. I am here to kill you, Thomas Benson.'

'Just Tom is fine. Dominika? A Russian assassin, eh? That's good. And you're here to kill me? All fine by me.'

Mary placed the nozzle against Tom's forehead. 'Hang on,' said Tom. 'Isn't there supposed to be a bit before you kill me? Er, not that I'd know about these sorts of things...'

'A bit before I kill you? Ah! You mean the usual torturing and stuff to get information first?'

Tom shrugged. 'We'll call it torture if you like, but I don't think it would be **that** much of a torture.' He smiled. 'You're super attractive. I think I might quite enjoy it. But I'll pretend it hurts if you like.'

Mary was becoming confused. Most people she held a gun to usually lost bladder function when she told them they were about to die. This balding man in cheap spectacles and pink pyjamas wanted to be tortured first? 'You seemed strangely unperturbed, Thomas Benson, by your imminent demise.' She started squeezing the trigger.

'No, no, no!' said Tom.

Good, thought Mary. At least he's going to plead for his life.

'You have to threaten me and rough me up a bit first... Not that I know about these sorts of things, of course. You don't kill me until afterwards.'

'You want me to beat you up before I kill you?'

Tom sighed. 'Well, not so much that it hurts or anything and **obviously** there's the bit in the middle, between the roughing up and the killing bit. Then after you've killed me we'll go for that coffee like I suggested. My treat. This house is too noisy for a decent chat, isn't it?'

Mary found herself agreeing that they were indeed having to speak louder than usual to overcome the rap music, smashing crockery and wailing from Room C. 'Wait!' she almost shouted. 'What do you mean? How can we go for coffee *after* I've killed you?'

'Goodness me, Dominika,' groaned Tom. 'This is your fantasy. I'm just going along with it because I like you – well a bit more than just like you, you know. I don't mind you being a bit forward. Er, some people might think that, but not me. Honest! I knew we'd made a connection when we...' he did quotation marks with his fingers, '... bumped into each other.'

'I'm not sure I understand, Tom,' said Mary because she did not understand. 'What fantasy are you speaking of? I'm here to kill you because I killed that person in the coffee shop and you saw my face. You might give my description to the police so I have to silence you.'

'Wow! Excellent background story, Dominika! Admirable, in fact,' smiled Tom, looking at her face and then the gun. He had a very close up view of it since the end of the silencer was pressed against the top of his nose. He stopped smiling. He pointed at the gun. 'That's a real gun, isn't it?' She nodded. He looked up into her eyes. 'You really are here to kill me aren't you?'

'Sorry,' said Mary because, given the circumstances, it was the polite thing to say.

COPELAND JOINS JANE IN THE BAR.

Bursting into the bar as if he was on a mission, Copeland loudly proclaimed, 'Jane! I need to tell you something. That Tom Benson chap didn't kill Inspector Lord, but I think I know who did. When I saw the news I saw... Why the heck is Mrs. Smith lying on the floor?'

Pouring the remnants of the Jack Daniels into her glass, Jane swished it around as she said, 'She fell off the bar stool. I think she's drunk,' then emptied the glass into her mouth.

Rushing over and kneeling beside the sprawled Mrs. Smith, Copeland picked her hand up and started tapping the back of it, as if it had some remote chance of reviving her.

Jane put her hand inside her black jacket, rubbed her stomach and cried, 'Woof! Good stuff that Jack Daniels. Mrs. Smith is really Alison Taylor, er, Sir.'

Copeland continued to tap the back of Mrs. Smith's hand. What Jane had said suddenly hit him. He knelt further over the prostrate body in the overly tight red dress, looked intently at the face, turned to look up and over his shoulder at Jane sitting legs crossed on the bar stool and said, 'She doesn't look much like she does in her photos.'

Jane was sceptical. 'You've actually looked at the photos I sent?' she said, sounding too much like the voice of his conscience for Copeland's liking.

Copeland was hurt. Anyone would think he was somehow averse to any sort of work. 'For your information, Detective Sadler, I don't spend all that time when I'm on toilet seats doing nothing you know! I've even read all the post mortem reports. Well, some.' He looked back at Mrs. Smith. 'Are you sure it's her, she's so...'

'I know, Sir! Isn't she just! How she got in that dress beats me. But it is her. She told me so before she toppled over,' said Jane, smirking.

Copeland stared at the comatose Alison Taylor and said, 'She's like something from a fairy tale.'

'Humpty Dumpty, Sir?'

'Sleeping beauty,' sighed Copeland, now holding Alison Taylor's podgy hand between his and staring wistfully into her unconscious face. Jane stared down at Copeland. She pinched herself. Nope, this really was real. Her concern grew into alarm as, in a far-away voice, Copeland said, 'She's just so perfect...'

Alison Taylor's eyelids opened. Alison Taylor's squinty eyes looked at Copeland. In a drunken version of her harsh nasal voice Alison Taylor slurred, 'Who the hell are you, fatso?'

Copeland smiled, stroked the back of Ms. Taylor's hand, and softly said, 'I'm Inspector Lawrence Copeland, at your service my dear lady.' He lifted her hand and kissed it.

Hey! Copeland! What are you doing kissing her hand?

Leaping down from the barstool, Jane stood behind Copeland and said, 'I think you need to get her to her bed, Sir.'

Just what I was going to suggest! Kissing her hand is just wasting time!

Copeland did not move, except for stroking the side of Alison Taylor's chubby cheek. 'You have the face of an angel and the voice of a nightingale, dear lady,' he sighed. Alison gave a crooked smile before her head flopped to one side. She snored.

'And the nightingale angel smells like cat piss,' added Jane. She was about to give Copeland a shake when she stopped and put her face in her hands. To no one in particular she groaned, 'Pheromones!'

The bed creaked as Alison Taylor's semi-conscious body was dropped onto it. Jane leant on her knees and tried to regain her breath. Copeland may have had Alison's arm around his neck, but it was Jane who had propelled them up the stairs and along the corridor to get Alison to her room. When Jane had regained her breath enough to lift her head, Copeland was kneeling by the side of the bed, stroking Alison's hair as Alison grunted every breath in and wheezed every breath out.

'Sir?' panted Jane. She got no response. 'Sir! Inspector Copeland! Larry! You've got to get a grip! I think it's the perfume, Sir. Midnight Intoxication. She invented it. It smells like cat piss to women, but to men... Pheromones, Sir! She found some way to add just the right mix of pheromones to hit all the right spots in the male brain. It's a damn good job it smells so awful to women and its sales were next to none or... Sir. Sir! Sir!'

BENSON AND MARY.

Staring at Mary's black trainers, Benson protested, 'You can't shoot me.'

The end of the silencer between Benson's eyes did not waver. 'I have to,' apologised Mary. 'I just can't take the risk.'

'No,' said Tom looking up. 'I mean you can't kill me here. This isn't my room. It wouldn't be fair to have my brains splattered all over Jesus' mattress.'

The pistol barrel wavered. 'Jesus?' asked Mary.

Tom smiled to himself. 'Yeah. We swopped rooms. When the police come to arrest me for murdering that guy in the coffee place they'll burst into my room and find Jesus there. Great plan, eh?'

'I think they might check the rest of the house as well,' Mary pointed out.

'Oh,' said Tom, deflated. 'But I still think you should shoot me in my own room though. Jesus won't mind changing back. I've already paid his rent for the next month.' Tom laughed. 'We'd best not tell him you're going to kill me though or you'll have to kill him as well.'

Mary was not used to this. Normally people she was about to kill rarely made jokes. She felt her hand slowly moving down to her side. She jerked it back so the silencer pointed at Tom's forehead again. She was not particularly worried about this Jesus person seeing her, or about his room being covered in blood and brains since she had inadvertently already gassed Jesus to a terrifying hallucinatory death, but thought Tom deserved his last request to at least die among his own belongings. It would also save the police the trouble of searching the rest of the house for him. 'Very well, Mr. Benson. I will allow you your last request and kill you in your own room. But allow me some professional curiosity and tell me why you seem so untroubled about all this.'

Tom put his chin in his hand. He had to move the gun barrel to one side with a finger to do this. Pink pyjama cross legged on the edge of the mattress on the floor, looking thoughtful and mostly bald, he said, 'Bad relationship. No, good relationship. Bad end. Nothing to live for anymore. New job coming up but I'll be rubbish at it just like I was at my last job and they'll soon fire me. What's the point? I tried to finish it all a few times. Well, I thought about it. You'll be doing me a favour really... Out, out, brief candle! Life's but a walking shadow, a poor player that struts and frets his hour upon the stage...'

'Why is your finger pointing to the ceiling?' asked Mary.

Tom lowered his quote finger. He went to say something, then felt it might be a bit awkward mentioning 'The Scottish Play' and bringing bad luck just before he was about to be shot in the head. He stood up, went to the window end of the narrow room, shuffled his feet and returned to stand in front of the pistol barrel. 'Ready,' he said.

'Rabbit slippers?' Mary asked, beginning to wonder if she had inhaled some of the poison gas and was having her own hallucinatory side effects.

'I'll just unlock the door with my spare key, send Jesus downstairs and then come and get you,' suggested Tom.

Mary thrust the gun's silencer into Benson's chest. 'Very clever, my cute little friend. Your plan is to leave me here while you jump out of the window in your awful pink pyjamas and ridiculous rabbit slippers!'

Tom was shocked. 'Jump? From one floor up? That would be crazy. I might hurt myself.'

Mary's eyes narrowed.

'You have really nice green eyes,' said Tom.

Mary gave him a prod. 'Let's go. Together. Jesus is already dead. I flooded the room with poison gas. Don't worry. It'll be safe now. After five minutes it becomes inert and undetectable.'

'You killed Jesus!' Tom retorted, hands on hips. 'That really wasn't very nice, Dominika!'

'Mary,' said Mary. 'And he would still be alive if you hadn't switched rooms, so technically it's your fault he's dead. Let's go.'

Shaking his head, Tom shuffled sideways to the foot of the mattress and out of the door. With the gun at his back he put the key into the lock of his own, room D door. He paused with the key half turned. 'We're not going to find Jesus half melted away, are we? It wasn't that Nosoi gas you used was it?'

Mary was about to answer when the door opened, leaving Benson half bent with the key in his hand. A figure from Raphael's Transfiguration of Christ stood in the open doorway. A white bed-sheet was doing a good job doubling as a glowing robe. 'Oh, hi Tom,' said the figure, 'I thought you were the police so I opened the door before they bashed it down and made a mess.'

'Er, right. Thanks, Brian,' nodded Tom.

Brian smiled. 'Thanks for calling me Brian, Tom. You know I like to keep my real identity a secret until the time of my second coming is right. Not that I ever left really... But I see you have a friend with you...' He stepped forward. Tom moved aside and saw Mary with one hand behind her back and the gun nowhere in sight. Her mouth was open. Her eyes were wide.

'I have this effect on people,' remarked Brian.

'This is Dom... Er, Mary,' said Tom as Jesus/ Brian took Mary's free hand and shook it. 'You are very beautiful,' commented Brian, holding Mary's hand far too long. 'You remind me of Mary Magdalene. You have a destiny. I see a great depth of goodness within you.' Mary appeared more shocked. He finally let go of Mary's hand and turned to Tom. 'I had to open your window, Tom. Did you know it was stuck? But I banged it open using the strength of ten angels. I had to. A strange odour had filled the room while I was having a brief chat with my heavenly father. I think I might be eating too many baked beans. I'll leave you with your friend in the spacious comfort of your own room. I'll go downstairs and watch out for the police coming to arrest you for the murder you didn't do. Nice to meet you, Mary.'

Mary watched him glide along the landing, pass door C and wave as he turned to go down the stairs. By the time she had shaken her head to dispel her disbelief Tom was already inside his own Apartment D. 'Want a drink?' he shouted. With her eyes fixed on the top of the empty stairs, Mary slowly entered the room. Tom was ferreting inside the bottom of the wardrobe opposite the door. 'I've got some bottles of water in here,' said Tom. 'I never drink the tap stuff because of the stuff they put in it.'

'You mean the chemicals?' said Mary, closing the door, bolting it and withdrawing her Beretta.

Tom looked over his shoulder. 'That's right! They put chemicals in it to control your behaviour and make you believe what they tell you. Aha! Here it is. I knew I'd put a couple of bottles in there somewhere.' He stood holding the two bottles. 'That's strange. It's gone red. He must have done his changing water into wine thing on it again.' He unscrewed the top and handed a bottle to Mary, who took it with her free, non-gun holding hand.

'It's blackcurrant,' she said, sniffing before she drank.

'Jesus must be off his game,' grinned Tom. 'Either that or they're the two bottles I filled with Ribena. At least he's not dead. Maybe he was but came back to life again?'

'Obviously the gas was old and its potency had gone,' rationalised Mary. 'I'll sort him out later. Now, where would you like me to kill you? It'll be in the side of the head and then I'll put the gun in your hand so it looks like suicide. So where would you like to be found? On your bed underneath your Yoda poster? Perhaps at your desk under your poster of... By all the gods and Trotsky's ice-pick! I don't believe it! That's an original poster of Invaders from Esbos! It's my favourite film. Rachel Duval is just an amazing role model for professional women like me.'

'Hmm... I suppose she is. She does kill a lot of aliens before making friends with that purple one in the poster,' agreed Tom. 'I have it on DVD. It's the best film ever. Shall we watch it before you kill me?'

'What?' said Mary, seemingly transfixed by the original movie poster. She whirled round. 'You have a copy? There were only a handful sold in the whole world! Is it the extended version?'

'There's an extended version?' cried Tom, sounding and looking amazed.

'Only five copies, I believe,' Mary said despondently.

Tom sagged onto the edge of his bed. He put his blackcurrant down on the bedside table and put his head in his hands. He muttered, 'Darn it! I'll never get to see the extended version now you're going to kill me... Our wills and fates do so contrary run.'

Despite his finger not being raised, Mary guessed he was quoting from Hamletski, Prince of Moscow. She looked down at Tom with concern. It was a new look for her. He was clearly sad he was going to die without seeing the extended version of 'the best film ever', even though it only just about made it on to DVD and was considered so bad not a single cable channel had ever screened it. For the first time in her life Mary showed something other people called empathy. 'I understand, Tom,' she said with her gun pointing at the floor. 'Will you let me have your poster and your DVD?'

Tom brightened up. 'In exchange for not killing me? I really want to live now I have some purpose again.'

'Er, I was thinking about you letting me have them after you were dead. You know, sort of letting them go to a good home where they would be looked after and appreciated. I'm not a thief, you know.'

Tom put his chin back in his hands and shuffled his rabbit slippers. 'OK, you can have them on one condition. Tell me why you shot that Inspector Lord in the coffee shop anyway.'

Mary sipped from her plastic bottle and thought. She put her Beretta back into the back of her belt. She placed her bottle beside Tom's and sat alongside him on the bed. She said, 'I could still kill you with my bare hands if you try anything.' He nodded. 'The truth is I missed my target for the first time ever. I was supposed to kill the woman who was sitting at the same table. They moved. My phone went off. I missed her and hit him.'

Tom turned his head to look at her. 'Why did you want to kill the woman?'

'Money. It's my job. Since dead men tell no tales, I might as well tell you. Someone who goes by the name of Atticus hired me to kill four people who worked at a lab. She was the receptionist there and a late addition to the other four. Atticus said they wanted her killed too, but then they changed their minds.'

'They?' asked Tom

Mary shrugged. 'I've no idea who Atticus works for. All he ever said when there was a problem was he had to consult the family, so I guessed he meant Mafia... What?'

Tom had leaped up. He rushed over towards his Rachel Duvall poster and turned on the laptop on the desk underneath. 'Are you sure he said The Family? He didn't call them anything else? Not ever?' Mary shook her head.

As Tom waved his hands about in an effort to get his laptop to come on faster, Mary leaned back with her elbows on the bed and said, 'I'm not usually curious about exactly who my employers are, as long as they pay, but you have piqued my interest, Tom.' She did not mention there was still the issue of an outstanding amount being withheld because she had failed to eliminate Alison Taylor: as far as Mary was concerned, she had killed three out of four workers at the lab so should have got three quarters of the money and she had only got half so far, so there might be a time when she had to track down Atticus and politely ask for the rest of her money while he was suspended over a vat of acid.

'How much did they pay you?' asked Tom.

'That's none of your...'

'How much, Mary?' demanded Tom.

'A hundred thousand per head, but they've yet to give me...'

'It **has** to be **the** The Family... The other groups who call themselves that just wouldn't have the resources. The Foundation call themselves the family sometimes, but they're conservative Christians and they're only interested in America and I doubt this Atticus works for the rock band with the same name... This **must** be The Family that some people call The

Fyli – that's Greek for family.' Tom was logging into the Dark Web. 'Hold on,' he said, swivelling round. 'This lab wouldn't happen to be one in Dorset owned by Dr. Lynn and her Uroboros Rejuvenation Limited, would it?'

'It was in Dorset but I have no idea who owned it. Why?'

Tom nodded, confident his advance body reading skills confirmed she was telling the truth. He turned to lean over his wooden chair and rapidly clicked on links on the laptop screen. 'Look!' he said pointing with a flourish.

Mary went over to look. She read. She scrolled down. She read. She looked at Tom. She read. She said, 'This can't be true, can it?'

'This is what they own,' said Tom, clicking.

Mary scanned the list. 'Der'mo!' she exclaimed. She waved a finger at the screen. 'That's not true – they can't own...'

'Through holding companies, majority shares, proxy CEOs, all that shit. *They* pretty much own the world, Mary.'

After reading everything there was to read about the so-called Family *(Grk.= Fyli)* on the Dark Web, Mary remained seated on Tom Benson's wooden chair in front of his desk, staring at the laptop screen. Eventually, without conviction, she said, 'This has to be all made up. No one group could own all this, surely? Shipping, electronics, real estate... the list is endless.'

'It's all come from people who say they used to work for *them*, or knows someone who did, or someone who knows someone who knows... Anyway, nothing has been posted about *them* for years now. Some of us who are dedicated to exposing the truth – we call ourselves TICs – think *they* somehow got control of what goes on the internet once *they* had taken over Knight Information Secure Systems. I just think *they* have tightened *their* security.'

'Yes, I noticed it said they owned K.I.S.S. electronics. Haven't they just taken over lots of machines that do credit card transactions? My God, these people run the world!'

'No, Mary, they don't **run** it, they **control** it. Apparently, The Family mainly like stability. Their game seems to be maintaining the status quo so they get more money, influence and, of course, power behind the scenes. If *they* don't like some government doing something they can just turn off the credit card machines or stop a lot of ships going there for a few days... Imagine no food in the supermarkets, no medicines, no fuel... But why are they hiring you to kill four scientists in some remote lab in Dorset? It's not usually their style.'

'Beats me. I think they were just making some sort of drug they were testing on animals there,' muttered Mary, closing the laptop. She stared at her hands on the closed screen. 'You know they paid extra for me to make it messy? I think they wanted the murders to be some sort of message or something. I don't usually do messy – I always make it look like an accident or suicide. Occasionally I plant evidence so someone who has killed someone else gets arrested. Lots of my hit-man rivals have ended up in prison. But this Atticus person said they wanted it messy, so messy is what they got. That included the Sharma family who would have been OK if Atticus had let me keep to my original timetable and put a bomb under Reema Sharma's car when she went to play football on Sunday. Waste of time making a perfectly good bomb really.' She picked up her Beretta from the desk and went to sit beside Tom on his bed. She held the pistol on her lap.

Tom Benson adjusted his spectacles and looked at her. 'You don't really want to kill me, do you?' he said.

Mary turned to look into his spectacles. She thought they needed a good clean. 'What makes you say that? I've killed scores of...'

'I can read your body language. I'm an expert at it,' said Benson. 'And your gun's safety catch is still on. It has been the whole time we've been in this room.'

Mary raised her pistol from her lap and looked at it. She raised her eyebrows. The safety catch was indeed still on. She lowered the gun back onto her lap. They sat in silence staring at the fluffy pink rug for what seemed a long, long time. A minute later, Mary said, 'I have strange feelings. Feelings for you, Tom.' She turned to Benson and said, 'I don't really enjoy killing people, you know. Not when there's no money in it. And it interferes with my gym classes. I really want to give it all up. Maybe I could start afresh if I found someone, you know, someone special... Tom... You're very cute with your little cherub face... If I let you live would you lie to the police for me?'

Tom Benson smiled. He had never been told he had a cherub face before. He supposed a cherub and a gnome were quite similar really. But could he lie for her after all she had done? It was a conflict between morals and her dreamy green eyes. With an air of defiance he said, 'Mary, if you're turning over a new leaf, then I think I could lie for you. After all, you didn't mean to shoot Inspector Lord. It was an accident. You meant to shoot someone else... Er, yes, quite, er, yes, I could give them a false description. I could base it on an actress or something.'

Mary nodded. 'I was suggesting you lie for me by telling the police it was you who killed Inspector Lord.'

'Oh,' said Benson.

'But I like your false description idea. An actress... I mean actor... Yes! Maybe you could tell them I look like Scarlett Johansson? I like her.'

Benson looked hard at Mary. He studied her hair, her eyes, her nose, her lips. 'Er, maybe I should go with someone else, someone who looks a bit less like... I know! Maybe Rachel Duvall? I know what she looks like really well. I stare at that poster above my desk every night... Er, well, not *every* night. Honest.'

Mary laughed as she nodded. Still smiling she unscrewed the silencer from her Beretta and rose from the bed. Standing directly in front of Benson, she pointed the shorter barrel at Benson's head and said, 'Right, Tom. Now, where were we? I'm a Russian assassin here to kill you. My name is Dominika. Let's see what happens before you buy me that coffee you promised. Maybe later you could have a turn at being the assassin as well...'

COPELAND, JANE AND NINA AT THE BAR.

By the time Jane and Copeland were seated on the bar stools with a fresh bottle of Jack Daniels, the friendly proprietress Nina had returned from her golf and joined them. Jane had risked a quick private word with Nina. They would sit either side of Copeland and grab him if he tried to make a break for it to see the new love of his life. All they had to do was to wait for the pheromones imbued into Midnight Intoxication to work free from his brain. To help them in their endeavour to keep Copeland at the bar they had recruited the aid of Mr. Jack Daniels, ably backed up by Captain Morgan.

Jane tried to explain pheromones as simply as she could to Nina, and how they influenced behaviour throughout the animal kingdom, such as aggression in bees, alarm in plants to avoid being eaten, signalling pheromones in cats and rats, and, in many species including our own, the desire to produce offspring and all that *that* grisly business entailed. Perfume manufacturers had never quite got it right, but Alison Taylor had and had used it in L'Argent's 'Midnight Intoxication' brand. Unfortunately, as a perfume, it was not a roaring success. While it may well have subliminally influenced men and 'brought out the beast in your man', the olfactory sense of women had not evolved to respond to the same pheromones: to women the perfume's smell was reminiscent of cat urine. Unsurprisingly, women shoppers chose a different brand. Alison Taylor, however, had stoically stood by her product and sprayed it on liberally. Between bouts of drunken sleep and Jane trying to tear the besotted Copeland away from her bedside, Alison Taylor had been coherent enough to tell of the consequences of her loyalty to Midnight Intoxication.

Copeland stirred. 'But my sense of smell is completely shot, so why did it get to me?' he asked in a distant voice.

'It doesn't quite work like that, Sir, but even so, I would guess your partial lack of smell gave you some protection. You got an emotional effect, whereas most males would get a more physiological effect too.'

Nina raised a finger. 'Can I just try to understand this a bit better, young lady? Are you saying this pheromone thingy in this perfume sort of magically makes men, you know, sort of... er, physically attracted to whoever is wearing it?'

'It's not magical, Nina,' Jane clarified, leaning on the bar, looking round Copeland's girth and shaking her head. 'It's just biology. But yes, any man within twenty feet of a woman wearing this Midnight Intoxication stuff would be like putty in her hands to wind around her little finger, if that's not mixing metaphors. The effects on society would be catastrophic. Men would become like slaves.'

'Sounds OK to me,' said Nina, rubbing her hands together.

'Tell Nina,' mumbled Copeland, rubbing his nose and squinting his eyes. 'Nina needs to know everything. Someone has to keep an eye on Alison when we're not here.'

'Sir?' queried Jane. 'Surely she should go into protective custody?'

'Jane... I'm trying to think straight again. No police. No phone calls. I'll explain later. Just tell Nina while I get my head together and finish this whiskey. That's an order, Detective.'

'Absolutely, Sir!' responded Jane, forcing herself not to salute, and telling Nina everything.

'So,' said Nina when Jane had finished, 'until Mrs. Smith – I mean Alison Taylor – just told you in her drunken stupor that she was the one who went to the lab that night, saw Mr. Smith's body – I mean Jonathan Carter's body... Where was I? So until just now, you didn't know it was her who turned the lights back on and left them that way?' Jane gave a big nod. 'And she's the only one left alive out of the four scientists who worked at the secret lab making some sort of new drug?'

Jane nodded again, saying, 'And I just managed to get out of her that they had finished a few days before the killings started, just like the Inspector had surmised.'

Nina patted Copeland on his stomach and said, 'Well done, Big Larry.'

Copeland turned to smile benignly at Nina. 'Thank you, Nina... You know you're a very attractive woman...' His hand started sliding across the bar towards Nina's.

Jane leaned across, tugged it back and placed it around the whiskey glass. 'It's just residual effects, Nina. I'm sure he doesn't think you're attractive really. Anyway, I tried to get Ms. Taylor to confirm they'd made some new senolytic drug – to lessen the negative impacts of old age, you know – but she just started giggling and that's when the Inspector started unbuttoning his shirt so I thought it best to get him out of there.' She turned to Copeland. She looked concerned. 'Sorry again about having to punch you on the jaw, Sir, and I do hope dragging your unconscious body down the stairs hasn't resulted in too many lumps on the back of your head.'

With Nina the friendly hotel proprietress left on guard duty to protect Alison Taylor in case a fully armed, highly trained, ex-member of the Russian SVR turned up to kill her, Copeland and Jane set off to see Nancy Carter to diplomatically ask her why she had taken out life insurance that specialised in murder just a few months before the husband she despised met his untimely demise. Copeland let Jane drive so he could keep his emotions and aching jaw in check by swigging from the Jack Daniels bottle.

'I believed I was totally in love with her and she was the only thing that mattered in the world,' confessed Copeland with sadness. 'Now I feel like I've lost the love of my life.'

Jane tried to console him. 'We're all just made up of chemicals, Sir. We're just a sack of skin around waves of gushing hormones and electrical impulses. You got a tsunami of hormones and your brain short circuited, Sir.'

Copeland felt so suitably consoled he gave up his belief in free will.

They had passed the turn for Charmouth and were nearing the minor road leading to Nancy Carter's before Jane asked what had been bothering her. 'Why not police custody, Sir?'

'Dominika probably monitors police calls and any police chatter,' Copeland said, knowingly. 'That's what spies do in all the films.'

'Better safe than sorry, I suppose,' conceded Jane. 'Miss Piggy should be safe at the hotel.'

'Detective Sadler! Don't ever refer to the beautiful, svelte, lovely Alison as Miss Piggy ever again!' He swigged. He considered. 'I suppose she's a bit on the largish side, isn't she?'

Jane gave him a look. She accompanied it with a slow nod.

Copeland swigged from the medicinal bottle and looked to the heavens, which currently looked like the plastic roof interior of a Fiat 500 an inch above his head. 'What I was going to tell you when I came into the bar and saw the woman I thought was Mrs. Smith lying there, just like Snow White waiting for... I'll just get some more of this medicinal Jack Daniels inside me... That's better. When we saw the news footage about Giles Lord's murder I recognised someone. It was my old boss. Remember I told you the Pickfords didn't exist? Well, they do. I worked for them doing research before I moved to this new Department C. The Pickfords are in the removal business – the people removal business. They fund themselves from their activities and are pretty much outside the remit of the J.I.C. – the Joint Intelligence Committee – and get rid of crime bosses, unfriendly heads of state and so on. For lesser folk the Pickfords just ruin their careers or siphon off their bank balances, but whatever they do is for stability and order. I think they killed Giles Lord before he could become an M.P., Home Secretary and Prime Minister.'

'He seemed like a harmless idiot to me,' said Jane, watching out for the turn-off.

'Not with someone as corrupt as his father, Robert Lord, pulling the strings behind him. Imagine his account in the

Cayman Islands bulging with our taxes? Or the police and security services, or even the armed forces, being privatised and run by his companies?'

'Like your Department C being sponsored by companies like Uroboros and Dr. Lynn?'

'That's different,' retorted Copeland. 'But forget that. I saw Beryl Pickford, the actual chief honcho of the Pickfords – that's not her real name by the way, well Beryl is, but Pickford is more of a title – she was there, in Honiton, at the scene of the killing, coming out of the coffee shop.'

'But the news said that Inspector Lord was shot by Thomas Benson from across the street, Sir, not by someone who was actually in the coffee shop.'

'So I saw, but I know Tom Benson and he wouldn't hurt a fly,' laughed Copeland, starting to feel cured of his lovesickness but making sure with another mouthful of Jack Daniels. 'I owe Tom Benson, Jane, and as soon as we've sorted this I'll be going to help him clear his name. But you're right about the shot coming from across the street. Beryl was probably just having a day out and there to confirm the kill.'

'We're here, Sir,' announced Jane pulling up the handbrake, swivelling to face Copeland and asking, 'And are you suggesting these Pickfords killed the lab workers as well, Sir?'

Copeland laughed. 'Of course not. I phoned Beryl and she assured me the Pickfords had nothing to do with Jonathan Carter's death. Anyway, why would they kill innocent lab workers?'

Jane shrugged. 'Beats me, Sir. Unless they see your Department C as some sort of threat and getting money from seizing the assets of organised crime which they would have got and they didn't like the idea of one of Department C's sponsors like Dr. Lynn and Uroboros Limited having billions more in funds from a new drug so she could increase her contribution and your manpower?' Jane ended with a sarcastic smile and got out of the car.

MARY AND BENSON.

Portentous dark grey, late afternoon clouds were gathering above Bricknall. Dominika had become Mary again but seemed in a state of shock. Tom Benson was sure it was because he had put on his blond wig and big green spectacles and become John Elton again so they could safely leave the house for coffee without him being recognised. They had barely left the house when Mary went to her nearby car to get her bag so she could pay her share, then she remembered she needed to go back in to get her empty not-so-deadly gas canister and her plastic tubing.

After the toing and froing they were eventually half way to the coffee shop just around the corner and Tom knew his John Elton disguise was working well when an elderly man told him he liked his pink suit and asked for his autograph. It brought Mary out of her trance, made her giggle behind her hand and afterwards whisper that the old man must have been short sighted. The incident seemed to have an undue influence on her because all she could say as they drank their lattes and had two cakes each to replenish their energy was, 'I just can't believe what happened.' But she seemed to go back to thinking about The Family when she spooned her latte's remains into her mouth as she repeated, 'Who would have thought that was possible? Amazing!'

'So what are you going to do now?' asked Tom.

Mary looked as vacant as the rest of the coffee shop.

'About your contract with The Family?' prompted Tom.

'The Family?'

'Yes, that's what you keep calling amazing, isn't it?'

'What? The Family..? Oh, yes, of course... The Family... Yes, I was talking about them being amazing. Of course I was. Honest.' She reached across the table to hold Tom's hand. 'They seem pretty all powerful according to your conspiracy friends so I suppose it would be best not to cross them, so I still have to find Alison Taylor and kill her – she's the last of the four scientists who worked at the lab who's still alive.'

'Ah, yes. Alison Taylor,' nodded Tom. 'The inventor of Midnight Intoxication perfume. She may deserve to die for inventing rotten perfume but I thought you said you would reform. And you promised not to kill anyone else ever if I...'

'Yes, I did. And you did. Twice. But I can't have this Family on my back, can I? I'll be looking over my shoulder forever and it's bad enough with Uncle Vasily and the SVR after me for breaking my oath to the Motherland, but I promise once I've killed Alison Taylor I will completely reform. From then on I will only kill bad people.'

'I'm not sure that's really reforming, Mary,' said a sceptical Tom. 'And the longer you carry on with your line of work the greater the chance your Uncle Vasily will find you and from what you said between when we, er... and we, er, and then we, er... well you said he was a particularly nasty piece of work. You should give it all up. Why not become Jennifer Green full time and just stick to running your charity and your shop? It makes sense, especially with Copeland on your trail.'

Mary tensed. She gripped Tom's hand. 'Copeland? Larry Copeland? Not *THE* Copeland?'

Clasping her hands between his as he laughed, Tom said, 'Must be a different Larry Copeland. This one's a tallish guy with silver hair and a huge stomach.'

Mary wiped a bead of sweat from her forehead. She spoke quickly. 'The rest of them could be outsmarted. They were predictable. But this Copeland wasn't. We studied him. He always got the better of our agents. He never did what was expected. No-one could understand how he thought.'

'Could be the same person, then,' grinned Tom. 'He's working for a new department of MI5 now, called Section C or something like that. I met him a couple of times when he started looking into the murder at the lab.'

Mary instinctively pulled her hand from Tom's and reached behind her for her gun before she remembered she had left it on Tom's bedside table. She slowly placed her hand back on the table again, leaned forward and whispered, in a menacing sort of way, 'Are you friends with him?'

Tom screwed his gnomish face as he thought. 'Not really. We just crossed paths on a case he had a few years back and we sort of helped each other out.'

Mary leaned back. She winced. She slapped the table top with her hand. 'Damn! Why is he tracking me? I left the usual bloody footprint message that this was not a security thing when I killed the Sharmas.'

'Er, you may not want to say that sort of thing quite so loudly, Mary.'

She leaned forward again. 'You won't tell him about me, will you Tom?'

'Or you'll kill me?' Tom smiled.

'I hope not to, Tom. I like you far too much to do that.' She tenderly took his hand across the table again. 'But I have found out where your parents, grandmother, your brother and his children all live.'

Tom swallowed. 'I have no intention of telling anyone about you, Mary,' he gulped.

'Why not, Tom? I mean besides keeping your family alive. Why would you want to keep my identity secret when you know I've killed scores of people, including three relatively innocent but boring ex-husbands – or is it four? – and you know I'm going to get Alison Taylor sooner or later – despite Uncle Vasily and Larry Copeland – and you know I'll carry on killing – but only bad people, I promise. Maybe a few who are sort of in the middle who might become bad given the chance. But you promised to keep my identity secret even after I said I wasn't going to kill you anyway and before we played assassins. You even vowed it with your hand on your holy book – the *Why Aliens Built Atlantis* one – and that was after you knew I'd found where your family live. I need to know why Tom. Why have you promised to keep my identity a secret? I need to know the truth before I give you the antidote to the poison I put in your latte.'

Tom looked at Mary across the table. He looked down at the empty glass mug in front of him. He picked it up, smelled it, put it down again. 'I thought that coffee was below their usual standards,' he said. He put his hand on top of hers. 'When I promised to cover for you I didn't have a reason except I like you. Apart from you being really attractive and having a sexy voice, I don't know why I do, but there it is. Agreeing to lie for you really had nothing to do with the fact you were going to kill me when I had found a reason to live again. Hon... Really it didn't. I was just being logical. I figured if I was dead I couldn't tell anyone, so what difference does it make if I'm still alive and don't tell anyone? And since I said I'd give the police a false description of you we, er, hmm... you know, we got to know each other better. You even let me hold your gun. Besides, Brian was in his full Jesus mode when he said he saw good in you, so perhaps you are destined to do great things and save the world by getting rid of The Family now you know about them. Can I have the antidote now please?'

'Thanks for that,' Mary said, patting Tom's hand. She burst out laughing, 'There's no antidote, Tom. Just my little joke. It was just poor coffee. No wonder this place is empty. Your face..! Sorry. But I'm not going to risk crossing swords with this all powerful group calling themselves The Family, even if it does really exist as your conspiracy theory friends claim. Not on my own anyway. But perhaps together...' She leaned across the table and kissed his lips. She cleaned the lipstick off with a serviette and said, 'Together we could track them down, Tom, and be happy... You're so unique, Tom. Just the sort of special person I've been hoping to find.'

COPELAND AND JANE REVISIT NANCY CARTER.

They had to ring the doorbell twice before Nancy Carter opened the door with a red, frowning face. When she saw them she huffed and made it clear she did not like her daily exercise routine being interrupted before she grudgingly showed them into her green pastel sitting room to wait while she put her designer grey tracksuit on over her white tee shirt and shorts. Jane and Copeland twiddled their thumbs for a few minutes before the recently bereaved, tracksuited Mrs. Carter reappeared with a white towel draped around her shoulders. She sat on her armchair, half facing them on her sofa, with her arms folded. She soon cheered up when Jane asked her why she had taken out extra life insurance on her husband which would make her a multi-millionaire if he was, by some mischance, murdered. Her exercise glow turned into a glow of pleasure. She leaped out of her chair with her arms raised and skipped around the room shouting, 'Yes! Yes! Yes!'

Copeland coughed a polite, 'Ahem!' to regain her attention and she moderated her glee with a few fist pumps, a little shimmy of her hips and a final cry of, 'Yes! Eat dirt, Jonathan!'

'I thought he was being cremated,' said Jane, looking confused.

'Yep!' announced Nancy, doing a happy-feet shuffle. 'The flames will get him used to where he's going next!'

Copeland decided to take charge of the situation. Pheromone love had made him completely forget about lunch and now he had (mostly) recovered his normal composure he needed a pie, as well as a pint to wash down all the Jack Daniels. 'I take it,' he observed, 'that you were unaware the insurance policy had an additional payout for murder?'

Jane put her hand in front of her mouth and whispered, 'She may be acting, Sir!'

'Aha!' Nancy Carter exclaimed, pointing at Jane. 'I heard that. I'm not acting but I'll put this moment in my repertoire for when I need to act happy.' She sat and clapped her hands. Still grinning she explained, 'I had no idea what the insurance policy said. I was advised to take it out a few months ago and all I did was sign a few forms and set up the direct debit. Ernie looked into our finances for us and said we really needed extra life insurance cover but Jonathan...' She pretended to spit. 'Jonathan said I didn't need extra cover because if I died he'd be better off without me spending his money anyway.' She rubbed her face with her towel.

Copeland looked at Jane. She was looking at him. He said, 'Ernie advised you? This is the same Ernie who was here playing scrabble? Ernie Rebus, your neighbour?'

Nancy's actress face reappeared from behind the towel. 'That's right. He's got his own business and is good with finances.'

'He's an accountant?' asked Jane.

Nancy laughed. 'I think he's everything,' she grinned and, leaning forward said, 'They're stinking rich you know – both of them. Some sort of family business. They bought that house next door for the full price. It's way bigger than this one. They've got houses all over. New York, L.A., Rio, Cape Town, Athens, Sydney...'

'And they chose to live here?' asked Jane with a pained expression.

Nancy laughed again. 'It's a very nice place to live, at least that's what my estate agents will be saying soon, Detective Sadler. But Ernie and Niks have only been here for about a year. They're great fun though. They love games.'

'Like scrabble and monopoly,' said Copeland forcing back a smirk.

Nancy screwed her face in his direction. 'So you probably want to talk to Ernie to confirm my story about the insurance. You'll have to see him some other time. They left in their private helicopter this morning to visit family up north. They're back tomorrow. We've got a game of charades planned.'

'And something exciting for Saturday like Twister, no doubt,' Copeland said, unable to help himself.

With another scowl Nancy replied, 'No, we played that last week to cheer me up when I found out Jonathan was dead and he wasn't going to get his huge bonus before I divorced him. There wasn't much else to do without the usual Saturday night veggie burgers on the barbie.'

'Veggie burgers?' muttered Jane, wishing she hadn't.

'And veggie sausages for the wholemeal rolls. Niks and Ernie are vegetarians. Apparently, their whole family is. And they do a lot of charity work for animal welfare. Now was there anything else, or are you going to arrest me for killing Jonathan this time? Why not ask me where I was when Reema Sharma got shot as well?'

'I suppose you were next door playing Snakes and Ladders with Mr. and Mrs. Rebus,' said Jane, not concealing her sarcasm. Copeland grabbed her forearm and put his other palm up to stop Nancy Carter retaliating. 'My apologies, Mrs. Carter,' Copeland said, standing and jerking Jane to her feet. 'We'll leave you in peace.'

TOM BENSON AND MARY BLACK.

Picking the last cake crumbs from his plate and Mary's, Tom Benson fastened a single button of his pink suit and followed Mary out of the coffee shop into the indecisive spots of early evening rain. Mary had assured him the police would take at least a few days to track him down because all his information was still registered at his old address near Lincoln so they had all evening to eat the sandwiches she had just bought and keep researching the activities of the nefarious group known as The Family. At least that was what Tom assumed Mary meant when she said they should go back to his flat and carry on from where they left off.

Any more carrying on, however, was not meant to be. As soon as they rounded the corner of Tom's road they saw the flashing blue lights. They stopped to watch the armed police patrol outside the terraced house that had recently become a five room 'luxury' apartment block. They began to gingerly step backwards to disappear back around the corner when they saw a figure in a dark hooded waterproof poncho bought from Lidl running towards them. Tom recognised the billowing poncho and recognised the bare legs and sandaled feet of the runner. They waited for him, out of sight, around the corner. Mary briefly clasped Tom's hand before she let it go again.

Brian almost fell out of his sandals when he skidded to a halt and gleefully said, 'I knew my Dad would keep you safe!'

'Your dad? Who's your..? Oh, *that* dad. Er, thanks Brian. How did you get my poncho? Forget it. Keep it. What the hell is going on with all the police?'

'Someone phoned them because of all the screaming coming from your room. It was pretty loud. They said a woman was being attacked. It must have been the woman downstairs. She told me it woke her kids up.'

'She complained about the noise? In that house? Come on, Brian! And her kids should have been at school!'

'School?' said Brian, looking at Tom as if he was mad. 'Anyway, my son, they sent a couple of uniforms first but when they found the gun on the bedside table the armed police came as well, then they found photos of you in your drawer and more armed police came. And you don't need to call me Brian when we're alone, Tom.'

'But Mary is...' Tom began, looking over his shoulder. He sighed. He looked back at Jesus and smiled. He took off his blond wig and exchanged the Elton glasses for his black plastic rims. He patted Jesus on the shoulder, closed his eyes, thought of the face on the poster above his desk so he could describe it in every detail, and walked with his hands aloft towards the flashing blue lights outside his home.

Mary had not appreciated the phrase 'Jesus Saves' before but when Brian started verbally attacking the police officers who were handcuffing Tom Benson, Mary gained a modicum of belief in divine intervention because the situation escalated when Jesus pushed a police officer away and grabbed Tom Benson with a cry of, 'Get thee behind me, Tom!' Mary thought that was a possible misquote, but took the opportunity during the Jesus inspired kerfuffle to amble to her car and sedately drive away. It seemed a good idea to leave before the police searched cars and found a high velocity sniper rifle in a silver attaché case in her boot. She felt a little sorry for Jesus. He was being thrown to the floor and possibly kicked in the ribs while he shouted, 'No one listens! It's just the same as last time!'

NINA CATCHES THE KILLER.

When Copeland and Jane returned to the little Lyme Bay View Hotel that did not have a view of Lyme Bay even if you stood on the roof, the friendly, golf playing proprietress Nina, who was not from Torquay, was there to greet them. Nina looked pleased with herself as she launched off one of her bar stools and greeted them in the reception area, which consisted of a dull, patterned rug between the bar and breakfast area. Nina stood before them, arms folded, smiling wide, holding a greasy, burned frying pan. All she said was, 'I got her.'

Jane and Copeland glanced sideways at each other. Copeland cracked first. 'And just who have you got?' he asked.

'Ha!' laughed Nina. 'You said to look after Ms. Taylor and watch out for a highly trained Russian assassin woman who might come to kill her because she might have the secret to making some sort of drug that can stop people getting all achy when then get old like you are Big Larry.'

Jane's round blue eyes widened. 'You got someone?'

'HA!' laughed Nina, louder than before. 'I got someone, alright! She pulls up in front of the hotel and walks in here as bold as brass. But I was waiting for her with my trusty frying pan. She walked through the door and never saw it coming.'

'You're sure it's her?' beamed an enthusiastic Jane.

'Ha! Who else would it be coming here?'

'Er, Nina, this **is** a hotel,' pointed out a more dubious Copeland.

Copeland! Why is your glass always half empty and not half full?

'Ha!' laughed Nina. 'A hotel! Oh... I see... She may have been coming to stay... No, that's silly. No one stays here except you and Mr. and Mrs. Smith. And it's the off season... Do you think I may have hit a new guest on the head with a frying pan?'

'Where is she?' asked Copeland.

'Ha! I tied her to a chair in the kitchen before she came round again... Er, maybe I shouldn't have gagged her mouth with that greasy tea-towel. She's not going to want to stay anymore is she?'

Copeland wanted to put Nina's mind at ease. He held out a horizontal hand and tilted it side to side. 'Fifty fifty,' he said encouragingly, with an exaggerated wince.

Jane had already bolted into the kitchen. She stopped a few paces in, appalled. Had she really eaten a breakfast cooked in this kitchen? How come she hadn't died of botulism? Was that blue stuff rat poison? Tearing her eyes from the grime on top of the once-silver topped cooker, Jane walked slowly towards the woman tied to the chair. Three paces later she was standing over her. Jane knew she did not know much about Dominika, except that she could probably change her identity and appearance at will, but she had assumed Dominika was fairly young, perhaps no more than mid thirties, which seemed young to someone like Jane who had crossed the threshold into her forties. She had not expected Dominika to be **well** over fifty, which the woman tied to the chair clearly was, and if this was a disguise then it was a good one, right down to the grey hair in a little bun, the wrinkled skin and the height and weight of an anorexic escapee from a geriatrics home. Jane sensed Copeland and Nina were behind her in the doorway.

'Bloody hell!' exclaimed Copeland. 'Beryl? What the hell are you doing here?'

The small thin woman with the grey bun and tea-towel in her mouth replied, 'Uking uneye eee cokland.'

Now standing beside Jane, Copeland said, 'Jane, this is Beryl. We go way back to our uni days. She was my boss until recently. She's the one who runs that secret organisation called The Pickfords – the one I told you about that's in the removal business. Like I said, they sort of remove people who are a bit on the unsavoury side. Remember? I also told you how The Pickfords are very, very top secret and no one is supposed to know about them... Ooops...'

'Ucking unie meee Cokland!' repeated Beryl with more urgency.

I think she wants to be untied, Copeland, suggested the inner voice.

'Issen to yor inker oice, Cokland!' suggested Beryl with gusto.

'Yes,' continued Copeland. 'We've known each other for so long it's almost like she can read my mind.'

Jane was on her knees and undoing the knotted rope binding diminutive Beryl Pickford to the kitchen chair. She was struggling. She looked at Nina in the doorway and frowned. Nina shrugged and said, 'I was a girl guide. Youngest Puerto Rican ever to get my knots badge.'

Copeland nonchalantly took a chopping knife from a scarred wooden worktop and applied the blade to the rope. After some fruitless sawing Jane took the knife from him and sliced Beryl Pickford free. Beryl tugged the rancid tea-towel from her mouth, spat out nothing a few times, glared up at Copeland as she pointed at Nina in the doorway and angrily cried, 'That woman is a psychopath! She says she owns this hotel but the first thing she does is whack me over the head with a frying pan when I walk through the door!'

Attempting to make amends, Nina gave Beryl a glass of water in one of her less dirty glasses while Copeland explained about Alison Taylor, Dominika and what he called 'the minor misunderstanding'. Jane tried to help with, 'I really like your mustard cardigan with the designer holes in it, Mrs. Pickford.'

'Right!' said Beryl, standing up. She rose to her full height, which was slightly higher than it had been when she was sitting down. She looked up at Copeland. 'Sit down on this chair, Lawrence, so I can look you eye to eye. And you, Detective Jane Sadler, who got third place in your sixth form one hundred metres breaststroke, should remember you signed the Official Secrets Act so any mention of my Pickfords and you will spend twenty years in solitary confinement, if you're lucky, and you Nina Diaz... Well, I'll be back to see you soon. Probably with the offer of a job since you managed to catch me unawares, but in the meantime you will forget you ever saw me. Am I clear? Good. Now I have you sitting comfortably and almost at eye level Lawrence, I've come to see you because we have a problem.'

'You're on your way back from Honiton,' said Copeland. 'You were in the coffee shop when Inspector Giles Lord was shot.'

Beryl Pickford was amazed. 'Your deductive powers amaze me, Lawrence. How the hell did you know that?'

'I saw you on TV,' said Copeland.

'Ah, yes. I've had myself air-brushed out now. The Crown did not want someone like the son of Robert Lord going into politics and becoming the Prime Minister. I was there to try to talk young Giles out of going into politics. Failing that I had a poisoned sugar cube for his coffee. But some young woman barged me out of the way and sat at his table first and, as you know, someone else then removed the Giles problem for us. Anyway that's all irrelevant now. We have a bigger problem. M.I.6 are in a frenzy. It seems the Russians have found out MI6 have an agent right inside the Kremlin, and in a very senior position too. The Russians must have got this information about a British agent from a traitorous double agent. How else could they know there's a top level MI6 operative within the Kremlin unless someone's blabbed? The Russians are rounding up everyone for interrogation. MI6, as usual, have no idea what to do so we want you to keep your ears to the ground and help us find out who leaked the information to the Russians.'

'Oh, dear!' thought Jane, or words to that effect, as she recalled the incident with Colonel Vasily Goraya and his gun in a hotel room in Slough the previous evening, and how Inspector Larry Copeland had 'misled' Vasily by telling him there was a British spy inside the Kremlin. Jane suddenly became very interested in Beryl's shoes. She thought small heels rather than flats would be better for someone of Beryl's height.

'I'll certainly keep my ears peeled,' said Copeland, innocently.

You'd best not talk to yourself then, Copeland.

'Yes, keep your ears peeled, Lawrence,' said Beryl. 'Because when we find out who the mole is that told the Russians about a British agent inside The Kremlin I'll suspend him from the ceiling by his...'

'Toes?' suggested Copeland.

'Quite so Lawrence. By his toes. Do not tell Wendy Miller or anyone else at your new Department C about this. MI6 think it's more than a coincidence that there's a leak within days of your new Department C being set up.'

She wants you to be her spy inside your own department, Copeland! But you'll have no trouble finding the source of the leak, will you, since it was you?

'Ah, of course, Beryl,' nodded Copeland. 'You can count on me. I'll be sure to let you know if one of the others in Department C is leaking information to the Russians,' he added, completely honestly.

Beryl leaned forward so the tip of her nose was almost touching his. Copeland forced himself not to blink. She moved her face away and with a little hesitation said, 'Right. Good. Keep your ears peeled and watch everyone in your new Department C like a hawk. We Pickfords may be happily handing over a lot of our minor domestic cases to them, but this private business financing of your Department C still troubles me.'

'It's only until...' began Copeland.

'And that reminds me,' continued Beryl. 'Why haven't you sorted this case out yet? It's been almost a week since that conceited braggart Jonathan Carter was killed. Time you caught the killer and found out who hired her, Lawrence. Still, you did good work nailing those bonobo smugglers.'

'To be fair, Beryl, that was all Inspector Sadler,' admitted Copeland.

Raising an eyebrow, Beryl turned to Jane and patted her shoulder. 'Well done. Excellent police work, Jane,' she said. 'I have to go now and coordinate The Pickford sting operation on illegal oil smuggling to an unfriendly foreign country. Tut! Bloody French! Get this killer and get back to Slough to find out who this traitor is, Lawrence.' She pecked Copeland's cheek and left, wagging a finger at Nina as she went past her.

'Don't worry, Beryl!' shouted Copeland. 'You've just given me the last corner of the puzzle!'

Jane looked hard at Copeland. 'Does that mean we have the corners of this jigsaw puzzle and now all we have to do is fill in all the rest?'

With both thumbs up to Jane, Copeland replied, 'Yes! But let's see if Alison Taylor has regained consciousness yet, Jane. It's time to answer the question I had when this all started. It's time to find out why Jonathan Carter was wearing that snazzy suit when he was killed. I don't think he was wearing it – or had those biscuits – to impress Alison Taylor.'

DINNER AT THE HOTEL.

The Indian takeaway delivered to the hotel was soon being devoured by all three hotel guests. The food filled one of the red and white check, plastic table cloth covered, circular breakfast tables and extra rice, side dishes and naan breads filled another table near enough for Copeland to reach for them without having to raise himself from his chair. Nina had eaten more frugally, had drunk less liberally and had left after the starters when a friend of hers from the golf club arrived. She had taken him straight off to show him her trophies.

Even though Copeland seemed over his Midnight Intoxication pheromone inspired love for Alison Taylor, Jane had taken no chances. She had made sure Alison handed over all remaining bottles she had of the offensive perfume for safe keeping and insisted she showered thoroughly and, to make certain there would be no repeat firing of Cupid's arrow, Jane bagged Alison's over-tight red dress and gave her one of Copeland's light blue shirts to wear. Alison was not pleased to have her glamour diminished, but Jane thought the shirt was plenty big enough and could easily double as a night dress, even for Alison.

As they ate, Alison worked her way through a second bottle of wine and talked about her favourite subject. She told them how she had waited for Jonathan to show up at the Lyme Bay View Hotel for their usual Friday night tryst after his meeting but she had grown bored waiting for him so had gone down to the hotel bar where Nina was chatting-up some tubby old guy with silver hair, which had been moderately entertaining until they banged on about golf, at which point she had enough and got a taxi to see why Jonathan was still wasting time at his meeting in the lab when he should be at the hotel for his nostrils to get their latest dose of Midnight Intoxication before the effects wore off.

As the food and wine diminished she told them how once she had gone through the lab's doors, put the lights on and seen Jonathan's body, she had left as fast as possible, not even daring to call a taxi, and walking back down the dark country road all alone, throwing her phone off the bridge on the way back to the hotel and more or less hiding in her room ever since.

'You poor thing,' said Copeland, which may have got Jane worried he was still suffering from "Love hangover" if he had not immediately stuffed another forkful of beef madras into his mouth and smiled contentedly. Jane knew the old Copeland was back.

'You have a big appetite inspector,' commented Alison, who had shown a more than meagre appetite herself.

'We've only had a Tesco sandwich since breakfast,' Copeland said to justify his hunger.

'Or two triple-decker all day breakfasts in your case, Sir,' Jane reminded him. 'Along with two packets of... Hang on, Miss Taylor. Why didn't you phone the police when you found Dr. Carter's body?'

'Jane, Jane. Let the poor woman eat in peace,' admonished Copeland, shaking his head at Jane.

Jane was not deterred. 'And what meeting was he having, Miss Taylor? Had some of the other workers stayed for a meeting?'

'Jane, please. Let her eat. That's an order, Detective. Could you pass the pilau rice please? I'm sure Miss Taylor will tell us all about the meeting Jonathan Carter had with the rival company when she's ready to.'

Alison stopped with a fork halfway to her mouth. 'How did you find out about that, Inspector?' she asked, astonished. Jane wasn't astonished. She knew it wasn't until Alison had just answered that Copeland knew Jonathan Carter was meeting with a rival company.

Copeland seemed only interested in his food. 'Hmm, nice rice this. More naan bread, Miss Taylor? So how much was this rival company offering? Must have been at least four hundred, eh?'

'Five,' said Alison, trying to flick off the chicken korma she had spilled down Copeland's borrowed shirt. She successfully flicked it onto Copeland's trousers as she said, 'Jonathan didn't tell me their name but they paid him fifty grand just for seeing their representative.' She turned to Jane. 'Why didn't I call the police? At first I thought Nancy had found out about us and would kill me just like she'd killed Jonathan as soon as I showed my head outside this hotel. When Reema was killed too I was overjoyed Nancy had got the wrong person. Then I thought maybe Jonathan was seeing that young bimbo as well and maybe Jonathan was having an affair with both of us and that really upset me and I cried on that Puerto Rican woman's shoulder right over there in what this rubbish hotel calls a TV lounge.' She pointed a brown, korma stained finger across the entrance area to the far side of the bar where a sofa sat in front of a TV in the corner before she tore off a thick chunk of naan bread, scooped her korma into her mouth and spluttered, 'But then I realised he could only love me, couldn't he? I mean, what would Jonathan see in an immigrant like Reema when he had me? Then I knew who had killed Jonathan and Reema. It was *them* – the other drug company. Now you've told me slitty-eyed Wang is dead too it confirms it. They obviously don't want **my** new drug on the market. I'm the last one left so I'm not going to trust the police. They could easily be bribed by this other drugs firm. All police are corrupt, aren't they? So here's pretty little me, working out what to do next.'

It took a moment for Jane to get over Alison Taylor's racism, being told she was corrupt and Alison referring to herself as "pretty", let alone "little" before she blurted, 'That's why he was wearing the sharp suit, Sir! He was meeting with a rival company after all! His bonus from Uroboros would have been huge and he was selling out for a mere five hundred thousand pounds.'

'Five hundred million,' Alison corrected her. 'But oh-hum, now they're all dead and when all this has blown over I'll tell grumpy Dr. Lynn how to make her wonder drug.'

'Ah, yes, Miss Taylor,' nodded Copeland. 'I daresay you will, providing she agrees to give you your deceased colleagues' bonuses too.'

'You make me sound greedy, Inspector,' sniffed Alison Taylor. 'As the last member of the team left alive I deserve all the bonuses. But the bonuses will still be a lot less than we would have got by selling the secret to another company. Jonathan and I would have lived like royalty for the rest of our lives. We would have been on our own Caribbean island in no time. Those Asian foreigners Wang and Reema would have got nothing! Ha!'

Jane bit her lip and sweetly said, 'Nancy Carter would have taken her husband to the cleaners.'

Alison laughed. She was well into her second bottle of wine. Jane wondered if Alison's laugh also sounded like a horse with nasal congestion when she hadn't been drinking. Ending with a loud snort, Alison grinned, 'Nancy? Ha! Jonathan had a plan for *her!* She would have slipped on the rocks, hit her head and been found... No she wouldn't! She wasn't going to drown. Honest. She would have been set up for life too. Honest.'

Copeland soothed, 'Of course she would have been, my dear lady.'

Alison glared. 'I have half a doctorate in molecular biology, so don't patronise me, thicko,' she snarled as she covered more of the borrowed shirt with brown sauce from her chin.

'Of course not! My apologies.' Copeland put his knife and fork together and bowed his head. 'How could I forget you were the genius who discovered that missing ingredient to make your senolytic wonder drug work so much better than all the others?'

'Better?' She turned to Jane. 'Is he always this stupid?' Jane hedged her bets and shook her head diagonally, but knew Copeland was still fishing. Alison tutted and turned back to Copeland 'Better? It wasn't just bloody better!'

'Of course not, dear **Doctor** Taylor,' flattered Copeland. 'It's the crème de la crème, isn't it? You tested it on the mice, then on the bonobos...'

'And we took some ourselves,' admitted Ms. Alison Taylor. 'And just look at me! Aren't I looking just great?'

Hold that laugh, Copeland! Look! Jane is holding hers. Admittedly, she does look like she's about to wet herself.

Copeland put his knife down and placed a hand on Alison Taylor's forearm. 'You'll be able to take your discovery to Dr. Lynn soon. We'll catch the killer within the next few days.'

'We will?' asked Jane, a little surprised.

Copeland smiled. 'Yes, Jane, and the person who paid her.'

'You did a lot of thinking while you were on the toilet earlier, didn't you Sir?' Jane said sarcastically and wished she hadn't because Alison laughed and her mouthful of korma was now down Jane's white blouse. Alison became serious. Trying to wipe the korma off and wincing Jane said, 'It's OK, Miss Taylor. I have the blouse I wore earlier.'

'Sod your blouse, Detective,' said Alison, turning back to her left and staring at Copeland. She went to speak and closed her mouth again. She tried again. 'The pills we made were in the lab... Do the police have them?'

'The pills? I'm afraid not,' said Copeland, sounding concerned. 'The killer must have taken them after destroying the computers, smashing the lab and killing all the test animals.'

'Shit!' screamed Alison. She slammed her cutlery down. The korma went up. Copeland thought there was a certain symmetry now his suit jacket was just as splattered as Jane's blouse. Alison Taylor emptied another glass of wine. She filled the glass in her hand again. Copeland grimaced. It was white wine. 'Shit shit shit,' repeated Alison Taylor, slamming her glass down so that her liberally sprayed food now had some nice cheap Chardonnay to go with it and, to underline she was less than happy, she thrust her fingers under her plate and levered it between Copeland and Jane. It landed face down on the embroidered armchair in the bay window. Jane stared at Alison Taylor, then stared at her lap where some of the korma had decided to leave the plate and make a soft landing before it hit the armchair.

'Er, Dr. Taylor, you do know what the final secret ingredient of the drug was, don't you?' asked Copeland, unphased except for being miffed it was white wine rather than the usual red down the front of his jacket.

Alison banged the table. She grabbed Copeland's lapel with her chubby, korma-coated fingers. 'Of course I know the final ingredient. That's what made it *really* work. It was that know-it-all Reema's idea but Jonathan told me what it was. I haven't forgotten what it was! Honest. It was... It was... A secret! And we were going to be rich and together for always and forever once we had sold the formula and got rid of Nancy... but I can't talk about that, can I, or you'll arrest me, won't you?'

'Of course not, dear Alison,' smiled Copeland, gently prising her grip from his lapel. 'You haven't been cautioned and we have no evidence you were planning to kill Nancy Carter, do we?'

'I wasn't going to kill anybody! I was only his helper,' confirmed Alison, releasing Copeland's lapel and looking at Jane, who sat with her hands in her lap nodding understandingly. Copeland winked at her while Alison wasn't looking.

Alison stood up, swayed a little and said, 'I'm going to bed. You two can go to my flat tomorrow and get me lots of clean clothes. I'm not risking my life, it's too important, but I suppose if there's a bomb there or poisonous snakes in there or something no one will really miss you two, will they? Goodnight.'

Jane copied Copeland and gave Alison Taylor a little smile and a wave as she staggered across the entrance mat, knocked over a bar stool and disappeared up the stairs beyond.

'What a delightful woman,' Copeland said with a grin.

'No she's not, Sir! She's a narcissist and an alcoholic,' Jane said, emptying her glass of wine before getting up to stride through the bar and make sure Alison and the splattered shirt were safely up the stairs.

When she returned to her seat, Copeland said, 'Do you have your gun, Jane?'

'Pardon, Sir?'

'Your gun. You're firearms trained and after the way the Sharmas were killed they must have issued you with a gun.'

'Er... Glock 17, Sir. But it's in the boot of my car, which is still in front of the Sharmas' house.'

'OK. We'll get it tomorrow.'

'On the way back to Slough to see Vasily, Sir?'

'Is that tomorrow? So it is. I think I'll allow myself a little drink now. Listen, I got Nina to put you in the room next to Alison Taylor's so if you hear anything like someone trying to kill her in the night you can go and stop them.'

'Gee. Thanks, Sir.'

'Oh, just take a knife from the kitchen. If Dominika sees it she will run a mile in case she gets infected by it. Oh, Jane! Don't worry. Dominika has no idea where Alison Taylor is.

Not yet anyway.' He looked down at his jacket. 'On second thoughts, if Dominika does come to kill Ms. Taylor, just let her kill her. She's ruined a perfectly good suit. I don't think I'll be wearing this chicken korma suit again. Hey, if I'm going to get a bottle from behind the bar you'd better have this before we leave it here again.' He took his hand from his pocket and tossed the flash drive to Jane. 'I doubt there's anything useful about Dominika's identity on it, not if Vasily has already had the information for months and hasn't been able to track her down, but have a look if you like. You can use my laptop while I tidy up down here.'

Jane put the flash drive in her trouser pocket. Copeland flicked his head for her to go. She fetched his laptop and, just in case, went back down to the kitchen to get one of the larger kitchen knives. Copeland was halfway through a bottle of Merlot from behind the bar when she passed him scraping food remnants onto plates and dropping the foil containers into a waste bag. Jane thought Copeland looked deeper in thought than she had ever seen and she wished she knew what he was thinking.

As Copeland tidied and picked at the last of the naan bread a voice inside him said, *You're thinking you should have had the Claret rather than the Merlot, aren't you Copeland?*

271

7. Friday, March 22nd.

BREAKFAST AT THE LYME BAY VIEW HOTEL.

Considering the state of the kitchen, Jane chose to stick to muesli for breakfast but still carefully examined each raisin to make sure it had not come from the posterior of a rodent. Copeland stuck to his usual double full English, telling Jane she was too fussy and a bit of ingrained grease added a maturity of fried flavour not found in lesser hotels.

'You were right, Sir,' said Jane ignoring him. 'There was nothing on the flash drive to help us with Dominika.'

'I thought not,' said Copeland, diligently making a fried bread and black pudding sandwich. 'As I said, Vasily has had that information for months and not been able to find her, so I'm not surprised.'

Since there was nothing else to see at the Sharmas', the press circus had finally subsided. The news cycle had moved on and was now full of police statements about the apprehension of the cold blooded killer, Thomas Benson, so retrieving Jane's firearm from the boot of her car still parked outside the Sharmas' was easily accomplished, as was stopping off in Weymouth for Jane to get more clothes and journeying back to the hotel in Slough, where Copeland had a room service lunch and an afternoon nap.

Jane skipped lunch, went for a run, showered and paced her hotel room. She felt like she knew so much but knew so little. At least she now knew Carter and his team had made a major breakthrough with the senolytics drug and a rival company had offered half a billion for the secret, but they had double crossed Carter and sent a Russian trained assassin to erase him, his team and, for some reason, all evidence of their breakthrough. Jane was sure Dr. Lynn did not have the secret, even though she had been paying Erica Young to covertly download the lab's data and send it to her. What she did not know was if Copeland really knew who had hired Dominika, as he had claimed to Alison Taylor, because every time she asked him he annoyingly told her to be patient, or more annoyingly told her she could work it out for herself and the only clue he would give was that it had to be someone who not only knew what they were doing at the lab but also knew they were on the verge of a major breakthrough... which brought her back to Dr. Lynn as the chief suspect... She kicked the waste bin across her hotel room.

One thing she did know for sure was that if they did not return Vasily's flash drive to him in a few hours time then Vasily would undoubtedly carry out his lightly veiled threat to harm Copeland's daughter, and Jane knew whatever happened she could not let Vasily harm Emily. She also knew they could not give him the flash drive. Feeling stuck between the Devil and the deep blue sea, Jane decided it was time to face up to the Devil and get rid of him. She took her Glock 17 pistol from her bag and spent the rest of the afternoon dismantling and cleaning it in readiness for Vasily's arrival.

BENSON IS INTERROGATED.

'Superintendant Clare Harper with D.C. Fellows. Third interview with the cop-killer, sorry, I mean the murder suspect Mr. Thomas Benson. I hope you are fully recovered from your journey, Thomas. I understand the handcuffs and manacles might have chaffed a bit on the way down and when you arrived here you also fell out of the van, er, several times. Now you are here I hope you are enjoying the delights of our Devon cells, Thomas, including your very own, exclusive bucket and the lights needing to be left on all night because we have you on suicide watch. Now I'll just turn the tape on again... So, would you confirm you have turned down the offer of a solicitor, Mr. Benson?'

'I can't afford one and it seems I'm not poor enough to be entitled to legal aid.'

'Would you like a solicitor present for this interview, Mr. Benson?'

'No! I'm innocent! I've never committed any crime. Honest.'

'Saying honest is a sure sign you're lying, Mr. Benson. I read it in a book.'

'OK! You got me. It's a fair cop, Superintendant. I haven't got a TV licence.'

'And you are the murderer of Inspector Giles Lord, are you not Thomas? Tell us where you learned to shoot a high velocity sniper rifle? Where did you hide it Thomas?'

'I told you it wasn't me. It was the woman I bumped into.'

'Ah, yes, the woman. Let me just refer to the notes here. You gave a very accurate description of this supposed assassin. Five feet six and a half inches tall, twenty seven years old, straight shoulder length brown hair, hazel eyes, shoe size four, and measures thirty six, twenty five, thirty eight... Big hips, eh? And you say she was wearing a short silver skirt, silver bra and over the knee silver boots. I'm surprised none of the other witnesses spotted her.'

'She was wearing a raincoat.'

'What colour?'

'Er, yellow.'

'We have an artist's impression for you to look at, Mr. Benson. If you please Detective Fellows. Take a good look Mr. Benson. Is that the woman you saw with the silver attaché case?'

'Yes.'

'And was a ray gun in the case, Mr. Benson?'

'What?'

'Well, you seem to have given us a description of an actor name Rachel Duval, apparently dressed as she was in an awful film called Invaders From Esbos. Is that true?'

'No! It's not true. It's a brilliant film.'

'Believe me, it's not Mr. Benson. It's probably the worst film of all time and Rachel Duval has the acting skills of a wooden puppet.'

'If I wasn't handcuffed to this table I'd... I'd wag my finger at you for that! Anyway, I know you're lying. No one has ever seen the film except a handful of people.'

'I know. I fell asleep. But let's cut to the chase. We know you went to the police station looking for Inspector Lord and you told the receptionist you were going to make sure justice was done. You said, and I quote, "I will have my revenge in this world or the next." You also gave a false name. You said your name was Maximus Decimus Meridius. That lie will not help your case in court. You have motive and we know you were in the right place at the right time, so you might as well make it easier on yourself and confess. I should tell you we also have a reliable eye witness. She saw you fire and shoot Inspector Lord from the window above the stationer's shop across the road from the coffee place.'

'An eye witness..?'

'Normally we would not divulge the identity of such a crucial witness, but she has specifically said she wanted her name mentioned to you otherwise she would not give her statement, so I can tell you her name is Jennifer Green. She is a pillar of the Dorset community. She runs a coastline preservation charity and owns a shop selling fossils and sea shells.'

'...Oh, crap!'

'And we have a Beretta M9 pistol found in your room, Mr. Benson. It's the same type of weapon that was used in other recent multiple homicides. Forensics are examining it now but they have already discovered only one set of fingerprints on it. The fingerprints are yours, Mr. Benson.'

'...Oh, crap!'

MARY DOES HER MAKE-UP.

Smiling to herself, Mary patted the wavy haired auburn wig draped on her wig-stand. She checked she had cleaned the vivid green contact lenses and put them back in their box, alongside the container which held the prosthetic skin she used for the bit on the end of her nose and the pieces that enhanced her cheek bones. Content, she nodded, then frowned when she saw how much of the lip solution was left. She reckoned she only had enough remaining to inject her lips another ten or twelve times to make them appear fuller. She looked in her dressing table mirror and worked her lips to make sure they were back to their normal size then picked up the false eyelashes and dropped them in her waste bin where they landed on top of the discarded syringe.

Improvisation was something they said she excelled at when she was training near Moscow. Plan A had been to gas Benson, but then she'd had the idea to pick the door lock, press his dead fingers around her Beretta and leave it on his bedside table. The police needed a culprit for the murders of Jonathan Carter, his team, twelve dead bonobos, many dead mice and, if they cared, the murder of Inspector Giles Lord, the son of the not-convicted embezzler Robert Lord. Once Thomas Benson's face had appeared on TV Mary had decided he fitted the culprit bill just about adequately. A dead Benson who had apparently died of heart failure brought on by his stressful life as a hired assassin would have been good, and one with the murder weapon in his room better, but once the insane man who thought he was Jesus had survived the out of date gas and had opened the door and seen her she had instantly known Plan A had to be abandoned.

Use every resource available to achieve the success of your mission was what she had been taught, but it had still been all too easy. As soon as she had seen the poster she had known how to form a bond with Benson. He had even believed her story about there being an extended version of that space invaders film she had never even heard of until she had seen the poster. Until then she had worried he would soon be begging her to actually kill him to put him out of the misery of his pathetic failed relationship. This troubled Mary. She could not comprehend how someone could care about someone else so much to want to not go on living without them. She cheered up when she reflected on what the rest of Benson's life was like: he had plenty of other reasons to want to die. Then, of course, she had seen the book carelessly discarded on his desk and had the idea to nurture his crackpot ideas about some organisation called 'The Family' controlling the world. Seeming to believe his nutty theory was all it had taken to get his trust, but to cement his gullibility she had played the silly assassin role-playing game. She had expected to have to pretend to enjoy it, but no pretence had been necessary. After all that, or rather all those, it had been plain sailing. He had lapped it up. She found herself smiling to herself again. He had looked at her with his innocent, puppy-dog eyes and readily believed her story about her having no choice but to kill the whole Sharma family because they had rushed at her with kitchen knives; he had eagerly held her gun when she had let him play at being the pretend assassin; he had believed her when she had said all she needed was a good man like him and she would retire from killing and just run her little sea shells and fossils shop; he had believed she needed to keep her satin gloves on the *whole* time because she had a skin allergy; he had waited patiently outside after she got her bag from her car then, feigning forgetfulness, went back into the house to collect the empty gas canister and plastic tubing and, of course, make a phone call to the police about a woman being attacked in Room D. She burst out laughing. Mary could not help herself. She was imagining Tom Benson giving her description as Rachel Duval to the police. She wondered if he had described her wearing that stupid, sexist, space uniform? Mary thought Rachel Duval must really know how to act if she had performed wearing *those* boots with *those* heels. She laughed again. She could just see Benson's face when he found out her alter ego Jennifer Green had come forward as an eye witness to his murder of Inspector Lord – even starry eyed Thomas Benson would finally realise he had been used. But what would he do then? He would give her description to the police of course and the police artist would produce a face that looked uncannily like the wonderful Scarlett Johansson. After describing two Hollywood legends as being the real murderer, any vestige of Benson's credibility would be completely shot. Mary briefly considered if that was a fair assessment. She concluded it was – Rachel Duval could be called a legend because no one had heard anything about her for years.

And what else had Tom Benson got in his favour? A deluded man who thought he was Jesus who, after a little prompting from Mary, had got himself arrested for assaulting a police officer? Would Tom Benson's defence lawyer call Jesus the son of God to the witness stand? Mary doubted it. She had covered her face and feigned laughter behind her hand when the old man had asked Tom for his autograph and the only other witness to her and Tom being together was the man serving in the coffee shop. Even though Tom had been in his John Elton disguise, Mary was glad she was always prepared and had enough change on her to pay for their take-away sandwiches. She had paid the coffee shop man with her special coins. She'd taken the whole lot just in case she had to treat everyone in the coffee shop and give mothers, children and pensioners some. By about now the poison she had sprayed on her special coins would have penetrated the coffee shop man's pores and he would be thinking about visiting a doctor with exactly the same sort of stomach cramps Wang Linpeng was getting when he boarded his flight to Spain. It was only a small dose sprayed on each coin but if the police ever did get round to checking Tom Benson's story they would first have to find which intensive care ward the coffee shop worker was in a coma in. Mary was sceptical the police would have ever bothered to interview the coffee shop worker but her motto had always been 'better safe than sorry'.

Mary looked into her mirror and smoothed her ultra-short black hair. She put her long platinum blonde wig on and put the blue contacts in her eyes to complete her transformation into Jennifer Green. She didn't like being Jennifer all that much because of the nose and her tendency to wear flowery dresses, not to mention the fake weight gain, but being Jennifer seemed appropriate since she was about to leave for

Honiton Police station to give her official eye-witness statement.

Looking at her face from different angles and glancing at her Jennifer Green photograph to make sure she had got everything right, Mary considered her next move. Alison Taylor was still the fly in the ointment causing a deficiency in her bank balance. Now that Thomas Benson was in custody – with the murder weapon found in his unsavoury little room to ensure his conviction – Mary could refocus on killing the elusive Alison and get the rest of the money Atticus owed her. Alison's body would never be found of course, she would bury it so deep no post-mortem would ever discover Alison had died while Benson languished in a prison cell... Or... Where had she put it? There was still the car bomb she had made for Reema Sharma's Land Rover. It would be riskier, but if she added a little more C-4 explosive there wouldn't be enough of Alison Taylor left for anyone to identify. Mary hated waste and really felt like the bomb needed to fulfil its purpose in life.

COLONEL VASILY GORAYA GETS NEW ORDERS.

'Colonel Vasily!' cried Ambassador Yashin, smiling like a lizard readying his tongue to catch an unwary fly. Vasily tried to stop his stomach rolling over while he waited to be snatched into the Ambassador-lizard's bottomless abyss of doom, which today was probably taking the form of a deep salt mine in Siberia. He remained at attention, saluting, with his eyes fixed on the plump oligarch Ambassador leaning back on the front of his elaborate office desk, forcing his gaze not to look at the paper the Ambassador waved in his hand.

Vasily knew in his heart of hearts that his time had come. The ever-wise President in Moscow had woken up in a bad mood and had decided it was time Vasily extracted some desperately needed salt, even though Dominika had not been dealt with. No doubt his successor would be tasked with solving the problem of the errant Red Cuckoo and Vasily's suspicions were confirmed when the Ambassador sternly said, 'Vasily, it seems your ducks have come home to roost!'

'Permission to speak, Mr. Ambassador?' asked Vasily, sweating inside his medal-laden uniform.

'No,' replied the Ambassador. 'But you may finish your salute and take your uniform off.'

This was it! Colonel Vasily Goraya knew it. After giving countless selfless years to the Motherland for nothing in return except caviar, champagne, a Ferrari, the weekly party with the silver disco-ball and, of course, power, he was now going to be ruthlessly cast aside, stripped of his uniform and sent back in chains. His hands shook as he began unbuttoning his jacket, his hands trembled as he loosened his belt, his hands clenched with shame as he lowered his trousers and wished he had not worn the boxer shorts with the red spots on them. It got worse. Ambassador Yashin pressed a button on his desk and a young female captain entered carrying a coat-hanger with a suit cover suspended from it. They were going to humiliate him further and dress him as a criminal in the grey suit with the little arrows on it before they manacled him. Vasily just knew it: he had done exactly the same thing on many occasions to soldiers in the lower ranks who had not saluted him fast enough.

Ambassador Yashin nodded to the young captain and she started to unzip the suit cover. Vasily could not bear it. He grimaced and closed his eyes. He opened one when the Ambassador cried, 'Da da!'

Vasily opened his other eye. The captain removed the cover completely. Ambassador Yashin explained, 'The President has made you a general, Vasily!'

Vasily did not like to mention this was usually done by replacing the insignias on the current uniform. At least this way he was getting a new uniform and he'd been wearing the other one since he had been an 'advisor' in Georgia and he'd become more portly since, so he was not overly upset. The captain helped him put the new uniform on and with the usual Russian efficiency made sure it fitted him in all the right places while she whispered how she would like to be a major soon.

'You have permission to speak now, **General** Goraya,' Ambassador Yashin informed Vasily with a smile, which still looked like a reptile's to Vasily.

'The president is most wise,' said Vasily, tactfully.

Ambassador Yashin waved the captain away, put the sheet of paper on his desk and poured two single malts. 'No vodka rubbish at a time like this, eh?' he said, handing Vasily a glass. They clinked. 'It seems, General, you have got all your geese in a row. Our glorious President is most pleased with you. The information you obtained about a British double agent in the Kremlin was correct. Our efficient interrogators spoke with many generals and senior ministers and discovered the British spy.'

Vasily managed half a smile. 'You mean they were tortured.'

Ambassador Yashin frowned. 'Only a little. Quite a lot survived. Nearly half in fact.'

Vasily was sceptical. 'A British spy would never admit his true identity,' he said.

'Aha! You are correct. This is how we knew it was him. The rest admitted they were British spies. Well, at least those who survived the interrogation did. So it seems we are now a few generals, along with a few senior ministers, short. So the President has made a few new ones! Well done you, Vasily!'

'This is good news,' said Vasily, taking a very large mouthful of his Scotch. 'For a moment I thought the piece of paper you were holding had some new orders for me.'

'Oh, yes! I almost forgot. Indeed it does have your new orders.' The Ambassador turned, picked up the sheet of paper and handed it to Vasily.

Vasily read it. 'I don't understand,' he said. 'Italy? Florence?'

'Well, Vasily, you know what they say. All roads lead to Florence. You could go to Rome if you prefer. I'm opening a new franchise in Italy. Mostly gambling. Lots of Chinese tourists there, you know. The President is worried about the Chinese getting too rich so we are setting up what you might call "establishments" in their favourite tourism places to fleece them out of their money. You get to run the ones in Italy. I'm afraid the pay isn't good, just ten percent of the profits, so you'll only make three or four million Euros a year, and the villa where you'll be based is modest with only twenty or so servants, but there you have it... Bob's your Aunty, as they say here. Take it, or leave it and stay here. Your balls are in your court.'

Vasily did not have to think for all that long. 'I will do my duty and suffer the hardships of Italy,' he said.

'Good! Oh, yes! One more thing. The president says you are not to go until this Red Cuckoo sleepy agent thing is cleared up and you have found... What's her name?'

'Dominika,' said Vasily feeling like the ground was slowly opening beneath his feet.

'Yes, Dominika. She has to be found and eliminated before you take up this new post.' Ambassador Yashin laughed at some private joke. He put a squidgy hand on Vasily's new shoulder insignia and, as if it were a schoolboy secret, hissed, 'He says because she has disobeyed orders and has gone around all nilly-willy killing people for money he wants you to take her head to him on a silver platter, whatever one of those is. And if you don't find her, the President says you're off to supervise the inside of a salt mine in Siberia. You have one week to find her, counting today of course.'

Vasily strode back to his rooms stony faced. Everyone he passed saluted extremely promptly. He got into his sitting room and closed the door behind him. He went into his bedroom and undid the top button of his new uniform's collar. He punched his pillow for ten minutes.

BENSON IS INTERROGATED AGAIN.

'So, Mr Benson, now you claim the murderer was this woman?' said Superintendent Clare Harper as she thrust the new artist impression across the table for Benson to examine.

'Yes! That's her.'

'So, first you gave us the description of Rachel Duval wearing a silver costume and now you're saying she looks like this?'

'Yes.'

'Like Scarlett Johansson?'

'Sort of.'

'And her real name is Dominika?'

'Yes.'

'And she was trained by the Russian SVR?'

'Yes.'

'Are you going to tell us she looked like Jennifer Lawrence next?'

'Why would I do that?'

'Your whole story seems to now be based on the film Red Sparrow, which starred Jennifer Lawrence.'

'She deserved at least an Oscar nomination for that. But *my* Dominika wasn't fictional.'

'No, your Dominika looked like Scarlett Johansson with a sun tanned face.'

'She was sun tanned all over.'

'And how do you know that..? My goodness, Mr. Benson! Are you telling me you..?'

'Yes.'

'Stop grinning! You're telling me you and this woman who resembled Scarlett Johansson slept together?'

'Of course not! There was no sleeping involved. First we...'

'Stop right there! This is just fantasy, Mr. Benson. Even if I believed this woman really existed, I could never believe someone who looked like that would even consider having intimate relations with someone who looked like you.'

'That's a tiny bit insulting, Superintendant. None the less, it's true.'

'Are you trying to get a psychiatric plea, Mr. Benson?'

'What about her car? I gave you a description, Superintendant. Have you used your police data base thing and tracked it down? Or had officers scouring CCTV footage for it?'

'Quite frankly, telling us it was blue didn't give us much to go on, Mr. Benson.'

'Light blue. I said it was light blue.'

'Yes, right. Let's move on. Do you know who this is?'

'No.'

'This is a photograph of someone you said you knew, Mr. Benson.'

'Never seen her before.'

'You have claimed that this Mary, also known as Dominika, is also the person who claims she saw you shoot Inspector Lord. Is that true?'

'Yes. Jennifer Green. She has a shop. She sells sea shells by the sea shore.'

'Well this is a photograph taken at a local golf club charity event by the local newspaper. As you can see, Jennifer Green has long blonde hair and a rather conspicuous nose.'

'And she's a bit chubby.'

'I'm glad you pointed that out, Mr. Benson. So the question is, Mr. Benson, is this the person you claim killed Inspector Lord, all the people at the lab near Axminster, tried to gas your neighbour, Brian Cox, who believes he's Jesus, and tricked you into handling her firearm before you...'

'Went for coffee. Yes. Er, no. Well yes. She's obviously a master of disguise because the Russians trained her.'

'Very well, Thomas. Detective Fellows, please show the suspect the print-outs.'

'Print-outs of what? Hey! These are from my laptop! They're personal! It's all my chat-room stuff with my fellow anti-conspiracy friends!'

'It may help your insanity plea. Please look at the highlighted section, Mr. Benson. Read it aloud for the recording, if you please.'

'I've nothing to hide so fine! Er... the highlighted section? Ah, yes...Here it is. It says... "I agree, Mint Saviour, Alison Taylor is a threat to civilization and something must be done to stop her." How was that? Did I elucidate OK?'

'I'm sure the tape picked it up just fine, Thomas. Now, tell me... What did you do with Alison Taylor's body?'

'Superintendant! Really! I never touched her body!'

'I mean her dead body, Thomas. For the recording, Mr. Benson is refusing to answer what he did with the body of Alison Taylor. He now seems lost for words. It's time to cut the bullshit, Mr. Benson. Forensics have confirmed the gun found in your room is the same gun that killed Dr. Jonathan Carter, Dr. Reema Sharma, her mother, father and brother, and twelve helpless bonobos. You may want to change your plea, Thomas. The court may go easier on you if you confess and tell us who hired you. Right now, you are looking at six counts of murder with six consecutive thirty year sentences, plus twelve consecutive five year sentences for killing primates of an endangered species, plus a one thousand pounds fine for not having a TV licence.'

THE LYNNS.

Jeremy Lynn was feeling pleased with himself. He nodded to Finch as the faithful servant poured him a second cup of Earl Grey and snuggled back into the armchair which he had turned around so he could look through the French window into the garden and enjoy the first scents of spring. He smiled to himself. He was bound to be in his wife's good books at last. Just as she had 'requested' he had taken the flash drive posted to him by Erica round to her Uroboros clinic as soon as it was delivered to his office. Dr. Evie Lynn had been more excited than a three year old on Christmas morning when he handed it to her. She had thanked him for taking it to her so promptly, and had even given him the smallest of kisses on his cheek before she had bundled him out of the door. He let his eyelids close and his head sag as he blissfully sank into a contented slumber. The contended, floating feeling was disturbed by something hitting him on the head. Holding the side of his head, Jeremy Lynn sat up and looked to his right, having correctly surmised whatever projectile had collided with his cranium this time had originated from that direction and was smaller than the airplane. His surmise was well-founded. Dr. Evie Lynn was standing with her hands on her hips a mere few feet away. He further surmised she was not in such a good mood with him as she had been an hour earlier when he had taken the flash drive to her. Her scowl had enough ferocity to possibly ignite what was left of Jeremy's hair.

Evie Lynn screamed, 'What the hell is that, Jeremy?' pointing.

Jeremy followed the line of her pointing finger. 'It's Earl Grey,' he answered. He gathered it was not the right answer when she cuffed him across the head and through gritted teeth growled, 'Not the... eight, nine, ten... sodding tea! That!'

Jeremy looked between the little, tea bearing table and his feet. He rubbed his head and further surmised this was the offending projectile. He picked it up. 'Aha! It's one of those plastic things that goes into the side of one of those computer things. Got it! It's a flash drive!'

Jeremy wondered why his wife's hand was around his throat. Finch, who had already retreated two paces from the back of Jeremy's chair, took two more and pretended to be watching some flowers bloom in the garden.

Squeezing Jeremy's throat, Dr. Lynn snarled, 'You've messed up again, Jeremy. This isn't the right flash drive. Where's the one Erica sent?'

'Glurgh,' said Jeremy with both hands pulling at Dr. Lynn's wrists and trying his best to swallow.

'This one is just a lot of women's photos and their addresses? If you live long enough to tell me we'll discuss who they are and why you have them when you tell me where you left the real flash drive!'

'Same one,' croaked Jeremy.

Finch thought it was time to intervene before he became a murder witness. 'Would you care for some tea, Ma'am?' he asked. He did some surmising of his own and guessed the look he got meant that not only did Dr. Lynn not presently care for tea, but that he should make himself scarce. 'I'll just be in the kitchen preparing dinner for later then Ma'am,' he said with a nod of his head and a rapid retreat into the adjoining kitchen.

'I swear, Evie,' gasped Jeremy, feeling her gaze scour his soul before the pressure on his throat slightly eased. She released her grip, and slumped onto the arm of his chair, looking out of the window as he had done not long before. 'Tell me,' she said.

Glad to breathe freely again, to Evie Lynn's back Jeremy said, 'It got delivered and signed for then my secretary brought it in to me, just like always. I didn't even bring it home like normal. I took it out of the squidgy bag thing and brought it straight to you like you told me to.'

Dr. Lynn said nothing for a few moments until she bowed her head and rubbed her hands deliberately back and forth over her scalp, muttering, 'Then Erica Young has screwed us, Jeremy. She's sent us a different file with lots of women's faces and lots of addresses on it, probably women she used to work with at that seedy lap-dancing men's club where you recruited her. She's taunting us. No doubt she found out about the deaths of her fellow workers and still has the information she downloaded from the lab. She must have figured out we'd pay a lot more for it now.'

Jeremy didn't like the words "we'd pay" because he knew which one of the "we" usually ended up paying, then felt comforted when he remembered Evie had often explained how they shared everything and she would often say "what's his is theirs and what's hers is hers". She was such a dear. He thought she needed consoling so he stroked her back and softly said, 'Don't worry, dear. I'm sure we'll get the real flash drive soon. And then you'll be able to make lots of money when you make that new Viagra.' He had no idea why Dr. Lynn grabbed his throat again.

MARY.

Mary sighed. 'You can't be serious, Atticus? You phone me and interrupt me while I'm busy making a better bomb to tell me you want her dead – again?'

Pause.

'Oh, it was an emergency decision, was it? I suppose this matriarch person decides everything, does she?'

Long pause.

'Oh right! She does except when it's a family board decision? And that takes too long, does it Atticus? So she's made an executive decision? I see. Well I'm not doing it. Once Alison Taylor is out of the way I'm having a break and spending the rest of the money you'll be putting in my bank account.

'You'll pay me how much? Just for one murder? And you don't care if it's messy or not as long as it's quick?

'OK. Consider it done. Erica Young will disappear soon. Now, about that nom de plume phrase you asked me to find out about... Hello? Are you still there? Atticus? Hello?'

COPELAND IS VISITED BY VASILY.

Scurrying down the short hallway next to the ensuite, Copeland stopped by the side of his bed and whispered, 'I think Vasily's here, Jane. I saw a shadow under the door. I think he's waiting until I go into the bathroom before he comes in. That's what he always seems to do. It's uncanny the way he knows when I'm in there.'

'Perhaps some air freshener **before** you've used the comfy toilet seat might help, Sir?' Jane suggested in her own whisper.

'Right! Good thinking, Detective. I'll use the comfy seat and no air freshener so he knows exactly when to come in.'

'Er, OK... No air freshener. And you want me to hide in here, really near the bathroom?'

'Yes! Behind the curtain. Just beside the chair where he always sits. Have your gun ready.'

'Gun, Sir?'

'Jane! The whole plan depends on...'

'Just kidding, Sir. Gun at the ready it is, Sir.'

'Ah, good! I'll just go and use the comfy toilet seat then. That madras last night, you know. You may want to put the TV on in case I'm a bit loud.'

As far as Copeland was concerned it was a very quick use of the comfy toilet seat but Vasily was sitting in his usual visitor's armchair in the corner when Copeland emerged. Vasily did not have a gun, or even the clicking table lamp switch, anywhere in sight. Copeland finished fastening his belt and sat on the side of his bed. 'Hello Vasily,' he said, producing the flash drive from his pocket. All he had to do now was say the words "flash drive" and Jane's gun holding hand would be thrust from the edge of the curtain and they would have the drop on Vasily. That was Copeland's plan.

And what happens after that, Copeland? Vasily runs off with his tail between his legs and forgets all about your daughter? asked his inner voice. Copeland felt he should have perhaps thought a bit further ahead.

'Pardon?' said Copeland.

'I said keep it, Comrade,' repeated Vasily. 'Things have changed. I want you to find Dominika again.'

'You can't be serious, you piece of Russian scum!' cried Jane, emerging from behind the curtain with her Glock 17 pointed squarely at Vasily.

Vasily smiled up at her. 'I wondered where you were. Of course, I saw the shoes sticking out from under the curtain, but I thought they were Larry's.'

Unwrapping herself from the rest of the curtain, Jane stood at the foot of the bed and looked down at Vasily. 'These are women's shoes,' she said.

'I don't judge,' shrugged Vasily. 'So, my friends, it seems I am promoted to general and I'm being reassigned to a cushy Mediterranean location.'

Copeland folded his arms. 'Well, Vasily. You've really fallen on your toes, as we English say. That's another one for you to use and share with your ambassador. But I suppose your new title and job require you to find Dominika first?'

Vasily's head wavered from side to side as he considered his answer. 'Sort of, my old comrade. I just need her head. The President wants it taken back to Moscow on a silver platter. You don't happen to know where I can get one of those, do you?'

'Please, Sir,' pleaded Jane. 'Can I just shoot him, Sir? He's going to threaten to hurt Em... Er, your daughter again if we don't find Dominika for him. I can put a little hole in his head so there's not much mess, Sir. We can put his body in the boot of the car and bury him in the woods.'

Hey, Copeland, she's thought the plan through far better than you did, though I can't see Vasily fitting in that Fiat's boot.

'No threats against your sculpture making, hockey playing daughter, Comrade Larry,' said Vasily, looking at the Glock 17. 'Let's go back to our original deal. I'll give you twenty thousand roubles for finding Dominika for me.'

'Two hundred and forty seven pounds and sixty six pence?' queried Jane.

'She's good with numbers,' Copeland told Vasily. 'And I think you offered me twenty thousand *pounds*, not roubles.'

'Let me kill him. Please, Sir. We can't take the risk.'

Copeland watched a bead of sweat trickling down Vasily's forehead. It told him Vasily knew as well as Copeland did that Jane was not bluffing. Copeland had not figured Jane to be a killer. He doubted she had ever shot at anyone, let alone hit them, before, yet here she was, completely prepared to put a hole in Vasily's head. *She seems very motivated to kill him for some reason, Copeland!* Copeland rolled his eyes and said, 'Alright, Vasily. Dominika is a killer and we need to find her. We're still investigating the murders of some people we think she's killed in Dorset. When we arrest her we'll let you know – IF you swear not to ever harm my daughter in any way... or order anyone else to.'

Vasily's head tottered again as he considered. 'I need her within one week, counting today,' he said.

'We'll have her in custody within a couple of days, tops,' said Copeland.

'Then we have a deal, Larry,' said Vasily.

'Awww, Sir!' moaned Jane. 'I cleaned my gun especially.'

BENSON HAS A VISITOR.

'Aha! Here's the man himself in his grey boiler suit! Mr Thomas Benson, I'm your lawyer, Jeremy Lynn, and this is my associate Mr. Crisp. Do sit down, Mr. Benson.'

'I can't afford a lawyer.'

'It's all part of your new employment package, Mr. Benson. It's not just health care you get but legal cover too, and we at Lynn, Jeremy and Archibald aim to give the best money doesn't buy.'

'Is your middle name Archibald by any chance?'

'Goodness me, Mr. Benson! However did you know that?'

'And are you by any chance married to Dr. Lynn who owns Uroboros Rejuvenation? And also owns the lab where the scientists worked I'm accused of murdering?'

'Er... Possibly... But let me assure you, Mr. Benson, there will be no conflict of interest. Mr. Crisp here will be your actual lawyer. He specialises in criminal law. I just do contracts, but I needed to get out of the house to escape from a little marital disagreement, you know? Now, Mr. Crisp here thinks he can get you off with a just a fine, and he should know – he's never lost a case!'

'Am I right in thinking this is his first case?'

'No, no, and thrice no. That's very cynical of you Mr. Benson. He did another one. He got someone off with a fine for having a parking ticket.'

'And he really thinks he can get me off murdering six or possibly seven people with a fine?'

'What? No. For not having a TV licence. He thinks you've no chance of beating the murder charges.'

'Oh, right. I see. He doesn't say much does he?'

'He's very shy and tends to get very stressed if he has to do any sort of public speaking.'

'And he's going to represent me in court?'

'He's passed his advocacy exam. He's fully qualified. Besides, as we understand it, the evidence is pretty damning, and the lies you've told about this fictional Russian hit woman haven't helped. We advise you to plead guilty and throw yourself on the mercy of the court, Mr. Benson.'

'Listen, Mr. Jeremy Archibald Lynn, I'm innocent!'

'It's OK, Mr. Benson, you don't have to lie to us as well. There is such a thing as solicitor client confidentiality. Or is it client solicitor confidentiality? I can never remember? Ha!'

'She got me to hold her gun when we... You don't need the details of that part... It was her gun! She killed all those people not me! I've never even been to that lab!'

'So how did you get the photograph?'

'What photograph?'

'Come, come, Mr. Benson. The photograph in your bedside table drawer. The one with the lab workers holding a plate with the big eureka banner behind them. The one where you'd put a big red X across each of their faces.'

'She must have put it there when she went back up to get the gas canister and plastic tubing she had used to try to gas Jesus in my room.'

'Do you often see Jesus in your room, Mr. Benson? Can anyone else see him? Does he speak to you?'

'I don't believe this! I see him almost every day. He usually lives next door. And of course he speaks to me. He always thanks me when I make him some beans on toast.'

'Beans on toast. Of course. Mr. Crisp, please write down Mr. Benson sees Jesus in his room and makes him beans on toast. Now, besides the lab workers, there's this other murder, but I suppose you never went to Honiton and shot Inspector Lord either?'

'No!'

'Aha! You were filmed in Honiton! Stop lying Mr. Benson and tell us the truth so Mr. Crisp can help you put together a mitigation plea. Pleading insanity is your best chance.'

'... Oh, crap,' said Benson.

JANE AND COPELAND RETURN TO KILMINGTON.

As soon as the little white Fiat pulled up in the Lyme Bay View Hotel car park Alison Taylor was outside the single-door entrance and staring at them. Heaving himself out of the car, Copeland saw she was wearing more make up than could possibly exist in the entire world, heels that could have doubled as lethal weapons and his light blue shirt covered in chicken korma. Copeland was sure he had once seen a shirt just like it hanging up in a gallery at The Tate Modern.

Contemptuously throwing her straight and apparently recently badly re-dyed, multicolour blonde hair over a shoulder of the stained shirt Alison Taylor shouted, 'I hope you two dimwit PC plods have got me my clothes!'

Copeland smiled as he called back, 'You forgot to give us your house key, Miss Taylor.'

'But, Sir,' began Jane, 'her door lock was changed. I've already got the... Sorry, Sir.'

'She's stormed off back inside anyway,' said Copeland. 'You know something, Jane? I think I've gone right off the new love of my life! No doubt she's gone to get her keys so we can drive back to Charmouth right away to do her bidding.' He laughed but his inner voice went into mild panic as it said, ***Copeland! You can't seriously be contemplating this as a plan, can you?***

Once through the entrance door Copeland resisted the urge to tell his inner voice to shut up and the urge to roll his eyes, shake his head and put his face in his hands when he saw Nina and her grimy saucepan standing at the threshold of the kitchen looking pleased with herself. She did not have to say anything. She made the walking motion with two fingers of one hand while the other hand briskly brought down the frying pan like a tennis serve. 'And before you say anything,' she said proudly, with her chin held high, 'it's not a potential resident. At least I hope not. Not in *that* dress!' She stepped aside and gestured with her trusty frying pan for Jane and Copeland to enter her kitchen and inspect her latest captive.

'Oh, my goodness!' exclaimed Copeland once they passed Nina to see who she had tied to a chair this time.

'I don't believe it!' exclaimed Jane. 'Look who it is, Sir!'

'Er, who is it, Jane?'

Jane did some eye rolling and a little head shake of her own. 'You haven't got to her face yet, have you Sir?'

'Er, no... Not yet.'

'It's Erica Young, Sir!'

'Oh, yes! So it is. I was distracted by the kitchen. Look, Jane. Someone's cleaned it...'

'Yes, Sir. I couldn't sleep last night so I came in and... Forget that! It's Erica Young, Sir!'

Once Erica was untied and free of the recently laundered tea towel mouth gag, and once she had found out Jane was police and Copeland was sort of MI5, and once she had hugged them and cried on their shoulders, and once she had been given a nice cup of tea, a digestive and some of Nina's more modest clothes to wear, and once they had hidden themselves from Alison in Copeland's room, and once Nina had gone to make Copeland some bacon sandwiches with perhaps a fried egg or two (once she had learned she would be letting yet another room and Copeland's Department C credit card would be paying for everything including her old clothes), Erica told them her story. Her story ended with her waking up in a farm shop car park a few hundred metres the other side of the A35 and her car refusing to start, despite the attempts of several men who seemed more than keen to help her once they had seen her leaning over the engine, so she had found the nearest hotel.

Throughout Erica's story of how she had been recruited by the Lynn's to download and send information from the lab, how she had worked there being bored on the reception desk and cleaning out the frequently replaced old bonobos, to how she had just sent the last flash drive and ended up at the same table as Giles Lord when he was shot, to how she had slipped out of the hospital and found a tracker on her car, Jane had been all ears. 'You know what this means, don't you Sir?' she eventually said, mouth agog.

'Hmm, yes,' said Copeland. 'It means we now know the farm shop just down the road is where Nina gets those really good sausages from and I can get some before I go back to London after we've wrapped this up tomorrow. The puzzle is finally complete, Jane. I know who hired our unfriendly neighbourhood assassin, Dominika.'

Erica smiled. 'Now you've just told me it was the police and not the Lynn's who changed the lock on my door, so do I,' she said. 'But I do wonder what happened to that notice you say the police put on there.'

'I'd guess it's back on your door, Miss Young,' speculated Copeland, 'probably covering up the window pane where you smashed it. Otherwise I think we would have got a call about someone breaking and entering.'

...Not far away in Axminster a teenage boy sat on the end of his bed still sulking because his mother had made him stick the really cool police notice he had put on his bedroom door back where he had got it from.

TOM BENSON GETS ANOTHER VISITOR.

'You look awful, Tom.'

'Probably not as bad as you, Brian. At least I only have one black eye.'

'And they've returned my celestial robes to me! You didn't mind me using your spare sheet did you?'

'I don't think I'll be needing it ever again, Brian.'

'Don't worry, Tom. It's alright. We're alone. You can call me by my real name.'

'I think they may be behind that big mirror listening to us, Brian.'

'No, that's just you and me in the mirror, Tom. It's just something called perspective that makes us look like we're really behind it.'

'Er, if you say so Brian. But how come they're letting you talk to me, and alone like this?'

'They said they thought I might talk some sense into you, Tom. They want me to get you to admit killing all those people and say you did it because you had voices telling you to do it.'

'Voices?'

'Yes, Tom. They said you think you talk to Jesus and he tells you to do things like kill bad people. But I've never told you that, have I Tom? I'm a pacifist. I didn't even push that policeman when that nice Mary lady told me to go and save you. He just walked into my hands when I was trying to stop him walking into me. But they seem happy enough to let me go now they've beaten me up a bit.'

'You should make a complaint, Brian.'

'Oh, no. I'm happy to get off without being crucified. It ruined my whole weekend last time.'

'At least you've got the weekend this time then, but if they're letting you go, have they given you some more of your medication to go home with, Brian? Please tell me they have... Why are you winking, Brian?'

'I know you didn't kill anyone, Tom. I told them you had an alibi last weekend. I told them you were in your room alone the whole time and didn't open the door to anyone. I told them I know that because I knocked quite a few times and you didn't answer. Or was that Monday when you went for your medical at that clinic? The days seem to blur when you're over two thousand years old, don't they Tom? Anyway... Come closer so I can whisper just in case you're right and those people who look like us in the mirror aren't really us... Good. I just want you to know that I have your stash Tom, so don't worry. They won't get you for drugs as well as for the murders and not having a TV licence.'

'What stash, Brian?'

'The stash of drugs on your bedside table. I've got them. I went into your room to get my sandals, my guitar and my gourd when you went out with that Mary Magdalene lady. You know, after she went back to get that gas cylinder. I thought you wouldn't miss one or two of the little white tablets so I took the tissue they were wrapped in and tried one. I have to tell you, Tom, it was rubbish. Absolutely no effect. I think you've been ripped off. Now I know a guy... He's a drummer...'

'Brian! I have no idea what pills you're talking about. I don't do drugs. Apart from the occasional pint and beef and ale pie, my body is my temple.'

'Hey, that's a great phrase Tom! Your body is your temple... It needs work, but can I use it? Oh, hang on a minute, I already did, didn't I?'

JANE CAN'T SLEEP.

With just over a week to go before she once more ceased to be a police officer, Jane reflected how appropriate it was she would become a teacher again on April Fools' Day, but this was a fleeting thought as she tossed and turned the early hours away. She would have got up and cleaned the kitchen again if Copeland had not told her to get a good night's sleep because she would need it. That was just before he had also told her to sleep with her gun under her pillow in case she heard Dominika coming to kill someone during the night.

Jane rolled onto her back, opened her eyes, threw her arms wide and listened to the rain pelting against the windows. She knew Copeland had been teasing about Dominika but she was still glad she had made sure all windows were shut and all doors locked before they had all gone to bed. Copeland had assured her he had a foolproof plan to catch Dominika and those who had hired her but had insisted on not telling Jane any details and like a broken record kept telling her she should work it out for herself. Jane rubbed her face, rolled over and switched on the bedside lamp. She sat on the edge of the double bed for a moment before going into the little en suite and splashing cold water on her face. What did Copeland know that she didn't? She knew whoever it was that had hired

Dominika must have known what they were doing at that lab and was worried enough to stop the discovery of some new, age easing senolytic being made public. But who would know that? If Erica Young was to be believed then not even Dr. Lynn knew the great drug breakthrough had been made, otherwise the Lynns would not have been so keen to give Erica five thousand pounds to send the last flash drive. Dr. Lynn may have hired someone to kill her lab workers *after* she had their discovery safely in her hands, but not before.

The amount of money given to Jonathan Carter just to get him to meet with a representative of the rival drug company also troubled Jane. If they were willing to give Carter fifty thousand just for a meeting, how much were they paying Dominika to silence all the lab workers? The amounts involved ruled out Nancy Carter, Alison Taylor and most definitely Erica Young, who was also clearly a target of Dominika's as well and had only been saved by a sloppy kiss. As far as Jane could see that left precisely zero suspects. She reached under the bed and took out Copeland's laptop. She waited for what seemed an age while it booted up. She clicked on the unnamed file icon she had created and typed in the password, smiling to herself at how clever she had been to think of it. The file blossomed to life and she read it from start to end again. Whatever Copeland knew, Jane knew she knew something he did not know and she knew he did not know she knew.

8. Saturday, March 23rd.

COPELAND ENJOYS BREAKFAST.

The breakfast sausages tasted better than ever to Copeland now he knew the pigs had been slaughtered and passed through a meat grinder locally. Erica Young joined him wearing Nina's jogging bottoms, some sort of baggy maroon golf top and without her large circular earrings. She apologised to Copeland for her rudeness in the Uroboros Rejuvenation clinic when they first met, and told Copeland how glad she was to have met him because she had no idea what she would have done otherwise – that was when Detective Jane Sadler walked resolutely into the dining room and pointed her Glock 17 at Erica.

'She's Dominika, Sir!' asserted Jane.

Copeland was so taken aback he squirted far more brown sauce onto his bacon than he had meant to. 'Is she one of the identities you've seen on the flash drive Vasily gave us, Detective?' he asked.

'Well, no, Sir. Not exactly... But how come she's here? It can't be a coincidence! She's tracked Alison Taylor down and is here to kill her!' Jane clasped her left hand under her right to steady the gun and point it at Erica's head.

Erica went to twiddle an earring, found she was not wearing it, twiddled an ear lobe instead and said, 'As much as I'd like to kill Miss Piggy Alison, I'm not going to. I didn't know she was here. I thought she might be, though. It's like this. I was supposed to use my charms – you know, my charms, like?' She put her shoulders back and the baggy maroon top suddenly wasn't quite so baggy. 'To use my charms to get slimy Jonathan Carter to trust me so I could keep downloading all the research from his computer and send it back to Jeremy Lynn so he could give it to Doc Lynn. Anyway, like, he seemed more interested in Miss Piggy than me. I mean Jonathan Carter not Jeremy Lynn. I couldn't figure out why he would prefer her to me. I mean, come on! So when Wang told me he ate a lot of mints and stayed away from Alison as much as he could because she had invented some sort of perfume that had got something called ferry moans in it which, like, made men all soppy or, you know, worse than soppy like, well I knew something was up so I followed big-head Jonathan from the lab one Friday and he ended up here with her. It was the ideal place for them to meet, like, wasn't it? No one else ever comes here, do they? So I'm over the road in the farm shop car park when the car won't start so I can't go back to London and stay with some of my old friends I used to know when I worked at the lap dancing club so I thought Hey! there's that little hotel where nobody goes. I'll stay there for a few nights and then do a runner before I have to pay like. I hadn't worked out how to get some clean clothes without Giles Lord's brains and blood splattered down them, but thought I could probably steal some from some washing hanging on someone's line, like, but then I walk in here and the first thing I knew was whack and a saucepan has floored me and then I wake up tied to a chair with a tea towel stuffed in my mouth, like, then you two guys show up.'

The gun in Jane's hand began to lower as she said, 'That sounds plausible...' and Copeland said, 'Lap dancing club..?'

The Glock 17 was firmly clipped back in Jane's shoulder holster and Nina had just brought a fresh pot of tea when Alison Taylor made an appearance looking a little worse for wear still wearing the korma stained shirt, having apparently run out of make-up and seemingly misplaced her hair brush. Alison Taylor's mood was not enhanced by seeing Erica Young, possibly because Miss Young instantly pointed at her, laughed, sniffed and said, 'She certainly doesn't smell of those ferry moans now! More like a wrestler's armpit!' at which Jane giggled behind a serviette, possibly diminishing Miss Taylor's mood even further because she threw a bunch of keys onto the breakfast table, told Erica she was an uneducated harlot, told Copeland and Jane to fetch her clothes because they were public servants and she was a member of the public, used some colourful adjectives about police officers and demanded Nina take a breakfast of kippers, two lightly boiled eggs, toast, marmalade and coffee to her room immediately before turning on her stiletto heel and walking out.

Copeland picked up the bunch of keys Alison Taylor had indelicately flung, examined them and said, 'Excellent!' while his inner voice screamed, *This is a crazy plan, Copeland!*

While Jane used the key to Alison Taylor's new lock to go inside her house in the back streets of Charmouth to get Alison Taylor some fresh clothes, Copeland stayed outside and pressed the car key on the bunch Alison had flung onto the breakfast table. The side lights of Alison Taylor's red Audi flashed. Copeland ran his hand under the sills and inside three of the car's wheel arches before he stood, gave his back a rub and smiled to himself.

When Jane appeared with a holdall Copeland said, 'You drive the Fiat back and I'll drive the Audi.'

Jane dropped the holdall. 'Are you mad, Sir?'

'Quite right! Good thinking, Detective,' said Copeland with a firm nod. 'I'll drive the Fiat. The Audi might have a bomb under it. Best get down and have a good look. I'll hold your jacket for you.'

'Thanks, Sir!' huffed Jane. 'But I think I'll get the car mats out to lie on.'

As Jane's fingers went under the door catch and lifted it Copeland said, 'The bomb might go off when you open the door.' Jane froze. 'Don't worry, Detective,' reassured Copeland. 'Killers like to stick to the same modus operandi and our Dominika likes to shoot people in the head at the moment, so a car bomb is really unlikely, isn't it? But just to be on the safe side, I'll just walk down the road a bit before you open that door.' He smiled, sauntered some distance away, stopped, turned and gave Jane a grin and the thumbs up.

Wishing she had let him take her jacket because it suddenly seemed to have got very hot wearing it, Jane closed her eyes and opened the car door. 'Told you so,' shouted Copeland. 'Now check underneath but don't touch anything that says Semtex or C-4 on it, OK? If there's a ticking clock then pull out the green wire. It's always the green one. Unless it's the red one.'

Being very thoughtful, Copeland took some photos of Jane with her head under the car engine which he showed to Jane afterwards. 'I hate you, Sir!' said Jane, picking up the holdall and throwing it into the back of the Audi. 'Why didn't you tell me how big my bum looks in these trousers!'

Jane had gone beyond eye rolling. She was into fully blown head in hands and on the verge of tearing at her curly blonde hair. 'That's your plan? Sir, that's madness! You've brought Alison Taylor's Audi back here to the hotel because there's a tracking device under the wheel arch so Dominika comes here to kill her? And when she comes into the hotel you will be sitting right there, just like you are now, there in the bay window and from that very armchair you will say "Hello Dominika" and when she steps off the entrance mat and comes round the corner then I come out from behind the bay window curtains behind you with my gun and we arrest her?'

'Brilliant, eh?' grinned Copeland. 'Just like we surprised Vasily in that other hotel with the self service breakfast which I've finally decided is not as good as a proper home cooked one like here.'

Jane tugged her curly blonde hair. 'Brilliant? Brilliant? Vasily saw my shoes poking out under the curtains and could have shot me before I breathed if he'd had a gun. And these curtains finish at knee height!'

Copeland peered round the side of the armchair. 'Ooh, that leaning over is a bit of a strain,' he said. 'But you may just be correct there about the curtains being a bit on the short side. I hadn't noticed that. Good detective work, Detective.'

'For Pete's sake, Sir! And she's a bloody Russian secret service trained killer! Do you think I'll emerge from the curtains with a gun in my hand and she'll just introduce herself?'

'Hmm... Are you saying she may be quicker on the draw, as it were, than you are?'

'Bloody right, Sir! Especially if I have to fight my way out of the curtains after she's just seen my legs sticking out!'

'Aha! Got it! Put your body armour on!' suggested Copeland. He wondered why Jane squatted down with her face in her hands and began hopping like a frustrated frog. 'Is that one of your special exercises?' he asked.

Jane's hands went up and her two fists waved about high above her curly blonde hair. Her round face was very red and her big blue eyes were firmly screwed shut. 'I haven't got any bloody body armour and Dominika kills with head shots anyway!'

'Hmm... You don't seem totally on board with my plan, Detective. Perhaps you should come up with a better one before she arrives,' suggested Copeland, rising from the armchair, feeling his backside where remnants of chicken korma had stuck to it and going passed Jane's hunched and sobbing figure to the bar. Since he was staying in complete control for when Dominika arrived he only poured himself a double brandy.

It was one o'clock in the morning. Copeland hoped Dominika would arrive to kill Alison Taylor soon. He was already more than a bit peckish and if she didn't arrive within the next hour the packet of digestives he had just eaten wouldn't sustain him for much longer and then he would have to leave his post and go and search in the kitchen. He wasn't sure if leaving the bay window armchair was such a good idea. It would mean getting up and going all the way round one of the little circular breakfast tables to reach the kitchen door. He was feeling tired and the kitchen lights were off so that meant when he went in search of further supplies he would have to raise his arm and switch the kitchen light on. The next ten minutes was a battle of wills between his stomach on one side and, on the other side, his legs and arm, which seemed to have conspired to form a united front against actually bothering to move.

'Are you still OK there?' he whispered.

'Uh-uh,' came the voice from behind the curtain.

'Won't be long now. Sorry I forgot to share the biscuits.'

'Uh-uh,' said the curtained voice.

'Shush! She's here!'

This Dominika is good, thought Copeland. She took no more than a few seconds to unpick a five tumbler security lock! Now she's waiting to see if anyone heard her open the catch. Here she comes...

'Hello Dom... Oh, you're already over the reception rug and pointing a gun at me. That was quick. Jolly well done!'

'Who the hell are you?' asked Dominika, also known as Mary White, Mary Black, Jennifer Green, a few others who had come and gone and, as far as Dominika was concerned, a few who were yet to be. 'I'm only asking who you are because I like to keep a list of people I've killed. A sort of aide memoir if you like.'

'Splendid,' said Copeland, who would have raised an emphatic finger if he had not thought it might get him shot. 'I'm Inspector Larry Copeland, formerly Special Branch, then S.O.15, a researcher with a group whose name should remain a secret called the Pickfords, and now I'm an agent of the new Department C with the designation double-o-seven.'

Dominika raised her eyebrows. Only slightly. 'You're Copeland? Really? You've changed haven't you? But I won't insult you before I kill you, that would be uncalled for, but you should have left me alone, Inspector. I even left the usual bloody footprint warning to back off at the Sharma house so you should have known better. Having said that, it will still be a great honour to terminate your life,' Dominika assured Copeland.

'An honour? Really? Ah, yes. I see. To terminate the new James Bond will be a feather in your cap!'

'No. But terminating Inspector Copeland will!' She took aim.

'Really? That's very flattering, Dominika.'

'So you know my Russian name, do you?' sneered Dominika, aka Mary White, etcetera. 'Perhaps I will put a bullet in your knee cap first and you can tell me how you know that while I stand on it, but first I think the woman behind the curtains should come out.'

'Goodness me, Dominika! However did you know she was there?'

'Ha! They told me you were good! What nonsense. Besides the fact I can see her legs under the curtain, I could see her through the window from outside.'

Blimey, Copeland! Even Jane hadn't thought of that. Though, to be fair, she did say your plan had zero chance of working so I suppose one could say it was quite irrelevant how the plan actually failed.

Frowning, Dominika said, 'Why do you seem as if you're listening to someone else? Do you have an earpiece in? Forget it. You'll be dead before any back-up arrives. Hey, you behind the curtain. Come out before I shoot and put holes in those antique curtains.'

The curtains rustled and with some difficulty a hand appeared and pulled a curtain back.

'And who are you?' asked Dominika. 'Just for my list, of course.'

'I am Nina Diaz, the proprietress of this establishment, and I resent you referring to my curtains as antiques. They are not antiques. They are just old,' said Nina, sounding quite cross.

'And,' said Copeland, 'behind you with her Glock 17 is Detective Jane Sadler.'

'So don't move a muscle,' said Jane, who had silently emerged from the darkened kitchen.

The stand-off lasted for nearly five minutes and ten rumbles from Copeland's stomach before Mary lowered her gun and handed it to Copeland. She conceded it was logical to assume there was a high probability that Jane would shoot her as soon as she shot Copeland. Copeland was rather glad Mary saw sense. Giving Mary the extra incentive of the deal he and Jane had devised had helped but Mary still made Copeland promise he would honour it by swearing on what he considered most sacred. The five minutes was consequently mostly used up by Copeland deciding on whether he should show his commitment to honouring the suggested deal by swearing on a bacon sandwich or a chocolate muffin. He was tending towards the muffin after eating the really nice, home-made one he'd eaten at the Lynns' when Nina eventually got strands of frayed curtain from her mouth and reminded him he had a daughter, and Mary was happy to accept Copeland's oath when he swore on Emily's life.

Jane waited for Nina to use her rope knotting expertise to tie Mary to a chair before she lowered her gun, glared at Copeland and snarled, 'You bastard!' and, grabbing Mary's reserve Beretta M9 from the tabletop, stormed out of the breakfast room. Copeland wondered if Jane thought he had gone a bit soft by letting Nina tie Mary to one of the cushioned breakfast room chairs rather than the wooden seat one in the kitchen, though Mary had not made things much better by telling everyone present she had made no promises to uphold the deal like Copeland had and if she ever got free she would kill them all in a heartbeat, then go and kill Copeland's daughter too for good measure.

A second packet of digestives had been found and half consumed by the time Jane returned. She looked like she had splashed water on her face to wash away the tear streaks down her unusually pale cheeks. To Copeland's surprise, she gave the Glock to Copeland and the Beretta to Nina. To Copeland's greater surprise, she offered to stay up and keep an eye on Mary. To Copeland's greatest surprise she fetched a rolling pin from the kitchen and said she would break Mary's arms if she even tried to get free of Nina's knots. Copeland went to bed shaken in his belief that nothing surprised him anymore. He could not work out any possible reason for Nina having a rolling pin.

9. Sunday, March 24th.

THE LOVELY ALISON SOCIALISES.

On hearing the news her would-be murderer was tied to a chair in the hotel's breakfast room, Alison Taylor joined them for breakfast after a mere hour spent doing her make-up and squeezing herself into a white dress. It hardly seemed worth it. All she did was ask Mary what had happened to the little white tablets from the lab, heard Mary say she'd got rid of them, slap Mary's face, sneer at Erica, order kippers again for breakfast and sit at the four seater table in the corner, scowling.

Copeland apologised to Mary/ Dominika for the slap, Jane practised her eye rolling and Erica continued to feed porridge into Mary's mouth. Copeland apologised for that as well. Mary shrugged and told them she had known worse, such as when she was first recruited as a Red Cuckoo novice – when 'Uncle' Vasily had put twenty of them in a windowless room with one bowl of porridge each day. At first they had all agreed to share the bowl between them, but after five days it was dog eat dog, after ten the first killings had started, and after twenty days Uncle Vasily had let the three remaining skeletal members out to experience the next part of their training. 'So the first eight people I killed were with my bare hands,' admitted Mary, 'and one of the other two who survived was my best friend Katarina. I had to kill her to graduate.'

Jane harrumphed, 'I'm surprised there was enough of you left to actually become Red Cuckoos.'

Mary explained there were lots of training camps and many parents gave their offspring up to the Motherland because it was both a great honour and a way of avoiding the Siberian

313

salt mines. She swallowed another mouthful of porridge, looked squarely at Erica and said, 'If it's any consolation, you were worth five times as much as Miss Piggy over there. I was getting a million for getting rid of you.'

The spoon the stunned Erica was holding dripped porridge back into its bowl. 'A million? For me? Why? I don't know anything. I'm not a scientist. I was just the receptionist and the cleaner and the animal feeder. A million?'

'It was only half a million last time – when you moved and got that Giles person killed. But Atticus, my employer, cancelled that one. Then he phoned again yesterday and offered me a million. I guess the extra was because I had to torture you first so you told me what you'd done with the flash drive.'

'The flash drive?' queried Erica, with wide-eyed Jane leaning forward onto the table and Copeland pouring himself fresh tea. 'You mean the one with all the data from the lab I downloaded onto it?'

Alison Taylor was hovering over Erica in a flash. 'You downloaded the data!' She pulled one of Erica's chestnut pigtails. 'When did you download the data last? Tell me!'

'Ms. Taylor. Please calm down,' said Copeland before sipping his tea.

'I'll let go of her hair when she tells me!' snapped Alison. 'That's all our work and I deserve the credit for it. And it's worth millions! No! Billions!'

'Ow! Wednesday – the last download was a week last Wednesday. It was after your little champagne and cakes celebration, which you still haven't paid me for! Ow! That hurts,' said Erica.

Jane felt herself about to move to protect Erica, but something was holding her back. She wanted answers as badly as Alison Taylor did. She felt better when Erica winked at her and said, 'Whatever you do, Alison, don't rip my earrings out – that will really hurt!'

'Right! Now I've got hold of your ugly big round earrings,' announced Alison Taylor because she had got hold of Erica's ugly big round earrings. 'Where's the flash drive, slut?'

'I posted it,' said the trembling Erica. 'To Jeremy Lynn like always. Just before I met Giles Lord in the coffee shop. I texted him to let him know I'd posted it minutes before Giles was shot.'

'Interesting,' said Mary. 'That's just about the same time I got a text from Atticus calling off the first hit on you, Miss Young.'

'Oh, dear,' sighed Copeland. 'I bet that was the flash drive you left in your flat, wasn't it Erica? The one near the front door by the empty blue plant pot? I had it in my hand, you know, but Jane here made me put it back. If only I had kept it...' (Sigh.)

Mary frowned. 'Listen, Erica, even I'm curious now. If you posted it days ago it should have got to Jeremy Lynn by now. So why was I being hired to kill you and get the flash drive from you and not from Jeremy Lynn?'

'Good question, Dominika!' agreed Jane.

'I'm Mary,' said Dominika.

'So...' said Jane. She looked sideways at Copeland. '... Jeremy Lynn is the person who hired Dom, er Mary. He's this Atticus person, Sir!'

'That doesn't make sense,' Mary pointed out. 'Jeremy Lynn gets the flash drive in the post and then I get the contract to get the flash drive and kill Erica Young..? Oh, I see. He's told his wife he doesn't have it but wants Erica's body to look like it's been tortured – nothing personal Erica. Dr. Lynn would assume Erica had been tortured for it so she then believes her husband when he says he doesn't have it.'

'Ow! Alison!' said Erica. 'I think it's Jeremy Lynn as well. He did my contract, like, and knew all about the flash drives. And no one is as stupid as that, even if they did get hit on the head by a model airplane. It's just an act, like. He delays paying me the money I asked for, like, so I don't post the flash drive and then he hires Mary to kill me because he thinks it's still in that flat in Axminster 'cause he doesn't know I can't get in like and he can come and get the flash drive once I'm dead. Then he finds out I've posted it when I text him and he calls off the hit, like. Then he gets the flash drive and tells his wife he hasn't, like Mary said, but he has, like. He hates Doc Lynn being richer than him and wants to sell the new Viagra drug thing to another company like.'

Jane said nothing.

Copeland smoothed his hair back. 'OK, then. Now that's all sorted it's time to get you into the car, Dominika. I suppose we should let you use the toilet before we go.'

'I'm still Mary for the time being and I can hold it, Inspector,' smiled Mary. 'I **was** trained, you know.'

Alison had not been the centre of attention for far too long as far as she was concerned. 'I never liked you,' she growled as she tugged down on both of Erica's large round earrings. Waiting for Erica's screams she held them proudly in her hands until she exclaimed, 'What the..? These are clip-ons!'

BENSON IS OFFERED A DEAL.

'No tape running to record my confession then, Superintendant Harper? Shouldn't my solicitor be here?'

'Er, no, Mr. Benson. This is a more informal meeting between just the two of us. You seem to be agitated, is everything alright?'

'Sure. Everything's fine. Just trying to get comfy, Superintendant.'

'Good. Now, Mr. Benson, after I'd gone back to Plymouth I understand you had to share your cell with someone else who was arrested yesterday evening. I hope you weren't inconvenienced by having to share with Mr. Banner.'

'You mean Mick "the Hulk" Banner? Big lad isn't he? And an inconvenience isn't exactly what I'd call sharing a cell with him, Superintendant. A pain in the...'

'That's good to hear, Mr. Benson, and yes, he is a rather large fellow. He's a member of the Devil's Own biker gang, you know. He was arrested for grievous bodily harm and they had nowhere else to put him. Honest. Of course, the charges against him may well have been more severe if he had worked out how to actually turn the chainsaw on rather than just bash a few people with it.'

'He told me that himself, Superintendant, while he was showing me his tattoos. I was amazed someone could have tattoos all over their body like Mick-the-Hulk has.'

'Yes that is amazing, Tom – may I call you Tom, Tom?'

'Just Tom is fine, Superintendant.'

'I hope he... you know... didn't hurt you, Tom. Are you sure you're alright? You seem to be finding it hard to get comfortable.'

'These are hard seats, aren't they Superintendant? No Mick-the-Hulk was fine. As gentle as a seven feet tall guy could be, really. And that was even though the police officers who put him in there with me made it clear I had killed a police officer and they didn't really care if Mick was feeling a bit aggressive because they would witness how I attacked him first. Given our size difference, I was presumably going to head butt him in the knee cap or something, was I?'

'But he didn't hit you did he, Tom?'

317

'No, he didn't hit me, Superintendant. Can I have a cushion please? Like I said, he was a really big guy...'

'Yes, he is, Tom. Are you sure you have no injuries at all?'

'My knees are a really sore as well. Does that count?'

'I meant something more like broken bones, ruptured spleen, gauged eyes... No, that's silly. I can see you still have your eyes. So, the thing is, Tom, you will be sharing the cell with Mr. Banner again this evening.'

'...Oh, crap.'

'Unless, of course, Tom... Unless you want to make that confession now?'

'...Oh, crap. I'm going to need a really big cushion by tomorrow aren't I, Superintendant?'

MARY GOES ON A JOURNEY.

With hands tied behind her and feet bound together, Mary sat in the rear of the little two-door Fiat. She found it impossible to move, mainly because Copeland had sat in the back beside her and he was taking up so much of the seat Mary was pinned against the side of the car. Arriving at their hotel in Slough, Jane pulled into the underground car park. A black SUV with darkened windows pulled up near them. Two dark suited, burly young men got out. One opened a rear door for Beryl Pickford to emerge, approach the parked Fiat, open the Fiat's passenger side door, tilt the seat forward and wait for the occupants in the rear to get out.

Beryl had been waiting for some time before Copeland's voice called, 'Help!'

Jane caught her breath. Had Mary somehow got free and wrapped the rope that tied her around Copeland's neck? Jane dared to look. Copeland was half out of his seat and struggling to get through the gap to get out. Beryl Pickford and her two assistants waited while Jane went round and dragged him out.

'Well done, Lawrence,' said Beryl Pickford.

Copeland caught his breath after his exertions. 'It was all Jane's plan really,' he panted.

'I meant getting out of the car,' said Beryl. She nodded to her two younger accomplices and they easily hauled Mary out through the passenger door.

Held up by the two burly men and quickly perceiving Beryl Pickford was in charge, Mary regarded her sceptically and said, 'So you're MI6?'

Beryl laughed. 'Nothing so mundane,' she said. 'But we are the people who are going to get you back to Russia. Tomorrow, via Geneva as it happens. Get her in the car and give her the injection boys. We don't want her to know where we're taking her for her debriefing, do we?'

Copeland and Jane watched Mary being literally dragged off, given some sort of injection and thrown into the back of the black SUV. 'So,' said Beryl Pickford, 'this was all your idea, was it Detective Sadler? I'm sure you will do well in your new career, but it's a shame you're leaving the police force.'

'Thank you, Ma'am,' said Jane, smiling. 'But it seemed an exchange of Dominika for the captured MI6 agent seemed a good idea. I wouldn't have said this a few weeks ago, but she doesn't deserve to live in a British prison after all the deaths she's caused. Letting the Russians execute her seems more appropriate. It's a good thing she doesn't know her fate, eh, Ma'am?'

'And,' laughed Beryl, 'it means Vasily Goraya will not get the credit for her capture and will end up in disgrace and in Siberia, but to be on the safe side we've set him up with some offshore bank accounts the Russians will soon trace. Lawrence's daughter will be safe.' She winked to Jane.

'You know about that?' Jane asked, wide eyed.

Copeland, who had been staring at the SUV and not paying much attention, sighed heavily and placed a hand on Jane's shoulder. 'They're The Pickfords, Jane. They know just about everything.'

'Oh... Oh!' said Jane. 'How?'

Copeland smiled, 'Well, they know about Vasily's threats against Emily because I told Beryl when we arranged this pick-up for Dominika.'

'Now, Detective Sadler, I'd like a quick chat about old times with my old friend Lawrence, so I think it's time you got back in the car,' Beryl said with a smile that meant, 'That's an order!'

'Yes, Ma'am,' said Jane, saluting before she got back into the Fiat to stare straight ahead.

'Does anyone salute anymore?' asked Beryl as she took Copeland to one side.

Copeland sighed again as he lazily half-pointed to the SUV. 'Sleeping beauty in there has no idea they'll kill her once she gets back, does she?'

'Lawrence, really! The off-shore accounts that can easily be traced back to Vasily make it look like Dominika was paying money into them – as if she was acting on his orders the whole time. We'll give Dominika all the bank details so she can tell the Russians when we hand her over.'

They're going to turn her, Copeland! They'll give her the bank account details only if she agrees to work for them and they'll threaten to expose her if she ever tells them Vasily was set up!

Watching Copeland's eyes flicker, Beryl said, 'Look at it this way, Lawrence. Vasily will be out of the way and the

Crown will have another overseas asset... Which reminds me... Your Department C is off the hook. MI6 are sure no one outside their department knew about their man in the Kremlin. Actually, now the MI6 agent will be swopped for Dominika, it's all worked out rather well. The Russian President used the excuse of finding an MI6 agent to have a big purge of anyone he vaguely didn't like and then promoted lots of the people who suck up to him. Our Pickfords agent in the Kremlin has been promoted to Deputy Defence Minister. It helps his chances of becoming the next president. We Pickfords like a more stable world and all that, you understand, Lawrence.'

Copeland did not sigh, he gasped. 'The Pickfords have someone inside the Kremlin? Deputy Defence Minister? Next president? Right... Er, OK, Beryl...'

'One more thing, Lawrence,' Beryl said, facing Copeland, looking intent and gripping his elbow. 'Tread carefully from here on in and try not to upset people too much.' Still stunned, he nodded. She smiled. 'And do tell Detective Sadler she should be proud of herself. Goodbye for now Lawrence.'

Night had long fallen before the little Fiat stopped at The Butchered Calf. Copeland and Jane went in for a much needed pie and pint. The pub had not changed since they had last been there, just as it had not changed since 1889. As they ate and supped, Jane told Copeland how pleased she was Mary would get what was coming to her and Vasily would soon be in Siberia because the Pickfords would make sure of that, even though they didn't exist as far as she was concerned. Copeland nodded sagely.

As they behaved like model patrons and gathered their empty glasses and plates to take them back to the bar, Jane said, 'Dominika didn't look like I expected her to though. I thought she'd be more...'

'And me,' said Copeland, 'and with more hair.'

'That's because she wears wigs, Sir!'

Seeing an all too familiar eye roll Copeland said, 'You forget, I haven't seen her disguises on the flash drive that Vasily gave us like you have Jane. Oh, that reminds me. Can you let me have my laptop and that flash drive back when we get to the hotel please?'

With half a nod Jane started carrying their empties to the bar.

'Hi, Jane,' greeted the man sitting at the bar. Copeland vaguely recognised him as one of the builders who had played pool with Jane.

'Oh, hi, Kev,' replied Jane. 'How's the building business been going today?'

'Been over in Honiton. Just telling Debbie here how we heard the blast even over there.'

'And it shook our windows,' said Deb, who seemed to be the woman behind the bar.

'What blast?' asked Jane, grabbing Copeland's jacket cuff as he turned to leave.

'You didn't hear it, Jane? They say it was a car...'

'On the main road,' added Deb. 'They say it had just pulled out onto it from almost opposite that big farm shop...'

'They say it was blown to bits and whoever was inside it was completely... You know...'

'I heard even the teeth were all over the place...'

'Just a few bits of red metal left from the car...'

'Someone told me someone told them they had spoken to someone who saw the truck behind the car actually leave the ground before it turned over...'

'I heard that. And someone said it was a red Audi that had pulled out right in front of that truck...'

'Red Audi? Massive explosion? Oh, goodness!' said Jane turning to Copeland. 'I think we might have missed something, Sir.'

'Ooops,' said Copeland.

10. Monday, March 25th.

LARRY AND SADLER MOVE OUT.

Their rooms were empty and the little Fiat was full to the brim, mainly with clothes needing a washing machine and supplies Copeland had purchased from the farm shop just over the road once it had reopened after a certain red Audi had been blown to shreds right by the entrance.

Cramming another box of locally brewed ale onto the back seat Copeland said, 'Sorry you've missed seeing your partner for a second weekend, Jane.'

'It's OK, Sir,' replied Jane stuffing a carrier bag full of what Copeland had called unmentionables behind the back seat. 'I've spoken to her most days and she's as keen as I am for us to see this case through to the end. And she says to thank you for massaging my calves again, Sir.'

'You're welcome. There, the car's pretty full but that's about the lot, I think,' huffed Copeland, leaning on the open car door. 'One more visit to make on the way to Weymouth for you to unload your stuff. Are you sure they've picked up the car from the Sharmas' drive?'

Jane leaned her elbows on the roof of the dirty white Fiat and said, 'Yes, Sir. My Inspector from the Weymouth station phoned me yesterday morning to say they were collecting it. What visit are we making on the way, Sir? I thought we were going to Bricknall to arrest Jeremy Lynn?'

'Oh, yes, we're going to the Lynn's alright,' smiled Copeland. 'That reminds me! I'm just going back in to see Erica and make sure she knows she should stay here until I clear everything up with Dr. Lynn for her.' He pushed off from the driver's door and went round the rear of the car towards the hotel entrance, but stopping halfway and calling back, 'Oh, and I have to thank her for helping me delete that file with the password Dominika from my laptop. I suppose you put it on when you downloaded Vasily's file? We don't need it now, do we?' Jane said nothing and shook her head slowly. 'Or this,' continued Copeland, pulling out the flash drive Jane had returned to him from his pocket. 'I suppose I should find a safe place for it, eh?' Jane said nothing and slowly nodded. Copeland dropped the flash drive back into his pocket and went into the hotel.

It was easier than usual pulling out onto the A35. There were temporary traffic lights while emergency repairs were done to fill in the crater in the road and someone in the queue let Copeland pull across. Jane winced as they passed the site of the previous day's explosion. Nina had told them what had happened...

Alison Taylor came down to breakfast in her black velvet pyjamas and in her usual mood, and after scowling across the room at Erica, told Nina she wanted a change from her rancid kippers and ordered the full English. When she speared a whole (locally produced) sausage with her fork and raised it to her mouth she dropped the fork, leapt out of her chair and rushed back to her room. Within the hour Alison Taylor's case was packed, her make-up caked, her hips squeezed into bulging black leggings and her quilted cream Burberry jacket somehow zipped. She demanded her car key from Nina, who told her Inspector Copeland had clearly said she should stay in the hotel until whoever had hired the murdering Dominika was in custody. Alison flew into a temper and with her finger in Nina's face screamed at Nina, telling her how a stupid hotel worker like her would never understand, but she had remembered the key ingredient that made the drug *she* had been working on *really* work! And she was going to see Dr. Lynn and get *all* the bonuses *she* deserved! She wanted her keys 'NOW!' and wanted to get into the imbecile Detective woman's room to get her perfume back 'NOW!' too. Alison Taylor resorted to physical threats but Nina remained resolute, at least until Alison pinned Nina against the bar, cast aspersions on Puerto Ricans not being able to play boring golf and, even worse, told Nina she would give her a bad review on Booking.com. Nina began to waver. Having watched on from the adjacent breakfast room Erica put her coffee down and told Nina she may as well give Alison what she wanted because she had seen how nasty Alison could get not only first hand, but with anyone delivering the blood bags to the lab and be especially nasty using the cattle prod on the bonobos. Nina shook her head despairingly, fetched the perfume and gave Alison Taylor her key to her red Audi.

With her last bottles of Midnight Intoxication laid carefully on the back seat, Alison Taylor wound down her window, gave a parting rude gesture to Nina and drove off, unaware that as the engine warmed the bomb under her car was gradually waking up and realising it had a destiny to fulfil after all. (It was a destiny Mary had devised but her curiosity had betrayed her and she had really needed to know why a woman was in the bay window hiding behind the curtains.) While Alison Taylor waited to turn right onto the A35, the bomb patiently waited and considered its place in the wider scheme of things. As Alison Taylor put her foot down, accelerated across the road and cut in front of a Waitrose lorry, the Audi engine heated and with a flash of understanding the bomb comprehended its purpose in the universe and happily fulfilled its full potential.

When Nina had told Big Larry and Jane all this, she had been quite pleased with the way she had anthropomorphised a self-aware bomb and had the sense not to tell them she had kept a full bottle of Midnight Intoxication for personal use.

When Copeland turned the Fiat off the main road Jane assumed Copeland was driving them to see Nancy Carter. Despite getting some sleep now that Mary had been handed over to be sent back to Russia, Jane was still too tired from the previous nights to ask why. She also wanted to give Copeland some slack since he had given her the credit for the plan to catch Dominika: she was smart enough to know he had led her there with his plan to hide her behind the curtains and then further provoked her to come up with her own better plan. She was also preoccupied with other thoughts – mainly getting to Bricknall to arrest Jeremy Lynn for hiring Mary Dominika and then staying there to finally see her partner again – but she also had a feeling of guilt. Jane felt guilty because Alison Taylor had been blown to little pieces, quite literally, and she didn't care. For a moment she worried she was becoming callous like Dominika and almost missed seeing the entrance to Nancy Carter's drive go by. By the time she had turned to frown and ask where they were going, Copeland was slowing down and pulling into the driveway of a neighbouring house. It was a long driveway.

'Oh, I almost forgot,' said Jane. 'We need to ask Mr. Rebus about the murder insurance Nancy Carter took out to see if he confirms her story and that it was his idea. No loose ends, eh, Sir?'

'Quite so, Jane,' said Copeland bringing the little Fiat to a halt and pulling up the hand brake.

'This is a lot bigger than Nancy's house next door, isn't it Sir?' Jane said, staring at the front of the home of Mr. and

Mrs. E. Rebus. 'This looks like a stately home I once paid to get into.'

Crossing the gravel drive they went up the three deep stone steps between the Romanesque colonnades and Copeland banged the brass dragon head against the double oak doors. A short wait gave enough time for Jane to step back and look up at the three stories of Georgian windows above her. The door was opened by a man in his early thirties impersonating a Victorian butler, right down to the white waistcoat and the morning coat with tails.

'Inspector Copeland and Detective Sadler to see Mr. Rebus,' said Copeland as he and Jane held up their I.D.s.

'Very good, Sir,' said the man from a Dickens novel. 'But I see your membership of Blockbuster has expired.'

Copeland looked at the card he had produced from the top pocket of his only remaining decent dark blue suit and said, 'So that's where that's been since the nineteen eighties.'

Alfred was the name Jane was already giving the man at the door. She had not read Dickens recently, but knew her Batman and this was definitely a younger Alfred, right down to his deadpan voice which said, 'The Master is not at home, but I could tell Madam you are here if you wish.'

Copeland nodded and with equal expressionless said, 'That will be satisfactory, Alfred.'

Jane giggled. Unsmiling, Alfred said, 'Your cinematic reference is very droll, Sir. Please come in.'

They followed 'Alfred' through a tiled entrance hall with a double staircase and were shown into the library. 'I will see if Madam is available,' said Alfred, closing the library's double doors as he backed through them. He was back before Jane and Copeland had found more than a dozen first editions among the floor to ceiling bookshelves. 'Madam is reading in the conservatory but she will see you now.'

Jane hoped tossing an original *Origin of Species* onto a table was deemed to be OK and followed Alfred and Copeland towards the back of the house and into the conservatory. The conservatory also happened to have a swimming pool the size of a tennis court. Half way down the poolside Mrs. Rebus was reclining on a sun lounger in a swimsuit which matched her long raven hair.

As they approached her Jane whispered, 'I wish I looked that good in a swimsuit.'

'Wish I did too,' whispered Copeland, 'but without the... er... you know... the... er...'

Niks Rebus lifted her sunglasses and smiled, 'Hello Detective Sadler and... Why are you holding your hands in front of your chest as if you're clasping something to it, Inspector?'

'Er,' stammered Copeland, 'Just telling Detective Sadler I used to be much bigger, Mrs. Rebus. Honest.'

Niks Rebus laughed. 'I can't see how that can be true, Inspector. I mean, how could you be bigger than..? Yes, well, enough said. Hobson, get some seats for our guests.'

Damn, Copeland! He's not Alfred, he's the one John Gielgud played in 'Arthur'.

Hobson hesitated. 'Shall I fetch wicker ones or the deck chair ones, Madam?' he asked.

Niks sighed, 'It's your choice Hobson.'

Copeland shuffled his feet, Jane looked around the swimming pool, Niks placed her book on the circular, glass topped table between her and Copeland and Jane, saying, 'Fascinating book this. It's about a sea captain called Ahab who obsessively drives his crew to hunt down one particular white whale.'

'Hmm,' said Copeland, nodding, 'the whale is the death of them all in the end.' He wondered why Niks Rebus suddenly looked a bit cross, especially when he'd saved her so much time reading the rest of the book.

Servant Hobson and a grey frocked maid from Downton Abbey brought two white wicker chairs and placed them next to the round table. 'Please sit,' said Niks Rebus with a gesture. 'And do call me Niks. I simply detest being called Mrs. Rebus. It's so old fashioned, isn't it?'

Jane used the arms of the white wicker chair to lower herself gracefully while Copeland collapsed into his, making it creak. Jane was only half seated when Copeland said, 'So you like games, don't you Niks?'

Niks raised her sunglasses and rested them on the front of her dark, swept back hair, smiled her broad Angelina Jolie lips and said, 'You could say that, Inspector Copeland.'

'Good. Let's play a game then,' suggested Copeland. 'We only tell each other the whole truth and nothing but the truth. OK? I'll be asking the questions...'

Niks held a finger up. She curled it. Hobson appeared at Copeland's shoulder. Without lifting her gaze from Copeland, Niks said, 'Hobson, the Inspector looks rather warm in here – we keep it at thirty in here, Inspector. Take his jacket, if you will, Hobson, and bring us some refreshments.'

'Hmm,' hummed Copeland, standing to remove his jacket. 'If you have them, that home-made lemonade and some muffins would be good for elevenses...' Hobson was behind him, slipping the navy jacket from Copeland's shoulders. 'Hang on,' said Copeland, 'just need to get my hand from my pocket... There. Thank you, Hobson.'

With a slight bow, Hobson retreated down the side of the pool carrying Copeland's cheap jacket in front of him as if it was radioactive. Back in his chair Copeland nodded to the reclining Niks Rebus, who said, 'Let's start with a more simple game than yours, Inspector. Not the whole truth and nothing but the truth, but we'll both agree not to tell any lies.'

'Fine,' said Copeland. 'I always speak nothing but the truth.'

'Ahem!' said Jane with her hands in her lap, her black jacket still on and feeling somewhat ignored. 'It wasn't true what you said about them all getting killed by that whale because one of them survives... Oh. Sorry, Sir...'

Niks laughed. 'I rarely have a good laugh these days, but seeing your face then, Inspector. Thank you, Detective. So, Inspector, now we have established the rules of our game, you can go first. What can I do for you?'

Copeland folded his arms across the top of his voluminous stomach in an attempt to give himself more gravitas and said, 'What did you think of Dr. Jonathan Carter, Niks?'

There was the briefest silence while Niks interlocked her fingers across her flat stomach before she answered, 'He was probably a genius in his field, but he was also a conceited, self-centred know-it-all who only talked about himself and treated poor Nancy with disdain, but Ernie knew him...'

'Ah, yes, he and Ernie would drink until the early hours at your famous barbecues,' said Copeland.

Why are we wasting time, Copeland? Ernie Rebus isn't here anyway to confirm he got Nancy Carter to take out the insurance so we should be on our way to arrest Jeremy Lynn for hiring Dominika!

'They were vegetarian barbecues, Inspector. Every Saturday night. Under the heated gazebo during the cooler evenings of course. But you're right, Ernie and Jonathan got on quite well,' confirmed Niks.

'Now,' said Copeland, 'I understand from another source that Dr. Carter got intoxicated quite easily.'

Niks laughed. 'It was hardly a secret, Inspector Copeland.'

'And, if I may ask, Niks, is it true Dr. Carter got even worse when he'd had a drink or two?'

'Worse, Inspector?' queried Niks, her manicured eyebrows frowning.

'You know,' said Copeland, 'he'd become even more conceited and talk about nothing else except how brilliant he was and what clever chemical wizardry he'd performed – such as making those diet suppressant pills for that Uroboros Rejuvenation company. That's just an example.'

Niks' frown did not subside. 'As I said, he liked to talk about himself and was extremely vain,' she said. 'Aha! Refreshments! Well done Hobson. On the table if you please.'

Feeling redundant, Jane said, 'That was quick.'

Copeland turned to one side and spoke to Jane. 'I'm sure they had some ready, Detective. Look, muffins and lemonade! And it looks like that real home-made lemonade.' He turned to Niks and asked, 'Everything is all home-made, isn't it?'

'Yes, it is,' replied Niks, smiling. 'Please help yourselves.'

Jane lifted the nearest glass and sipped. Copeland watched. Jane sniffed the lemonade. Copeland asked, 'Is it good, Jane?'

'Very,' said Jane. 'It's got... Is that cinnamon?'

'Well spotted, Detective,' said Niks.

'And a hint of lime?' asked Jane after another sip.

Niks smiled. 'Is she playing this game too, Inspector? I don't want to have to give away the third secret ingredient!'

Copeland laughed with her. 'I'm sure you don't, Niks! I bet it's all from old family recipes isn't it?'

'Yes, it is!' laughed Niks. She abruptly stopped laughing and stared at Copeland as he reached towards a chocolate muffin.

Jane thought Copeland was either ill or still full from his double English breakfast as she watched him break off only a small piece from a muffin and put it in his mouth. 'Very nice,'

Copeland said, approvingly. 'And these are these home-baked? Old family recipe as well?'

Scratching the side of her slender neck, Niks sat upright and asked, 'Are you here to arrest anyone, Inspector?'

Copeland smiled and replied, 'Is it my turn to not tell lies already? Am I here to arrest anyone? Hmm, I don't know. Is there anything you want to confess to, Mrs. Rebus?'

Niks bridled. She raised a finger and bent it. Hobson appeared at the other side of the sun lounger. She beckoned him closer and whispered something. He nodded and left. She turned back to Copeland and Jane. 'No, I don't want to confess to anything and I think I can speak for Ernie too when I say he does not want to confess to anything either. Do you want to give me one of your famous police cautions, Inspector?'

Jane, with lemonade glass poised, said, 'What's going on, Sir? I thought we were here to confirm Nancy Carter's story about the life insurance taken out on Jonathan Carter being Ernie Rebus' idea?'

'Oh, I can confirm that,' said Niks.

Copeland nodded. 'Good. Thank you, Niks. We'll be on our way then.' He shuffled forward in his seat as he added, 'I suppose you and Ernie had a soft spot for Nancy, didn't you?'

'Yes, we did and we still do,' answered Niks. 'Jonathan Carter treated her terribly. But you're not going anywhere before I have my turn, are you Inspector?'

'No,' admitted Copeland, shuffling back into the wicker chair with his arms folded across the top of his stomach again. 'I suppose you want your turn to see if I can avoid telling lies as well as you can,' he said.

Jane sipped her lemonade and watched Copeland and Niks staring at each other. She was glad she had not agreed to play this 'don't tell any lies' game, not when she had a couple of secrets of her own she had been keeping from Copeland. She was wondering what Niks was waiting for when Hobson appeared at her shoulder with something black and the size of a postcard in each hand. Niks pointed to Jane and said, 'Give them to the detective while the Inspector and I play at staring at each other.' Hobson handed the items to Jane, who took them, read the front, opened them and said, 'These are Mr. and Mrs. Rebus' passports, Sir. They're Greek diplomatic ones.'

Copeland smiled, unfolded his arms, reached forward over the plate of muffins and between the two remaining cloudy lemonade glasses, opened his hand and dropped its contents on the table near to Niks. 'I'd like one more, final turn of our game, Niks,' he said. 'Do you know what that is?'

'It's a flash drive,' said Niks, flatly.

Damn! That was your last question, Copeland!

'My turn to play our game, Inspector,' said Niks. She pointed at the flash drive and asked, 'Where did you get that?'

'From Erica Young's flat in Axminster when Detective Sadler took me there last week. You see, I had another one in my pocket at the time and they sort of got mixed up. By accident. Honest.'

Niks smiled. 'I have no interest in what's on it, Inspector, but tell me this... Has whatever there might happen to be on that flash drive been downloaded onto any other device?'

Copeland played a straight bat and answered honestly, 'I can assure you, Niks, the information on that flash drive is not on any other device. I have never even opened it and looked at its contents.'

Jane swallowed hard and sipped her lemonade.

Niks stared at Copeland.

'You can keep it, Niks,' Copeland said.

'I see,' said Niks. 'You wouldn't be giving it to me if you were lying, so... Hobson! Come here!' Hobson rushed from his holding position at the end of the pool. 'Hobson, take that,' ordered Niks, pointing. Hobson picked up the flash drive. 'And destroy it,' said Niks. 'Do it here and now, Hobson.'

Hobson looked around the poolside and asked, 'What with, Madam?'

'Just crush it under your heel or something, Hobson!' snapped Niks, not taking her eyes off Copeland, who heard a crashing noise as from the corner of his eye he saw Hobson repeatedly raise and smash down with his foot until he bent, picked up the cracked flash drive and handed it to Niks Rebus. Niks looked at it, nodded and dropped it into her cloudy lemonade. 'I think the acidity of the drink should make doubly sure. Satisfied, Inspector?' she asked.

'Pretty much,' replied Copeland.

'Thank you, Inspector,' Niks said without enthusiasm. 'I take it that is the end of the matter?'

'No,' said Copeland. 'We still have an arrest to make. Someone has to be held responsible for hiring Dominika to kill everyone at the lab and, inadvertently, Inspector Giles Lord, lots of white mice and twelve helpless bonobos.'

'And Reema Sharma's family, Sir!' added Jane. 'Ask her if she knows Mary White! She knows we can't touch her with her diplomatic passport!'

Niks turned her gaze to Jane for a few moments before returning it to Copeland. 'If you asked I would tell you in all honesty that I have never heard of Mary White or Dominika or ever spoken to either of them about killing anyone, or asked anyone else to murder anyone for that matter, and it saddens me deeply that our animal cousins were also unfortunate victims, but I understand you have a job to do

Inspector Copeland and there will be those seeking answers so, for the sake of closure, by all means arrest whoever you think is responsible for hiring the killer. We will not interfere.'

Driving beyond Bridport and along the coast road to Weymouth was a silent journey long enough for Jane to realise she might have missed a few things she may have well worked out earlier if she had not been so concerned about keeping secrets from Copeland.

She stared through the side window of the Fiat and eventually said, 'So Ernie and Niks Rebus work for a company who bought the house next door so they could befriend the Carters and get Jonathan Carter drunk at Saturday barbecues so he shot his mouth off and bragged to Ernie Rebus about their senolytics work and how close they were to a major breakthrough.'

'Worse,' said Copeland. 'I think he told him they *had* made a major breakthrough and how good it was. Dr. Jonathan Carter signed his own death warrant.'

'But we can't arrest Ernie Rebus, can we Sir? He's got a diplomatic passport,' sighed Jane.

'We have no evidence either, Detective Sadler,' said Copeland.

'He bankrolled the whole thing though, didn't he, Sir?' Jane said, finally turning her gaze from the side window and looking at Copeland, who was staring at the road in front with the intensity of a learner driver. 'They certainly seem to have enough money to hire an assassin, Sir, and arrange for money to go into Jonathan Carter's bank account so he agrees to meet Dominika because he's vain and greedy and they knew... Oh, gosh, Sir! *He* didn't, did he? *She did!* Nicola Rebus! If Ernie

Rebus was running the show she wouldn't have destroyed the flash drive until he gave her the ok... But surely that's what it was all about? If they wanted Carter's team's research why did she destroy it?'

'And why, you may ask, did Mary destroy the labs computers when she could have easily got Jonathan Carter to give her all the pass-codes or, for that matter, used her skills to hack them? Remember the Devon Police tech people said the computers hadn't been switched on for days?'

'We should have asked her, Sir – Niks Rebus was eating out of the palm of your hand once you suggested it was a game,' said Jane resignedly. 'She'd have told you anything you asked.'

Copeland managed a smile. 'That's exactly why I didn't ask,' he said. 'Some secrets are best left alone.'

And you didn't want some new hired assassin after you either, did you Copeland?

TOM BENSON HAS SOME NEWS.

'As flies to wanton boys are we to the gods; they kill us for their sport.'

'Is your finger in the air because that's some sort of quote Mr. Benson? I hope so. Otherwise I might think you seemed a bit down, and we've given you a really nice cushion to sit on. Please stop saying "Lear" and hitting your head on the table, Mr. Benson. It's government property.'

'Right! Fine! What now, Superintendant? I see the tape is running and Mr. Crisp is finally here all the way from London to represent my interests. By the way, try not to look directly at him. He's very shy. He might cry. So what new charge am I facing?'

'Er, right... Actually, there have been certain developments, Mr. Benson. It seems our main witness, Miss Jennifer Green, cannot be contacted. At first we assumed one of your associates had, you know, terminated her so she could not give evidence against you, but it transpires she has been taken into custody by the security services.'

'Aha!'

'And another witness has come forward who says she saw you walking along the street just before the shooting of Inspector Lord, so you could not have been firing from the window above the stationer's shop. You have a Mrs. Beryl Pickford to thank for... You know, Mr. Benson, I'm sure I've heard that name somewhere before. You're smiling. Do you know her?'

'Never heard of her, Superintendant. Never met her and never had lunch with her in a fancy London hotel. Honest.'

'Hmm... Then do you know an Inspector Copeland?'

'Larry? Tall guy with silver hair and a double Santa size stomach? No. Never heard of him either, Superintendant.'

'Do stop grinning, Mr. Benson. It's quite unsettling. Inspector Copeland says he knows you. He's sent a statement vouching for your character.'

'Oh! That Inspector Copeland? I know him. We were sharing a bottle of wine at my place only last week.'

'Er, OK. That sounds like him. Do stop grinning or I'll arrest you for possessing those teeth as an offensive weapon. Now there's the matter of the other murders. Why didn't you tell us you had an alibi, Mr. Benson?'

'Perhaps because you didn't tell me when I supposedly killed people?'

'Yes, well... It seems you were at a work conference at a Hotel and Spa with your future work colleagues...'

'You mean when we were getting massages and drinking champagne in the Jacuzzi? I don't work there yet but they'd just landed a big new PR contract and the company's owner treated everyone and thought I should be included for, you know, team building or something.'

'Well, Mr Benson, it seems the owner and the office manager had not seen any news for a few days but have now both confirmed you were there. You look very happy about something, Mr. Benson.'

'Gosh! The office manager? Sam? Gosh! I didn't even think she'd noticed me. She's *so* attractive, Superintendant. In fact, she's the most beautiful woman in the world. She didn't come in the pool or Jacuzzi though. She said she didn't have the figure for a swimsuit. Could've fooled me! She seemed to prefer getting her legs waxed a couple of times a day... Seemed to get a sort of shadow around her chin in the afternoon too...'

'Er, right... So, Mr. Benson, it seems you have an alibi for both Friday the sixteenth and the following two days when you were at the hotel.'

'That's sort of about ten days ago, then? That's when the people who worked at that lab were shot? Er, OK... I was definitely at the hotel then. Honest. The hotel thing definitely wasn't the weekend before that and the reason I moved to Bricknall early. Honest.'

'I wish you would refrain from using the word honest, Mr. Benson. It sounds like you aren't being truthful.'

'You're right, Superintendant. I won't use the word honest again. Honest.'

'Ow... kay... So, you're free to go, Mr. Benson. But before you do, and for the record, I just want to check you have been treated properly and do not want to make a complaint about anything.'

'You mean apart from a wrongful arrest, being roughed up, put in a cell with only a bucket and having to share with a seven foot guy who had tattoos **all** over his body? Have you seen his stretching concertina?'

'Er, no, but I should tell you, Mr. Benson, that if you make a complaint the paperwork will take several hours and then you'll have to wait while the complaints people get here and, I'm sorry to say, the only accommodation available is back in your cell, along with Mr. Banner of course. And, just so you know, we're just about to move one of his friends in there with him too – Terry "The Thing" Grimm – and I'm aware you already need that very deep cushion and already have very sore knees... So, Mr. Benson... Just for the recording... Do you wish to make a complaint about anything?'

'...Oh, crap... Er, no complaint, Superintendant. Everything was absolutely fine. Honest.'

JANE AND LARRY HEAD HOME.

Jane took her dirty clothes into her Weymouth flat and brought out a bag with fresh ones for her stay at her girlfriend's and they stopped in Dorchester for a four course lunch paid for by the Department C credit card. The meal had a finality about it. They shared their food and talked about irrelevant everyday things like politics. Copeland changed the mood and told Jane about his failed marriage and how he had been barred from ever seeing his daughter Emily again. His ex-wife had said he put them at risk because he associated with violent criminals, paramilitary groups and armed foreign agents. Copeland admitted he had not challenged the claims not because of the official secrets act, but because they were true – his work did put his daughter in danger and hadn't their recent experience with Vasily only proven the point? Jane listened as if she had not heard it all before when Copeland was drunk the first night they had met and ended up sharing a bed in the Kilmington hotel. He messed with the cheese board and admitted he had often wished he had quit his job so he could see Emily, but at the time he saw work as his only refuge and volunteered for the Irish undercover assignment. Jane wondered why he was telling her all this.

Back on the A35 road to Bricknall Jane thought at least one little confession of her own was called for and said, 'I saw what was on that flash drive.' Copeland silently watched the road. 'You can read it too, you know, Sir. Deleting it hasn't removed it completely from your laptop. It can be retrieved.'

Copeland looked at her and chuckled. 'No, it can't,' he said. 'Erica helped me. She's pretty good with computers. She knew how to make it irretrievable. Apparently there was a guy who worked at the lap-dancing place she used to work at and they sometimes got raided by the police. They had a lot of what Erica called special clients on their database so it was crucial any data was wiped before the police seized the computers. He showed Erica and some of the others how to completely wipe a data base in case the police ever raided when he wasn't there.'

'Oh,' said Jane. 'Maybe it is completely wiped then... But I know what it said though.'

'No you don't, Jane!' snapped Copeland, gripping the steering wheel.

'It said they were working on a senolytic based on blood plasma and growth factor fourteen just like the other senolytic drug places are...'

'Jane, you don't know anything!' barked Copeland.

'But Reema Sharma had the idea of using an enzyme called telomerase – it helps extend telomeres on the ends of chromosomes...'

'Jane! Forget you ever saw it!'

'Telomerase is why older men can still have children. It preserves the genetic integrity of sperm cells. It's an enzyme found a lot in the testes, Sir.'

Aha, Copeland! That's why Alison Taylor remembered when she bit into that sausage! Copeland winced. He turned to look at Jane. 'Listen, Jane, you have to forget you ever saw anything on that flash drive. Lots of people have been killed because of that discovery. You must never tell anyone – especially not your partner!' He returned his eyes to the road ahead.

Jane folded her arms across her black jacket, shuffled in the passenger seat and moodily grumbled, 'It's not fair, Sir! It should be made available to everyone, Sir. Why would Niks and Ernie Rebus hire Dominika to stop it being made, Sir? It's not only worth billions but it's just not fair to withhold it from the world. I read their research. Each pill they made in that lab took years off the life of those bonobos – and without the makeup, did Alison Taylor really look like she was in her forties? It didn't just do what all the other senolytic drugs claim they do. They had made something that didn't just stop ageing but actually partially reversed it.'

Copeland indicated to overtake a tractor. It was the first slower vehicle they had passed on the dual carriageway. He pulled back into the inside lane a few minutes later and quietly said, 'Who would have thought it? You're saying they invented a sort of immortality drug.'

Jane huffed. 'No, Sir! Not immortality, Sir! It's called amortality! Remember?'

COPELAND AND SADLER VISIT THE LYNNS.

The street lights were flickering on as Copeland switched off the Fiat's windscreen wipers and they stepped out into the drizzle and breeze to press the bell on the front of the mock Tudor house. Jane was glad Jeremy Lynn would soon be in custody.

Jeremy Lynn himself answered the door. 'Inspector Copeland! Evie said you phoned her to say you were coming,' he beamed, innocently. 'And Inspector Lord! Goodness me! Inspector Lord! I heard you'd been shot. Are you better? Those head wounds can be nasty, so well done you for making such a speedy recovery. Jolly good show and all that, what? Please come in and join us in the dining room.'

Jane closed her open mouth and whispered, 'He keeps the act up well, doesn't he, Sir?'

Copeland smiled and ushered Jane to go in first. With Copeland behind her she followed Jeremy Lynn down the hallway, past Finch in the kitchen and into the dining room with its ten-seater table, where Evie Lynn was already seated at the far end with espresso and water. Compared to her husband Jeremy, still in his lime green pin stripe shirt and yellow tie, Dr. Evie Lynn looked relaxed in her jeans and loose, speckled-grey sweatshirt, but her demeanour told a different story. She seemed to have consumed one espresso too many. She was twiddling with her straight blonde hair as she chewed an end. Her steel grey eyes had the signs of recent tears. As they entered she looked up at them with a pale round face, forced a wan smile and gestured for them to sit near her on her left. She pointed at Jeremy and then to a chair on her right and, with shoulders hunched, he trudged to his designated seat as he muttered, 'My dear wife's not her usual self, Inspectors. I don't know why, but she hasn't been herself since you phoned and told her the flash drive we had been expecting from Erica had been accidentally destroyed when Alison Taylor took it from her and had it on her to bring here when her car happened to explode,' by which time they were all sitting comfortably around the end of the dining table.

Copeland was startled when a voice at his shoulder said, 'Shall I bring your guests refreshments, Ma'am?' and he turned to see Finch had silently followed behind him from the kitchen. Jane responded first with, 'We're fine. Let's get this over with.'

Copeland's inner voice was not in total agreement, grumbling, *What? Copeland! Say something. You were looking forward to those muffins again.*

'Yes, let's get on with it,' said Evie Lynn, looking at Jane seated next to her and lightly placing a palm on Jane's jacket sleeve. 'I suppose my thanks are in order. Despite the loss of the flash drive containing two years of research and possibly the formula for making the most revolutionary senolytic drug ever, I understand you have apprehended the murderer and know who hired her to kill my team?'

Jeremy was taken aback. 'Evie? Did you say "her"? The murderer is a "her"? I thought it was that Thomas Benson chap, and I should know. I'm his lawyer and he seems pretty guilty to me. He's short, wears glasses *and* he's almost bald – all sure signs of guilt in my experience!'

Jane, with detectable repressed aggression, said, 'Not in this case, Mr. Lynn. Our evil-doer is elderly, tall and thin, grey haired and hook nosed!' She turned back to Dr. Lynn and more calmly said, 'I'll let Inspector Copeland explain.'

'What?' said Copeland, who had been hoping Jane would do all the tiresome arresting stuff while he looked forward to a celebratory bottle of red wine or two after a quick stop at the local nick and dropping Jane off at her partner's. He shuffled on his seat and said, 'No, you carry on Detective. You deserve this arrest.'

'Gosh! Thanks, Sir!' Jane said with her typical enthusiasm. She freed her arm from under Dr. Lynn's hand and pulled handcuffs from her jacket pocket. Copeland raised an eyebrow. She pulled back the side of her jacket to reveal her Glock 17 in its shoulder holster. Copeland raised his other eyebrow. She placed her elbows on the table with the handcuffs dangling from her hand, glared across at Jeremy Lynn and in her sternest voice said, 'Jeremy Lynn, I'm arresting you for conspiracy to commit murder. You do not have to say...'

Shame you don't have another eyebrow, eh, Copeland?

'Jeremy?' Evie Lynn blurted. 'Jeremy?' Evie Lynn laughed a tired laugh. 'Don't be silly, Detective! How could it have been Jeremy? Since his head injury he hasn't got the wit to...'

'Shush, Evie,' Jeremy said, sitting on the edge of his seat. 'This is all terribly exciting. I've never been arrested before. I say, do I need a lawyer? Silly me! I am one.'

Jane looked at Evie Lynn, who shrugged; she looked back at Jeremy Lynn. He gave Jane a broad smile and waved a hand to encourage her to go on. Taking her notepad and pen from her inside pocket, Jane slid them over to Jeremy. 'You can make a written confession, Mr. Lynn.'

'Would that help?' asked Jeremy. 'Sorry, what am I confessing to again? Oh, yes, that business with the flash drive and the lab making the new Viagra. What exactly did I do?'

'You hired someone to kill everyone who worked at the lab and destroy all the evidence of their work, Mr. Lynn,' Jane said to remind him.

'Did I?' said Jeremy. 'My memory isn't what it was since that airplane hit me you know.' He picked up the pen. 'OK.'

Ready. Just say it again, Detective Lord. I hired someone... yes... got that. What was his name?'

'Dominika,' said Jane, beginning to have doubts. 'She was once a Russian secret agent.'

Jeremy's eyes widened. 'Really? Like Jennifer Lawrence in that film? She deserved at least an Oscar nomination for that, you know. Now, what *was* that film called again?' He started looking around the mock oak panels of the dining room for inspiration.

Evie Lynn had had enough. 'Look, I told you he can hardly put two thoughts together since that model aeroplane hit him on the head. And why would Jeremy want to sabotage the work in the lab anyway? Please don't tell me he was jealous of my success and tried to stop me making billions from the most wanted rejuvenation medication since the dawn of time.'

'Exactly!' said Jane. 'We know it's him, Dr. Lynn, because apart from you, he's the only one who knew Erica Young was going to post that flash drive, then he called off the hit when he knew she had, then ordered it on again when the wrong flash drive came. It had to be him. Besides Carter and his team, who else knew what Jonathan Carter and his team were up to at that lab? He had the chance to look at all those flash drives Erica Young sent to his office before he handed them over to you when you got home.'

Jeremy slammed the table, 'My goodness, I'm good aren't I? I did all that? And I don't even need that new Viagra so I had another motive there as well... Shall I write that down, Detective Lord?'

'And,' continued Jane, ignoring Jeremy and looking at Evie Lynn, 'we know Jonathan Carter would boast incessantly when he'd had too much to drink and, by his own admission, your husband told us how Carter had told him how he made the appetite suppressants, so it stands to reason Carter also boasted about how the new lab was going to make a revolutionary new senolytic that would be worth billions. That's when your husband contacted a rival company who are, no doubt, developing their own drug. They wanted to make sure you didn't get it first. They sent people to befriend the Carter's. They got him drunk every Saturday so he would spill the beans on where the research was at and paid Jeremy a small fortune, obviously, for his inside information and offered even more if he made sure the drug was never produced.'

'Am I rich then?' asked Jeremy.

Jane turned back to Jeremy Lynn. With her elbows on the table and her fingers locked, she placed her chin on the back of her hands, glared at Jeremy and said, 'You can stop the act now, Mr. Lynn. The game's up. Just hand over your phone and we can see all the calls you've made to the other company who paid you – money *you* used to hire Mary White.'

Jeremy remained poised to write his confession. 'Mary White? Who's Mary White? I thought you said I hired a Russian called Dominika? Tut! My memory, what? My phone? Of course. Here it is in my jacket pocket... No, it isn't. I haven't got my jacket on, have I? Now where did I..? Finch! Finch! Have you seen my phone, dear boy?'

'Coming, Sir,' called a baritone voice from the kitchen. They waited. Dr. Lynn held her head in her hands and shook it in disbelief. Jeremy made a start on his confession. Jane continued to glare. Copeland tapped his thighs impatiently, knowing that cheese board after the other three courses would not keep him going forever. Finch appeared carrying Jeremy Lynn's shiny grey jacket in front of him. 'You left it on the sofa, Sir,' said Finch, 'as you always do when you come in from a hard day at the office.'

'Aha, Finch!' said Jeremy, wagging a finger at Finch. 'I'll have you know it always finds its way back into my wardrobe on its own, though.'

'Er, quite so, Sir,' said Finch, handing over the jacket and retiring back to the kitchen.

Jeremy put his hand inside his jacket pocket and stopped. 'What was it you wanted, Detective Lord?' he asked. 'Ah, yes. My phone. Here you go.'

Evie Lynn lifted her head from her hands to mutter, 'The pin number is his birthday. It's...'

'Twenty three twelve,' said Jane, tapping the number in.

Jeremy had a dangling jacket in one hand and a limp pen in the other. He seemed dejected. While Jane scowled her way through the calls and texts on Jeremy's phone Copeland thought he would join in with the interrogation and said, 'Mr. Lynn, I need to ask you something. Do you get less birthday presents because your birthday is so close to Christmas?'

Dr. Lynn audibly groaned. Jeremy Lynn's face lit up as he told Copeland about the injustice of people telling him they had bought him a 'combined present'. Seeing a kindred spirit he asked Copeland if his bithday was at Christmas too. Copeland told him it was in May. Jeremy gave him a look, dropped his jacket on the floor and went back to writing his confession. Copeland leaned forward to upside-down read what Jeremy had written. It began, "Once upon a time I was born from a lady called Mother who told me it hurt a lot and when I was two I broke my rocking horse and when I was two and a half..." Copeland thought it could be quite a long confession.

'Damn!' Jane exclaimed. 'Nothing here! Just texts from Dr. Lynn, Erica Young and his office saying he doesn't need to bother to go into work...'

Dr. Lynn groaned, 'I wonder why...'

Copeland stirred. It was time he was assertive and made a meaningful contribution. He leaned across Jane and tapped Evie Lynn's elbow. 'Can we have those refreshments now, Dr. Lynn? I'm feeling a little peckish, and I'm really thirsty,' he said.

Dr. Lynn nodded solemnly and called to Finch before putting her head back into her hands. Jane continued to scroll through the phone, looking increasingly exasperated. Jeremy was turning to page three of his confession and had reached his fourth birthday. Copeland drummed his fingers on the front of his taut blue shirt and wondered if the picture on the wall opposite was an original Constable. Finch appeared with the refreshments and placed glasses and plates in front of Jeremy and the two visitors. Copeland smiled. Finch had given him a blueberry **and** a chocolate muffin.

Scrolling one-handed, Jane nodded her thanks as Finch turned to stroll back to the kitchen. She subconsciously picked her drink up as she scanned the next message on the phone's screen. She lifted the glass to her lips and sipped the drink. She sipped it again. She smelled it. She put down the phone. She sipped again. 'It's...' she began, sipping and sniffing again. 'It's home-made lemonade.'

'It is?' said Copeland, swallowing home-made chocolate muffin.

'You agree, Sir?' said Jane. 'But you haven't started yours yet. Try it, Sir.'

Copeland did. 'It's very refreshing, isn't it?' he commented with an approving nod.

With her hands on her ears, Dr. Lynn looked up and weakly said, 'Look, I've lost my research and my research team are all dead, you're arresting my husband, I've had an awful day and I have to phone and somehow tell the other investors

Alison Taylor and the flash drive have been blown to smithereens, and all you two care about is bloody lemonade!'

'And muffins,' Copeland added. 'I care about the muffins, too. Especially the chocolate ones.'

'Lemonade!' cried Jane. 'Home-made from an old family recipe!' She slammed the table so hard even Jeremy Lynn stopped writing his confession for a few moments. 'Jeremy Lynn isn't the inside man, Sir!'

'Really?' said Copeland, looking down to see where that whole chunk of his broken muffin might have just landed so he could kick it over to Jeremy's side of the table.

MARY GOES HOME.

Mary was surprised to have her shackles removed and to be met by the new Deputy Defence Minister of the Russian Federation when she landed in Moscow. She soon explained to him how she had been duped by Vasily Goraya into carrying out various heinous acts of murder and mayhem for organised crime syndicates so Vasily could make money out of them.

Percy Asquith-Blakeney, codenamed 'Pimpernel' and known to Mary as Deputy Defence Minister Aleksei Denisov, seemed to be very efficient and had proof of General Vasily Goraya's illegal offshore bank accounts within no time, almost as if he already had the information to hand. Over dinner at a top Moscow restaurant, Mary confirmed they were indeed the bank accounts belonging to 'Uncle Vasily' and the very same ones that she had been paying into for many years. She did not mention all the accounts seemed to have identical sums in as hers had done before she had been caught and had agreed to work for The Pickfords.

The deal Copeland had offered her seemed to be working and all the briefing information given her by that strange elderly Beryl person seemed to have got the Deputy Defence Minister thoroughly convinced she had always been nothing but loyal to the Motherland. The false bank accounts also easily convinced him Vasily Goraya was not so loyal, and he told her General Goraya would be dealt with as a traitor forthwith. Mary thought the use of the word 'forthwith' was rather unusual for a Russian.

Deputy Defence Minister Denisov even offered her a new job. Until then she had not been aware that France and Germany were the 'old enemies' and with the prospect of Britain not being there to stop them collaborating inside the EU any longer, it was her job to train a new generation of Red Cuckoo agents to infiltrate their governments and sow mutual distrust. And, just in case, some were to be trained as slumber agents for Scotland too.

When she was told the salary and the many perks the role had to offer, she was keen to take the job. It had the extra bonus of overseeing the 'deployment' of military personal, such as a certain recently promoted general, to the Siberian salt mines. And the pay was in addition to what that Beryl person had offered her for being a double agent. And there was a gym nearby. It apparently had some excellent group classes. Mary was happy to become Dominika again.

COPELAND AND JANE DISAGREE.

So that was it, thought Jane. It was all over. The servant Finch had said "it was a fair cop" and confessed to hiring Mary (Dominika) White and Jane had handcuffed his hands behind his back before she and Copeland had led him out of the Lynn's house. Jeremy had insisted on keeping the pages from her notebook he had already used, claiming it would make a good opening to his autobiography. He had told her this just after he had slapped Finch on the back and told him he was 'a jolly decent egg' and gave him a firm handshake and an unmissable wink, as if he had no idea what Finch had done. Jane put Jeremy's behaviour towards Finch down to his head trauma. (Jeremy's, not Finch's, because, as far as Jane knew, Finch had not been hit by a model plane.)

She sat, unmoving in the passenger seat of the little Fiat, waiting for Inspector Copeland to say something now he had stopped the car, but he was as motionless as she was and, like her, was sitting looking through the windscreen with a thousand yard stare.

Jane broke the tension. 'So Finch was Atticus all along. He even admitted it and agreed to make a full confession – he admitted he hired Dominika, er, Mary White, to kill the workers at the lab and destroy all the evidence of the work they had done. Shame really. They were making a new senolytic that actually worked,' she mused out loud.

'Uh-uh,' said Copeland, rubbing the end of his nose. 'Atticus was Finch. We should have worked that out a lot sooner really. Gregory Peck...'

'Who?' asked Jane. 'Oh, I see. That's Finch's real name. The police data base had hardly anything so you used the MI5 database. Well done, Sir.'

Larry Copeland basked in the warm praise for a moment before his conscience snapped, *COPELAND!*

'Well done to you, Detective Sadler,' Copeland said. 'You worked out the lemonade link. Finch infiltrates the Lynn household as a servant, looks at the flash drives every time Jeremy Lynn leaves it lying about and accesses Jeremy Lynn's phone whenever he wants to.'

'Yes, Sir!' enthused Jane. 'And the postmark on the jiffy bags the flash drives arrived in gave him the location so all the company he worked for had to do was find a nearby house registered to Dr. Jonathan Carter and send someone there to pose as new neighbours and befriend them, get Jonathan Carter a bit drunk every Saturday evening and get the latest inside information. If it wasn't for their home-made family recipe lemonades being the same I would have arrested Jeremy Lynn by mistake! But you would have stopped me, wouldn't you, Sir? You knew it was Finch, didn't you?'

Answer her honestly, Copeland!

Copeland laughed and turned to Jane. 'You know, Jane, when I first started this case Chief Inspector Harper said she thought the wife did it. I told her it was the butler who did it. It seems I was right.'

At least that's true, Copeland, sighed his inner voice.

'You're a genius, Sir!' Jane exclaimed with a clap of her hands, which she kept clasped together as she nervously wrung them together and said, 'I still don't get why they paid Dominika to destroy all the research when she could have just stolen it for them. I checked the databases while we were driving here and there's nothing at all on Mr. and Mrs. Rebus and that scumbag Finch refuses to say who he works for, but whichever company they all work for could have made billions marketing that super-senolytic, so why destroy it?

Anyway, I'm glad the assassin-hiring low-life turd will go to prison.'

'I am still here, you know,' said a baritone voice from the rear of the Fiat. Copeland and Jane turned their heads to look into the back seat. Finch smiled at them. 'You two still seem to have a lot of questions.' He laughed. 'At our family get-togethers we sometimes play a game where we have to answer questions honestly. My grandmother loves that game. I have no intention of playing such a game but I will tell you a few things that won't be in my confession.'

Copeland sighed. 'Can you make it quick? Turning round like this is hurting my neck and those muffins won't keep me going forever either.'

Finch laughed heartily. 'Ha ha ha,' he more-or-less said. 'Always the joker, eh, Inspector? Getting people to drop their guard by appearing to be disinterested and only concerned with food, eh?'

Copeland! Don't let him insult you like that! Tell him you're interested in alcoholic beverages too.

'But I will try to be quick,' Finch continued. 'Although I am still mildly annoyed you saw fit to handcuff my hands behind me after I gave my word to come quietly and give a more-or-less full confession. I am a man of my word, Detective Sadler. Firstly, may I congratulate you both on my arrest. I thought you would dismiss me as a suspect when you found out I had begun working for the Lynns years before the lab began its work.'

Copeland said, 'You did?'

Jane said, 'You're quite right, Sir. He did.'

Finch said, 'It was the genetics lab Dr. Lynn set up that got us worried, so I was sent to be the perfect servant. We bought off the other candidates of course. After three years the genetics lab was getting nowhere and I was about to leave when Dr. Lynn hosted a dinner party for the team appointed to work at her new secret lab. That was the turning point. I overheard Jonathan Carter boasting about his appetite suppressant to Jeremy Lynn, but then he started saying how he would soon invent a senolytic that would stop ageing and change history. We couldn't risk that, especially with Reema Sharma on the team. But we didn't know where the lab was located and didn't know how to stop them. Fortunately Dr. Lynn got annoyed about the lack of information she was getting from Carter and infiltrated Erica Young into the lab to send her a monthly download on a flash drive. The postmarks on the flash drive packets Miss Young sent told us where the lab was and, as you've guessed, members of our... our organisation bought the house next door to the Carters. Even though the house wasn't for sale the occupants couldn't resist our generous offer. My, er, associates, soon befriended Nancy and within weeks Jonathan Carter was getting intoxicated and being his usual boastful self. We were relieved to discover they weren't really getting anywhere special – just the usual stuff with blood plasma from young donors infused with extra GF14. That stuff might help for a few months, but nothing serious. We were thinking of buying Carter and his team out anyway just in case, but we waited too long. Quite unexpectedly, one of Carter's team had an idea to make their drug *really* work. It was probably the brilliant Reema Sharma's idea, but Jonathan Carter boasted about it being his after a few beers. We knew they had found that one missing ingredient to make their senolytic drug work far too well. It was too late to buy them out. They couldn't unknow what they knew, could they? We could not allow their drug to be made so, with great regret, we had to make sure what they knew never came out. We had to revert to plan B. I'd already found Mary White on the Dark Web and had hired her to keep tabs on the team, and for the right price she was willing to kill Carter, the rest of his team and destroy all evidence of their work. Jonathan Carter was vain and greedy, so it was easy to dupe him into a Friday night meeting with what he thought was another company willing to offer him billions for his discovery and he let Mary White in, not knowing she was really there to kill him. We didn't know about the poor bonobos any more than Dr. Lynn did, and murdering Reema Sharma's whole family was not something we sanctioned either.'

Jane sneered, 'But you did **sanction** the deaths of Reema and the rest of the lab team, and then Erica Young when you thought she had the final flash drive, didn't you, *Mr. Finch*?'

'Yes, Detective,' sighed Finch. 'But consider the alternative. What if they had made this new drug and Dr. Lynn had started to sell it? How much would it have cost? Who would have been able to afford it? What happens when those billions of people who can't afford it find out there's a drug that rich people can buy that stops them ageing? How long would it take before the fabric of society was torn apart or people would start going to any lengths to get this new wonder drug? We do not like change. We had to weigh-up the deaths of the four researchers at the lab against the possible deaths of countless millions, perhaps even billions. Which would you choose?'

'That's nonsense,' scoffed Jane. 'Everyone could just have been given the drug once they got old. Say when they were fifty.'

Copeland frowned. It had been a long time since he'd been fifty.

'Oh, sure,' said Finch. 'Uroboros Rejuvenation giving away a free wonder drug? When was the last time a drug company did that? But let's say they did. Or someone else made a cheap generic version? What then?'

'People live longer,' said Jane. 'And they don't get all the chronic diseases of old age like rheumatism or...'

'No, Jane,' sighed Copeland. 'He means what happens if people start living for, say, another thirty years? We have another elephant in the room, Jane.'

Jane's face fell. Her eyes went left and right until she whispered, 'There could be fifteen billion people by the end of the century. Twenty billion by...'

'Close, but we calculate more,' said Finch from the back seat, 'unless conflicts to get hold of the drug virtually wipe civilisation out. And the Inspector's thirty years figure for increased lifespan is quite a conservative one. Once the drug is out there it would be improved on and then, sooner or later, people would live another fifty years, then a hundred and then, all too soon, become amortal and live just about forever. The world just does not have the resources for the people on it now, so what happens when the human population quadruples and keeps on increasing? Please don't say forced sterilisation. We played out that scenario as well. It just takes us back to global civil wars.' There was a silence.

'Right,' said Copeland. 'My neck is killing me turning round like this, so let's get you inside this police station, Mr. Atticus Finch, and find a nice cosy cell for you.'

JEREMY.

After phoning the other investors, Lynn returned to the dining room to find Jeremy at the dining room table rubbing his head with one hand and typing with the other. She went to stand behind him, moved his hand from his scalp and felt it herself while she looked at what he was typing on the screen. She said, 'You have a nasty lump there, Jeremy.'

'Yes, I know, Evie,' said Jeremy, without turning to look at her. 'A lump of chocolate muffin was on the floor where Inspector Copeland was sitting. I went to pick it up and banged my head really hard on the table when I stood up. To be honest, I feel a bit strange. As if my mind has cleared, you know? Like it was before that aeroplane hit me.'

Evie Lynn squeezed Jeremy's shoulders. 'That's good news Jeremy. It would be good to finally have the old Jeremy back.' She kissed the top of his head. 'I see you're typing up your memoirs, then?'

'Yes, Evie,' Jeremy said as his fingers danced across the keyboard. 'But I think I'll have to use a false name for them, won't I?'

'You need a nom de plume,' suggested Dr. Lynn.

Jeremy stopped typing. 'That means *name of feather*, doesn't it Evie? You know, I've often wondered... Do you happen to know why it's called that?'

PARTING OF THE WAYS.

Looking at her watch, Jane hoped Copeland would be true to his word and make the briefest of visits into the shady terraced house to check Tom Benson was home and well. She was thinking about phoning her partner to tell her she would be late because the processing of Finch had taken longer than anticipated, but she didn't like lying. Copeland had actually produced his Department C card before producing any other card, for once, and the processing of the new prisoner Finch had been quicker than Jane had ever seen. She worried that Finch seemed completely at ease with the idea of spending a long time in prison for multiple counts of conspiracy to murder. She also could not understand why Finch had not got Dominika to steal the formula for the drug – whatever organisation he and the Rebus's worked for was obviously fabulously wealthy and, even if they did not need the money selling the senolytic wonder drug, they could have made it and used it themselves. Her mind flipped back to Finch, who seemed to think many decades in prison was not such a long time, especially when he was sure he would get time off for good behaviour.

As Copeland came out of the house Jane realised the truth. She was momentarily distracted by Tom Benson waving from the doorway being joined by another figure who seemed to be wearing a flowing white gown. What caught Jane's attention was the way the gown, along with the hair and the beard of this second figure seemed to be glowing. The car sagged to one side as Copeland got in, said, 'He's fine,' and started the car.

'Wait!' cried Jane. 'Who **is** that with Benson?'

'Oh, that's just Jesus,' said Copeland. 'Tom's finally persuaded him all the Romans have gone.'

'He's glowing,' Jane pointed out, still staring out of the passenger window with her mouth open.

'What?' said Copeland, leaning over Jane's side to look at the house doorway. 'So he is. Tom says he thinks Jesus got some glow in the dark stuff leftover from Halloween and has been sprinkling it over himself for days.' He laughed. 'So, Mary got Tom's confidence by, er... amongst a few other things we don't need to go into... by telling him there was an extended version of Tom's favourite film – Invaders from Esbos – and how she led him to believe she was being hired by The Family – not the seventies rock group, but a secret organisation that's very rich, controls the world and has existed since ancient Greek times.'

'Sir! That's true!' shrieked Jane.

Copeland recalled how Jane had spent hours through the night talking to Dominika. He said, 'It's true?'

'Wow, Sir! You know it's true it as well?'

'I do?'

'I'm so glad you know it's true as well, Sir,' grinned Jane with a sigh of relief. 'I know it's almost unbelievable, Sir, but I actually own a copy of that extended film version... It's not an illegal copy, Sir. Honest.'

'Er, right, good for you...' said Copeland. He put the car in gear and drove off, leaving a doorstep waving Tom Benson and a glowing Jesus behind.

'I think they already have it,' said Jane quietly, as if she feared being overheard.

'I don't think they do,' said Copeland.

'Hmm... I understand, Sir. We must pretend we don't know they already have it. But, between you and me, I think they've had it for a long, long time.'

Copeland would have frowned if a cat had not run out in front of the car and he had to emergency stop. He thought he would change the topic of conversation: as far as he was concerned, arguing about whether Tom Benson and Jesus possessed a copy of the extended version of a minor film seemed fruitless. He asked, 'Do you love your partner, Jane?'

'Pardon, Sir? Do I...' Jane hesitated. 'I think so, Sir.'

Copeland pulled away again and headed to the semi-derelict block of flats Jane had directed him to so he could drop her off to visit her partner. 'Perhaps you could tell her a bit about me,' he said. 'Just the good stuff, maybe...'

That won't take her long then, will it Copeland?

Jane said nothing. She had vowed not to admit her secret to him. She looked at Copeland, who may have been watching the road but, as the light of a street lamp flashed through the car, there was a glistening on his cheek. Jane relented. 'You know, don't you? How long have you known?' asked Jane.

Copeland shrugged. 'The back of your neck went red when we first mentioned her name and then you were willing to risk Vasily shooting you when he threatened her at the hotel. I figure if you're willing to be shot to protect her, then she couldn't ask for anyone better.'

Jane gulped. 'Thank you, Sir. That means a lot. But doesn't our age difference bother you, Sir?'

'No, but this does...' said Copeland pulling the car up near the monolithic grey block of flats. He turned to Jane. 'This place is bleak. Give me your bank account details. I'll transfer some money. You can live somewhere better. She need never know...'

'No, Larry! You can't,' protested Jane. 'It breaks the court order – indirectly yes, but still... Anyway, we're fine. My teaching salary will be enough. Just. And she's going to be a famous sculptor soon...'

Copeland flopped back in the car seat. 'OK, fine,' he sighed, looking up at the eight storeys of lights from the windows of the concrete slab in front of them. He rummaged in his pocket. Jane thought he was about to cry when he pulled out a tissue. She was intrigued to see him unfurl it and hold it in the palm of his hand. He said, 'Tom Benson gave me these. He said he'd had enough involvement with the police for one lifetime and didn't want to be arrested for possession of class A drugs. He thinks they're ecstasy tablets. When Dominika tried to frame him and left her gun with his fingerprints on it and the photo of the lab workers celebrating, she also left these tablets wrapped in this tissue. Tom told me the Jesus chap took them to save him from being charged with possession as well. Tom said Jesus told him he's quite good at saving people from all sorts of possession. So, what do you think the tablets might be, Jane?'

'My God, Sir! Dominika said she had got rid of the tablets she took from the...'

'I think they're just aspirin, Jane,' Copeland interrupted. 'You **do** agree, don't you?'

Jane looked up from the tablets in Copeland's palm. She looked him in the eye. He was nodding encouragingly. She said, 'They look like aspirin to me too, Sir.'

'Good,' smiled Copeland. 'Now that we both know they are aspirin and absolutely **not** anything else that may have been made in a certain lab in Dorset and they are definitely **not** tablets which not only stop ageing but might even reverse it... I'll keep some to share with Beryl, but would you like to take a couple as souvenirs? You never know, when you get a little older, you might get a headache and need an aspirin.'

Printed in Poland
by Amazon Fulfillment
Poland Sp. z o.o., Wrocław

52557147R00214